FACETS OF THE JEWEL SPELL

For centuries, Piyanthia has known peace, governed by the Diadem Lords and Ladies: Diamond, Ruby, Emerald, Topaz, Citrine, Aquamarine, Sapphire, Amethyst. Now one is dead, one is under a wizard's spell—and at least one holds a terrible sorcerous secret . . .

JENA: She's a hero with a wizard's power, a gemcutter's craft—and a woman's heart . . .

LADY KESTRIENNE: She may seem like a doddering dowager—but an unpolished stone can hide the greatest treasure . . .

LADY RHUDDLAN: The Diamond Heir, she must persevere through the greatest crisis in the history of the Diadem . . .

LORD DUONE: Will he be the next Emerald Lord—or an assassin's next victim?

"A delightful read, inventive and intriguing. The plot's sly humor grows into genuine wisdom by the book's very satisfactory end."

—LOIS MCMASTER BUJOLD,
bestselling author of *The Spirit Ring*

"Mannerist fun crossed with gem magic and a sense of humor about adventure—that's Peg Kerr's EMERALD HOUSE RISING. Wonderful to have a new and charming voice on the fantasy scene."

—JANE YOLEN, author of *Briar Rose*

EMERALD HOUSE RISING

PEG KERR

ASPECT®

WARNER BOOKS

A Time Warner Company

WARNER BOOKS EDITION

Copyright © 1997 by Peg Kerr
All rights reserved.

Aspect® is a registered trademark of Warner Books, Inc.

Cover design by Don Puckey
Cover illustration by Kevin Johnson

Warner Books, Inc.
1271 Avenue of the Americas
New York, NY 10020

Visit our Web site at
http://pathfinder.com/twep

Ⓦ A Time Warner Company

Printed in the United States of America

First Printing: June, 1997

10 9 8 7 6 5 4 3 2 1

For my parents,
the first to tell me I could write

and for Rob,
with love

Acknowledgments

With thanks to my tutor, Joel Rosenberg,
    who glared at me and told me I could do it (even
    providing the computer so I'd have no excuse), and
    so I wrote the book because I didn't dare disobey him;

To my mentor, Pat Wrede,
    who sat patiently through endless phone calls and
    long sessions at the Good Earth, asking me the ques-
    tions I needed to answer to bring the story to life, and
    who even made emergency house calls when I
    panicked;

To my fellow journeymen, Bruce Bethke, Carolyn Ives
    Gilman, and Kij Johnson,
    who read the manuscript in all its various stages and
    offered their comments and encouragement;

And to my partner, Rob Ihinger,
    who offered love, meals, and baby wrangling above
    and beyond the call of duty.

Special thanks are also due to,
    Richard Johnson and Kij Johnson for technical com-
    puter support, to Pamela Dean for insight, perspec-
    tive, and guidance on grammar nitpicks, to Leslie
    Foreman for her helpful information on gemstones,
    and especially to the Anonymous Benefactor (you
    know who you are).

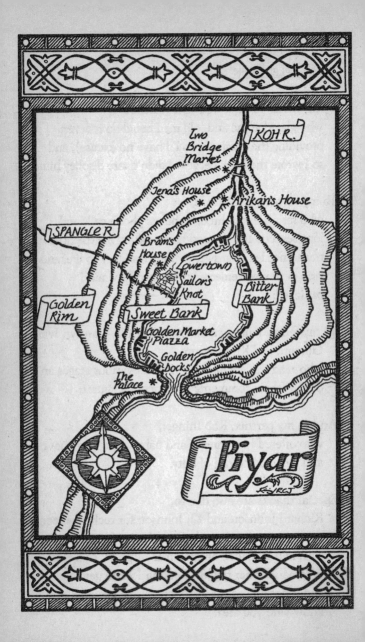

CHAPTER
⊙ONE

In the summer of her eigh-
teenth year, every evening she could get away from her
household duties, Jena came to the acacia grove to watch the
sunset over the harbor of Piyar. The weather was oppres-
sively sultry that year, shortening the tempers of everyone in
the city. But in the grove at the south end of her father's garden, high above the central city, Jena forgot the heat, and the
flies, and the stink of the pushing crowds.

The city had been constructed on a series of semicircular
terraces cut into the hillside from the top of the ridge down
to the Koh River. The residents imagined the city's layout as
resembling a set of nested rimmed bowls of graduating sizes.
By custom, the uppermost terrace was called the Golden
Rim. Beneath that, each "rim" was numbered, starting from
the top, and corresponded to the slope, or "bowl," below it.
Collas the Gemcutter's residence, along with others of the
wealthier merchant and artisan classes, stood on the terrace
known as the Rim of the Third Bowl. Only the nobles'
houses, built on the First and Second Rims, and the Winter
Palace itself on the Golden Rim, were built higher up. Here
in the garden, the flower-scented breeze through the grove
was cool, and Jena's favorite stone bench offered a splendid

view. She would bring her mending or embroidery to work on as she sat in order to placate Collas, who could not bear that anyone should ever be idle, least of all his only child. Most often, it was only a pretense: although she began her stitches dutifully enough, eventually her work would fall forgotten to her lap as she looked out over Piyar, drinking in the view long after her eyes could possibly distinguish the color of the silks in her bag or find her needle if she dropped it.

At the end of one such evening, just as Jena was gathering her handiwork to go inside, she heard the scraping sound of footsteps. A man was climbing up the terrace staircase from the street below. She could make out that he was tall, with narrow shoulders, and his silhouette suggested a summer-weight cloak partially draped over a long knife. When he came to the top of the stairs, he called out to her: "Mistress? Is this the way to the home of Collas the Gemcutter?"

"This is his home," she replied. "I'm his daughter, and his apprentice."

"His apprentice? And you are?"

"Jena, sir."

"Jena. Is your father within?"

"May I tell him your name and business, sir?"

"I should like to speak with him about a commission." He stepped closer to her, and in the faint light from the rising moon, she saw for the first time the thickly knotted cord at the shoulder of his outer gown.

She dropped a hasty curtsy. "Your pardon, my lord—"

"It's of no consequence," he said smoothly. "Is he engaged?"

"No, my lord." Jena did her best to hide her surprise. How strange for a lord to be coming up from the inner city rather than down from the Golden Rim, or the First or Second Rim. Moreover, for a lord to deign to come calling at the home of a gemcutter, even the best gemcutter in the city, was most unusual. Generally, nobles expected Collas to wait upon them in their palazzi and to be grateful if they didn't leave him cooling his heels in one of their anterooms for half the day.

Despite knowing her name, he clearly didn't intend to offer his own. She knew better than to allow any annoyance at the insult to show. After all, he was a lord, although one wouldn't have been able to tell from the hour he chose to come calling for gemcutting commissions. As Jena's father had often pointed out to her, there was no use in taking offense at anything a lord did. Much more to the point was avoiding having a lord take offense with you. "Follow me, if you please," she said quietly.

He followed her through the grove, up the steps, and into the sitting room overlooking the garden. The shutters stood open, leaving the furniture just visible in the last of the fading twilight. "There is a chair by the window, my lord, which I hope you will find comfortable." After putting her embroidery bag away in a storage cupboard, she twitched a straw from the broom in the corner and lit one end in the small corner brazier.

"I'm sure it will serve." He seated himself as she brought the burning straw over and lit the candle on the table at his elbow.

The flame caught, and as the light strengthened, she saw him frankly appraising her. He looked younger than she had supposed from his voice, perhaps ten or fifteen years older than she. His pourpoint and jerkin were lightweight silk dyed a rich blue, without the slashed sleeves or exaggeratedly high collar most nobles were wearing this season. A color that dark was usually worn to set off jewelry but, except for the small round brooches holding the pleats in place at the shoulders of his outer gown, he wore only a simple gold chain. His hair, under a matching blue velvet cap, was russet or brown; the uncertain light made it difficult to tell. The shadows exaggerated the line of a jaw which, she reflected, would probably be judged by most as being too angular to be handsome. His neatly trimmed mustache completed the violation of the courtly standards of fashion. Jena liked his face the better for it.

She blew out the straw and reached out to place it on the candleholder base. Somehow her hand collided with his as he brought it up to rest it casually on the table. At the touch, Jena felt something that somehow *jolted*. She gave a little gasp and clutched at his hand for balance.

"Is something amiss?" he said pleasantly enough, but his eyes narrowed as they studied her.

With an effort, she pried her hand from his, her face heating in embarrassment. "Pardon, my lord. I'm not usually that clumsy. Something . . ." she stopped. Her hand still tingled, the way it did sometimes when she slept on it wrong and then awoke and tried to move it.

"Yes?" he asked solicitously.

"I touched something cold. It startled me, somehow." He moved his right hand, and she saw the ring glittering in the candlelight on his fourth finger, a large piece with the rich sheen of a heavy grade of gold. "It must have been your ring."

He did not answer at first, but curiously, she had the impression that somehow she had in turn immensely startled him. "My ring?" After a moment, a rather forced smile quirked the corner of his mouth. "I suppose you must share your father's professional interest?"

"Yes, I do, my lord." She bent forward to study the gray, faceted gem; was that stone cut in the brilliant style? The candlelight glinted off the top facet in an oddly bright reflection. She tilted her head to avoid the tiny glare and drew in a surprised breath. The facets seemed to disappear with her change of angle, so the stone now appeared to be a smoothly rounded cabochon. And it was no longer gray, but black. Like obsidian, perhaps. No . . . there was a subtle glimmer suspended in the black, rather like the flecks in goldstone, only finer.

Something about it nudged a memory. A picture welled up in her mind, superimposing itself over the gem. Of course, how silly of her! She wasn't looking at a ring gemstone at all. No, she was leaning over something . . . she thought she felt rough-hewn stone and mortar under her palms. She was leaning over the lip of a well she had seen once as a child, peering down into the velvety black water. The sun shone directly on it, and suspended particles of minerals glimmered up at her, dazzling her eyes. But the blackness remained as obdurate as ever, hiding its secrets even as it drew the eye in, so that she could no longer see the stone edge of the well, the gold setting of the ring. It thwarted the sunlight, ate up the candlelight. It made her vision go dim, and a distant hum rang faintly in her ears. *Now, what does that remind me of?* she wondered fuzzily. *Oh, yes, the time when I was twelve, when I fainted; am I fainting now?* The hum grew louder and the thought drifted away, down into the waves of soothing dark nothingness.

And then she found herself blinking stupidly at the polished tabletop. The nameless lord's hand had withdrawn from the circle of candlelight. How much time had passed? A moment? She shivered once, violently. "I . . . I will fetch my father for you now," she stammered.

"Thank you." He nodded to her graciously.

In the hallway leading back toward the workroom, she stopped to lean against the wall and take a deep breath. What had happened to her? Hallucinating with her eyes open! Surely she wasn't sick? Her knees shook, and she tucked her trembling hands under her arms, trying to make them stop.

Well, if she wasn't sick, what else could it be? *There is a reason for everything.* The magician Arikan, who had tutored her in her letters, always said that. Jena caught her breath and frowned, remembering another time she had shaken like this. The time she fainted. She had surprised Arikan, walking in on him in his shop in the middle of the casting of a major spell, and so he hadn't prepared any wards to protect her.

Was it magic, then, she had felt just now? She remembered how Arikan had held her for a long time afterward until she stopped shaking, and he hadn't even scolded her for interrupting the spell.

Her father had done that for him, when he found out.

Her father. Jena pushed herself away from the wall and looked back doubtfully. The hall was dark. Perhaps she should go back and get another candle?

No. She didn't want to go in there alone. Instead, Jena walked forward, following the glimmer spilling around the corner from her father's workroom.

Inside, candles set in sconces and lanterns warmed the large room with golden light. From force of habit, Jena looked around with a critical eye, but all was ordered with Collas' characteristic neatness. A large oak cabinet domi-

nated the wall opposite the window; here the gemcutter kept
his polished and unpolished stones, sorted into tiny hand-
tooled drawers by type and color. Sketches of commissioned
pieces hung tacked in orderly rows on the walls; dop sticks
and jamb pegs for faceting work bristled in stands along the
work counters underneath. In a corner beside the small fireplace, a free-standing frame held soldering irons and heavy
spools of gold, silver, and brass wire, organized by thickness.
The parquet floor was swept clean; at least the servants were
getting that right now. The smell of clove and wintergreen
oil filled the air.

Collas, clad in his usual sober black, sat hunched over the
central worktable, his narrow fingers tinkering delicately
with the disassembled links of a heavy necklace. He was an
unprepossessing man with receding light brown hair and soft
blue eyes, at the moment squinted in concentration. Jena
sighed inwardly at the sight of the almost untouched dinner
plate he had, as usual, absently shoved aside. Putting down
an engraving tool, Collas saw Jena and gave her his quick
smile as he rose and went over to the racks by the shuttered
window to find another.

"Well, then! Come to say good night?"

"Not yet, Father," Jena replied, twitching her skirts out of
the way of the lap-wheel benches as she came forward into
the room. "There's a lord waiting to see you in the sitting
room; he spoke of a commission. . . ." She ran a testing finger over the splash guard on the nearest wheel. The wood
felt dry and rough to her touch; she'd have to remember to
coat the guards with linseed oil tomorrow to keep them from
warping.

"A lord come here? At this hour?" Collas removed the
loupe from his eye and stretched, wincing. Jena went over to
massage his shoulders. "Mmm, thank you, my dear. Well,
who is he, then?"

"I didn't recognize him, and he wouldn't give me his
name." She hesitated, wondering whether to tell him about
the ring.

"Strange." Collas sighed. "I hope it doesn't mean he won't
pay for whatever he orders." He reached over his shoulder to
pat her hand on his back. "Perhaps you could bring some

wine to the sitting room, while I speak with this mysterious gentleman."

So Jena fetched a jug of wine from the cold room and brought it on a tray, along with two of her father's prized blue-stemmed glass goblets and a plate of cheeses, to the sitting room. Collas, already seated and chatting with the lord, nodded toward the table. "Put it right down here. Would you honor us, my dear, by pouring the wine, and then light more candles?" He cut a few slices of cheese as she filled the goblets and set them down very carefully on the table. "So, then," Collas continued, addressing his guest again as Jena went toward the cupboard that contained the tapers, "there is no change in the Diamond's condition?"

"I'm afraid not. He did rally a bit after Equinox, but now he is worse. The physicians have declared he can't be moved."

"Hmm, yes. It seems quite strange for me to be calling on the members of the Court here at this time of year rather than at the Summer Palace in Chulipse." Collas shook his head. "This is the first summer in twenty years I've stayed in Piyar."

"Oh? You follow the Court then, too?"

Collas smiled. "I follow my business, my lord."

"Yes, I have heard of your work from a number of your patrons. Your skill is renowned throughout Piyanthia and highly recommended in Court circles, Master Collas."

"I'm honored." Collas acknowledged the accolade with a little nod. "And you, too, have a summer home? Your ancestral seat?"

"Yes."

Collas waited, but the visitor didn't offer the name of the house, which would reveal his identity.

Eventually, Collas cleared his throat as Jena finished lighting the last of the tapers. "Thank you, my dear," he said to Jena, and she turned to go.

"No, stay," said the lord, putting down his goblet. "I understand, Master Collas, that your daughter is also your apprentice?"

"Jena has applied to the Guild to be elevated to journeyman."

"Well, then," the lord said, reaching for a pouch on his belt. "Perhaps she'd like to see the stone I want you to cut for me."

At a look from her father, Jena swallowed her first impulse, which was to reply she'd seen all of his lordship's jewelry she'd care to see. Her father leaned forward to examine the stone in the visitor's palm. "Hmm. You want this prepared for any particular setting?"

"I'd like to wear it as a ring, and I'll leave the setting to your discretion."

"A ring, yes. We'll take your size before you leave tonight, my lord." Collas' voice, although polite, sounded puzzled, and Jena could appreciate why. The stone in the lord's palm was notably unspectacular. Just a mottled gray, which, unlike the stone in the ring he was wearing, had no inner fire or interesting crystalline structure whatsoever. Why, wondered Jena, would a nobleman want to use such an ordinary stone as an adornment?

Collas gently took hold of the nobleman's other hand and turned it over. "I should think an oval would suit the shape of your nails best. You'd like it to be smooth-polished, perhaps?"

"It can't be faceted?"

Collas shrugged. "Well, the stone is opaque, my lord. I hardly see the point." He reached in his pocket, pulled out the hand-length polished hazel wand Arikan had given him, and extended it to touch the stone.

But the lord's hand jerked back. "No."

The gemcutter looked up in surprise. "Forgive me, my lord, but it's a very simple spell."

"I know. But I don't want it done."

Collas assumed his most reasonable voice, the one he used when humoring highly unreasonable nobility. "It won't hurt the stone. It's simply a protective procedure to keep it from being stolen while it's in my custody. I've known the magician Arikan for years; we have a longstanding professional relationship."

"Nevertheless," the lord replied, smiling, but with a definite edge to his voice, "I would prefer that you not use the spell. Call it a whim of mine, if you will. I'll assume the responsibility," he said, lifting his hand as Collas tried to speak again. "Besides, it's generally known you do place a guard on stones customers bring you, am I correct?"

"Yes."

"Well, then." The lord waved a hand. "I imagine you haven't had any attempted thefts in years, have you?"

"No."

"Of course not. Why would any thief bother, since that is common knowledge? At any rate"—he gestured, holding the stone between thumb and forefinger—"if, by a remote chance, a thief should break in during the next day or so, I don't think this would be the first thing he'd try to take, do you?" He glanced at Jena. "It is a very ordinary stone."

"As your lordship wishes," Collas said after a pause. He fished his string of sizing rings from his pocket, and the visitor tried several on until he found one that fit.

Then the lord smiled, placed the stone on the table, and rose. "When can you have it ready?"

Collas rose, too. "Would three days be soon enough? I can have it finished by midday."

"Excellent." He reached into a pouch at his belt and placed some coins on the table with a satisfying golden clink. "I hope this will be sufficient?"

Collas eyed the small pile. "More than sufficient, my lord."

"If not, let me know, and I will give you more when I return to pick it up." The lord nodded at Jena. "Thank you for the wine." And then he was out the door. Jena could see him through the window, striding swiftly along the garden path leading to the terrace steps to the street.

Collas slowly sat again and thoughtfully reached for his wine. Jena sat down opposite him in the seat the mysterious lord had just vacated. "You didn't recognize him, either, Father?"

"No." His eyes looked troubled.

Jena placed her hand over his. "What is it?"

"I don't like not being allowed to use the warding spell." He withdrew his hand from hers and picked up the gray stone to hold it up to the candle.

"I don't see why he wants it that way, either."

Collas tucked the stone into a pocket. "Jena, would you carry a message to Arikan for me tomorrow morning? Tell him to stop by, that I'd like to consult with him on something." His lip curled in a smile. "And if that old windbag doesn't want to come, tell him I just received the first pressings of last year's North Cilea vintage. That will get him here in a hurry."

Jena laughed. "I'm sure it will."

CHAPTER TWO☉

THE DEATH OF JENA'S MOTHER six years before had left the responsibility for running the household squarely on Jena's shoulders. Collas (everyone assumed) should be left free to concentrate on the gemcutting and jewelry-setting skills that made his name a byword among the nobles. No one, least of all Jena herself, questioned that she should deflect all cares and problems from him by assuming them herself. Unfortunately, this often meant she had less time to spend on her own apprenticeship studies than she would have liked.

There were servants, of course, and usually other apprentices who helped with errands. This summer, however, the household was unusually small: one young man, Baldesar, who had studied with Collas for the past five years, had been elevated to journeyman and posted to another city the previous winter. Another boy had proved too sickly and been sent home, leaving Jena as the only apprentice. For once, Collas didn't have a journeyman working with him, either. Fewer people meant fewer responsibilities because the household was easier to manage, but also fewer hands to share all the work that needed to be done to keep Collas' business running.

Buying the supplies for the shop, among other chores, had fallen to Jena. The following morning, after a simple breakfast of porridge and fruit, she took her basket and hat and slipped out the street door of the house. Now, before the heat of the day arose to sizzle away the dew, the morning air hung heavy with scents from the gardens lining the street. Jena breathed in deeply, swinging her basket as she walked. After descending the public stairway leading to the Fourth Bowl, she turned left, heading east for the Two Bridge Market.

The rising sun brightened the white limestone of the Palace above the city to a dazzling glow and warmed the pale terra-cotta roofs in Lowertown below. Through a break in the houses, she could see the white sails of the tiny pleasure sailcraft venturing out from the western moorings to dart back and forth between the ferries across the wide area of the river. Mirrored amulets hanging from the masts caught the light, winking across the bay. Some of the boats headed south for the sea, disappearing through the strait guarded by the rocky outcropping upon which the Winter Palace stood.

The crowd heading for the Two Bridge Market grew steadily the farther east she went. Some smaller stalls already lined the street here, their colorful, flapping awnings shading tables and rush baskets piled high with cloth, vegetables, fish, bread, fruit, and cheese. "Buy my bread; buy my wine," toothless women called out shrilly to her as she passed. "Oranges and grapes, fresh and sweet!" Mouthwatering smells from skewers of roasting meat and vegetables wafted from other stalls.

Just before one of the public stairways leading down to the next rim, she ducked up a quiet lane to knock at the door of Arikan's lodging. He was out, and so, disappointed, she left a message with the housekeeper. Collas would have to wait until tomorrow.

But the North Cilea white proved to be even more effective a lure than she had suspected. By the time Jena returned home, trudging back up the private steps to the garden, the magician had already arrived and was deep in consultation with the gemcutter. As a longstanding family friend, Arikan had long ago ceased to stand ceremony in the sitting room where Collas met formally with his clients. Instead, the two sat at a small table Collas had brought out from the work-shop and set up in the garden to take advantage of the faint morning breeze.

Jena smiled at the sight the magician presented, for a greater contrast to Jena's neat and reserved father could scarcely be imagined. Collas wore black while Arikan de-lighted in expansive, brightly embroidered coats and equally expansive gestures. Collas sat in his chair in a self-contained manner, always keeping his elbows out of other people's way, never even creasing his clothes. Arikan overflowed his chair, his barrel chest and powerful arms making him look more like a blacksmith than the popular conception of a ma-gician: thin and pale from moping over dusty, arcane books. He kept his white hair and beard cut short, and it almost bris-tled with a kind of vital energy. Nevertheless, despite or per-haps because of the differences between them, the two had been firm friends for years.

Arikan broke off the conversation to hail Jena familiarly as she approached them. "There you are, you heartless minx. How could you leave me a message to visit, and then not be home to greet me? Off mooning after that tailor of yours. Staring rapturously into his goggle eyes, no doubt."

Jena blushed and then grinned, setting her basket down on the grass and plopping down beside it. "No, I wasn't seeing Bram," she said, removing her hat. "I was buying linseed oil and polishing cloths. Oh, and I took that message to the wholesaler, Father, about including more dopping cement and bort with the next order."

"Ah," said Arikan. "How unromantic."

"And Bram doesn't have goggle eyes."

"Oh, no, of course he doesn't! How silly of me." Arikan pretended to cower behind his wine cup. "Protect me from your daughter's towering rage, Collas," he said out of the corner of his mouth. "How ruthlessly she flies to her lover's defense!"

"Arikan, you are ridiculous." Despite herself, Jena laughed. "Besides, you had Father to keep you company."

"A poor consolation." Arikan gave her a ferocious scowl. "A most inadequate substitute."

Collas smiled. "You'll tolerate me, though, in order to drink my wine. How kind of you, Arikan."

"Never let it be said I don't make allowances." Arikan took a deep draught from his wine cup, eyes crinkling at Jena over the rim, and then set it down, smacking his lips with a satisfied sigh. Abruptly he frowned and reached for the gray stone resting innocently on the table at Collas' elbow. "So he wouldn't let you use a warding spell, you say?" he said to Collas. "*My* warding spell?" Jena and her father exchanged smiles at Arikan's tone of aggrieved professional pride as the magician turned the stone over in his hand.

Arikan had a serious side as well, one often obscured by his frequently noisy exuberance. He had taught Jena to read and cipher, to help her learn the business, Collas insisted, although she suspected this was only a pretext. Certainly the two encouraged her to continue her studies long past the point most would have considered necessary for a crafts-woman. In time, her tutor and father's friend became her friend as well. She found him to be a kind and thoughtful counselor whenever she brought him her concerns and questions.

He looked particularly thoughtful now. Putting the stone back down on the table, he reached for a grape on the plate by his elbow and leaned back in his chair. "Most curious," he muttered, and popped the grape into his mouth.

"What's curious, Ari?" asked Collas.

"This stone. It carries no impression of its owner."

"I thought if you touched things, you could read who the owner is. Can't you do that?" Jena asked in astonishment.

"My dear, what a crude way of putting it." Arikan sighed heavily. "Sometimes I despair; have I really managed to teach you nothing?"

"Nothing about magic, at least," Jena retorted tartly.

"You think not?" He fixed her with a stern eye. "Then an-swer this for me: what do you think magic is?"

"Any child knows that," Jena replied. "Magic is seeing possibilities and then acting upon them."

"No!" Arikan's meaty fist crashed down on the table, and Jena jumped. "You speak like a child, when you mouth part of the answer, without understanding, and mistake it for the whole."

Collas grinned and took a sip of wine as Jena bristled.

"Listen, Jena," Arikan went on. "A magician is one who can see possibilities, true, and who knows how to make them happen. But that is only part of it, and that's because not all possibilities should be acted upon. It isn't enough just to see the possible roads; anyone who wishes to be an adept can only do it by learning how to decide which road to take."

Jena tried to keep a defensive edge from her voice. "So what does this have to do with not being able to read that stone?"

"Ah, yes, this stone." Arikan picked it up again. "My point is that when I scry an object like this, I don't simply read it. It's not that easy, not like a book I can simply open. I have to interpret it—look at the possibilities of who has touched it, as well as the not-possibilities, and balance one against the other. That's what scrying *is*: it means to succeed in discerning, or to make out, dimly."

Jena sniffed. "Sounds like quibbling to me."

"If you like," Arikan replied serenely. "The difference is real."

"Ha. Then what you're saying is you can't *interpret* anything at all about this stone."

"No, I can't. And that is unusual."

"What could be the cause?" Collas asked.

"The possibilities, you mean?" Arikan laughed shortly. "That's the precise problem. The possibilities are in flux. Perhaps the owner is undecided about it in some way that involves the actual ownership. He may keep it, he may give it away, but he hasn't decided which, so he doesn't yet think of it as his own." He raised an eyebrow at Collas. "And you say he wouldn't give you his name?"

"No."

"Well, that may be another reason. The stone carries no trace because his wish to remain anonymous is strong, and he knows enough magic to hide his own possibilities from others. Powerful, and subtle." He reached for his cup. "Jena, tell me your impressions of this eccentric lord. Perhaps you can remember some detail that would help me identify him."

"I'm not sure I can. I saw the knot on his cloak, of course, but no device stitched to it that I could see. No device on his hose, either."

"Did he wear an enseigne brooch on his cap? Was there anything on the sheath of his knife?"

Jena shook her head. "No, nor on his ring."

"His ring? What ring?" Collas asked sharply.

"Why, the ring on his hand," she replied in surprise. "His right hand, I think."

"He wore no ring."

"But he did, Father. It was a plain setting of yellow gold, with a dark central stone." She frowned.

Arikan studied her face intently, but Collas was saying, "Remember, I sized his hands, Jena. Both hands, in fact. I saw no ring. I certainly would've noticed any jewelry he wore, to make sure I matched the style with the ring he commissioned."

"How interesting," Arikan said.

"He must have taken the ring off," Collas said.

"When I came to fetch Father," said Jena, puzzled. "After . . ." Her words trailed off uncertainly.

"After?" Arikan prompted after a moment.

"That ring. It had a strange effect on me."

"What do you mean? What kind of effect?"

"Remember the time I interrupted one of your spells, Arikan? I became dizzy. Like that."

A heavy silence fell for a moment. Arikan broke it, combing his fingers through his beard as he fingered the gray stone. Finally he handed it back to Collas.

"My advice to you, my friend, is to refuse the commission. Give Milord of Mystery his stone back, along with his money."

Collas looked surprised. "Do you think that's necessary?"

Arikan smiled. "Of course not. It's simply advisable."

"Why? What would happen if Father cuts it?" Jena wanted to know.

"Many things could happen. Some are more likely than others."

"But what could—"

"If your father follows my advice," Arikan interrupted,

"we'll never know, will we? You are going to follow my advice, aren't you, Collas?"

"I always have before," Collas replied slowly. "I don't see any reason to stop now."

"There, you see?" Arikan dismissed the question with an airy wave of his hand. "It's immaterial. Poof."

Jena glowered at him but knew not to press any further.

"And now, Collas," Arikan said, "you are a busy man. Doubtless you have better things to do than dance attendance on me. Besides, you've had enough wine. Go make some lovely jewelry and leave me alone with your lovely daughter."

Collas shrugged good-naturedly and stood. "If I've had enough, so have you," he said, reaching for the jug, but Arikan whisked it neatly out of his reach.

"Almost enough." The magician refilled his cup to the brim. "Don't forget I have a monstrously higher capacity than you."

"Oh, I never forget." Collas took the jug when Arikan relinquished it and strolled away toward the house as Jena appropriated her father's seat.

"I don't understand why Father lets you talk to him that way."

"It amuses him. He gets tired of your whey-faced pliant obedience, my dear. I offer a refreshing change."

"Ha. And I don't know why you call me lovely in front of Father, but as soon as we're alone, you start twitting me about my looks."

"Any young girl like you who wears her hair like that deserves twitting," Arikan said unexpectedly.

"What?" Despite herself, Jena's hand went up to touch her black braid reflexively. "What's wrong with my hair?"

Arikan raised an eyebrow. "Do you really want to know?"

"Of course."

"Perhaps you might consider releasing it from that stranglehold once in a while, eh? You scrape it back from your forehead so tightly I can see the skin pulling at your cheekbones. It makes your eyes look like cat's-eyes."

Self-consciously, Jena lowered her hand. "I don't think—

that is—well, with the things I have to do, I can't have hair flying in my eyes all day."

"Of course not," Arikan said, his eyes twinkling. "Why, now that you point it out, your hair suits your lifestyle perfectly. What could be more suitable for the prim mistress of a busy professional household?"

With difficulty, Jena kept her temper. "Anyway, Father likes it."

"Of course. Interesting that you mention your father, rather than your fiancé." He waved her to silence as she opened her mouth to object. "But then your father's opinion is naturally very important to you. You have always excelled at pleasing him."

"And just what's wrong with that?" asked Jena, still nettled.

"Nothing," Arikan replied gravely. "As long as it doesn't mean you have trouble recognizing what *you* want. Anyway, in answer to your earlier question, perhaps you haven't yet noticed that your father is horribly biased where you're concerned, too. Of course I humor him; didn't you hear me explain earlier that I make allowances?" Abruptly, he stopped baiting her. "Now. Tell me about it."

"It?"

"Don't be stupid, Jena. Tell me about the lord's ring."

She did. She found it difficult to think, to choose the words to describe the experience. ". . . and then I found myself in the corridor leading to the workshop. I remember it was dark, and the darkness reminded me of the ring." She shivered.

"And then?"

"Well, I felt I needed a candle, but somehow I didn't want to go back in there without Father. So I went to the workshop to find him instead."

"You're sure he wasn't wearing it when the two of you went back to the front room together."

"I didn't notice. For some reason, I felt reluctant to mention it to Father. I almost did, several times, in fact. But every time, just as I was on the verge of saying something, I would forget about it instead. I don't know exactly why." She shrugged helplessly. Arikan stared at the table, gnawing pensively at his lower lip, until she broke the silence. "What do you think it means, Arikan?"

"It may mean one thing, it may mean another."

Jena sighed. Arikan might not look much like a magician, but he certainly knew how to sound like one at times. "Arikan, tell me."

"Do you think I must tell you everything, just because you pester me?"

"No, I don't. But I'm not pestering. And I'm not teasing. That's what I did when I was little, but I'm too old for such tricks now."

"Humph. They never worked much on me anyway."

"No, they didn't. What I'm doing now is *asking*. Because . . . because I think you should tell me."

"Oh, you do, do you?"

"Yes, I do."

"Perhaps you're right," Arikan said unexpectedly, rubbing the bristles on his chin. "Well. The ring, I suspect, among other things, is meant to serve as a detection device. To sense people who are sensitive to magic."

"But everyone is sensitive to magic."

"I mean"—Arikan gestured impatiently—"to detect potential adepts. People who are capable of becoming magicians."

"You mean me?" Jena straightened in her chair in astonishment. "Me, a magician?"

"Of course," Arikan replied blandly, as if the idea were the most natural thing in the world. "You have the potential, Jena. You always have."

"You knew?"

Arikan made no reply.

"You always knew?" Jena found herself almost spluttering in indignation. "You could have trained me. Why did you never tell me?"

"Because, my dear girl, you never asked."

"What difference does that make? If you knew something about me that was so important—"

Arikan snorted. "Important? How important could it be if you never even realized it? Magic is no use to those who do not want it—"

"You never even gave me the chance."

"—who do not discover it within themselves, by themselves."

"But now I have discovered it."

"Yes." Arikan sounded unhappy at the idea. "Because you had help."

Jena sat back in her chair, overcome by the idea. A magician . . . Suddenly another thought occurred to her. "Does Father know about this?"

Arikan hesitated, and in that split second, Jena felt sick. "He does know," she said. "You told him, but you never told me."

"It's not just that. I was the one who—" he checked himself.

"The one who what?"

Whatever he had been going to say, he changed his mind. "I did what I thought was best."

"I'm sure you did." Jena laughed bitterly. "That's what you always do, Arikan. Your best." She pushed herself back from the table and stood up. "The finest magician in Piyar; that's what Father always said—"

"As your father is the finest gemcutter in Piyar," Arikan interrupted smoothly. "Because that is what he wishes to do." Leaning back in his chair, he studied her with narrowed eyes. "Well, then, Jena. Now that you know—what is it *you* wish?"

Jena glared back at him, but was surprised to find no ready answer.

CHAPTER
THREE

WHEN JENA CAME INTO THE house after saying farewell to Arikan, Collas was nowhere to be found. Lila, one of the maidservants, told her that a messenger serving one of Collas' noble clients had come to the workshop to request that the gemcutter wait upon his master. "Lord Baro's man, I believe it was, mistress," Lila said as she laid out the midday meal of fish and salad greens. She arched an eyebrow with a significant look, and Jena sighed.

"Lord Baro? Then who knows how long it will be before we see Father again. Poor Father."

"I did give him a pocket of bread with meat and cheese to take with him, mistress," Lila said primly. "So at least he'll not starve, no matter how long his lordship keeps him waiting."

Jena spent the afternoon in the workshop by herself roughing out jasper cabochons on the lap-wheel. As she pumped the foot pedal, deftly turning each stone against the grinding surface to shape it, the rotating wheel thrummed and the water gurgled quietly in the sluice pan. The familiar sounds were soothing, encouraging a part of her mind to wander even as she worked, and she thought back over the morning's conversation with Arikan.

So she could do magic!—if she wanted to, of course. She wondered what she would have chosen to do if she had known before beginning her apprenticeship studies with her father. What would it have been like to learn to become a magician? Would earning a living that way be interesting? Arikan certainly seemed to find it so, but would it really suit her? How strange to find out that the potential had always been there!

And yet there was no reason she couldn't start learning now, she realized suddenly. The thought was so startling that she ceased pumping the treadle and simply sat, staring down at the half-formed cabochon in her hand as the wheel slowed and stopped. What—not become a gemcutter? She had spent years as an apprentice, fully expecting her life to follow a particular course. The idea of discarding those plans now to try something new felt alarming—and yet, she had to admit to herself . . . intriguing, too.

Frowning a little, she added more water to the sluice pan, reached for a new stone, and started up the wheel again. It was natural to be intrigued by the idea, she told herself. She had watched Arikan cast enough spells to understand that magic had its own kind of fascination. But she had invested so much time in learning how to do what she was doing now, and she loved it. Cutting gems and designing pieces of jewelry to set them off to their best advantage satisfied something in her that delighted in the beautiful, the colorful, the perfect. She had her father to consider; he had spoken of her taking over his business someday. And there was Bram, too. What would he think of marrying a girl who planned to become a magician rather than a gemcutter?

And yet . . . to be able to do magic . . .

She was still thinking everything over when Collas returned at sunset, with a commission for a fan-cut tourmaline cloak brooch, and a bemused expression. He greeted Jena with an absentminded kiss on the forehead and a word of critical approval for her afternoon's work. "I suppose Arikan didn't stay to dine, did he?" he asked.

"Why, no, Father. He left shortly before midday. I'm sorry; did you want me to invite him?"

Collas sighed. "I should have left that jug of wine after all.

Better yet, I should have told him where to find the whole barrel. That way I'd have been sure he would still be here when I returned."

"But then he might not have been of much use to you," Jena replied dryly. "Why do you need to speak with him again?"

"Well, *I* don't, exactly. But when Lord Baro gave me the fee for this new commission, he mentioned that he's lost that ring I delivered to him last Equinox. You remember, the one set with one of those very pale garnets I got when I traded that extra lapis with Master Cherno?"

Jena groaned. "Another ring? That must be the third this year! Father, that man would lose his head if it weren't attached to his neck."

"I suspect you are right, my dear."

"And I suppose he added ten more coins to the pile and said he would be grateful if you might, 'er, have any inspiration' as to where the ring might be found?"

Collas' lips twitched. "How did you guess?"

Jena sighed. "What a hypocrite. Very well. Would you like me to take the fee to Arikan tomorrow?"

"If you could, I would be grateful, Jena. I need to finish that series of mourning brooches for Lady Farraline."

Accordingly, the next day, for the second morning in a row, Jena presented herself at Arikan's door and asked to see the magician. This time, however, Arikan was in, and so the housekeeper promptly ushered her into Arikan's workroom.

Jena repressed a shudder as she looked around at the untidy heaps of books and parchments, scattered with half-melted candle stubs. Shelves lined the walls, heaped with stacks of bowls and jars holding herbs and tinctures, and boxes overflowing with a dizzying array of objects. Arikan stood bent over at one shelf, rummaging through a box and tossing the contents carelessly behind him as he consulted something on a parchment; some landed on his worktable and others careened off it onto the floor. The table already held a set of shipmaster compasses jumbled together in a wooden tumbler, a large pair of rusty scissors, a chicken skeleton, a lantern, charm bags, and three or four children's marionettes with tangled strings and sticks.

Jena ducked as several painted masks flew past her shoulder. "Arikan!" she exclaimed, half laughing.

Arikan looked up from the parchment he was studying. "Ah, Jena," he said vaguely. "Good to see you."

Jena looked around at the mess and shook her head ruefully. "I can't understand why you don't discharge your housekeeper."

"Why should I?" he replied, frowning as he came to sit at the table. "She possesses a masterly hand with pastry, and she keeps the rest of the house scrupulously clean enough to suit even you. She dusts in here, too, although she knows enough not to move anything. She hinders heedless young girls like yourself from interrupting me in the middle of spells. We deal delightfully well together. You really should confine yourself to managing your father's household and leave mine in peace."

"Hmph."

"Here, now, stop wrinkling your nose at me. Shift that pile of books from that stool. No, don't set them on that table, or it will undoubtedly collapse. Put them there on the floor, next to the canary cage."

Jena placed the books on the floor and sat herself upon the stool.

"Now," Arikan said, pushing a plate of figs in her direction, "how may I possibly be of service to you?"

Jena reached for a fig and drew from her pocket the pouch her father had given her that morning. "Father received a commission from Lord Baro yesterday. His lordship paid the stated fee, and then counted out these additional coins while asking whether Father had any idle idea where he might have misplaced a ring."

"Lord Baro, eh?" Arikan rolled his eyes. "I suppose that's about as subtle as he ever gets. What kind of ring is it?"

"It's yellow gold," Jena said around her mouthful of fig, "set with a pale red garnet. Father delivered it last Equinox."

Arikan reached out to take the pouch, hefted its weight, and grunted. He extracted a coin and handed it back to her. "See that Collas gets this, won't you? And thank him for acting as go-between." He heaved a sigh and scratched his beard. "Let's hope his lordship's avaricious mistress didn't filch this one, too. I'm certainly glad I didn't have to tell him last time."

"I know. Explaining that with the proper degree of delicacy was so awkward for Father's dignity." Jena shook her head. "It's ridiculous, Arikan. Why won't nobles ever deal with magicians?"

Arikan's eyes widened in mock surprise. "Why, Jena, whatever gives you such an idea? I positively batten on the largesse flowing from the coffers of our beloved noble class. You've no idea how often workmen consult with me about the best type of roof to put on milord's palazzo. Or a matchmaker sounds me out about the possibility of arranging an illustrious alliance between milady's pimply son and her best friend's pea-brained daughter. Why, this year alone I've received enough from locating Lord Baro's lost jewelry to buy me a whole new Festival wardrobe!"

"But they won't deal with you directly! They'll rage at Court about the evils of sorcery—"

"And then commission my services through intermediaries and look the other way while I receive my fee, eh?" Arikan gave her a crooked smile. "As long as the fee is paid, Jena. As long as the fee is paid."

Jena's eyes widened a little. "I didn't know you were so cynical, Arikan."

Arikan fell silent for a long moment. The canary took advantage of the pause in the conversation to burst into song, and with a look of long suffering, Arikan got up and threw a cloth over the cage, cutting off the sound abruptly. He turned to Jena with a thoughtful expression.

"Perhaps I'm not as cynical as all that, Jena. Not entirely. Oh, I admit I find gentlemen like Lord Baro quite tiresome. The lengths some nobles go in order to avoid any appearance of consorting with 'sorcerers,' the *knots* they tie themselves into—why, I might be tempted to bust my guts laughing, if only it weren't so insulting. But there is another kind of noble, too, you know: the kind who'll have nothing to do with a magician like me, even through an intermediary, because they truly despise magic. I have a bit more respect for those who think that way. At least they're not hypocrites."

He gave a short laugh as he seated himself again. "Hypocrites have their uses, of course. I have something the Lord Baros of this world want, even though they won't admit it publicly. And so they offer me some protection from the other type. If Lord Raffaello or Lord Oselare get too emphatic about driving magicians out of the city, why, I know Lord Baro or Lady Carlotta will say a quiet word into the appropriate ear, grease the appropriate palm, and I'll be left in peace."

"How can you call it being left in peace? The nobles won't let the magicians establish a school for study or a formal guild, or anything!"

"Perhaps that's not such a bad thing," Arikan said, surprising her. "Magic—proper magic, properly used—isn't necessarily something inherited or something that can be drilled into you. It just *is*, mostly. You discover it within yourself because it wells up inside of you, if you have a heart and a mind that are open enough to seeing possibilities. I picked up whatever else I needed to learn from books and from informal arrangements with whoever was willing to teach me."

"Yes, but wouldn't it have been easier if you'd had a school?"

"Magicians work best when they're not too hidebound. If a magic school were ever established and given a century or so to get steeped in tradition, I imagine it might drive true magic out of the hearts of hopeful students rather than cultivate it. And as for a guild, well, I've listened to your father's animadversions on guild politics often enough to think I'm not missing much. No, Jena. It's enough for me that the Diadem has never gone so far as to outlaw magic. Moreover— and this is what I mean when I say I'm not entirely cynical—I can't be too angry at the nobles. I pity them instead, I think."

"Why is that?"

"It's hard to hate someone who treats you badly when you know they're only doing it because they fear you."

"But why should they be afraid?"

"Oh, come now, Jena. What do you think started the Founders' War?"

Jena raised an eyebrow. "What—magic? The Founders' War was over the succession. Everyone knows that. *Keyan the Great sired strong sons eight/ The first, Lord Broderick—*"

"Try to think a little beyond the children's rhymes," Arikan interrupted scornfully. "I'm not asking you to parrot back to me which son or cousin killed which nephew or uncle. That's not the point."

"Well, what is the point, then?"

"It's what the nobles decided they had learned, rightly or wrongly, from that whole bloody fratricidal mess: never trust magic. Yes, it was about the succession. But it was started by a magician who started thinking about altering the succession because he misused his magic. I'll say this for the nobility: as stupid as they seem to me sometimes, I have to admit they have long memories. They haven't forgotten that lesson, even centuries later. That's why they refuse to acknowledge ever dealing with the likes of me."

Jena considered. "I still think it's absurd."

"Of course it is. But as maddening as it is sometimes, I must admit they are quite right to be afraid. History tells them what out-of-control magic can do."

"So you really think if it weren't for the Founders' War, the nobles would have no trouble with magic at all?"

Arikan leaned back in his chair, and his gaze out the window became abstracted. "I looked at that question once, when I was younger and more interested in doing pure theoretical research. What if Lord Broderick had lived to assume the throne, for example—instead of dying of a fever before his father, leaving the heirship to eight-year-old Ewan, and an ambitious uncle to assume the regency? What if Lord Vance hadn't perished at sea? What would Piyanthia's history have been like then?

"Scrying the past—that's what studying history is, after all—is complex. The further back in time a historical turning point is, the more difficult it is to see and understand the what-might-have-beens, the possibilities that didn't happen. That's because all the events that followed from the initial crucial event shape the events that follow *them* in turn."

"It's like cutting a stone, I suppose," Jena said thoughtfully. "I can take a stone some other gemcutter has started with a flat table cut and decide to make it either a basic round or a basic square. But once the square cut's been started, I can't go back and finish it as a pendaloque. I don't even see that as a possibility."

Arikan laughed. "Exactly. Or imagine if an engineer diverted a river. You see the valley the way it is with a new source of water. Trees grow up around it, and people come to live along its banks. Years later, if you try to imagine what the valley would be like if the river *hadn't* been diverted, you not only have to picture the river being gone, but the trees and cultivated farmlands and the cities as well. We reach the point that when we look at history, so much of what we see has sprung from that original point that we have trouble imagining it turning out any other way.

"Now, difficult as it is to scry the past, one thing is clear about the Founders' War. The nobles' fear of magic, the war itself, and the eventual establishment of the Diadem itself all sprang from one thing: it was the Regent Lord Stearn's terrible abuse of magic. He asked only one question, one that had gnawed at him the whole time his nephew was growing up and beginning to contract a marriage alliance: is it possible that I can be king? The answer, magic told him, was that it would be easy. To become king, he just had to do one little thing." He paused and lifted an eyebrow, a teacher waiting for a comment from his student.

"Kill Ewan," Jena said, "and seize the throne." She shuddered and reached for another fig.

"Exactly. Of course it wasn't that easy. Ewan's betrothed escaped and gave birth to a son in exile. Vance's heirs, too, had a better claim than Stearn did, since Vance was the second son and he was the third." Arikan sighed. "The nobles are right to call him Stearn the Black. That's what black magic is, to ask only 'Is it possible?' without adding, 'What will the consequences be? Is it right?' Stearn didn't bother to reflect whether he *should* usurp the throne or examine all the possibilities that would flow from betraying the trust placed in him as regent." He shook his head, a sober look on his face. "He finally understood in the end," he said softly, "when he was dying, alone in a dungeon, his wife and all of his children

dead before him. But by then it was too late. He had un-
leashed upon Piyanthia a wave of bloodshed and betrayal and
assassination by magic that wouldn't stop until Lord Erin became the first Diamond, ending the war and establishing the
Diadem. That didn't happen until years after Stearn's death—
and Stearn had magic enough to know it, too. A pity he didn't
understand sooner. He was a slow learner."

There was a short pause, and Arikan reached for the cup of
wine at his elbow and took a swallow. "So I think the answer
to your question is, yes, if the Founders' War hadn't happened, the nobles wouldn't be as bothered about the use of
magic. Oh, I'm not saying they would have no problem with
it at all, but at least they wouldn't be so frightened of it."

A rap at the door made them both look up. "Enter," Arikan
called.

The door opened, and the housekeeper poked her head in
around the corner. "Begging your pardon, sir, but it's Mistress Elspet to see you."

"Ah." Arikan nodded. "Show her in." As the housekeeper
withdrew, he hoisted himself to his feet and went over to a
shelf to collect a wide basket heaped high with pots and
pans. "She's come to collect these, I expect. Well, Jena, if
you will excuse me . . ." He gestured vaguely toward the
door.

"Could I—that is—" Jena stopped, and laughed a little
self-consciously. "Would you permit me stay, Arikan? Just
to watch for a little while, if your customers wouldn't
mind?"

"Watch?" Arikan, returning to the table, looked over at her
in some puzzlement. "Watch what?"

"Well, to watch you, I suppose. To see how a magician
spends his day."

"You've seen me in my shop before, Jena."

"Well, yes. But not since knowing I could maybe learn to
do magic myself."

Arikan studied her through narrowed eyes for a moment,
and then shrugged as he put the basket down. "That's true
enough. Very well." The sound of a step in the hallway diverted his attention. "Ah, my dear madam. I have the pots
ready for you, as you see."

"Do you indeed, Arikan?" The slight woman entering the shop spared Jena a single curious glance and then came forward eagerly, all her attention focused on the contents of the basket on the table. She lifted one griddle to eye level with work-roughened hands and squinted down the length of the handle. "They don't look any different," she said, a note of doubt in her voice.

"Of course they don't," Arikan said blandly. "I pride myself on keeping my style rather unobtrusive. You want pots and pans that work, don't you? Not cookware that will necessarily draw the eye of everyone who comes into the kitchen."

"That's so," the woman said hesitantly. She gave Jena another quick glance, and Arikan immediately took the hint.

"Madam Elspet, this is Jena Gemcutter, a friend of mine for many years. Jena, this is Elspet Washer, of Buckthorn Lane."

"Pleased to meet you, I'm sure," Elspet said. Her gaze strayed back to the basket, and she lifted out a hanging covered pot and held it up to admire. "For my daughter, d'ye see," she said with simple pride. "Her wedding is in a month."

Jena's eye quickly took in the patches on the woman's apron, the scrubbing paddle hanging from a cord at her waist, the careful, almost invisible darns down the length of her sleeve. The pot the woman held wasn't large, but Jena could tell it was a heavy grade of iron, with a well-fitting cover, and there was a larger one still in the basket, besides the griddles, bread pans, ladles, and skillets. The whole set must have made an impressive dent in a hardworking laundress' wages. "Oh, your daughter will be thrilled with such a wedding gift," Jena said. "I'm sure when I marry, I'd feel lucky to have a set half so fine."

Elspet blushed a rosy pink with pleasure. "Why, thank'ee kindly. I'm hoping my Nonie will like 'em. Aye, and use 'em well."

Jena gave Arikan a sidelong glance. "So . . . you brought them to Arikan . . ."

"A simple spell," Arikan said, "to decrease the possibility that the young bride will ever burn her new husband's meals."

"Oh, I see."

"My Nonie's a good girl, miss," Elspet said. A small

crease appeared between her eyebrows. "But she don't have much of a dab hand in the kitchen, if you know what I mean. She *will* scorch the soup every time. Now she's found herself a good man, and I don't want her to lose him, so I thought, d'ye see, perhaps a charm or so . . ."

"I can assure you," Arikan said, "I foresee a long and happy marriage for her and a wide reputation as a splendid cook. In fifteen years or so, her husband will be well on his way to a girth like mine. That is"—he raised a finger—"if you do what's necessary to finalize the spell. I left it for you to complete."

"What? Me?" Elspet put the covered pot back into the basket hastily and looked at Arikan in some alarm. "I don't know no magic."

"In a way, you do." Arikan smiled. "You have a month. Spend it giving your daughter concentrated cooking lessons."

"Oh." Understanding dawned on Elspet's face. "Aye, that would help, too, wouldn't it?"

"Yes, I think it would. And more than that," Arikan continued kindly, "it will give the two of you some time together. By the time the month's over, perhaps you'll feel more confident she's ready to begin her life with her new husband, eh?"

Elspet's forefinger slowly stroked the edge of one of the bread pans. "I just don't know whether I'm ready," she confessed in a low voice. She dabbed her eyes hastily with the hem of her apron and smiled at Jena a little tremulously. "She's the first to leave home, you see. Ah, well." Resolutely, she gave her eyes a last wipe, and then lifted the basket with a grunt and settled it against her hip as Arikan pulled the bellrope. "That's good advice, Arikan. I'll do what you say. Thank'ee! Good day to you both, then."

"And a good day to you too, madam," Arikan replied as the housekeeper appeared at the shop door, "and my very best wishes to your daughter upon such a happy occasion."

Elspet exchanged a friendly nod with Jena and followed the housekeeper out of the shop.

After the door had closed, Jena cocked her head at Arikan. "Will Nonie's marriage really be happy?"

Arikan considered the matter judiciously. "Well, all the

parties involved want it to be, including Elspet. I think it will—as long as Elspet doesn't defeat her own purpose by sticking in her oar too often. Some private moments with her daughter before the wedding might help prevent that."

Jena smiled. "I remember Father saying once that there were two parts to earning a living as a master gemcutter. One was learning to cut gems flawlessly. But the other part was harder, and maybe even more important, and some gemcutters never grasp it: you have to sense what it is that customers really want when they ask for something, because sometimes they don't even truly understand it themselves."

Arikan sat down again and refilled his cup of wine from a pitcher at his elbow. "Is that so?" he asked innocently, as if being presented with an interesting new theory.

Jena grinned, not in the least fooled. "Yes, it is, although I didn't understand until now it's true of magicians, too. I wonder if Elspet Washer understood she paid her fee as much for her own benefit as for her daughter's."

"No. But that's not important for the spell to work." He took another sip of wine. "Now, let's see if we can't discover where Lord Baro's ring might be hiding."

Jena stayed with Arikan for several more hours. By the time Arikan had finished a succession of scrying spells and determined the ring had probably rolled into one of Lord Baro's clothing storage chests ("It's buried somewhere among his underlinens, I believe"), several more customers were waiting. The first, a merchant whom Jena knew had a reputation of having a rather peppery temper, had come because he had quarreled bitterly with his son and now wanted a spell cast that would make the young man willing to speak with him again. Arikan refused to accept a fee and simply sent the man on his way with a polite but firm, "You don't need magic from me. Simply write to your son and tell him you're sorry."

He did cast a spell for the next person waiting to see him, a young fisherman about to go into business for himself, who had brought in a splinter of wood from a boat he was considering buying. Arikan scorched the end of the splinter in a candle flame and then rapped it sharply over a bowl of water and studied the patterns of bobbing ashes on the water's surface. "There are a few rotten planks on the starboard side near the bow. Keep that in mind when you're bargaining over the price. Replace those and it should remain seaworthy for ten to twelve more years—if you keep the hull scraped clean and caulk the seams every winter. Mind you get good sails, too. If you like, when you buy your nets, bring them in and I'll put a spell on them for you." And he gave the man an amulet to take with him to hang from the mast.

The rest of the client meetings went like that, mixing the application of magic, when appropriate, with common-sense advice. As Jena walked home afterward by herself, thinking over the morning, she realized that Arikan's use of magic had interested her, but she had actually been paying more attention to the different ways he had handled each customer— a jocular manner with one, a confiding air with another, a serious and quiet style with a third. He was even better at that sort of thing than her father, really.

He had not asked her to help him with any of his spells. That surprised her a little, since once the secret was out that she could learn magic, she would have thought he would have been eager to teach her. But then, she had to admit to herself, she had not asked, either.

A passing woman's heavy dangling earrings caught her eye as she mounted the steps leading toward Goldberry Lane. She spent several moments absentmindedly considering how they might be better designed when she caught herself and smiled at her own abstraction. Perhaps that was why Arikan had not jumped at the chance to teach her any particular lesson about magic that morning: he knew what it was she really wanted to do. She thought of the half dozen spinels she had waiting for her in the shop, rough-ground and set on dopping pegs, ready for the first cut. Maybe she could ask Father to demonstrate the briolette. She was ready for something challenging. Her step was light, and she was humming to herself when she came home to her father's shop.

CHAPTER
FOUR

In the afternoons, Jena joined her father in the workshop. Sometimes they worked silently side by side for hours, but at other times she would watch as Collas demonstrated to her techniques of his craft. The day after spending the morning in Arikan's shop, she was watching him painstakingly set a spray of opals on a brooch when a knock at the street side of the house interrupted their work.

Jena went to answer the door. It was a young apprentice from another gemcutter's shop, who handed her a folded piece of parchment sealed with a stamped blotch of indigo wax. "For Master Collas." He gave her a wave and a cheeky grin and was off at a run back down the street before she closed the door.

"Who was it?" Collas asked her as she came back in the workshop.

"One of Master Tiavet's apprentices. He left this for you."

Collas took the parchment, slit the seal with an engraving tool, and read what it contained. After a moment, he lowered the paper and looked at her, with an expression she could not quite read.

"It concerns you, my dear."

"Me? That is stamped with the Guild business seal, isn't it?" she asked.

"Yes. Master Tiavet is replying to your application to be elevated to journeyman."

"Already? But I thought the Guild didn't announce this year's elevations until autumn."

Collas nodded slowly.

Jena swallowed. "Father, what does the letter say?"

With a sigh, he handed it to her. It took her a few moments to grasp the contents. *Your rather unusual request . . . do not consider it necessary . . . precedent does not allow us to . . . trust you will, of course, understand . . .*

She looked up from the parchment in wonder. "They're rejecting my application?"

"Jena, I'd hoped—but of course, I could not be sure . . ."

She felt a heavy numbness creeping over her and sat down abruptly. "But why? I mean, weren't my samples good enough?"

"I suspect it has nothing to do with your work."

"I don't understand." She looked down at the parchment, blinking hard. "This letter hardly even mentions me."

Collas' answer was slow in coming. "There are not many women in the Jewelers' Guild, you know."

"But they can join! What about Beatrice? Or Elisabetta? Elisabetta is even a master! And there are others, too. Why should the Guildmasters refuse to even consider me?"

"The circumstances are rather special in their cases. Their membership is what is called hereditary, in trust."

"What does that mean?"

"To begin with, Beatrice's and Elisabetta's fathers were gemcutters."

"So? You're a gemcutter, too."

"Both their fathers were gemcutters who had died without sons," Collas said gently. "Beatrice and Elisabetta both wanted to join the Guild. I think they were only allowed to because their memberships were considered to be held in trust for their own sons."

"You mean they're not really members because of their own skill."

"No." Collas shook his head. "Elisabetta once told me that

was why she never married. If she should have a son, she would no longer have the right to make jewelry because the membership would pass to him." He tapped the parchment she held. "I had hoped this would not be a problem for you. But you see, I'm still making jewelry, and, well . . . they don't understand why you want to join. Since I'm still alive. Perhaps, when I'm gone . . . they will reconsider."

"They can't understand why I would want to make jewelry?" Jena said numbly. "They expect me to simply sit around waiting for you to *die*? They think the only possible reason I would have to join is to ensure a place for a son? Why do *they* want to make jewelry and join the Guild? Tell me that!"

Collas looked at her with compassion. "I'm very sorry, Jena."

Jena's gaze fell on the brooch on the table, and she had to dig her fingernails into her palms to keep the tears from spilling over. She folded the parchment back up along the creases and tucked it into her sash as she stood up. "I'm going to go see Bram."

Collas' voice stopped her in the workshop doorway. "Jena—there is a process for appealing the decision."

Jena shrugged and said, her voice cracking, "What would be the point?" It was only with a strong effort of will that she refrained from slamming the door on her way out.

Bram Tailor lived with his father, mother, two younger sisters, and a constantly fluctuating assortment of cats in an overcrowded brick house on Three Blossom Lane, down on the Fifth Rim. It was a cheerful, bustling household, although sometimes a bit noisy for Jena, accustomed as she was to the quiet order of her own home.

The oldest sister, Carina, a couple years younger than Jena, was tending the counter. "Hello," Carina said, smiling. "Come to order a dress?"

Jena felt herself warm in response. She liked Carina very much. "Wish I could, but not today. Father thinks I have more than enough clothes."

"Oh, go on, one more can't hurt. We can always use the business. No?" Carina gave a little shrug and laughed. "Well, at least Mother can't say I didn't try. I'll go tell Bram you're here." She hurried into the back room. "Bram!" Jena could hear her call. "Braa-am! Jena's up front!"

Jena waited, absently rubbing the chin of one of the cats; it had taken advantage of Carina's absence to leap up onto the countertop. Eventually Bram emerged from the back of the store and smiled when he saw her. "You shouldn't encourage him," he said, flicking the ends of the cloth measuring tape draped over his neck at the cat. "Shoo, Fishbreath, shoo. Yes, you, sir!" The cat hissed and swatted at Bram with an indignant paw and then hopped down and thundered off through the back doorway.

Jena did her best to smile. "What absurd names you give them."

"We try to keep 'em humble, but it's a losing battle, I'm afraid." He reached for her hand and drew it up to press a kiss on her palm, but his smile died as he caught a closer look at her face. "What's the matter?"

"I need to talk."

Bram pulled off the measuring tape, leaving it on a shelf with his thimble, and ducked under the counter to join her. "Father said he could give me a little time. Let's not waste it."

They hastened from the store into the street outside. "So, where do you want to go to talk?" Bram asked, throwing an arm over her shoulder and squeezing it.

"By the river? Maybe it will be cooler there."

"Don't think so." He sighed. "It's hot as a forge everywhere. But we can try."

A few lanes away from the tailor shop, the Spangle River poured down from its source above the Golden Rim, cutting a swath through the city on its way to join the Koh River. Walking along the Spangle toward Lowertown, Bram and Jena pushed through the crowds of laundresses drawing water, quay fishermen, food vendors, and other strollers-by. Finally, they broke through a clump of people and saw several worn wooden pilings in the shade. The Spangle ran swiftly here, falling down the slope of the Bowls, but far below them, where the two rivers joined, the Koh ran slowly, choked with low-riding barges poling along toward the sea.

"It is cooler here," Jena said, sitting down gratefully on a piling and lifting the braid at the nape of her neck to feel the air. Bram gave her a glancing kiss on the ear, and then settled down on the ground beside her and leaned against her thigh.

For a while they simply sat in companionable silence, enjoying the spray from the rushing water and watching the river traffic on the Koh below. Jena gently ran her fingers through Bram's curly black hair, feeling the sweat at his temples. The faint breeze over the water carried the smell of fish, wet rope, and the odor of cooking cabbage.

Finally Bram gave her foot a poke. "Now. Tell me what's happened."

"Father received a letter this morning." She pulled it from her sash and showed him the seal.

"What's it about?" He didn't take it from her; Bram could not read very well.

"My application for elevation was rejected." She unfolded the letter and scanned the words again, as if they would say something else this time. "It's just so hard to believe." She told him what Collas had explained to her.

"So you didn't expect this at all?"

"Of course not." She frowned down at him in surprise. "Why, did you?"

He shrugged. His head was turned from her so she couldn't see his face.

"Father told me I can appeal." She heard the plea in her own voice, begging him to say, *Yes, go ahead and do it. Make them accept you. You don't deserve this; you're as good as any gemcutter in the city.*

Instead he said, "Maybe it's for the best."

Her surprise stole her breath away for a moment, like a slap of icy water. "But I thought—Bram, we've always talked about when I take over my own shop."

"I know we've talked about it." Bram shifted to squint up at her. "But I suppose I never thought it would really work out that way."

Jena slowly refolded the letter and tucked it back into her sash. "Why not?"

"Well, I sometimes found myself wondering whether you

weren't making too many assumptions—like that the Guild would make it easy for you to go to Chulipse."

"I know I can't *start* as a journeyman in Father's shop there, since I was apprenticed to him. But there are lots of other good masters in Chulipse I could work under. And once I became a master—"

"No, I mean the Guild might've decided not to post you to Chulipse at all. What if they'd chosen to send you to Ponza or Almanea instead? It would mean years of separation, Jena. I know you didn't even think about it, but I did. A lot."

He paused to give her a chance to reply, but she remained silent.

"Even if it had worked out the way you'd planned," Bram continued after a moment, "and you went to Chulipse and the Guild eventually elevated you to master rank . . . well, wouldn't it just be too much? Having a gemcutter's shop and helping me out, too, I mean? Once a baby or two comes along . . ." He shrugged.

"But Father's shop in Chulipse's already established, so we wouldn't have to buy any new equipment. You'd get apprentices to help you out, and so would I."

Bram gently tapped the letter in her sash. "You forgot. The Guild isn't going to accept you as a journeyman, Jena."

"But if I appeal . . ." She stopped herself. "That might create a problem for Father. I couldn't let that happen." Old precepts, old customs, such as *avoid making trouble for Father,* died hard.

"With the Guild, you mean? Oh, I think his position is secure at least. I don't think you need to worry about that."

Jena nodded slowly. "I suppose so." She took a deep breath, trying to regain a sense of hope—and then remembered. "But if I do have a baby, a boy, it would all be for nothing, anyway." Another wave of numbing helplessness washed over her. "Perhaps you're right. Maybe it *is* for the best." Despite her best efforts to smile, the words tasted bitter in her mouth.

"Besides," Bram said, pulling restlessly at the grass at his knee, "Father and I were discussing the business last night."

As she had trained herself to do, Jena put aside her own

troubles to concentrate on another's concerns. "It's going to be a big change for him when you leave, isn't it?"

"Well, that's why I needed to talk with you. It seems it's not going to be very easy for me to go to Chulipse, either. Father asked if I . . ." he hesitated. "If we could wait. He wants me to stay and help him here in Piyar."

"For how long?"

"I think he was hoping we could put it off for a year. Maybe two."

"What? He can't be serious!"

Bram shifted to face her and rested his chin on his fist on her knee. "I'm afraid he is."

"I thought your uncle wanted to start that Chulipse shop before the end of the year."

"He does." His dark brown eyes were sober. "I've already talked to him. He said he'd have to find someone else."

"Someone else! Bram, this was your best chance to start your own shop, to work in Chulipse silks. It's the only way you can get into a position as a Court supplier." Something inside her realized, vaguely, that she felt more upset about Bram's setback than about her own.

"Don't you think I know that?" he replied sharply. He stood in a single swift motion and strode away along the water, kicking a stone aside angrily.

"Bram, wait. Bram!" When he stopped, she caught up with him and placed her hands on his shoulders. She could feel the tension coiled in his shoulders under the thin cloth. "I'm sorry." She gently turned him to face her. "Does he want us to wait on getting married, too?"

He couldn't meet her eyes. "Anesta's been so sick. It's left them short-handed. And they had to spend far too much on medicines—"

"I told you they should ask Arikan—"

"I know! But Father wouldn't listen. You know how he is about magic. The orders have been coming in for Equinox Festival . . ." He shrugged helplessly. "Try to understand, Jena."

"I'm trying." She felt her throat tighten, and the words that came out next surprised both of them. "All I understand is that your father's being a fool. And he's asking us to pay for it."

She saw the anger in his eyes flare to match hers. "He's my father."

"I know." Suddenly ashamed, she took him into her arms, held him tightly. "I know, Bram, I'm sorry. It isn't anyone's fault. I'm just upset about the letter, and this—it's such a disappointment on top of that. I wanted it so, for both of us."

"So did I." He buried his face in her hair. "Jena, maybe I'm just not meant to work for the Court. There's no shame in living out my life as a neighborhood craft tailor."

"Like your father?" She rubbed her cheek against his. "There is when you're capable of doing so much more. You could work miracles with that silk, Bram, I know you could."

"Perhaps." He kissed her cheek. "But I've wondered. Jena, could it be what you really want is to leave home, but you can't admit it?"

"What?" She pulled back and looked at him.

"It's just a feeling I get sometimes." He shrugged. "Maybe you don't like the responsibility of actually leaving your father or something. But anyway, it's much easier for you to think the reasons for leaving are mine, rather than yours."

"That's not true, Bram. You're jesting, aren't you?"

"No."

"Well, you're wrong. I'm sure of it."

"Perhaps I am," Bram said affably. They began walking alongside the river again. After a few minutes of silence, Jena spoke again. "Bram, do you think there's a chance your parents don't want us to marry?"

"What? Don't be ridiculous. You know they love you like I do."

"Well, maybe not quite the same way." At his grin, she went on. "No, but you know how your father hates magic. I was wondering if he had talked to my father, or perhaps to Arikan."

"To Arikan? You must be mad." Bram stopped dead in his tracks. "Jena, why would my father ever possibly talk to Arikan? What are you hinting at?"

She shook her head, suddenly regretting the way the conversation had turned. "It's probably nothing."

"What does magic have to do with us?"

"I don't know if I should tell you. Please, Bram, just forget it."

"I thought we could tell each other everything."

Too late, she realized she had really hurt him. "I mean, I don't know if I can explain it; I don't entirely understand it myself. Arikan told me a couple of days ago . . ." she faltered.

"Told you what?"

"That I could do magic."

He just looked at her, as if he didn't understand what she was saying.

"And I was wondering," she said a little desperately to fill the sudden silence between them, "if your father knew, like my father did and, well . . ."

"Magic." He said it so flatly she was afraid to look at him.

"Yes. At least, that's what Arikan said." She forced a laugh.

"No. No, I'm sure Father doesn't know."

"Because if he did know, he wouldn't have accepted me?"

"No, probably not." He studied her face, his expression as hard as a stranger's, and she felt a rising fear. Then he smiled; he was her Bram again, and she found she could once more breathe freely. "Mother and Father know you now, Jena," he said, slipping an arm around her waist. It felt the same as always. "They think of you as part of the family. Don't worry, everything'll be fine. You'll see."

"Just because I could do magic doesn't mean I have to do it."

This suggestion seemed to cheer up Bram even more. "You're right. You'd have to train, wouldn't you?"

"Yes. I don't see Arikan's in any hurry to take me on. Besides, who wants to start as a beginning student all over again?" They laughed, and the sound echoed sharply over the water, startling a flock of dusky geese floating at the river's edge into a flurry of hisses and honks. "See? They agree with me."

Bram gave her braid a tug. "Come on. It's time for me to be getting back." They turned and began retracing their steps along the water. "So why did Arikan decide to tell you this?"

he asked as they turned up one of the lanes leading away from the river.

"He didn't. Well, not exactly. There was a lord who came to Father with a jewelry commission . . ." she broke off, and her steps slowed.

"Yes? Well?"

"A lord we didn't know. He wouldn't leave his name. He left a stone . . ." The words came haltingly.

"A stone?"

"For a ring." She stumbled and stopped abruptly as her stomach lurched. "Bram, something's wrong."

He was back at her side in an instant. "What is it?"

"I feel sick." She thought he took her arm, but she couldn't feel it. "What hour is it? Is it after midday?"

He blinked in surprise at the question and then squinted up at the sun. "I think so. Why?"

"That's it," she breathed. "He's returning to the shop." Her lips felt numb.

"Who's returning? Jena—"

But she wasn't listening. The street had faded away, replaced by a cold, clear vision. The lord would return, and Collas would tell him he had decided not to do the work. The lord would smile and take back the money and the stone without a single protest.

And then he would smoothly draw his knife and stab Collas through the heart.

Jena saw the flaccid look of shock on Collas' face, the blood trickling out of his chest, dripping off the handle of the knife. His hands fumbled at it weakly and then fell away. *No!* she screamed, but the nightmare held her tightly in its grip, and her words made no sounds. Her hands fluttered like a ghost's, unable to touch her father's fallen body.

And then, mercifully, Bram's voice cut through the haze, saying, "Here, lean against this wall. It's right behind you; just step back. There." Piercing sunlight made her blink, and the vision fell away. She could feel the rough, sun-warmed brick through her dress, pressing into her, the grit falling down by her ankles, and then Bram's anxious face swam back into view. He smoothed the wisps of hair back from her eyes. "Jena, can you hear me?"

With an effort, she pushed herself away from the wall. "Father," she croaked. "The lord is going to kill him."

"What are you talking about?"

"I need a weapon. Bram, do you have a knife, anything?"

"Jena—"

She grabbed his shirtfront and yelled into his face, "I don't have time to explain! Do you— oh, here." Fingers fumbling, she seized the sharp cutting shears Bram wore suspended from a loop at his waist.

He tried to restrain her, but she brushed his hands aside as if they were dry leaves and lurched away up the lane. Her first staggering steps felt wooden, and then she ran in earnest.

"Jena, wait!"

Her fingers closed around the points of the shears to protect her if she fell. The cold metal felt good in her hand, driving away the last of her disorientation. She could no longer hear Bram, shouting behind her. She pushed through the startled crowds, shoving aside children, a cooper trundling a cart loaded with barrels, a flower seller. She crashed into a water seller who had unfortunately dodged the wrong direction to avoid her, and they both tumbled to the cobblestones. Jena retrieved the shears and scrambled, panting, to her feet, ignoring the water seller's outraged protests about his smashed pottery. Dripping, she kept on, up the terrace stairs to the Fifth Rim, two street levels below her house. Down another lane she dashed, her heart laboring hard, and then up another flight of stairs to the Fourth Rim. She felt a stitch cramping her side.

At the top of the stairs, she stopped and leaned against the railing, fighting to catch her breath. Sweat poured down her face and ribs and slickened her grip on the handles of the shears. She shifted them to her other hand and scrubbed her fingers on her skirt to dry them. Her heartbeat sounded loudly in her ears as she looked around the quiet lane. No pedestrians walked here. *Good*, thought a cold, unfamiliar part of herself. When her breathing slowed, she walked past three houses to the private stairs leading up to Collas' garden.

They had never seemed so long. Nerves taut, Jena stopped

every few steps to listen, but she heard nothing. At the top of the stairs, she slipped over to an acacia tree beside the path leading to the house. Was the lord already within? Maybe it wasn't too late. She should work herself closer and try to look within the front room, if she could do so without being seen herself. On the other hand, perhaps he hadn't yet arrived. Should she wait here to confront him when he came through the garden?

As she hesitated, unsure what to do, the door from the house opened. She threw herself behind the tree and closed her eyes at the wave of despair. *Too late.* The steps came closer, and she shifted her grip on the shears. The despair melted in the face of a burning rage. *He won't escape, Father, I swear.* Once he was past her, with his back to the tree . . .

But the footsteps slowed. Just opposite her, there on the path at the other side of the tree, they stopped. Jena held her breath. *Just a little farther.*

Suddenly a hand snaked around the tree and seized her upraised wrist. She jumped, dropping the shears, and the crushing grip dragged her around the tree, where she all but collided with the lord. He looked at her with a kind of mild amazement—yes, and something else, too.

She could have sworn it was pity.

She drew a breath and opened her mouth to scream and then stopped, arrested by a totally unexpected sound. Startled, she turned her head to listen, and then after a stunned moment realized what it was: her father's bright whistle, wafting from the workshop.

She stared at the lord. "You didn't hurt him?"

The lord dropped her hand. "Who? Your father? What conceivable reason would I have to do that?"

"I thought . . . I thought . . ."

His mouth quirked. "What? That I would be so insulted by a refusal to cut a stone, I would throw some kind of lordly tantrum?" His eyes widened. "Did you actually think I would *kill* him?"

Jena felt her cheeks grow hot.

He stooped to pick up the shears and hefted them in his hand. "And so you came flying to your father's defense"—

he shook his head in amazement—"with a pair of *sewing shears?*"

Face aflame, she tried to seize the shears back, but he held them out of reach. "Not a particularly good choice for a weapon," he said, cocking an eyebrow at her. "I suppose if your first attempt didn't work, you could always use them to cut off your hair. Then your lover would have a revenge-braid to hold while you chased after me." He jammed the shears into the trunk of the tree. "With something more lethal."

She turned to flee, to get away from him, anything, but he took her wrist again. "Jena, stop."

"Let go of me!"

"This is my fault." He gave her wrist a little shake, his voice serious this time. "I honestly didn't realize you were someone who could see possibilities so strongly."

She stopped trying to free her wrist. "Someone who could . . . see possibilities?"

"You caught me off guard when you looked into my ring; I'm not used to people even noticing it. I never would have allowed you to do so, had I known. I'm sorry."

"Not used to people noticing it—what are you talking about?"

"Look at me," he said kindly. When she did, reluctantly, he placed a fist gently over each of her temples for a moment and looked deep into her eyes. A part of her wanted to flinch away from him, but she couldn't reject that calm scrutiny.

Then he released her. "I see," he said softly. "You wanted to leave home. And this was a possibility you saw, one which would make that happen. You simply didn't understand it was only that: a possibility."

Jena said nothing.

"Is that the only way you can imagine leaving home?" he said, taking her hand. "Surely you can think of a different scenario."

"Such as?"

He took a step closer. "Such as coming with me, perhaps?" His voice sounded light again, suggestive. "I could open up some opportunities which might . . . interest you."

She looked down at his hand holding hers. "What are you asking me, to be your mistress or something?"

He stared at her, and she got the impression he was trying very hard not to laugh. "I'm disappointed. Such a lack of imagination! No, try again."

"Surely—" she stammered, "you're not asking me to . . . to marry you—"

His grin became a roaring laugh. "Worse and worse!" he gasped when he could speak again. "Now, that's a possibility that never occurred to me! You are capable of surprises." He gave her a mocking bow. Jena felt her face flare crimson again. "A very valuable characteristic for someone who wishes to learn magic," he went on. "I don't think, however, that such a match would add much luster to my family's name. No, it just won't do. Try again."

Goaded by his jesting tone, Jena demanded, "What is your name, anyway? You should tell me that at least."

"Should I?"

Her lips tightened. He took the gray stone from his pouch. Taking her hand and pressing the cold stone into her palm, he curled her fingers around it and then placed her fists at his temples. "There. Now you tell me."

She stared into his eyes. They were gray, with silver flecks which drew her in, as the golden flecks had drawn her into his ring. "Morgan," she whispered. "Your name is Morgan."

"Yes."

"And . . . I can leave home—"

"Why?"

Her hands dropped to her sides. "To be your pupil."

She saw his answering smile—and then the garden disappeared. The house, the terrace, all of Piyar—all gone. Jena looked around, blinking.

She stood in the dusty stone courtyard in front of an unfamiliar castle keep.

CHAPTER
FIVE

BEWILDERED, JENA CRANED
her neck to stare up at the massive keep and, as she turned, the outer ward walls. A line of about fifteen horses and riders were preparing to ride out the keep's outer ward gate, directly in front of her. Men clad in leather traveling gear were mounting up, shouting at boys fastening bundles to their saddles. A few women stood clustered nearby, skirts fluttering in the breeze, apparently waiting to say goodbye. Jena took a hesitant step in their direction and then stopped, swaying, as a wave of vertigo flooded over her.

A soft pop of displacing air made large puffs of dust skitter in all directions, like startled cats. "You little idiot!" Lord Morgan appeared suddenly beside her, white-faced and furious. He closed the gap between them with a couple of fast steps and grabbed her arm roughly. "By the first Founders, girl, what do you think you're doing?"

"I?" Jena gasped.

Lord Morgan took her other arm and shook her like a rag doll. "That was an easy way to get both of us killed!"

"Morgan!" The shout from the group by the front gate made them both look. The man on the most richly caparisoned horse dismounted and began walking toward them with a look of delighted surprise, drawing off his gloves. "Morgan, where in blazes have you been?"

"Ranulf?" Letting go of Jena, Lord Morgan looked around quickly, taking in the keep, the banners fluttering from the parapet, and the approaching courtiers. Turning back to Jena, he sputtered in an undertone, "How did you get us here?"

"I had nothing to do with it!" Jena choked out, fervently hoping she could keep herself from getting sick on the flagstones. "Where *are* we, anyway?"

"But it's a woman's spell—never mind that now," he said hurriedly, glancing at the approaching nobleman. "Just keep that stone a secret. And whatever you do, don't say anything about magic."

Then, breaking into a smile, Lord Morgan took one step forward, spreading his arms wide toward the other man for an embrace.

And vanished.

Jena squeaked in surprise, batting at the dust flying in her eyes. The other man dropped his gloves with a startled cry and drew his sword. "Morgan! Morgan, where are you?" His voice rose in panic as he spun around wildly. "Answer me, brother!"

"Call for the castellan, my lord," another man beside him advised, drawing his sword also. Jena took a stumbling step backward. The movement made her head swim again and she almost fell.

Other men ran up, sliding to a stop before them. One was the castellan, with the traditional ornamental gilded key to the keep hanging at his waist indicating his office. "My Lord Duone?"

"My brother, Lord Morgan," said Lord Duone through his teeth. "He was here but a moment ago, and he disappeared before my very eyes. Find him!"

"Disappeared, my lord? But where—"

"I don't know! Look everywhere!"

The castellan looked at Lord Duone doubtfully and then gestured quickly to his men, indicating they were to split in several groups to begin the search. As the men began hurrying off, the castellan's quick gaze rested on Jena. "Who is she, my lord?"

Lord Duone seemed to notice her for the first time. "I have no idea." Frowning, he sheathed his sword, to Jena's relief, and came toward her, his eyes narrowing. He was a half-head's height taller than Lord Morgan, and his hair a shade redder, with a few strands graying at the temples. She could see a family resemblance in the face; although Lord Duone's chin was blunter, he had his brother's close-set gray eyes. "Now, then, who are you?"

"I . . . I . . ."

"Well?" His fingers tapped impatiently on his sword hilt.

"My name is Jena," she replied, drawing her dignity around her as best she could, despite the trembling of her hands. Fortunately, her queasiness was beginning to subside. "I am the daughter and apprentice of Collas the Gemcutter."

"What are you doing here? How did you get here?"

"Why, I came with Lord Morgan," she temporized. The lord's frown deepened, and she could feel a fine sheen of sweat breaking out on her forehead. *Don't mention magic*, Lord Morgan had told her. Looking at his brother's angry face, Jena could guess why: Lord Duone was probably among those nobles who feared and avoided magic. Most likely, Lord Morgan had kept his abilities a secret. Then why, Jena thought angrily, had he abandoned her in a wretched tangle like this?

"And just what is your business with him?"

A man behind the castellan made a low-voiced comment she didn't catch, and several of the men quickly smothered uneasy laughs. Lord Duone's lip curled, and he looked her up and down deliberately.

Jena felt her face redden. "I am under his protection," she said as loftily as she could. That was true in a way, of course, although given Lord Morgan's warning she couldn't very well tell this imposing lord that she was under his brother's protection as a pupil of magic.

"Protection?" Lord Duone repeated skeptically.

"In my professional capacity." That, if anything made the snickers worse. "As a gemcutter," she added, belatedly. Stung, she reached for the letter tucked in her sash and showed it to him. "Perhaps you recognize the Guild seal?"

To her horror, he took her gesture as an invitation. Before

her fingers could tighten on it, he took the letter from her and quickly scanned it.

His face hardened. "This letter denies you have any standing with the Guild to take your own commissions."

Now what? Jena thought wildly. "Yes, yes, it does." She forced herself to shake her head mournfully. "Lord Morgan was most indignant."

"Indeed?"

"Of course. That someone of my caliber would be rejected on such a basis. He was outraged. Oh, it was a fine speech he made when I showed him the letter, my lord. It quite warmed my heart. Mind you, I was discouraged at the setback, of course," she went on with a confidential air. A part of her was listening to herself with amazed astonishment, stunned by the totally uncharacteristic string of lies she was inventing. "But he assured me that with his support, the Guildmasters would eventually change their minds."

Lord Duone blinked. "I don't follow you."

"Why, the appeal, of course. To the Guildmasters, to allow me to be elevated to journeyman. All they would consider at this point was making me a hereditary member in trust, and only if my father dies." Remembered anger made her throat tighten. "Lord Morgan is sponsoring my reapplication. He has been kind enough, on that basis, to commission some new settings from me, to give me the chance to show the Guildmasters what I can do." She remembered just in time not to offer the stone in her hand as evidence. As casually as she could, she slid it into her pocket.

"Strange . . . I've never been particularly aware of Morgan as a patron of the arts." He cocked a sardonic eyebrow at her.

"Give me the tools, my lord, and some stones to work. I will show you what I can do." *I hope.*

"I thought you said he had commissioned something from you. And yet you have no stones?"

Oh, help. "We were still in the process of designing the project, my lord," she said in her most reasonable tone. "It is pointless to purchase stones before you know what you are making. We happened to be speaking together in my father's workshop in Piyar. And then . . ." she hesitated.

"And then?"

"And then we found ourselves here."

A flurry of excited whispers greeted this statement. "You found yourselves here?" Lord Duone repeated, shaking his head in amazement. "Young woman, Piyar is leagues from here. My party and I were just taking leave for Piyar ourselves, and we could not expect to arrive there until just before the Equinox Festival."

Jena's jaw dropped, even as her heart sank. Equinox Festival would not come for another six weeks. "I'm sure you will pardon my curiosity, my lord, but where are we, exactly?"

"This is the Duone stronghold, in the Uriat Mountains. You could not have come here but by . . ." he paused, his mouth working distastefully. He was apparently unable to even make himself say the word *magic*.

How could she possibly be so far from home? Bram and her father would be frantic. She was at Lord Duone's mercy even more than she realized. And what would happen when his brother heard this tale, once he was found? Furiously, she cudgeled her brain, trying to think of everything she might remember about Lord Ranulf Duone and his family, including, presumably, Lord Morgan. It was precious little, although she thought she recognized "Duone" as the name of one of the minor lords of the Court. "How vexatious!" she exclaimed. "Why, I cannot possibly spare the time it will take to journey back to my home."

"Unless you return the way you came," he said darkly. He eyed her as if he thought she could not leave quickly enough to suit him.

"I am sure I have absolutely no idea how I got here, my lord," she replied with absolute truthfulness. "I must say," she blundered on hastily, trying to hide her weak defense with a strong offense, "I find this abduction to be outrageous. Most shocking."

Lord Duone stared at her open-mouthed.

"With all due respect," Jena went on severely, sweating, "I do not appreciate being spirited away from my work like this."

Lord Duone sputtered indignantly.

"I'm sure you will understand if I hold Lord Morgan responsible. A pretty kind of protection, indeed!" She shook her head.

Lord Duone looked murderous. "Where is he?"

"I'm sure I don't know," Jena replied as if surprised. "You know him better than I do. It is most strange." She shuddered delicately and held her breath.

"Yes, indeed. Very strange," said a new voice behind Jena. She turned and saw one of the ladies who had been standing before the keep's gate. Her startlingly black eyes, set in creamy, wrinkled cheeks, gave Jena a knowing look. She was a tiny woman, dressed in a tight-fitting gown of rich crimson, with hair like oxidized silver arranged in a complicated series of braids. She shook her head, and a pair of heavy garnet earrings swung from her ears, setting off the color of the gown admirably. "But very like Morgan. You know how scatterbrained he is, Ranulf. How I wish the dear boy had a better sense of responsibility. Not to mention propriety! Such a disappointment to his father, too. How did Tersat tolerate it?"

Lord Tersat Duone. Jena caught her breath. Why, she had heard of him before. Lord Tersat Duone had even commissioned her father once or twice for jewelry. He hadn't been from one of the seven great ruling houses of the Diadem. But he had been, she thought, the head of one of the minor houses directly underneath them.

"This seems to be a somewhat different kind of situation, Aunt," Lord Duone said, scattering Jena's thoughts again. "Morgan has . . . has disappeared."

"Exactly. Just as he went away six months ago, when you particularly needed help with the estates."

"No! I mean, didn't you see him vanish? Right before our very eyes!"

The lady shrugged, apparently unimpressed. "Well, no matter how he's managed to spirit himself away this time, once again he's left his obligation in your hands." She shook her head, tsking. "Of course the rascal knew you wouldn't let him down, which is more than you can say of him."

"Obligation? Whatever are you talking about, Aunt?"

The lady looked at him in surprise. "Why, to the young lady here, of course. Morgan took responsibility for her.

How fortunate you are here to prove that at least she can count on someone within the family!"

Through the keep's narrow windows above them, Jena could hear the thump of heavy boots on flagstone floors and the sound of doors being opened and shut as Lord Duone's men obediently carried out the search.

The lady held out a friendly hand to Jena. "I know your journey has tired you out, child," she said, with an emphasis Jena couldn't entirely read. "Come, we must find you a room. One of the ones in the northeast corner should do. It's away from the kitchens and shouldn't be too smoky."

Glad for the chance to escape, Jena turned to follow her, only to be stopped by Lord Duone's voice. "Aunt Kestrienne—"

Lady Kestrienne looked back at him, all innocence. "Yes?"

Lord Duone stared at her and then shrugged helplessly.

"You'll let us know when you find Morgan, won't you?" she said. "Meanwhile, I'll help the child get settled in." She took Jena's arm, the friendliness of the gesture somewhat belied by the firmness of her grip, and led her away at a surprisingly brisk pace.

"But—" Jena began.

"Shh. Wait until we have a chance to speak alone," Lady Kestrienne said to her in an undertone. She smiled brilliantly and inclined her head at two passing gentlemen and then led Jena through the keep's gatehouse doorway.

The plunge from sunlight into shadow darkened Jena's vision, and she slowed her steps. A peculiar mental sensation niggled at her attention. She blinked, waiting for her eyes to adjust. Whatever it was felt like pressure, like the weight of the massive stones looming over them. She looked up at the shadowed gatehouse ceiling. The stones were mortared tight, of course, but suppose they fell? Suppose an attack came which breached the gatehouse? Or perhaps the stones would stay firm forever, entombing defenders trapped in the keep during a siege? Her knees shook with a weakness like starvation, and she clutched at Lady Kestrienne's arm.

Possibilities. Not necessarily realities.

She heard a low chuckle in her ear. "You grow accustomed to it," Lady Kestrienne said.

"What is it about this place?" Jena's voice sounded hollowly against the stones.

"It is the Duone Keep," Lady Kestrienne replied simply. "Many find it imposing, I know." She gave Jena's arm a tiny shake and let go, walking on.

Had the noblewoman sensed the flux of magic? Or were her words meant to be taken at face value? Inwardly cursing Lord Morgan, Jena followed her through the inner gatehouse entrance into the sunlight of the inner ward.

"That is the Great Hall, just ahead of us," said Lady Kestrienne. "The kitchen is beside it in the southwest corner. The barracks are there," she said, pointing, "over to the right. This way, now," she said, starting across toward one of the doorways on the left.

"The warning is appreciated, my lady," Jena said, following her. "I'll keep my distance."

A snort of laughter greeted this mild sally. "You are wise, but there is really no necessity with Lord Duone's men. His discipline is firm, and his men respect him. And, after all," she added lightly, "you are under Lord Morgan's protection."

As they went inside, Jena gave her a sidelong glance, suddenly sick at the thought that Lord Morgan might reappear and deny everything. But Lady Kestrienne's eyes twinkled at her, and she patted Jena's shoulder. "Until we see him again, consider yourself to be under mine." She indicated a narrow circular flight of stairs and turned to lead the way up. "And don't worry, my dear. He will return." She said the last with the air of someone trying to convince herself, and two lines appeared between her brows.

"Are you sure?"

"He always does," Lady Kestrienne replied firmly as they reached the top and turned right down the corridor, but Jena thought her eyes seemed troubled.

The keep's living quarters rose two stories above the inner ward. The storerooms, Lady Kestrienne explained, were yet another floor below, cut directly into the cliff upon which the keep was built. Bright sunlight poured like warm honey through the narrow arched windows overlooking the inner ward. As the two women walked through alternating pools of light and shadow, the rays struck Jena's hair and shoulders in a successive wash of warm waves. To their left, doors opened into the apartments built into the thick keep wall. Directly ahead at the end of the corridor, Jena could see one of the decorated entrance doors to the Great Hall.

Now, safely out of range of the imposing Lord Duone's gimlet eye, she marveled anew at her own audacity. How, for pity's sake, had she managed to pull herself together in the face of intimidation like that and come up with such a fantastic story? Why, the words had all but tumbled out of her mouth, with a serene confidence she had never before experienced. If Lady Kestrienne hadn't unexpectedly swooped in and whisked her away, perhaps she would have even been able to screw up enough courage to ask for leave to join the party traveling to Piyar. She absolutely had to get home somehow!

The noblewoman *had* rescued her from further awkward questions, at least. Why had she done it? As they continued down the corridor, Jena studied her companion out of the corner of her eye. What did this noblewoman know about the afternoon's strange events?

Once more the warning came back to her, *Don't say anything about magic.*

She knows something, Jena argued silently. *I know she does. I have to find out what it is.* She drew a deep breath. "Lady Kestrienne?"

The quick look Lady Kestrienne gave her, however, quelled her mustered courage. Jena looked away quickly, undecided again. "Well?" Lady Kestrienne prompted after a moment.

"I . . . I'm sure I've never seen such thick walls before," Jena faltered, after a short pause spent scrambling for a suitable remark. "Not in Piyar or Chulipse, anyway."

"Oh, no, nor in Tenaway, either, although there are other castles like this scattered throughout the Uriat Mountains. Of course, a young girl like you hasn't had a chance to travel much and see them," Lady Kestrienne said, very kindly exonerating her. "This keep was built three hundred years before the Founders' War."

"It's that old?" Jena was impressed.

"Yes. There's no need to build such a fortress during these peaceful times."

Her tone sounded approving, but Jena reflected that Lady Kestrienne probably would have been equally at home in a more warlike era. Jena pictured this redoubtable lady on the battlements of the keep, shouting defiance at an approaching army. She blinked, and the vision disappeared. Or perhaps Lady Kestrienne would simply befuddle the enemy, as neatly as she had befuddled Lord Duone. Feeling rather befuddled herself, Jena asked, "Pardon me for asking, my lady, but where are you taking me?"

"To meet Lord Duone's wife, Lady Metissa Duone. She sews with her ladies every afternoon. Here we are," she said, stopping before a door, wider than the others lining the corridor. As she opened it, Jena heard from within the clear strains of a lute, accompanying a sweet soprano voice.

In the large room inside, a cluster of ten or so women sat grouped in a semicircle of seats by the unlit fireplace, embroidering. A few candles on tables supplemented the indirect light from the narrow windows. A young girl playing the lute broke off her song and looked around.

One of the women looked up from her sewing and smiled. "Ah, Kestrienne. Is my lord away safely, then?"

"I think his plans have changed, Metissa. You will have to inform your cook to throw more partridges on the spit. The party will not be riding out today after all."

Lady Duone arched her elegant eyebrows in surprise. She put aside her sewing and stood up, a little awkwardly due to her advanced pregnancy. She wore a simple dove-gray gown of fine wool, with no jewelry but a gold wedding band and an enameled chatelaine girdle, buckled low and hung with a heavy bunch of keys. "Has there been some news of Morgan?" she asked, coming toward them and looking inquiringly at Jena.

"Morgan actually appeared, albeit briefly," Lady Kestrienne replied smoothly. "He stayed only long enough to leave his protégée here to Ranulf's charge, and left again in a great hurry. Metissa, I present to you Jena, a gemcutter of Piyar. Jena, Lady Duone."

Lady Duone looked surprised as her eyes quickly took in Jena's simple morning work dress and flimsy sandals, but she inclined her head in acknowledgment of the introduction. Jena curtsied shyly, suddenly aware of the unraveling of her hair braid, the water stains on her skirt and the smell of her own perspiration, results of her desperate run through the hot, crowded streets of Piyar. In this gracious apartment, with its wall tapestries and frescoes, delicate tables, and finely dressed ladies, she felt grubby and rumpled.

"You are most welcome, Jena," Lady Duone said. "Perhaps you can tell us where Morgan has been, or when he might return? My lord and I have been so worried about him."

Jena looked at Lady Kestrienne nervously. "Actually—"

"I'm afraid he has left once again without confiding his plans," Lady Kestrienne interrupted, shaking her head mournfully. "Such an impetuous young man. If only he would follow dear Ranulf's example." She sighed. "Yet, if Morgan wishes to keep his comings and goings private from us, Metissa, he must have his reasons. It would be discourteous to press his ward for explanations he is unwilling to give."

Lady Duone looked doubtful. "But surely—"

"In the meantime, speaking of courtesy," Lady Kestrienne cut in briskly, "we have a guest to make comfortable. Morgan gave her absolutely no time to pack," she added with awful emphasis. "Such deprivations she has endured on the trip! Perhaps she could borrow some clothes and other necessities from one of your ladies?"

Lady Duone gave her unexpected guest another appraising glance, as Jena bit the inside corners of her lips to keep herself from breaking into hysterical laughter. What would Lady Kestrienne say next? "I believe she is about Liselle's size," Lady Duone said finally. "Liselle?"

The lute player carefully leaned her instrument against a stool and hurried toward them. "Yes, my lady?"

"Could you offer a few of your gowns to our guest here?

For Jena, I should say. Perhaps the new blue one? I think the color would suit her well."

"And some shoes, if we can find any the right size," Lady Kestrienne added brightly. "And handkerchiefs, as well as a few other items. Sleeping gowns, underthings . . ."

"A comb," Jena murmured, feeling absolutely ridiculous. "I should be very grateful if you could spare a comb."

The girl Liselle smiled warmly. It did wonders for her rather homely, freckled face. "I should be glad to. Would you like her to share my room?" she asked Lady Duone. "Or shall I bring the clothes elsewhere?"

"That's very kind of you, Liselle, dear," Lady Kestrienne said firmly before Lady Duone could answer. "But Jena will need her own apartment, with a separate room she can use as a workshop. She is engaged in creating a project for Lord Morgan." She had raised her voice a little, loudly enough to be heard by the other women in the room, and pressed her elbow lightly into Jena's ribs.

Cued by that touch, although she hardly understood why, Jena spoke. "It would be best if the workroom would have access to natural light. I need it to see the stones as I work with them." She blinked, surprised at herself. *Now what in the world made me say that?* "Although, of course," she added hastily, "I won't be staying very long. I really do need to return home as soon as possible, my lady. Do you think, perhaps, that Lord Duone—"

"Of course she won't be staying for very long," Lady Kestrienne interrupted yet again. "She will be returning home just as *soon* as she finishes her project for Lord Morgan." And when Jena opened her mouth to object, Lady Kestrienne elbowed her again, harder, under the guise of adjusting her girdle. Confused, Jena remained silent.

"There is a large room with good light available in the northeast tower, on the floor above us," Lady Duone said slowly. "I believe it is unlocked at present."

"Only one room? But then she would need to sleep in her workroom," Lady Kestrienne objected.

"I don't mind, truly I don't," Jena said quickly. "You are very generous, my lady, thank you."

Lady Kestrienne threw up her hands. "I should rather say,

your needs are modest. Very well, then. I'll take Jena to show her the room. Liselle, why don't you bring the clothes there directly."

"I will," Liselle said.

"Excellent," Lady Kestrienne said. "Come along, dear." Jena barely had time for another curtsy to Lady Duone before Lady Kestrienne encircled Jena's waist with an apparently affectionate arm and hustled her out of the room.

Out in the corridor with one hand on the door handle, Lady Kestrienne permitted herself a chuckle. "Better than I'd hoped," she said in an undertone. "We managed to get you a room to yourself." She started off down the hall in the direction from which they had come. "Thank you for your timely comment about the light, my dear. That was perfect. Brilliant."

Jena hurried to catch up. "But I don't see—"

"It kept Lady Duone from stashing you away with the fosterlings, didn't it? Now, then." She reached for a pouch knotted at her waist, pulled out some coins, and pressed them into Jena's hand. "That's all I have with me at present. Don't worry; I'll bring you more later."

Jena looked at the coins in her hand. They were small, but several were silver and two were gold. "I don't know when I can repay this."

"Oh, don't trouble yourself about it. You'll have to have money for the tools and raw materials you need for Morgan's project, won't you? If anyone asks, you can say Morgan gave it to you." She turned to lead the way up another narrow, spiral staircase. "And I shall get it out of Morgan's hide, never fear," she added a little grimly. "If we can find out where he is. You will let me know as soon as possible should he contact you in any way. Won't you?"

"Of course." Unnerved by the urgency in the other woman's voice, Jena cleared her throat. "Uh, Lady Kestrienne. About what I said in the outer ward, about that project for Lord Morgan—"

Lady Kestrienne threw her a startled glance as they rounded the head of the stairs and began walking down a new corridor. "Oh, bless you, child, you don't need to worry your head about that! I understand exactly how things are between you two. Now, then, here's your room."

I don't understand it, Jena wanted to say helplessly. Utterly bewildered, feeling as if she were being hurried along a path she couldn't see, she slipped the coins into her pocket and stepped into the room.

She groped her way over to the far wall, barking her shin in the process on a chair set against the wall, and opened the shutters on one of the recessed windows. Duone Keep was a castle, and castle rooms are cool. But the light through the window revealed this one to be quite clean and much larger than her bedroom in Piyar. A brightly painted fresco on the wall over the bed depicted a falconing party.

Lady Kestrienne opened the small chest at the foot of the bed, wafting the scent of lavender into the air. "You'll need a large worktable, of course, along with your equipment," she said, brushing aside tied bunches of dried herbs and pulling out sheets and blankets. "And perhaps Lady Duone might have a tapestry or two to spare for the walls. We'll see what can be had. The garderobe is down a small corridor past two doors to the left. We passed it on the way here. And there's probably a chamber pot under the bed to use at night."

Jena leaned against the shutter, breathing in the mountain air and looking out over the outer ward, and beyond that, to the steep cliff falling away from the castle's side to a river. The window faced the east; the light from the setting sun was turning the snowcaps on the mountains before her to a dull bronze.

She ached all over with weariness, and homesickness smote her heart, filling her eyes with the prickle of tears. What would her father think had happened to her? Bram undoubtedly had followed her and would tell him how she had run away in a frenzy. They would be so worried about her until she could make her way back; how could she get a message to them?

Behind her, Lady Kestrienne's voice continued: "Liselle can show you where to get coals for that brazier in the corner, as well as where the well is. I assume you'll want water for tomorrow morning. There's a pitcher over on that stand by the bed. You'll only need to do that tonight; servants will bring water every day, once they've been told Lady Duone is having you stay here. Candles are here in the chest. And there are—" She stopped.

After a moment, Jena wiped her eyes and glanced over her shoulder. Lady Kestrienne was kneeling on the floor with lengths of sheets spread over her knees, staring intently at her right hand.

"Lady Kestrienne?"

"Yes?" she replied, looking up.

"I'm sorry, what were you saying?"

"I was saying—yes. Well, it's nothing important. I must go now; someone is calling me."

"Oh," said Jena, puzzled. She had heard nothing.

"Liselle should be here shortly with some clothes. We will talk later." Closing the chest carefully, she placed the sheets on the bed and stood. "Don't look so forlorn, my dear. We'll find Morgan." She glanced out the window, and once again Jena was struck by the worry in her eyes. After a moment, Lady Kestrienne looked back at Jena and seemed to force herself to smile. "And until we do, I won't let you down." She raised her right hand in front of her face and gestured enigmatically with the fingers.

Jena stiffened. Lady Kestrienne's right index finger wore a ring which Jena hadn't noticed before. The gold setting was identical to Lord Morgan's, but whereas the stone in Lord Morgan's ring had been black with gold flecks, this stone was clear. That in itself was shocking. Only the Diamond himself had the right to wear clear stones.

"Your ring—" she began, but Lady Kestrienne touched the ringed finger to her own lips.

"Shh. Later." She slipped out the door and was gone.

Thoughtfully, Jena went over to the bed. The mattress tick, stuffed with feathers, felt luxuriously soft, but as she sat down on it, the contents of her pocket jabbed her thigh. She pulled the folds of her skirt out from underneath her leg and turned the pocket inside out into her hand. The coins clinked into her hand, and then Lord Morgan's stone tumbled out to rest on the small pile. Jena's hand jerked in surprise, scattering the coins and dropping the stone onto the bed.

An hour ago in the garden in Piyar, this stone had been

opaque and featureless, a dull gray, yet now it was clear and colorless, like an uncut diamond. No, not quite—gingerly, she picked it up and took it over to the window to look at it more closely, wishing for her loupe. Yes, it was transparent, except for some tiny gold flecks, like the flecks in the black stone in Lord Morgan's ring.

"Magic," Jena whispered. Her hand dropped to her lap, fingers clenching the stone tightly. The crystalline edges cut into her palm as she looked out unseeingly over the mountains. *I want to go home.*

CHAPTER
Six

A KNOCK ON THE DOOR EVEN-
tually roused Jena from her thoughts. She went back to the
bed, scooped up the coins, and put them with the stone back
into her pocket. "Come in."

"Could you get the door for me, please?" said a muffled
voice outside. "My arms are rather full."

Jena opened it to admit Liselle.

"Where can I set these things down?" Liselle said a little
breathlessly. "Oh, here." She put the clothes and a small pile
of other items down on the top of the chest and collapsed on
the floor gratefully. "Phew, all those stairs. Here, this is the
gown Lady Duone mentioned," she said, twitching one out
of the pile. "Will it fit?"

The material, dyed a deep periwinkle blue, slid softly and
richly under her fingers. Jena held it up to her shoulders. "I
think it's about the right length," she said.

"Yes, but it may be a little wide at the waist," Liselle said
critically. "You could take it in easily enough."

"You wouldn't mind if I altered it?" Jena sat down on the
bed and carefully laid the gown over her lap, smoothing the
pleats in the skirt. The sleeves, laced tightly to the bodice

with black silk ribbons, were detachable. "It's certainly finer than anything I'm accustomed to wearing."

"Oh, it's no trouble. Lady Duone is always generous with her fosterlings, and I have plenty of gowns to wear."

"Are you sure?"

"Of course. Really, I think that color suits you better than it does me, anyway. It makes my hair look dreadfully red."

Jena laughed shyly and studied her companion. Liselle was perhaps a year or two younger than herself, and a little plumper, with an open, honest face, a snub nose, and strawberry blond hair. She wore a finely woven gown of mossy green, along with a simple silver chain. Gold would really suit her coloring better, Jena thought privately, perhaps a necklace set with peridot to bring out the green in her hazel eyes. "Personally," Jena said, "I like red hair."

Liselle's eyes widened. "Really? Well, they don't in Niolantti. You should hear my brothers tease me."

"Is that where you're from? I've never been there."

"Haven't you? It's southeast of here, you know; you travel east along the Orbo River out there and then sail south along the coast, and you'll come to it. I came here because my mother grew up fostering with Lady Duone's mother. I like it here, but I miss the sea." Her eyes clouded briefly, but then she looked at Jena and smiled. "I heard Lady Kestrienne say you're from Piyar?"

"Yes, although my father and I usually live there in the winter and in Chulipse in the summer. He's Collas the Gemcutter, you see."

"Oh?" Liselle said, politely puzzled.

"Haven't you heard of him?" Jena asked, a little condescending in her turn. "He's one of the most famous gemcutters in Piyanthia."

They stared at each other and both burst out laughing, instantly friends.

"I brought you a few others, too, and some of the other things Lady Kestrienne mentioned," Liselle said. "Here's a girdle with some pouches you can use. Of course, you can change the sleeves around if you like, and I brought an extra pair. I see you're wearing a chemise, but here's another one."

"Thank you, Liselle."

"I don't know about shoes." Liselle lifted a delicately embroidered pair, looking speculatively at Jena's feet. "My feet are boats compared to yours. These will be too big, I expect."

"My sandals won't show underneath the hem of the gown; they'll do for now. Maybe I can sew some slippers that will serve until I get shoes."

"I suppose you'd like to change now? They'll be serving supper in the Great Hall soon."

"Oh." The thought of parrying questions over supper brought Jena's queasiness back again. "That is—well, I came here as a rather unexpected guest. Perhaps it wouldn't be exactly, er, tactful for me to appear?"

Liselle looked surprised. "Oh, no! Please don't feel that way. I mean, I know Lady Duone wouldn't want you to."

"Really, I'm so worn out from my, uh, journey," Jena pleaded. "I wouldn't be fit company for anyone. It wouldn't offend anyone, would it, if I just ate something simple here on a tray in my room and went to bed early?"

Liselle considered. "Well, of course if you're tired . . ."

"I am. I'll come to the Great Hall tomorrow night, I promise."

"We could go down to the kitchen to see if there's something you can bring back here."

"Thank you," Jena said, relieved. She picked up the pitcher from her bedside table. "Could you show me how to find the well on the way there?"

Soon enough the two young women returned to Jena's room, with a full water pitcher, a small scuttle of lit coals which Liselle emptied into the corner brazier, and a tray with a supper of roasted meats and vegetables. Jena placed it on a corner of the bedside table, jostling the basin aside and sloshing some of the wine out of her goblet in the process. Fetching a candle from the chest, she set it in a candleholder on the stone ledge at the head of the bed.

"I'd stay and keep you company while you eat," Liselle said, lighting the candle with a coal taken from the brazier with a pair of tongs, "but Lady Duone asked me to play at supper tonight."

"Did she? Then I must beg your pardon for not coming to hear you." The light sweetness of burning beeswax filled the air.

Liselle laughed. "Don't imagine you're missing such a treat. I haven't studied the lute very long, only about a year. My fingers still make mistakes." She dropped the coal back in the brazier and hung the tongs on a hook at the side.

"I'll hear you another time, I'm sure," Jena said. "Believe me, I'd like to. But I'm so tired, Liselle; I truly don't mind being left to myself tonight."

"Well, then, I'll say good night." Liselle paused at the door, a little shy again. "I'll see you tomorrow, I suppose?"

"I should be easy to find," Jena replied wryly. "Just keep an eye out for someone wearing a gown that looks strangely familiar."

"I will." Liselle smiled. "And don't worry, Jena. You'll like it here. You'll see."

"For as long as I'm staying, anyway. I really do want to go home as quickly as I can. But anyway, thank you again, Liselle. Good night." Jena shut the door after her.

She shook her head ruefully as she drew a chair up to her supper tray. *Don't worry, everyone says. Lady Kestrienne and now Liselle—ha! What would they do if they were whisked away from home and dropped in the middle of a bunch of strangers?* She found herself thinking longingly of Piyar, of her father's shop and Bram, and felt the lump coming back to her throat. Hastily, she cut off a piece of the roast and took a bite. Deliciously peppery, if a little cold. And the vegetables were crisp-tender, in a gingery marinade. She suddenly realized how hungry she was. No, famished. *Well, first things first.* She fell to the task at hand with relish.

All too soon, Jena had sopped up the last bit of gravy with a chunk of bread; she took a last sip and her wineglass stood empty. Then she leaned back in her chair, absently brushing at crumbs, and shoved the tray aside with a sigh. *Now what?*

Slowly, she pulled Lord Morgan's stone out of her pocket, drawing a candle closer to study it again. The flame caught the sparkles suspended in the crystalline structure, making them shimmer.

What had Arikan said about this stone, back in Piyar? That

the lord who brought it, Lord Morgan, could hide his possibilities, and that took a powerful and subtle power.

Lord Morgan seemed to think Jena could learn magic, too, but unlike Arikan, he was willing to teach her. It was almost, she thought, rubbing a thumb gently against an edge of the stone, as if Lord Morgan had actually awakened magic within her. What were these visions, these glimpses of possibilities she had been having all day, if not magic?

Only I have no idea how to use magic.

She had to find him. But how?

Perhaps . . . if she had magic now, and it came from Lord Morgan . . . well, then, if she could figure out how to use it, maybe she could do what Arikan hadn't been able to do? Learn about Lord Morgan by trying to scry the stone itself?

It was worth a try. Uncertainly, she cupped her hand around the stone, hefting its slight weight, trying to sense everything about it she could. *How do you see the possibilities in a stone?* she wondered, feeling faintly silly. *What are you supposed to do? Do you ask it? To whom do you belong?*

She waited, concentrating. The stone felt warm in her palm, the edges familiar to her fingers. Like . . . She groped in her mind for a comparison. Like the hairbrush she used every morning had molded itself to her grip over the years, its wooden handle darkening slightly from the oils in her hand. After a few more moments, she opened her eyes and sighed. She couldn't sense anything from the stone at all.

Well, what else had Arikan said? Jena turned the memory of the conversation over in her mind carefully, considering. The stone might not reveal its owner because the ownership was in flux. Could it be the stone felt familiar because Lord Morgan had decided to give it to her? Because it belonged to her now? Slowly Jena smiled and then laughed. Yes, that might make sense. Maybe.

Her eye fell on the pile of clothes Liselle had brought and left for her. Here was a way to find out. She got to her feet, untied her sash, and pulled her dress over her head. She tossed it over the chest and picked up the gown dyed periwinkle blue. Like cool water, it slid smoothly over her arms and torso. It had a square neck, cut low enough to allow her

chemise to show at the top of the bodice. The skirt settled
about her waist with a satisfying weight, the pleats flowing
from her hips to her ankles in graceful curves. Her fingers
unraveled her ragged braid, and then she took the comb and
smoothed her hair out over her shoulders. *Now. Concentrate.*
She sat down again slowly and shut her eyes, trying to focus
all her senses on the touch of fabric on her skin. *What do you
have to tell me about yourself?*

The sound of her own breathing filled her ears in the quiet
room. The gown felt like . . . well, like a gown. *Of course,
stupid.* Except that—she caught her breath. Except that she
could feel a slight, a *very* slight pressure on the material on
the right side of her lap. Yes, and at the right side of the
waist. As if . . . as if—her eyes flew open.

As if something rested against the fabric, pressing against
the fibers? Something like the belly of a lute? She felt a
surge of triumph. Yes! That was it. *Is this magic, then?*

The sensation felt odd, although not uncomfortable. It was
rather like something between sensing and intuiting, but it
clearly told her: this is Liselle's gown. She felt it in the
stretch at the waist (the gown fit Liselle more tightly there),
and in the play of the cuffs over her wrists, and even more, in
the essence of Liselle sunk into the material. More than a lingering scent, more than stray hairs clinging to the neckline:
Liselle had made the gown her own. And Jena could tell.

She picked up the comb and tried focusing on that. After a
few moments of puzzlement she understood: the comb didn't
belong to Liselle, but to someone else. She drew it through
her hair with lingering strokes. Yes, someone with rather
short, straight hair. Very fine hair, too. A child, perhaps?

As she put the comb down her fingers closed again over
the stone. It still told her, *I'm yours.* She felt a wave of frustration. *Well, what about the person who had you before me?
What can you tell me about him?* Abruptly, the sparkles in
the stone flared with light, and then her sight slid away into
another vision.

The floor swayed beneath her, gently, with creaking
sounds. The air smelled of salt and seaweed. She saw a tiny
room, lit by a guttering ship's lantern swinging from a hook
on the low ceiling. Crude furniture crowded the room: a table

and two clumsy chairs bolted to the floor, a curved-top trunk. Slung between two hooks on opposite walls, a hammock swayed heavily with the limp form of a man dressed in rich clothing. His russet hair was rumpled, his face deathly pale. Blood trickled from a cut on his temple. Was he asleep or . . . "Lord Morgan," Jena breathed. Just as she spoke, someone stepped into her line of vision, blocking her view of Lord Morgan. Then, as if frightened away by the sound of her voice or the other person, the vision faded. Once again, she was surrounded by the gray walls of her room in the Duone Keep. Desperately, Jena squeezed the stone, staring at it until her eyes prickled with strain, willing the sparkles to flare and the vision to return again. No use. The stone remained quiescent in her hand.

What could she do? Lord Morgan was somewhere, sick or hurt. Maybe even dead? Then she remembered the dreadful mistake she had made earlier in the day, when she thought Lord Morgan had killed her father. *Remember, what you see may only be a possibility.*

Jumping to her feet, Jena began to pace. How could she know? She needed more information, about magic and about Lord Morgan. How could she get it? By talking to Lady Kestrienne? Jena weighed this possibility and then, mindful of Lord Morgan's warning, reluctantly rejected it. No, she would not disobey his instructions until she had a good reason to do so.

Suddenly she stopped in midpace, struck by a sudden thought: what if she searched Lord Morgan's room? He might have books that could teach her about magic. She felt a quick rush of hopeful excitement, then ruthlessly repressed it to think the matter through. Of course, magic books wouldn't be conveniently sitting about on his bedside table. Given his brother's attitude, Jena suspected Lord Morgan had been forced to be discreet about practicing magic. But he had learned it somehow.

Moreover, if she touched some of his things, perhaps she could learn more about him, maybe even enough to puzzle out where he might have gone. Enough, she thought wryly, remembering her other problem, to give her a clue to what he might be likely to commission as a jewelry piece. She would need to tell Lord Duone something that wouldn't arouse his suspicions.

You're mad, an inner voice said. *What if you're caught rummaging around in a missing lord's private quarters? Do you have any idea what they might do to you? You wouldn't just be punished for thieving. Lord Duone already knows his brother's disappearance is tangled up somehow with magic. Do you want to do anything more to make his suspicions center on you? Such as getting caught red-handed in his brother's room with, say, a book of magical lore? Imagine the reaction if you said, "Oh, it's Lord Morgan's book; I was just looking through it."*

Jena quailed at this mental picture. No, no, it was impossible.

Or was it?

If she went after everyone had gone to sleep, she argued with herself, and was very careful, it might be worth the risk.

This isn't like you at all, the first voice said peevishly. *What has gotten into you, that you would even consider such a reckless, featherbrained scheme?*

And that was true. The girl she thought of as herself, living with and working hard for her father in Piyar and Chulipse, making plans to marry her fiancé (it seemed a hundred years ago already) would never do such a thing.

But then, that girl would never have stood up to Lord Duone, either; no, she would have crumpled into a heap. Was this what magic did to people who used it?

When you don't know what else to do, get moving. Arikan used to tell her that (sometimes a little impatiently), whenever she got stuck in a ciphering problem and floundered to a stop. *Make a mistake if you must; just move! If you make a mistake you can correct it, but you'll never get anywhere if you don't start.* She had always had difficulty following that advice, in more than just mathematics; doing nothing seemed easier.

But right now, after the day's adventures, the advice felt right. No more waiting for other people; she would make her own moves. Tonight.

*   *   *

The supper gathering in the Great Hall did not break up until a late hour. In the shadows of the corridor, at one of the windows overlooking the inner ward, she watched people drift out of the Great Hall and disperse in different directions, their voices and laughter echoing faintly off the ward walls. Some of the men headed into the barracks, housed in the opposite, western side of the keep. Other men and women headed toward the apartments on the eastern side, some returning to their quarters via the corridor inside. She could hear fragments of conversations down the hall.

Where would Lord Morgan's room be? In the barracks? She hoped not; she had no wish to explore that portion of the keep, but probably it wouldn't be necessary. Lord Morgan hadn't struck her as someone who considered himself to be more a soldier than a lord. At any rate, it would be unlikely he could keep any magical paraphernalia in a common barracks room.

That left the family's private quarters, which Liselle had pointed out to her as they walked through the ward on the way to the kitchens. Lord Ranulf Duone and his lady maintained their rooms in a short section on the south side, directly above a portion of the Great Hall. If she guessed correctly, Lord Morgan's would be there, too.

The ward eventually emptied of lingerers. She waited still longer, until the talk down the corridor stilled and echoes of shutting doors and silence convinced her that people had retired for the night. The only sounds floating through the windows now were the faint echoes from the paces of patrolling guards on the parapet high above the wall. Picking up the candle in its holder she had taken from her room, she began tiptoeing down the corridor toward the Great Hall, her heart thumping hard.

As she passed doors along the way, the urge to look back over her shoulder grew. But no one passed her. No one challenged her. Cold air flowed in from the inner ward windows, making her skin prickle. Except for the gentle scuffing of her footsteps, all was still.

At the end of the corridor, the passageway turned to the right. Jena paused, listening, and then edged around the corner. Ahead, she could see a long rising flight of stairs. *Last chance to reconsider.* Her heartbeat hammered against her ribs so hard that she leaned against the wall, and the cold touch of stone made her shiver violently. *Are you really going to do this?* She took several deep breaths and, after a few moments, pushed herself away from the wall. *Apparently, the answer is yes.*

Cautiously, Jena crept up the stairway which led into a wider passageway, a gallery running directly over the Great Hall. Here, as best she could tell in the flickering light from her candle, the ceiling rose higher, drawing the eye upward in a series of groined vaults. The gallery boasted a collection of portraits, interspersed with elaborately branched candletrees bolted to the walls. The candletrees were unlit. Curious, Jena raised her candle and looked up at the picture hanging beside the first candletree. It featured a middle-aged lady resplendent in dark blue velvet and jewels. The necklace, she decided after a few moments of study, looked particularly splendid, an exceptionally delicate pattern set with what looked like lapis lazuli, although the wearer's coldness of expression rather spoiled the effect. *Come, now, you aren't here to get new ideas for jewelry designs.* She turned to stare down the length of the gallery, which came to a dead end after about fifty paces. Tall doors lined the wall on the left at intervals between the portraits. *Which one is Lord Morgan's?*

Jena glided to the first, her candle making the shadows tremble on the bas-relief carving cut deeply into the wood. A scene set in a wood in springtime: she admired the detail of the blossoms on the flowering trees and the musculature on a dancer's outflung arm. Cautiously, her hand crept up and rested on the latch as she closed her eyes. *It is . . . a woman's room. Someone who looks a little bitterly at the scene on the door every time she opens it because it reminds her that she doesn't dance anymore. A . . . bad knee.* She sighed. *Ah, how it hurts when the weather changes. An older woman. Not Lady Duone, then. Lady Kestrienne? No.* Her hand dropped to her side, and she tiptoed over to the next door. The point was, it wasn't Lord Morgan's.

The next door showed a procession of ships on a river, beautifully carved down to the details of the shields hung on the sides and the swirl of water in the sterns' wake. *A man lives here . . . or did. He sometimes slammed the door in a temper, hurting the hinges. And then . . . the door opened to let many people in. People weeping, servants carrying things out of the room. A box scrapes against the doorframe. Someone has died? This door hasn't been opened for a long time.* She frowned. Whoever it was reminded her of Lord Morgan and Lord Duone, although it wasn't one of them. Perhaps an older relative? Their father or an uncle? She walked on, the eyes of the portraits staring down at her, making the back of her neck prickle.

On the next door, stooped laborers swung their sickles to bring in a harvest of grain from the field, and others gathered grapes from the vineyard, taking them to a vat to be trampled. A trio of tipsy revelers in one corner seemed to be sampling the final product. Jena smiled, and smiled even more broadly when she touched the handle. *No one lives here . . . yet. But someone comes in here often, to prepare the room, or just to sit and think. All sorts of jumbled fears and hopes, and great anticipation.* It was Lady Duone, Jena realized, as she took her hand from the handle. Lady Duone, waiting for her unborn baby, waiting to put it in its own bed for the first time. The magic in the door felt very strong. This room brimmed with possibility.

As she expected, the next door, showing a feast in a banqueting hall, revealed itself to be Lady Duone's. Servants carrying a dizzying array of platters heaped with delicacies converged from several directions to serve the richly dressed guests seated at table. *I think Lady Duone will be a good mother. She wants to be. And . . . she loves her lord very much.* She paused at the halfway point to the next door, sensing something beyond the wall. *Something else. Another door, inside, between Lady Duone's apartment and the next.* The corners of her lips twitched. Husbands and wives of the nobility customarily kept separate rooms, of course, but even through the wall Jena could tell, faintly, that the door inside often stood open. *Apparently, Lord Duone reciprocates the feeling.*

Although she already knew the next apartment would be Lord Duone's, she stopped to examine the door, curious to learn more. Here, a column of cavalry and foot soldiers led a siege against a castle. The foreground company leveled the battering ram, some fallen to one side, wounded by arrows shot by the crossbowmen stationed at the brattice at the top of the keep tower. Jena touched the handle. *He grasps the handle tightly when he opens the door, his grip strengthened by hours of swordfighting practice. He is worried, preoccupied, a man of action who frets because he doesn't know what action to take. When he decides, he will move resolutely, with relief.* She pulled her hand from the handle quickly. She would not want to be in his way when he did.

Jena moved on. The next door, featuring a tournament pageant with jousting, swordfights, and jugglers entertaining the crowd, wasn't Lord Morgan's, either. Nor was the one after that, showing a group of noblemen and -women assembled for a court dance, with musicians and singers. To one side in the carving, young lovers slipped away into formal gardens, presumably to wander up and down the avenues and flirt under the moonlight. She rolled her eyes up at the portraits in exasperation. *Was I wrong? Is his room in the barracks after all?* The portraits gazed sightlessly back at her, unconcerned.

But at the first touch of the handle on the eighth door, Jena started with surprise. *This is it!* Hot wax dripped on her hand at her sudden movement. Hissing, she switched the candle to her other hand, wiping her hand on the doorframe as she studied the carving. Lord Morgan's door showed a stag hunt, with lords and ladies dressed in splendid hunting gear following on foot and mounted on horses. The stag wheeled at bay, with one of the dogs frozen in midleap at its throat. She touched the desperate stag with gentle fingers. *Is there any significance to which carvings adorn which doors? If so, what kind of omen does this make on the door of my teacher?* Yet, there was an unexpected rightness to the scene, the door told her. *The man who lived in this room left . . . because he went hunting for something.* She stared at the stag wonderingly. *Was he hunting for me? And has he left now to hunt something else?* She pressed the handle down to open it.

The door was locked.

After a moment of disbelief, Jena all but laughed. *Well, of course, silly! What did you expect?* But before she could think of what to do next, she heard a sound that made her blood ice over. Her head snapped to the left, and she saw a wavering light creeping up the stairwell wall. *Oh, no.*

She looked around wildly, but there was absolutely nowhere to hide. No furniture to crouch behind, no tapestries to conceal her. The gallery was a dead end. The windows were cut too high and narrow for her to clamber up on a ledge. The doorframes weren't wide enough for her to press against one and hope she wouldn't be noticed.

She heard a voice: " . . . see to it that the men are ready to leave again early tomorrow morning, if you still wish to follow your original plan then, my lord. Shall I have you called at dawn?"

"That would probably be best." The second voice was Lord Duone's. "Oh, I must remember before we leave to speak to that girl, the gemcutter, to see if she can tell us anything else."

Oh, no, no, no! Furiously, Jena fought down panic. *Is there some magic I could use, some possibility that would keep him from coming up here?* The air felt heavy, as if before a storm. She wanted to run, but her limbs felt weighted down. *Scrape, scrape* came the sound of boots on the stairs; they were coming closer. The other voice sounded like the castellan's. She grimaced. *Oh, perfect. How convenient for Lord Duone to have someone along who just happens to be carrying the dungeon key.* Desperately, she rattled the door latch again. It refused to budge. *Think! What if they heard something in the courtyard and went out to investigate? Or if the castellan lured him away, telling Lord Duone there is something he should see?* The thickness in the air grew; she found she was panting for breath.

And then, just before Lord Duone and his aide finished mounting the stairs and Jena gave herself up for lost, a door down the gallery opened. The tension in the air snapped. With three swift steps, Lady Kestrienne stood at Jena's side, her eyes blazing. "That was Lady Brianna, my great-great aunt, who originally came from the Amethyst family," she said loudly. "A pretty work, don't you think? But I fear the artist succumbed to the temptation to flatter. Lady Brianna's contemporaries described her as having the face of a horse, although you certainly couldn't tell that from this picture. Besides that, she was always increasing—she had fourteen children. I wonder that the artist ever saw her otherwise, yet here her waist looks so narrow you'd think it would snap in half like a carrot if she bent over to pet the dog."

Dumbfounded, Jena stared at Lady Kestrienne, but the other woman was looking fixedly at the wall above Jena's head, and Jena followed her gaze to the portrait hanging there. "But then, I suppose," Lady Kestrienne rattled on as the footsteps behind them stopped, "it makes as much sense to wonder how Lord Tansing managed to get her with child so often. Apparently he had difficulty tearing his attention from his mistress. *She* had sixteen children."

"Aunt Kestrienne?" Lord Duone's voice sounded bemused.

"Oh, good evening, Ranulf, dear," Lady Kestrienne replied warmly, wheeling around to face her nephew. "Going to bed so soon?" Jena turned, too, feeling her knees shake with relief.

"What *are* you doing?" Lord Duone said.

Jena took a deep breath and spoke. "Why, I was asking Lady Kestrienne about your family's interest in art, my lord. She very kindly offered to give me a tour of the family portraits. Such an impressive collection! I suppose it is rather late—I'm sorry—but I found it utterly fascinating." She nodded to the woman beside her and gave her best smile. "And Lady Kestrienne has been so *very* gracious in answering my questions."

"I see. Well, then." Lord Duone shifted from one foot to another, somewhat at a loss. The castellan cleared his throat.

"I will say good night, then, my lord," the castellan said, bowing. "Unless there is anything else?"

"Hmm? Oh—no, thank you. That will be all. Good night." Lord Duone made a vague hand gesture toward the stairs and the castellan withdrew respectfully.

"I was hoping you would allow me to speak briefly with you, Lord Duone," Jena said, seizing her chance as the castellan's steps retreated. "About your journey to Piyar. You see—"

"Jena needs to secure some equipment for Morgan's project," Lady Kestrienne interposed. "She was hoping for your permission, before you left, to requisition the necessary supplies. Morgan has provided her with the money for materials, of course." She reached over to pat Jena's hand benignly. "She is most anxious to begin her work."

"Quite so," Lord Duone replied. Jena was about to protest, when Lady Kestrienne made a shooing gesture at her nephew.

"But, of course, any little details about that can be discussed tomorrow, before you leave. For pity's sake, Ranulf, go to bed. You were up before dawn; I know you must be dead on your feet. You needn't dance attendance on us!"

He rocked back on his heels a little, but recovered soon enough. "Good night, then, Aunt." He kissed her cheek and gave Jena a little nod. "And good night to you, too."

Helplessly, Jena dropped him a curtsy, knowing herself outmaneuvered. "Good night, my lord." She watched him as he retreated to his apartment, but Lady Kestrienne had already turned her attention back to the portraits.

"That dignified gentleman dressed in plum, the one with the bad case of dropsy, was Lord Garrick. A rather distant cousin. Quite a fine example of the style of the portraiture of the period, I believe, although I don't particularly fancy cherubs myself." The door to Lord Duone's apartment shut with a quiet thump. Lady Kestrienne wheeled on Jena fiercely. "So. Where do we talk?" she said in a very different undertone. "Morgan's room?"

Jena opened her mouth and closed it. "It's locked," she said finally.

"We'll see." She led Jena back to the door with the stag hunt, put her hand on the latch, and pressed firmly. The door opened with an audible click.

Jena's jaw dropped. "It was locked before," she said inanely.

Lady Kestrienne gave her a frosty look as she swung the door open. "It is possible for locks to break, you know. Inside, if you please."

Jena stepped over the threshold. Lady Kestrienne followed, swinging the heavy door shut behind them.

CHAPTER SEVEN

⚱

THE CANDLE JENA HELD ILLU-
minated only a few steps in front of them. Lady Kestrienne
deftly plucked it from her hand and lit a taper standing on a
shelf inset beside the door. Then she moved forward into the
room and lit a candelabra standing on a table beside the
canopied bed. The light grew, revealing a handsomely ap-
pointed chamber, smaller than Jena's tower room. If Lord
Morgan decorated his own quarters, he had fine taste. It was
in keeping with his sense of dress: confident in its simplicity,
rather than slavishly copying court fashion. No carved
nymphs, grapes, or animals interrupted the clean lines of the
massive, walnut-wood furniture. Tapestries depicting more
hunting scenes covered the walls, and dark green silk brocade hung from the bedcurtain poles, devoid of tassels, ruf-
fles, or embroidery. The candlelight captured the richness of
the heavy sheen in the folds, black edged with a glimmer of
gold. A small pile of richly bound books on the table beside
the bed caught Jena's eye, and she started toward it when
Lady Kestrienne's voice stopped her: "You won't find any
books on magic there."

"No?" Jena raised an eyebrow.

"That is one of the things you were looking for, wasn't

it?" Lady Kestrienne carried a thick candle over to the door and stooped there, tilting it to drip wax against the base of the door. A faint humming resonated in the air, masking any sound which might have intruded from outside the room.

"What are you doing?" Jena asked.

"Sealing the door so we won't be interrupted. The spell is based on metaphor, of course, but it's still quite effective."

Jena watched her in silence until she had dripped the last drop of wax and straightened up again. The humming ceased, but a dense stillness remained, as if the walls around them were muffled with velvet curtains, partitioning off the room. "So you are a user of magic, then," Jena said finally. Her voice sounded oddly muted to her ears, as if it had difficulty piercing the spell in the air around her.

"Of course I am," Lady Kestrienne replied, replacing the candle on a small shelf built into one of the bedposts. "And you, my dear, are a loose cannon on the deck of a ship."

"I'm a what?"

Lady Kestrienne plunked herself down in a chair set by the fireplace and regarded Jena severely. "A loose cannon. A menace. An accident looking for a place to happen."

Jena pulled a stool out from a corner and sat down beside her. "Whatever are you talking about?"

"You simply have no idea how much power you have right now, do you?"

Jena shook her head.

"I thought not. Well, consider this: you could have killed Lord Duone. When you were trying to think of a way to keep him from coming up the stairs, what if it had occurred to you for him to trip and break his leg? Or fall sick suddenly? Or worse?" Lady Kestrienne shuddered. "Now, I grant you, Ranulf can be stuffy at times, but I am rather fond of him. I would hate to lose him that way."

"I could have done that?" said Jena, appalled.

"Yes." Lady Kestrienne bit the word off neatly. "It's bad enough I had to risk discovery in the courtyard like that today. I was popping off spells like mad, trying to blunt everyone's reactions to your extraordinary arrival. And now this!"

"But Lord Duone—I wouldn't have—I didn't—"

"You didn't because I was monitoring you and interrupted you in time by offering a different possibility. You must *learn*," Lady Kestrienne said, jabbing the arm of her chair with her finger to emphasize the word, "to control yourself."

"I'm truly sorry," Jena said, "but please, try to understand: my teacher has disappeared. I was doing what I could to find him. If magicians must be monitored, well, I didn't know. Lord Morgan's the one who should have been doing that, anyway, isn't he?"

"Hold a moment." Lady Kestrienne cocked her head at Jena. "Your teacher? Is that what you think Morgan is?"

"Well, isn't he?"

Abruptly, Lady Kestrienne leaned back in her chair and laughed merrily. "Of course not. My dear, he is your partner. Your equal. He knows no more about being a wizard than you do."

Jena's eyes widened. "A wizard? Is that different from being a magician?"

"Yes, very." Lady Kestrienne hesitated. "So he told you he was your teacher?"

"Well . . ." Jena thought back on the scene in the garden at Piyar. "Not exactly. But he implied it."

"I suppose it's not surprising. I might have told him about wizardry, eventually. But the nature of wizardry is generally kept a great secret. I had no idea there was a chance he might partner so soon after beginning to learn magic. Most magicians never partner at all. He left the keep about six months ago, and we didn't hear from him for a long time. That was one of the reasons why Lord Duone was setting out today, to try to find him."

"Wait, go back. What do you mean by partnering?"

Lady Kestrienne eyed Jena for a moment. "Suppose you start, by telling me how you two met."

And so Jena poured out the whole story, starting from Lord Morgan's first visit to the workshop. It was a relief to tell it, although she found herself faltering when she came to the part about chasing after Lord Morgan with the shears. It was difficult, after all, to admit she had done so, especially after just being scolded for the danger she had posed to Lord

Duone. But Lady Kestrienne listened intently without interrupting, her face offering no clue to her reactions.

" . . . And so I said I could be his pupil. He didn't have a chance to say anything, but I think that's what he wanted to hear. And then we found ourselves here. It all happened so quickly." She stopped. "Lord Morgan said something about it being a female spell? I assume he means being picked up and moved like that. Did you bring us here?"

Lady Kestrienne sat up straight in surprise. "I? Goodness, no. You did it, Jena. It was your magic that brought the two of you to Duone Keep."

"Are you sure?"

"When wizards partner, particularly powerful ones like the two of you, the new possibilities this causes create a tremendous surge of energy and affinity which other wizards can sense, even from very far away. When you popped into the outer ward, I could tell immediately that you had done the transporting spell. Now mind, the power needed for a feat like that is truly immense. You felt disoriented right after you arrived, didn't you?"

Jena nodded.

"And you'll find yourself to be quite tired the next couple of days or so," Lady Kestrienne went on. "It won't be easy or perhaps even likely for you ever to be able to do that sort of spell again."

"But how did I do it? And what do you mean, powerful like the two of us?"

Lady Kestrienne sighed. "Very well. From the beginning. Adepts can be either magicians or wizards. Magicians work alone; wizards work in pairs. Always male-female pairs. It is possible, though rare, for someone like you, who has never used magic, to partner and become a wizard immediately without having been a magician first. Wizards are much more powerful than magicians."

"Why is that?"

"Because working with a partner broadens your ability to see possibilities. Alone, you have blind spots, areas you can't perceive because of your background, your sex, your age, whatever. But your partner can see them and cover them for you.

"The most powerful wizard pairs are those who are very different, because they bring a wider range of experience to the partnership. Each knows something the other doesn't know, and that is what makes them equals."

"Equals?" said Jena. "How could I possibly be equals with Lord Morgan? He's a noble, he's a man, he's older than me."

Lady Kestrienne smiled. "Wizardry requires a nontraditional kind of thinking. That's why," she said, wrinkling her nose, "it's rare among those who see life only in a certain prescribed way, like the nobility, for example. Yes, it's true Morgan is a man, that he's a noble and older than you. You, on the other hand, are young, a woman, and an artist. Those are things Morgan doesn't know about, that he must learn about from you. They are just as valuable." She tapped Jena's knee with her finger. "You must remember that, Jena. I'd suggest that you teach yourself to think of him as 'Morgan' rather than 'Lord Morgan,' because deep in your bones you must always know that you're his equal. When it comes to wizardry, he needs you just as much as you need him. You must never be afraid to challenge him. If you don't remember that, if you begin to defer to him, your partnership will unbalance and weaken. The two of you will fail to cover each other's blind spots, and that will get you both into trouble."

Jena sat quietly for a moment, thinking. "I wonder what made him pick me," she said finally.

"Oh, he didn't," Lady Kestrienne replied quickly. "I told you, he didn't know about this. No, when you met, magic had already been catalyzed in both of you, and your opposite natures—"

"Wait." Jena held up a hand. "I'm sorry to interrupt, but . . . catalyzed?"

"Oh. Yes. You know a male adept, don't you? You've been in some kind of student-teacher relationship with him?"

"Well, I know Arikan, a magician. He's been my tutor, and a friend of my father for years."

Lady Kestrienne raised her eyebrows slightly. "Hmm, yes," she said after a momentary pause. "People with the potential for doing magic are often drawn to adepts of the opposite sex. Your friend Arikan helped you begin to see possibilities. It's called catalyzation: the fact that he was your teacher awakened the possibility of magic in you. And this made you ripe for partnering when you met Morgan. It's not necessary for someone to be catalyzed in order to become a wizard, but it makes it easier."

"Arikan told me recently—right after I met Lord Morgan, in fact—"

"Just Morgan, remember."

"Oh. Yes." Jena smiled self-consciously. "That's going to take a little practice.

"Anyway, Arikan told me I had the potential to use magic," she went on. "I was angry at him because he hadn't told me for so many years, hadn't taught me."

"It wouldn't have been wise for him to have done so. You had to discover it yourself."

"But in fact, it's really because of Arikan that I became a wizard at all?"

"In all probability, yes."

"I suppose I owe him an apology."

Lady Kestrienne laughed. "I suppose you do. He may have finally told you about your potential after you met Morgan because he sensed the possibility you were close to partnering."

"I wonder if my father knew." Jena sighed. "He and Bram must be so worried about me."

"You needn't distress yourself about them, Jena," Lady Kestrienne said. "Your father and your fiancé know you're safe."

"They do? Really? How do you know?"

Lady Kestrienne seemed to struggle with herself for a moment. "We'll just say that they've received a message." She raised a forestalling hand as Jena opened her mouth to ask another question. "Never mind how for the moment."

Reluctantly, Jena left that particular point and turned to another question. "Did you catalyze Morgan, then?" How strange his name sounded without the title.

"Yes. I've lived with the household since before he was a baby—his father Tersat was my brother, you see. Morgan became a magician under my tutelage."

"Until he found me."

"Exactly. The opposition of your natures drew you to-gether, without any conscious choice on either of your parts. It's more than the difference of your sexes and social classes, too." She cocked her head, studying Jena. "Knowing that the two of you partnered, I could hazard some guesses about you. I've known Morgan for his entire life. He is impetuous, restless, forceful, decisive, and often arrogant and quarrel-some. Therefore, I would imagine you can be hesitant, quiet, and obedient to a fault. Rather a homebody. Probably a little mealy-mouthed at times. Am I right?"

"At least I'm never rude!" Jena flashed, and then stopped, abashed.

Lady Kestrienne rocked with laughter until tears came to her eyes. "Ah, not so mealy-mouthed now," she gasped fi-nally. "Well, that's to be expected."

"Just what do you mean?" Jena demanded huffily.

"When wizards partner, they suddenly draw upon the magic of someone very unlike themselves, who sees totally different possibilities. New wizards pull away from their old habits and act in opposition to their own natures. They take on their partner's characteristics. I know you surprised your-self several times today—in the outer ward with Lord Duone, for instance. Your bond with Morgan did that." She chuckled. "Morgan didn't understand the nature of a wizard partnership any more than you did. If he thought the two of you would be teacher and pupil, I suspect it may have even been in his mind to bring you here to train you, where he learned magic.

"But in the moment of partnering, the leader and the fol-lower changed places. You understood his intention in a flash. And you implemented it, bringing both of you here."

"Why is that a woman's spell?" Jena said.

Lady Kestrienne shrugged. "Ordinarily, women stay at home and men travel. And therefore—"

"I've traveled," Jena interrupted. "I've been traveling back and forth between Chulipse and Piyar all my life."

"Because your father follows the Court, I suppose?" Lady Kestrienne asked.

Jena nodded.

"Ah, you mean you've been moving back and forth between two homes. But you've never wanted to go anywhere that isn't your home, have you?"

Jena considered. "Bram told me my problem was that I wanted to leave home, but I just didn't know how and couldn't admit it. I told him he was crazy."

"Hmm. Morgan, in contrast, has sometimes seemed to me to be determined to leave home as far behind him as he can. Another difference between the two of you, you see? Although, I suppose," she added reflectively, "he may have been searching for his partner, without really understanding that was what he was doing. I could tell something was making him particularly restless in the months before he left.

"Anyway, partnering transferred that possibility to you, and since new possibilities are magic"—Lady Kestrienne spread her hands—"you brought the two of you here."

"Did these sorts of things happen to you, too? Becoming like your partner, I mean?"

"Yes."

"Who is he?"

The smile left Lady Kestrienne's face abruptly. "It's a good thing I'm tolerant. You couldn't possibly realize how appallingly rude that question is."

"It is?" Jena asked in surprise. "I'm sorry, but why?"

"Because your partner covers your blind spot and is the most important element of your practice of magic. If someone wants to hurt you, he or she will try to do it through your partner. Wizards made a great deal of ugly use of that particular fact during the Founders' War."

"Really?"

"Yes, that's one reason why wizardry is such a great secret now. And, by the way, that's also why the first Diamond renounced his own magic totally when he established the Diadem."

Jena gaped at her. "Are you saying . . . do you mean . . . the first Diamond was a *wizard*?"

Lady Kestrienne nodded. "Indeed he was. Lady Adrienne, his wife, was also his partner, you see. He always blamed himself for her murder: he knew she had been killed in an attempt to stop him. Wizardry makes an adept powerful, but wizards are vulnerable in a way magicians aren't."

"And my partner is missing," Jena said bleakly.

"Yes." Lady Kestrienne nodded slowly, her face extremely grave. "So you see now how serious this is. He must be found. As his partner, you have the best chance of doing it. Let me think." Lady Kestrienne rose gracefully and crossed to the table piled with books by the bed. A castle-and-siege game board stood there, too, and she fingered one of the playing pieces thoughtfully while Jena waited. Finally Lady Kestrienne gave the piece a final tap with a finger tip and turned. "Did Morgan give you anything before he disappeared? A ring, or a pendant, or some such thing?"

"He gave me this." Jena pulled the stone from a pouch at her girdle and brought it to Lady Kestrienne. "I'm glad you mentioned it; I need to ask you about it."

"Ah!" Lady Kestrienne all but snatched it from her hand to hold it to the candle. "Excellent. This will make things easier, I hope."

"It was gray before, and opaque. I've never seen a stone change like that."

Lady Kestrienne looked at her with a half smile. "How has it changed? What does it look like to you now?"

"Why, it's clear. With gold flecks."

"Did you ever notice whether Morgan had a black stone with similar gold flecks?"

"Yes," replied Jena. "He had a ring." She paused, remembering. "It was strange. When I first saw it, I thought it was gray, and faceted. Then I suddenly saw it as a black cabochon. Polished smooth, I mean, rounded, with the gold flecks."

"Describe the setting for me."

Jena did, and Lady Kestrienne sighed in satisfaction. "That is the ring I gave him when he became a magician. I gave him the stone at the same time, in case he should ever find a wizard partner. And he did." She patted Jena's hand. "We're in luck. Despite Morgan's disappearance, you had enough time together to key a pair of linked talismans. The gold flecks you see in both are the link between the two of you. Their presence means that your bond has been truly forged. Of course, I can't see the flecks at all myself."

"You can't?"

"No, not any more than you can see the flecks I can see in my stone. This is my talisman link with my partner." Lady Kestrienne waggled the fingers of her right hand, making her ring flash in the candlelight. "Because you are also a female wizard, the stone appears clear to you. Morgan would see my stone as an opaque black and, similarly, my partner's would look black to you."

"Doesn't wearing a clear stone get you into trouble?"

"No one can see talismans unless they are adepts themselves, or at least have a very strong potential to become so."

"That's why my father didn't see Morgan's ring!"

"Exactly." She shifted the stone in her hand, letting the candlelight play across its angles. "Hmm. It would be better if the stone was cut, in a shape similar to his."

"You mean the stone on his ring? I could cut this stone, if I had the tools."

Lady Kestrienne brightened. "I'd forgotten. Yes, you could! How singularly fortunate. Do you remember what his stone looked like? Could you duplicate the cut?"

Jena thought. "It was a little over a carat. Brilliant cut, a new style, but Father has shown me how to do it."

Lady Kestrienne returned the stone to Jena. "Splendid. Keep it quite safe, my dear. It may be possible to use it to communicate with Morgan."

"I think I already have." Jena squeezed the stone tightly. "Earlier this evening, I was trying to read it, the way Arikan scries objects. I saw a vision of him, on a ship, I think. He was lying on a hammock, hurt or sick. Could it have been a false vision? A possibility that isn't necessarily the truth?"

"Not if you were using the talisman," Lady Kestrienne said grimly. "Did you speak to him?"

"Someone came between us, and the vision faded. I couldn't make it come back."

Lady Kestrienne's brow furrowed. "Unfortunate."

"Perhaps if I cut the stone, that might help me reestablish the link?" Jena ventured.

"Perhaps. Something came between you, you say? How far away did you seem to be from Morgan?"

"I don't know. Ten or twelve paces?"

"Oh, dear." Lady Kestrienne sat back down, and Jena hastened to join her. "It doesn't sound like he was wearing the ring, then," Lady Kestrienne continued. "That may be bad."

"Why?" demanded Jena.

"Because I've never known Morgan to take that ring off since I gave it to him. In fact, I told him not to. It may have been taken from him against his will."

Jena sat very still.

"Unless he removed it voluntarily, of course," Lady Kestrienne went on, "and I cannot think why he would. If someone took it from him, that person would have to be an adept to see it in the first place. And if that person knew enough to take a wizard's talisman link from him, he or she is probably a wizard, too."

The two women sat in an uneasy silence for a moment, and then Jena spoke. "Something just occurred to me: you told me that my magic brought Morgan and me here. But was it my magic that whisked Morgan away again?"

Alarmed chagrin flickered over Lady Kestrienne's face. "What a dolt I am not to have considered that myself!" She closed her eyes. "I don't think it was," she said a few moments later, her frown deepening.

"You're sure?" Jena said anxiously. "I didn't . . . I don't know . . . find another place by rummaging around in his mind and send him off there?"

"No." Lady Kestrienne opened her eyes again. "No, this magic had a different essence than yours. Different echoes, you might say."

"And Morgan didn't do it, either?"

Lady Kestrienne's shoulders sagged. "No," she said bleakly. "No, he didn't."

"Could you recognize who did the magic? Was it more than one person?"

"I'm not entirely sure. Your joint appearance caused very powerful reverberations, after all. They hadn't entirely died down when Morgan vanished, and that masked the magic involved, in a way. But a transportation spell, as I've said, is generally the mark of a woman adept."

"And so," Jena said, "someone you don't recognize, probably a woman, made Morgan disappear. And then someone, probably a wizard, took his ring away from him."

"And they may be one and the same person, or not," Lady Kestrienne finished. "A very serious matter indeed."

Jena leaned forward. "Will you help me? I'll need to learn more about magic to begin the search, won't I? Would you teach me?"

Lady Kestrienne brooded silently for a moment. "There are balances to be maintained here. Ideally, a wizard should learn magic by working with the partner—"

"But my partner isn't here," Jena replied, exasperated. "If I am to find him at all—"

"Hush, child, I wasn't finished." She narrowed her eyes at Jena. "You've just partnered, so I must make allowances when you sound like Morgan. But even he was taught that interrupting one's elders continually is quite discourteous.

"As I was saying," she went on serenely as Jena blushed, "learning from one's partner is the ideal situation. But there is another side to that particular coin. I told you about tutors, wizards of the opposite sex who catalyze you before you partner. But there are also mentors, wizards of the *same* gender who help you *after* you partner. Even if I hadn't spoken to you this afternoon, you would have eventually found yourself seeking me out without understanding why."

Jena brightened. "So you will help me, then?"

"Ah, but you see, there is a problem: I was also Morgan's tutor. Unless that factor is balanced, your partnership will suffer strain, particularly because Morgan is not here to learn at the same rate as you. If I do become your mentor, I must take care not to teach you too much before you find Morgan."

"Do you mean . . . in order to balance, Morgan should use Arikan as his mentor, since he was my tutor?"

Lady Kestrienne seemed reluctant to answer. "Yes. In fact, that would make your partnership quite strong. That and—" She broke off.

Jena was about to ask her what she meant, but then she had a dawning realization. "Wait a minute. When you talked about tutors earlier, you simply said they had to be adepts. But just now you said they had to be wizards."

Lady Kestrienne looked a bit flustered. "Did I? Perhaps you misunderstood me—"

"Why couldn't I partner with Arikan? You said catalyzation wasn't necessary; it just made partnering easier. And if I didn't have to be catalyzed first, well, Arikan is even older than Morgan. That difference in age would have set up some powerful possibilities, wouldn't it? Except that I couldn't be a partner to Arikan—because he already has one!"

Lady Kestrienne closed her eyes. "May the ground open up and swallow me. Immediately."

"You're his partner, aren't you?"

Lady Kestrienne did not reply.

"You told me Father and Bram knew I was safe. Of course when Father heard Bram's story, the first thing he would do would be to consult Arikan. You said wizards could feel the power of partnering from far away. Arikan might have felt it himself. He might have felt us travel here. Maybe he even knew who Morgan was, because you were his tutor. That's why you left my room this afternoon. Arikan was calling you through his talisman!"

"Yes," Lady Kestrienne said heavily. "You are correct."

"I remember you told Lord Duone tonight that he shouldn't dance attendance on us. That is something I've heard Arikan say to Father."

"Is it? Dear me. I see I will have to watch my language around people who know us both."

"I'm sorry if you wanted to keep it a secret. I wouldn't use it against you, Lady Kestrienne, believe me. How could I? You're Arikan's partner, and he's been my dear friend. And you were Morgan's tutor."

"It would have been difficult to keep it secret, I suppose," Lady Kestrienne said philosophically, "considering the bonds between the four of us. Hmph. Well, I'm sure you can see how my partnership with Arikan creates an additional balancing problem, at any rate." She looked at Jena and smiled. "It is appropriate for you to call me just 'Kestrienne,' my dear, at least when we're alone. Since I'm to be your mentor."

"Thank you—Kestrienne."

"Now, then." Lady Kestrienne gave her an inquiring look. "What do you plan to do next?"

"Uh, couldn't you tell me?" asked Jena, taken aback.

"Oh, goodness, that's not for me to say! Dear me, what a poor mentor I'd be if I started out by making all your decisions for you!" Lady Kestrienne shook her head decidedly. "No, Jena. Choices must be made by those affected the most. Remember that, if you practice wizardry! This choice belongs to you."

"But I don't know what to do!" Jena pleaded.

"Don't you? You were already doing something tonight until I interrupted you, weren't you?"

"I was going to search Morgan's room," Jena said, a little shamefacedly. "I needed an idea for what to tell Lord Duone about what Morgan might have commissioned for a jewelry design, something that wouldn't arouse his suspicions. And I wanted to learn about Morgan and, well, about magic."

"An admirable strategy," said Lady Kestrienne warmly. "How very clever of you! Aside from the trifling matter of the threat your inexperience posed to hapless passersby such as Ranulf, of course." She stood and held out her hand to Jena until she rose, too. "No matter. I will stand guard to protect the innocent. Go ahead and put your plan into effect. Consider the room yours to explore."

CHAPTER EIGHT

Thus encouraged, Jena looked about the room with new curiosity. Where to start? "Since Morgan has been missing a while, haven't you already tried this? Touched his things to see what you could learn?"

"Yes," Lady Kestrienne admitted. "But I didn't absorb much. Arikan is better at scrying objects than me." She shrugged. "There are compensations. He tells me I'm better at interpreting people."

"Is there a way I might use the talisman stone somehow?"

"The only way to find out is to try it and see."

"You do sound like Arikan." After a moment's thought, Jena closed her hand over the stone and went over to the large chest pushed against the foot of the bed. She knelt and touched the lid, closing her eyes in concentration. After a few moments, she said tentatively, "I'm not sure—I mean, I don't sense that Morgan has touched this chest very often."

"Of course not. Mostly it is opened and closed by servants who help him dress and who put the clothes away again at night."

"Oh." Jena blushed. "I see. I didn't even think of that." She opened her eyes and looked at Lady Kestrienne. "My goodness, does Morgan have servants left behind in Piyar, at an inn or something?"

"I don't think so. Some of his clothes, perhaps, but no servants. He slipped away from the keep alone six months ago, shortly after returning from Piyar. That was one of the reasons Lord Duone fretted so about him. Going off without even a single attendant! Unheard of for a nobleman! Unthinkable! You would have thought Morgan was a stripling who had set out delirious with brain fever, or been kidnapped by outlaws for ransom." Lady Kestrienne sniffed. "I don't know what Ranulf thought some of the foppish menservants we keep around here could have done against outlaws. Taught them the latest court dance, I expect.

"I knew that in all probability Morgan was safe, of course," she continued, "although I didn't know where he had gone. But then Lord Duone received word that Morgan might have been seen in Tenaway a short while ago. Lord Duone planned to take that route on his way to attend the Equinox ceremonies at the Court in Piyar. That was where he was setting out with his men this afternoon when you suddenly appeared."

"So that's what the castellan was talking about," Jena said. "Lord Duone must have decided to head there tomorrow anyway, even after seeing Morgan this afternoon." With an effort, she swung open the lid of the chest. "Morgan certainly didn't take all his clothes when he left." Pourpoints, shirts, jerkins, and outer gowns were arranged in piles, all tidily sorted. Pairs of hose lay folded in narrow piles wedged near the front of the chest. "Even if you don't want to tell me what to do, couldn't you at least give me some guidance on how to do a magical search?"

"Starting with more light would help." Lady Kestrienne fetched the candelabra from the table beside the bed. "You must learn your own way," she said, sitting on the foot of the bed, so that the glow spilled into the chest's interior. "But perhaps I can give you a little push in the right direction.

"When you start to see possibilities magically, it's like acquiring a whole new sense, like being in darkness all your life, and then"—she gestured toward the candelabra she held—"opening your eyes and encountering light for the first time. Until you became accustomed to what seeing means, you wouldn't know what an object in front of you was until you used a familiar sense to identify it. You could 'see' something, meaning you would perceive shapes and colors in a new, puzzling way. But the shapes and colors would mean nothing to you until, say, someone plucked a string, and the sound made you realize you were looking at a lute. Then you would be able to recognize a lute visually in the future."

"Or you could touch something and only then understand it's a stool?" Jena asked.

"Exactly."

"I never thought of seeing quite that way before," Jena said.

"In the same way," Lady Kestrienne went on, "in order to interpret magical sensing, at first you will need to verify it with other, familiar senses until you can understand the magical sensing directly. Keep your mind open, quiet, and receptive. Touch the objects you're using in a search. Pick them up, smell them, taste them, stroke them. Use what you learn to begin forming tentative conclusions. If you're doing it right, you will begin to get magical 'hunches,' which you use to keep shaping your conclusions. Your senses will point the way to go, until you can feel the hunch clearly enough to follow the magic firsthand."

Jena ran a hand over the clothing in the chest, trying to merge her tactile impressions with the vague possibility sensations from the talisman stone. "I would guess, just from looking in here, that he likes to keep his clothes neat," she ventured. Her fingers stopped abruptly over the seam of a folded outer gown. "Here's a darn."

"What does that tell you?"

"I suppose . . . it means he cared enough to see that his clothes get mended."

"That's your deduction from your senses. Any magical hunches to back up your impression?"

Jena's forehead furrowed in concentration. "There's . . . distress from the tear . . . leading to a kind of urgency. One that has been relieved." She pulled out the gown and examined it. "I think he had someone repair this within a day of its being torn."

"Mmm, yes," Lady Kestrienne said. "You're right. He is fastidious. He once threw a boot at the head of a laundress who didn't get a spot out of one of his shirts."

Jena winced. "Ouch. I hope he won't throw one at me when he finds out I've been rifling through his things." She carefully refolded the gown. "But how am I supposed to see where he might have gone by doing this? I can't tell where he has worn his clothes." Jena picked up another garment. "This pourpoint, here, now; he felt very hot the last time he wore it. But nothing more definite than that. Perhaps the hose?" She selected a pair and gently turned over the feet, running her talisman stone over the sewn-in soles. "These have walked over gravel, and over sand and . . . and over ground." She sighed and replaced the hose among the others in the chest. "Only which ground? Even if I could tell, it wouldn't do us any good if he's somewhere now where he's never been before."

Lady Kestrienne shrugged. "If you don't think what you're learning here is useful, try something else."

After shutting the chest, Jena took the candelabra from Lady Kestrienne and brought it back to the table at the head of the bed. The shift of the light's angle made shadows play around the playing pieces positioned on the wooden game board. They had been carved from jade, and the border of the board had been inlaid with delicate twinings of mother-of-pearl. Jena traced them with her forefinger, allowing herself to take a moment to admire the artistry of the intricate design. At the edge of the board, her finger hesitated; she looked up and caught the sad half smile flickering across Lady Kestrienne's face. "You gave him this, didn't you?"

Lady Kestrienne blinked, as if startled out of her memories. "Yes, I did, for his twentieth birthday." She laughed. "It was a gift born out of desperation, really. He and Tersat were simply at each other's throats throughout that entire winter. Everyone in the household was in absolute despair over the two of them, and so to restore some semblance of peace I decided to teach Morgan to play castle-and-siege. I hoped it might keep him out of Tersat's way and perhaps help him develop some patience! He surprised me by developing quite a keen interest in the game, and we spent many an hour over the board.

"It didn't even occur to me when I gave it to him, but castle-and-siege is really an invaluable tool to develop the type of thinking used by the adept. After all, the player who wins is the one who can best see possibilities: How will my opponent respond if I move this piece here? What will the board look like three moves from now, or five moves? Playing castle-and-siege with me is actually what catalyzed Morgan, I think."

"Really?"

"Yes. And as his inner potential for magic began to stir, he began to sense mine and wonder about me. One night—I'll never forget it. He'd just beaten me soundly for the third time in a row. And as he picked up my lord and lady pieces, he looked me in the eye and said, "It's rather like magic, isn't it?"

Jena laughed.

"Oh, my heart was in my throat," Lady Kestrienne said. "I knew he wasn't simply making an offhand comment; he was testing me. I'd kept my own magic secret from the family all my life, but I said, 'Yes, it is.' And the very next morning, I started to give him magic lessons."

Jena picked up a pair of crossbowmen, dark and light, and smiled. "He prefers to play white."

"Yes. Do you know why?"

"Because he likes to go first." Putting the pieces down, Jena opened the cover of the top book on the stack beside the board, carefully, to check the title page, and then another and another. "You're right," she said when she finished going through the stack. "There aren't any magic books here."

"Morgan used mine, which I keep in my room. I flatter myself that no one will find them unless I intend for them to do so. Although," she added coming to peer at the books over Jena's shoulder, "books might be said to have their own kind of magic, since they open up new ideas." She fingered through the pages of one of the volumes. "Mmm. What do you make of his taste in reading material?"

Jena went through the stack again, ticking off the subjects. "Hunting . . . the study and use of arms . . . horsemanship—"

"Those don't surprise me," Lady Kestrienne interrupted. "But look at these: books on political thought ... rhetoric ... history ... music ... goodness gracious, *poetry* ..."

"Wouldn't they be natural things for him to read about, as part of a nobleman's education?" Jena asked.

"More than just that: they are subjects generally agreed to be essential for a courtier to master. Now, what would Morgan be doing with books like these? I've heard him say hundreds of times that he'd rather be drowned in boiling oil than rub shoulders with Court popinjays." She twitched a book out from under Jena's hand. "Look, this is Lord Omnahan's treatise on falconry. I *distinctly* remember hearing Morgan tell Ranulf that the day Lord Omnahan said anything worth hearing would be the day the Koh ran backward." Lady Kestrienne snorted. "And here he has spent who knows how many gold pieces on one of his publications?" She looked up at Jena sharply. "Did he buy it simply to mock the fellow's prosy stuff to his friends?"

Jena placed the talisman stone on the stack of books. "He's been reading all of them quite intently," she answered eventually. "Studying them, really, not skimming."

Suddenly a minute flash caught her eye: the sparkles in the talisman stone were flaring again. Another vision? No, she decided cautiously, but something in the room was tugging at her attention. She picked up the talisman, and it drew her fingers over to the left like a magnet approaching steel, until her hand hovered over another object. She drew the candelabra closer. "Do you know what this is?"

"That? It's from Lady Vianne Rhuddlan, the Ruby. A lump of gold ore, I believe; you know the Rubies made their fortune in mining, don't you? Morgan, Ranulf, Metissa, and I stayed at Rhuddlan Palazzo in Chulipse over the Midsummer's Eve Festival last summer, and she gave it to him then as a Festival gift. He uses it as a parchment weight."

Jena picked it up and gasped. "Kestrienne ..." She reached out blindly to grasp the bedcurtains, and the lump of ore dropped from her fingers. "Ohh, I'm getting dizzy again."

"Sit down on the bed. Down! Head between the knees, if you please. There." Lady Kestrienne expertly folded her into position and sat beside her until the dizziness passed. When Jena could raise her head again without the room swimming around, Lady Kestrienne fished a pomander from her girdle and, extracting a restorative pouncet bottle, waved it under Jena's nose. The stinging sweetness brought tears to Jena's eyes. "Better now?"

"Yes. Thank you."

"Perhaps you need to return to your room?"

"Tell me about the Ruby first." Jena looked at the gold nugget on the table. "How long has Morgan known her?"

"Why, most of his life, I expect. Her father, the former Ruby Lord Egen Rhuddlan, owned an estate adjoining some land belonging to the Duone family, just outside Chulispe. Vianne often spent her summers there. I believe both Ranulf and Morgan passed quite a bit of time with her as the three of them were growing up. They all studied under the same masters and sometimes took their lessons together." Lady Kestrienne's eyes narrowed. "Why?"

Jena silently handed the nugget of ore to her. Lady Kestrienne turned it over in her hand, eyes half closed. "I don't perceive anything unusual about it," she said finally, returning it to Jena. "But as I've said, scrying objects isn't my specialty."

Jena shook her head in wonder. "When I touch it, I feel the wash of feelings like a burn, they're so strong." She laid the nugget back on the tabletop. "Morgan and Lady Rhuddlan are in love."

Lady Kestrienne's eyes widened. "In love?"

"More than that. I think they are secretly betrothed."

Lady Kestrienne reached again for the restorative bottle in her pomander, this time for herself. "Morgan is betrothed to the Ruby? *The Diamond Heir*?"

Jena nodded.

Lady Kestrienne took a deep breath from the pouncet and began gurgling in laughter. But the smell started a coughing fit, and it took several minutes of strangled gasps, punctuated by waves of a handkerchief snatched from her sleeve, before she recovered her breath. "My, my, my," she choked finally, tears running down her face. "Don't I feel the fool, after telling you my specialty was scrying people. The sly rogue! I

had absolutely no idea." She wiped her streaming eyes.
"That explains the books, at least. Dear, headstrong, trucu-
lent, rebellious Morgan is studying to become the Courtier of
courtiers. The Diamond Consort!" And she went off into another gale of laughter.

"But . . . but not necessarily," Jena stammered. "He'll be
the Ruby Consort. If the Diamond lives through the end of
the year, the Topaz becomes the Diamond Heir."

"Aye, and it would be another six years before the heirship
revolves through the Diadem to the Ruby again. But"—Lady
Kestrienne raised a finger—"the Diamond is extremely frail.
It could very well be that Lady Vianne Rhuddlan will be the
next to mount the Adamant Throne. And a good thing for
Piyanthia it would be, too."

"My partner? The Diamond Consort?" Now the idea as-
tounded Jena as much as it had Lady Kestrienne. "But
I'm . . . I'm marrying a tailor!"

"I trust you don't mean that as a disparagement to tailors.
But yes, it's quite a disparity, and it will give your bond with
Morgan an even greater potency."

"I've never met Lady Rhuddlan, although I've seen her at
a distance, at festivals. Father has cut some pieces for her; I
remember a parure he designed," said Jena.

"A very kind woman," Lady Kestrienne declared. "With
an admirably keen intellect, although she keeps her accom-
plishments mostly to herself." She sighed happily. "Yes, she
and Morgan will make a good match."

"Kestrienne," said Jena slowly, "could Morgan's disappearance be related to this?"

The last of the laughter faded from Lady Kestrienne's
face. She gazed off vaguely into the middle distances with
half-hooded eyes, an expression Jena was already coming to
associate with the scrying of possibilities. "The potential is
there," she replied, after several moments of thoughtful silence. "Yes, you may very well be right. The betrothal is secret, you say? I wonder if anyone else knows of it." She
brushed her fingers over Lady Rhuddlan's gift, resting on the
table. "Tell me everything you feel when you touch the
nugget."

Jena picked it up. "There's a . . . a sense of Lady Rhuddlan at the center . . . like . . . the grain of sand at the core of a pearl. Her emotions were strong when she gave it to him. Feelings of love, and trust . . . but she suppressed them, somehow." She looked at Lady Kestrienne. "Were you present at the time?"

"Yes, we were all there, exchanging Festival gifts."

"That's why. It's a lover's gift . . . but she must hold herself back, so no one sees how she feels."

"I wonder why," Lady Kestrienne said softly.

"She is free to marry him, isn't she?" Jena asked, with an anxiety that surprised her. Perhaps, she reflected, it was Morgan's own concern she felt, resonating from the wizard's bond between them.

"I don't know. I haven't heard any rumors about any attempts to arrange a Ruby match."

Jena turned her attention back to the nugget. "Mostly what I perceive is . . ." she groped for words, "his memory of her. I think he has handled the nugget many, many times. He picks it up whenever he thinks of her. Or . . . longs for her." She blushed faintly. Did Bram feel this way about her? "It feels strange," she added in a low voice, "prying into something that is so very private."

"Your instincts do you credit," Lady Kestrienne replied gently. "But I'm afraid we have little choice. This has already taught us something important, and we will need to learn everything we can to find him."

It took Jena a moment to regain enough composure to continue. "He is happy and yet worried at the same time, wondering about . . . about obstacles?"

"Can you tell anything about what he was thinking the last time he touched it? Before he left the keep?"

"He has just returned from seeing her in Piyar. There is a strain . . . a trouble." Her breath quickened. "Some fear unspoken between them. Ah . . ." Unexpectedly, tears began rolling down Jena's cheeks. "I could lose her. She's frightened, Ranulf, frightened of the changes I'll bring. I can't tell you everything, not now." Her throat tightened in a sob. "But I love her so much and *I'm losing her* . . ."

"Jena!" Quickly Lady Kestrienne pried the nugget from Jena's hand and took her by the shoulders. "Jena, stop!" But

Jena only sobbed harder, until Lady Kestrienne slapped her sharply on the cheek. "Jena, look at me. Look at me!"

Jena stared at her, wide-eyed. "Aunt Kestrienne, what do I do?"

Lady Kestrienne looked startled for a moment and then drew Jena into her arms and stroked her hair, rocking her as Jena buried her face in the front of her dress. "There, child, there. There, now. You'll find a way. I'll help you. We'll think of something."

Jena still held her talisman stone. She clutched it to her heart, and a warmth sprang from it that soothed her; she began to relax again. After a few moments, she pulled herself away gently, with an embarrassed sniff. "I'm better now, thank you, Lady Kestrienne."

"I told you. It's Kestrienne. At least when we're alone." Gravely, she proffered her handkerchief. "I must beg your pardon, my dear. I've been remiss: magic can quickly over-tire and overwhelm someone not accustomed to it, and after all, you've only just bonded today. And the transporting spell, too! We should have stopped when you first became dizzy."

"Wait, I'd just like to talk a little more first." Jena finished mopping her eyes. "What I was saying just now wasn't what Morgan said, exactly. But it was what he felt." She heard the catch in her own voice. "It was very strong."

"He has talked with Lord Duone about this, though?"

"I . . . I think, yes, he did tell him. Or hinted at least, about the betrothal."

"Lord Duone would need to know, as head of the family. Hmm."

"But there was something he couldn't tell him," Jena said, puzzled. "Related, somehow, to the barrier between him and Lady Rhuddlan."

"*She's frightened of the changes I'll bring,*" Lady Kestrienne repeated slowly. Her shoulders sagged. "Of course. Morgan is an adept. He can't tell Ranulf that. And if Vianne knows, or suspects, she may be thinking of calling off the match."

"Oh, no, surely not. They really do love each other."

"You're a romantic. Natural enough at your age." Lady

Kestrienne smiled thinly. "But you must understand: those who can see possibilities encourage change. That's just what the nobility doesn't want, especially the seven major houses of the Diadem. I'm not certain Vianne's good sense will be enough to overcome years of indoctrination."

"But the Diadem does allow change," Jena objected. "Isn't that why the Diamond can't simply pass the crown to his or her own child? Isn't that why the Founders set up the revolving heirship, so one family couldn't monopolize the throne?"

"Change, pish! As long as it's tamed, predictable, under their own control. They pride themselves on a 'change' that has become little more than inertia. They think it's preferable to the wild magic that raged during the Founders' War. No, Jena. The first Diamond knew exactly what he was doing when he renounced magic and made sure no adept stood among the other founding Diadem families. And though some have been born since then with the ability to become adepts, they taught themselves early to strangle their own potential." Lady Kestrienne shook her head. "Such a pitiful waste.

"At any rate, whatever the Founders originally intended, the Diadem is now hopelessly intermarried. It isn't seven families anymore, but one. They don't want magic, but they need it. They need new blood. And new visions. Morgan could bring that to them."

"We must find him," said Jena. "And now not just for you and me, but for Lady Rhuddlan as well."

"It would relieve my feelings delightfully if he stood here, so I could scold him thunderously for keeping such a secret." Jena had no trouble sensing the deep apprehension behind her lightly spoken words.

"Aren't there some other spells we might try, if we used my bond with him to establish a direction?"

"A good thought, and we will try it, but not tonight. You are too strained for such exacting work."

"But Kestrienne—"

"And if you totally exhaust yourself, it may spill over into your bond and harm Morgan, too, particularly if he is in trouble already. Remember, he has no one to monitor him."

Jena was forced to see the justice in this. They sat in silence for a moment or two, and then a slow smile curled at the corner of Lady Kestrienne's lip. "I've just thought of something else. It occurs to me what we can tell Lord Duone about your commission from Morgan."

Jena sat up straight. "What?"

"Can't you guess?"

It took a moment. Whether she surmised the answer or saw it magically, she couldn't tell. "A betrothal gift for Lady Rhuddlan. Oh, what a splendid idea."

"More than splendid," Lady Kestrienne said smugly. "It's the perfect way for you to approach Vianne when you return to Piyar; you may be able to get at least some help from her. And it will convince Ranulf that you are deep in Morgan's confidence. As you will be, when Morgan returns, so that's all right. Now, what could you make? A carcanet?"

"Well, some of the ladies of the Diadem are beginning to wear larger ruffs. If the fashion takes hold, a carcanet wouldn't be as useful as a pendant would. Or perhaps a girdle buckle, in the shape of a truelove knot? I could adapt the design of the necklace and girdle links in Father's parure set, of course, or I could design something completely new." Then she remembered and slumped in dismay. "Oh, no, I forgot. I can't."

"Can't what?"

"Can't cut stones or make jewelry anymore. The Guild won't allow me to take my own commissions without journeyman standing."

"What does getting the Guild's consent have to do with it?" Lady Kestrienne asked tartly.

Jena stared at her. "Why, I can't make jewelry without the Guild's permission."

"Why ever not?"

"Because it's . . . well, it's . . ." Jena sputtered. "It's just not done!"

"Ah. It may be that it won't even be an issue. After all, you are going to be submitting a new application under Lord Morgan's sponsorship, aren't you? They could hardly forbid you to work on your reapplication piece."

"No," said Jena doubtfully.

"And once they've accepted your reapplication, how could

they possibly turn you down for membership? They wouldn't dare insult the future Ruby Consort or impugn his taste in gemcutters by suggesting his betrothal gift was anything less than a masterwork. Particularly when there's such a strong chance he'll be the Diamond Consort before the year is out."

"A masterwork?" Jena said faintly.

"Yes," Lady Kestrienne said firmly. "Make no mistake about it. The piece must be extraordinary. And anyway, Jena," she went on impatiently, "even if the Guild does turn you down again, what then? Why should you continue to press your dues money upon them if they are stupid enough to refuse it? It's their loss, not yours. You won't need them. After you create the Ruby betrothal gift, and perhaps even the wedding pieces, you will have all the patronage from the Court you need."

"Practicing *guildless*?"

"A new way of thinking, remember. That's what the Diadem needs, and doubtless the Jewelers' Guild does, too.

"And now," she said, standing, "it's very late. I will walk you back so there's no question about your being out of your room at this hour."

Jena stood, swaying with fatigue, and blew out the candles in the candelabra and on the bedpost shelf. Lady Kestrienne picked up the candleholder and, at the door, knelt and pried up two or three spots of wax on the floor with a fingernail. She crumbled the wax into bits, murmuring a few words Jena didn't catch, and then blew the pieces from her palm. "There," she said, dusting off her hands, and then opened the door. Jena blew out the last candle on the shelf and followed her through the doorway.

Out in the hallway, the echo of their footsteps on the stone resounded with a bell-like clarity; it startled Jena after the muffled quiet of Morgan's room. A wavering circle of light spilled from the candleholder Lady Kestrienne held, animating the figures carved into the doors with shifting shadows.

Partway down the hall, Lady Kestrienne stopped suddenly, holding up her hand.

"What is it?" Jena asked warily. "Is someone coming?"

"No." But Lady Kestrienne cocked her head, and a breathless hush enveloped them as if the air listened, too. After a moment, she raised the candleholder and looked at the door abreast from them, which belonged to Lady Duone.

"What *is* it?"

"Probably nothing," Lady Kestrienne replied after a pause, but she didn't sound very sure. She stirred eventually and smiled at Jena. "At least, nothing that's of any concern to us tonight. Come along, dear."

Nothing more was said until they stood before Jena's door. "There you are, then, child," said Lady Kestrienne. "Oh, I almost forgot. Here, take this." She unlooped a pouch from her girdle and pressed it into Jena's hand. "Some more coins to hold you until we find Morgan."

Jena hefted the bag and felt a quick rush of gratitude. "Thank you, Kestrienne. You've been so kind, and I'm very grateful for all your help."

"Not at all, child, not at all. I've received the same help from others in my time." Unexpectedly, she leaned forward and kissed Jena on the forehead. It made Jena think of her father, which brought another wave of homesickness, but the kiss comforted her, too. "Sleep well, my dear. Mind you, keep your talisman nearby. A pouch next to your skin would be best, until you can cut the stone into a ring."

Inside her room, Jena lit a candle with an ember from the brazier and undressed quickly. She tucked her stone into one of Liselle's pouches and looped it over her neck and then got into bed and blew out the candle.

At least I'm warm, and safe, and among friends, even if they're new to me. Morgan, I hope you are as lucky. Within moments, she was asleep.

CHAPTER NINE

CURLED INTO A BALL, JENA floated in darkness, warm and comfortable, safe and secure. How long had she been here, cradled by a familiar, soothing presence? She didn't know. The presence had always been here, and would always be here, protecting her. It surrounded her, supported her with love and peace, and she trusted it, although she had no name for it. Nothing could bother her.

But then she became aware of a creeping weakness, growing slowly, stealthily. She tried ignoring it, but then she realized the presence she trusted was growing weaker, too, and that frightened her. The darkness ceased to be her friend, becoming instead a swallowing nothingness. She tried to surface through the weakness, to claw her way up, up out of the blackness, but something was holding her limbs, and she fought with ebbing strength, flailing in panic. "Oh, no! Oh, please, help!"

Someone clamped a hand over her mouth and hissed "Shhh!" in her ear. Jena abruptly came awake, heart thumping madly. Whoever it was fumbled with the pouch at her neck, and then she felt her talisman stone being pressed into her hand. "Hold that. Don't open your eyes. Just concentrate on the stone. Don't think of anything else."

Jena clutched at the talisman. It grew warm in her hand, feeding her strength, and gradually the darkness faded, compelled back by a murmuring voice. She could feel light fingertips pressing on her eyelids.

Eventually the murmuring stopped. "There, now," the voice announced as the hand withdrew. "You may open your eyes again."

Jena peered through the early morning dimness at the face hovering above her. "Why, La—uh, Kestrienne," she said in bewilderment. "Whatever are you doing here?"

Lady Kestrienne looked solemn. "You tell me."

"I was having a dream. About . . ." Jena gasped. "The baby. Oh, is Lady Duone all right?" She sat up in bed. "Is the baby—"

Lady Kestrienne placed her hand over Jena's. "This was a possibility I felt long ago, and so I already had protective spells in place. As soon as I sensed the trouble, I sent for the midwife, and then I came here. I knew you'd need help."

Jena rubbed her eyes hard; she still felt sleep-befuddled. "But . . . why?" she said, a little thickly. "What is it about the baby—"

"Think about it," Lady Kestrienne interrupted gently. "An unborn baby is all potential, all possibility. That's why you could sense it, because right now it's radiating more magic than just about anything else in this keep—except for you, since you're a newly partnered wizard."

"But something's wrong with it now?"

Lady Kestrienne hesitated. "Yes, and so its magic is fluctuating rather strongly. You've partnered so recently that right now your sensitivity is at its height, and your powers aren't yet completely under your command, especially since your partner's missing. And so I knew you might need a little monitoring to keep your magic from, well, getting mixed up with the baby's."

"If my magic's so powerful, did I . . . hurt it somehow? Interfere with it?"

"There, child, don't look so stricken. It's not your fault."

"It's not?" Jena whispered.

"No. Your awakening magic sensed the baby's distress,

and yes, if I hadn't stopped you, you might have made it worse. But you didn't cause it. It may be you can help."

"How?"

"I need to speak to the midwife to find out exactly what the problem is." She slipped off the edge of the bed. "Don't allow yourself to dwell on what might go wrong. Babies are very attuned to magic, and we must use ours to help it find the way to be born safely."

Jena's voice stopped her at the door. "Kestrienne?"

"Yes?"

"Do you know whether it's a boy or a girl? It might help if I knew."

"It's a boy," Lady Kestrienne replied, and smiled slightly. "But mind you don't tell anyone."

"My mother died in childbirth," Jena said, her voice trembling a little. "And my baby brother died a day later. Are you sure they'll be all right?"

Lady Kestrienne hesitated. "I won't lie to you. Magic becomes muddled when confused by lies. They have a chance. We must help them both make the most of it." She slipped out the door and shut it carefully behind her.

Jena flopped back on the feather tick with a sigh. After a moment, she realized she still had her talisman stone clenched tightly in her hand. She opened her fingers and looked at it. The sparkles were still there, but they looked smaller, and that worried her. She would have to ask Kestrienne about it later. She pulled the pouch from around her neck, dropped the stone back into it, and then got out of bed.

After splashing cold water on her face from the basin, Jena chose another one of Liselle's gowns and put it on over her chemise. This one had a rose-colored bodice and skirt, heavily pleated and trimmed with silver beads and embroidery. Like the rest of the clothes, it had no pockets, so she buckled on the girdle and looped Lady Kestrienne's money pouch off to one side. Her talisman stone remained in the other pouch, which she fastened around her arm and tucked into one of her sleeves. She combed out her hair and was just beginning to plait it when she noticed a hairnet trimmed with the same silver beads on the pile Liselle had left for her. With a little hesitation she gathered up her curls with one hand and rather clumsily folded them into the net. Despite her best efforts, tendrils escaped, puffing out over her forehead. *I suppose it will be falling in my eyes all day, but at least Arikan won't be able to say I'm scraping it back too severely.*

Silly, she thought. *Arikan isn't here Why should you worry what he thinks, anyway?* But the weight resting on the back of her neck felt oddly satisfying, and she decided to leave it the way it was, at least for one day. *I wish Bram could see me now, at least. I wonder what I look like, dressed like a noblewoman? Except for the sandals, of course. And I need jewelry, too.*

She put her few things, including the borrowed ones, into the chest at the foot of the bed and drew the bedcovers up as tidily as she could. Then, out of excuses, she picked up the dinner tray from the previous night and headed for the kitchen.

Outside, dew beaded the grass and made the dust on the flagstone paths of the inner ward smooth under Jena's sandals. The keen scent of mountain wildflowers mingled in the morning air with the smell of horses and the tang of woodsmoke rising in delicate curls from the kitchen. From the blacksmith's quarters in the northwest corner she heard the ringing clang of hammered blows, and the hiss of heated metal plunged into a water barrel to cool. The well stood in that corner of the ward, too; there, several laundresses hovered over a wooden trough, pounding and rinsing out sheets. A couple of men lounging by the barracks archway threw sticks for a dog to fetch.

In the middle of the ward, another small knot of men in traveling garb stood clustered around the castellan, listening to him intently as he spoke. Jena recognized several from the group who had been preparing to ride out the previous day. *I suppose Lord Duone has canceled the trip yet again, and the castellan is telling them why he hasn't made an appearance yet.* She sidled past them, gaze downcast upon her tray, feeling obscurely guilty about her expedition the previous night.

She followed the path toward the southwest corner, through the vegetable and herb gardens to a low archway. Here, a boy sitting on a low wooden stool leaned against the propped-open kitchen door, yawning as he plucked a goose. Through the doorway, Jena could hear the clatter of bread pans, and the chopping sounds of knives and cleavers against wooden blocks. The aroma of roasting meat and baking pastries drifting toward her made her mouth water.

Inside, the slope-ceilinged room seethed with activity. Three women bustled past Jena with long-handled wooden trays heaped high with loaves of manchet bread, fresh from the oven. A girl stooped by one of the fireplaces, basting coneys on the turning spits. Other men and women worked at the tables and counters, scaling fish, sorting greens, and stuffing capons. A couple of dogs scuffled snarling in the corner over a bone; one wrestled it away from the other and loped past Jena with its prize, hotly pursued by the other.

"Do you want something—oh, there's one of the trays!" One of the cooks, a short, squinting man, put down his knife and hurried forward, limping, to relieve Jena of her burden. "I couldn't imagine where they'd all gone. Kennet, take the dishes and cutlery to the scullery. Nanine, is that broth and manchet ready for Lady Duone yet? And where's the tankard of small beer?"

"No beer," Jena heard Liselle's voice say. "She needs a tea, with yarrow and raspberry leaves." Liselle came around a corner, presumably from one of the storerooms, her hands full of dried herbs. "I found those. I need blackberry leaves, too, if you have any. And can you tell me where the cinnamon is? Oh, hello, Jena, good morning."

"My beer," began the cook wrathfully, "is as fine as any my lady could want!"

"I'm sure it is, but the midwife and Lady Kestrienne say she mustn't have it."

"Is something wrong with Lady Duone?" Jena asked cautiously. She noticed the sounds of chopping around them had ceased.

Liselle threw her a significant look. "The cinnamon, please?" she said to the cook.

"I'll grind it out," the cook said, still not entirely appeased. "I'll not have you fosterlings wasting it."

"I wouldn't," Liselle said patiently. "And you can hardly complain about waste for the fosterlings when it's the lady of the keep who's drinking the tea." When the cook limped away, Liselle spoke in an undertone to Jena. "There is some trouble about the baby. I'm going up to her room now. Did you come down to break your fast? They set out bread and beer in the Great Hall for people who wish to eat. I'll meet you there after I've brought the tray."

One of the pages obligingly directed Jena to the door leading directly from the buttery into the Great Hall. It was a huge chamber, over one hundred feet long and graced with three fireplaces. Corbels soared upward, bracing the timber framework that cantilevered out from the walls, supporting the ceiling. Jena blinked at the light pouring in from glass windows, set high above the doorways lining the inner ward.

Four trestle tables had been set with platters of bread and tankards. Some fifteen or twenty people sat at these, eating and talking. They sat with no particular attention to rank that Jena could see; apparently the first meal of the day at the Duone Keep was a casual affair for those who chose to take it. Jena took a half loaf of bread from one of the platters and found a seat at a corner of one of the tables. The man seated across from her broke off a conversation with the boy beside him to pass her a tankard of beer. "Good morning," he said, smiling.

"Good morning," she replied cautiously, accepting the tankard, but he immediately resumed talking with his companion (something about fighting with quarterstaffs), to her secret relief. She ate and drank slowly. The bread, made with manchet, a finer grade of flour than she usually ate, tasted very good, but she found herself wishing for a plateful of porridge instead, her usual breakfast. As she reached for the pitcher to refill her tankard with more beer, she saw Liselle walking toward her table, and so she slid over to make room.

Liselle sat down on the end of the bench with a sigh. "Is there any bread left? I'm famished." Jena passed a platter to her, and Liselle helped herself to a loaf. "They came pounding on my door before even the larks were up."

"Who did?"

"Lady Elladine, for one. Lady Kestrienne sent her, I think, because she heard me say once—" She broke off, glancing at the man and boy seated across from them, and took a bite of her bread.

Understanding the look, Jena resigned herself to having to wait yet longer to learn more. At that moment, however, their companions chose to leave the table. A servant came by to clear their tankards and flick bread crumbs off the table surface into a bowl. As he moved on, Jena asked, "She heard you say what?"

"That I helped deliver two of my younger sisters."

"Really?"

"Mother never had much trouble having babies. Goodness knows she's had enough practice: I have nine brothers and sisters. And I know something about herbs, too, and that helps. But . . ." Liselle moodily crushed the edge of her loaf into a small pile of crumbs.

"But you've never had to face anything quite like this before?" Jena asked gently.

"No." Liselle bit her lip. "At least the keep has a good midwife; I'm glad of that. I wouldn't want to be entirely responsible. How much do you know about how babies are born?"

"Not much," Jena admitted. "I know it hurts, and there's blood." She stopped herself, remembering she needed to hold on to possibilities that were true, yet would keep the baby safe. "But despite all that, women go on having them."

"Maybe only because they don't have any choice," Liselle said gloomily.

"Please, Liselle, what's wrong?"

Liselle lowered her voice. "Lady Duone is bleeding slowly, but she's not in labor. The midwife says it's because there might be something wrong with the placenta, the part where the mother and the baby are attached. It might be growing over the opening of the womb where the baby is supposed to come out. If it grows over all the way, Lady Duone will bleed to death when she goes into labor, because there's nowhere for the baby to go. And then the baby will die, too."

Jena took a deep breath, trying to keep a strong grip on her reactions. Now she understood what she had to do, even if she didn't entirely know how. "You said *if*? The midwife isn't sure?"

"No. But anyway, Lady Duone will have to stay in bed until the baby's born. If it's born."

"Don't say that," Jena said quickly.

After a moment, Liselle nodded slowly. "You're right, I suppose. Although I don't know if it makes any difference."

Jena considered for a moment. She had a lot to learn about manipulating possibilities. Simply refusing to consider what might go wrong, she suspected, would not make unhappy events go away. She would need to talk with Kestrienne about that. "I don't mean we should try to ignore the worst, exactly," she amended, "but I think it's important Lady Duone should be at least able to hope everything will go well."

"She has had some luck already. Lady Duone's maid told me about it: usually Lady Duone rises before dawn, but she hadn't even gotten out of bed this morning when Lady Kestrienne burst into her room for some reason or another, as bold as you please. Usually Lady Kestrienne doesn't rise until just before noonday dinner."

Jena suddenly knew Lady Kestrienne habitually rose much earlier, but kept that fact a secret so she could practice magic in the early morning hours if she wished to without anyone the wiser.

"Anyway, she began chattering at Lady Duone about a needlework pattern or bread recipe or something ridiculous like that, before Lady Duone was barely awake. And then suddenly Lady Kestrienne spotted some blood on the hem of the gown Lady Duone had worn the night before. Lady Duone hadn't noticed it at all. She'd undressed in the dark last night and thrown it over the chest at the foot of her bed, and her maid hadn't had a chance to put it away.

"So Lady Kestrienne told her *don't move* and sent for the midwife and for me. It's a wonderful stroke of fortune she did, because the midwife said if Lady Duone had gotten up as usual, she might have started bleeding in earnest."

Jena hid her smile. "Yes, very good fortune, indeed."

"At least Lady Duone won't have to worry about managing the keep. Lady Kestrienne will take over doing that, of course."

"It must be a tremendous job," Jena said, thinking of her own household.

"Yes, it is, but Lady Kestrienne did it for years, you know. Her brother, Lord Tersat Duone, was widowed quite young, and there was no one else to do it until his son married." Liselle laughed. "Now, Lady Duone is an excellent house-keeper, but I'll wager you that within a week Lady Kestri-enne will have every servant in the place both so charmed and so terrorized that every room in this keep will be cleaner than it's been in years. And she's canny enough that she'll be sure to visit Lady Duone every day with some questions—just enough to make Lady Duone feel she's still needed and in charge even if she's in bed, but not enough to make her feel she has to worry at all that the keep might come tum-bling down around our ears."

Jena smiled, pleased to have an opportunity to learn a little more about her mentor. "You like her, don't you? Lady Kestrienne, I mean?"

"Oh, yes, everyone does. Some think she's just a harmless biddy, and when it suits her she'll let them believe it, but don't ever let her fool you. She has a trick of sizing a person up in an instant, and although she's very kindhearted, she has a mind that's sharp as a razor."

Liselle took another bite of bread and washed it down with beer. "Anyway, I really think I need some more herbs. If they aren't in the dispensary, do you want to walk down with me to town? There's an apothecary I can speak with, and you might be able to get some shoes."

Jena hadn't even realized there was a town. "Do you know if there's a jeweler or goldsmith? One who might let me bor-row or rent time with some equipment?"

Liselle shook her head. "I'm not sure, but I don't think so. I remember Lady Duone asking Lord Duone if he could bring one of her brooches with him when he went to Ten-away, to get the clasp repaired."

"Ah, well." Jena sighed. "Is there a papermaker? I need to start working on some designs."

"You can buy paper; one of the shopkeepers trades down-river for it."

Besides, a trip to town would keep her out of Lord

Duone's way a little longer. "That's a start, at least. Yes, I'd be pleased to join you."

They stayed in the town most of the morning. Liselle consulted with the apothecary, who had a small supply of the herbs she needed. Jena bought a slate, paper, and wax to begin work on a model, and she had the cobbler measure her feet for new shoes. They ate meat pies bought from the baker's street stand for their noonday meal and then walked back up to Duone Keep.

Liselle went off to confer with the midwife, leaving Jena to her own devices. She had no wish to get impressed into service doing the usual afternoon needlework with Lady Duone's ladies, and so she cloistered herself in her room, curled up on the cool stone window seat, sketching rough studies on the slate. A girdle buckle would be best, she decided after several hours of concentrated drawing. Yes, a buckle, without enameling. Jena didn't mind detailed goldwork but preferred emphasizing color in the jewels rather than the setting. She wished for one of her father's sketches of Lady Vianne's parure set. Had the stones for the girdle been rose or round cut? Had he used the single or double S-shape to connect the links? In the middle of a furious scribble, she heard a bell and dropped her slate pencil with a start.

Supper. There was no help for it; she would have to face Lord Duone and the rest of the household eventually. Reluctantly, she set aside her work and left her room, steeling herself for an ordeal.

The trestle tables in the Great Hall had been set up in the shape of a staple. Liselle, standing with the other fosterlings along one of the side tables, saw Jena when she entered and beckoned her over. "Hsst, Jena! Come and sit here beside me." Jena slipped into the spot beside her, and the other fosterling girls jostled aside to give her room, like so many complacent cows.

"Why is everyone still standing?" Jena asked low in Liselle's ear.

"They're waiting for Lady Duone—oh, well, for Lord Duone, I suppose."

"Wait, Liselle," said Jena, craning her neck and looking down the table. "I can't sit here, it's above the salt."

"Too late," said Liselle, her hand on Jena's arm. The castellan walked forward from the eastern door, followed by Lord Duone with Lady Kestrienne on his arm. As Lord Duone and Lady Kestrienne took their places at the head table, the castellan knocked sharply on the stone floor three times with the butt of his staff, and then, with a rumble of scraping benches and a rustle of clothes, everyone seated themselves. A rush of servants carrying bowls and serving platters streamed out from the kitchen; others came from the buttery, carrying wine. "Don't worry; no one will know," Liselle assured Jena.

And in truth, no one would know she was seated above her social station, Jena reflected, not with the clothes she wore.

"So Lady Kestrienne heads the board tonight," said a short, cheerful-looking girl with a rather long nose, sitting across from Jena and Liselle. "That's one in the eye for Lady Lenette, anyway."

"Oh, hush," someone else reproved in a shocked whisper. "You mustn't speak so, with Lady Duone so ill."

"Mustn't I?" The first speaker winked at Jena and Liselle. "I think Lady Duone would say the same, if anyone could make her admit it."

"Who is Lady Lenette?" Jena asked, as a servant offered a bowl of rosewater and a napkin.

"A cousin of Lady Duone, who's said to envy Lady Duone's place more than a little," the girl said, flicking rosewater from her fingers and drying them on a napkin offered by another servant. She lifted an eyebrow at Jena. "I beg your pardon, I don't believe I've had the pleasure of your company before," she said, looking pointedly at Liselle.

Liselle made some rapid introductions, too quickly for Jena to be sure which name went with which face, although she caught the name of the girl sitting across from them, Cestilline. "You can't say Lady Lenette has ever had any encouragement from Lord Duone," Liselle went on, tweaking slices of roast duck from a platter to her plate.

"No?" Cestilline's tone indicated polite disbelief.

Liselle shook her head decidedly. "Certainly not. Why, he

sat with Lady Duone almost the whole day; it drove the ladies attending to her to distraction."

"He's only worried about his heir," someone observed impatiently.

"Lady Lenette would be glad to provide another," the dark-haired woman on the other side of Liselle remarked, and two or three of the fosterlings giggled.

Liselle scowled. "I don't think he would want to take another lady very quickly, should the worst happen."

"Certainly not as quickly as your father did when your mother died, Phellia," Cestilline added pointedly. The dark-haired woman's gaze dropped to her plate.

"Of course he's concerned about his heir, as he should be," Liselle went on. "I heard him say he intends to stay here now with her until the baby is born, rather than leaving for the city. But he also truly cares about his lady. He held her hand all day long, even when she slept."

"He makes himself ridiculous before his men," Phellia muttered, not entirely quelled. Jena wondered if she favored the hopes of the thwarted Lady Lenette.

"If it pleases his lady, how does that hurt them? Or you?" Liselle retorted.

They all glanced furtively up at the head table, where Lord Duone sat, toying with his food. Lady Kestrienne leaned over to speak to him and seemed to be urging him to take some fritters onto his plate; he shook his head.

Jena turned her attention back to her plate as the fosterlings gossiped. The bantering made her feel homesick and ill at ease. How different the quiet suppers she was accustomed to taking with her father seemed from this crowded, splendid meal. Well, not always so quiet, actually: some of Collas' gemcutting apprentices had bickered terribly at the table over the years. Jena smiled to herself and then sighed. Collas must be missing her dreadfully tonight, even if he did know where she was. Would Arikan be keeping him company? She hoped so. It made her desperately sad to think of her father eating all alone.

She had just reached for a flagon to refill her wine cup, when she felt something, another fluctuation in magic, and put the flagon down hastily before she dropped it. *Lady Duone again?*

No, she decided finally, after an anxious moment or two. *They are still safe, and resting.* What she had sensed this morning when they had been in danger had felt close and agonizingly sharp, like the stab of an icy stiletto. This, now, too, was cold. But it was at once both bigger and more distant, as if she heard the sea thundering in her ears, and the sound made her remember faintly the inexorable tug of an ocean wave, rushing her away from shore. Jena took a deep breath. The possibility ripple she had felt was powerful, she felt sure, but it had not touched her very directly. She fumbled for the pouch holding her stone in her sleeve and glanced up at the head table.

Lady Kestrienne's face was the color of ashes. Even at that distance, Jena could tell she was drawing in labored breaths, clutching at the rim of her plate. No one at the head table had noticed yet. *You must go to her,* something inside Jena told her after a moment of stunned disbelief. *She has felt it, too, and although you escape the brunt of it, she will drown in it. You must help her as she helped you this morning.*

She looked around wildly. *I can't just walk up to her without everyone seeing. How can I get her out of here?*

Afterward, Jena never could quite reconstruct the paths of the three pages and two dogs or even say exactly what caused them to collide. Suffice it to say that when the din had died down, no one could have glimpsed Lady Kestrienne's pallor under the gravy, wine, and beer dripping from her brow to her toes. Jena sat in rigid horror as a hush fell over the Great Hall.

Uh, maybe I overdid it.

Lord Duone, shocked out of his self-preoccupation, bent over Lady Kestrienne. His voice was clearly audible in the silence. "Aunt, are you all right? You haven't been burned?"

To Jena's relief, Lady Kestrienne answered him, albeit in a shaky voice, "I . . . I am unhurt. I think." She tried to stand up, but fell back upon her seat. "Although I fear my dignity is shredded." Another page, gobbling with consternation, stepped forward, feebly waving a towel. The cloth was laughably small for so grave a situation. "Perhaps if one of the fosterlings could help me to my chamber . . ."

Hearing her cue, Jena leaped to her feet and hurried forward, snatching towels from dumbstruck pages as she went. "I will assist her, my lord," she murmured, and helped Lady Kestrienne to rise, soggily. Under the guise of wiping her face and hands with one of the towels, she rotated Lady Kestrienne's talisman ring on her finger so the stone faced the palm, and closed the older woman's fingers over it. Lady Kestrienne's knuckles turned white, but Jena saw, with relief, that a tinge of color was creeping back to her face. "Here, lean on my arm, my lady." They left the Great Hall slowly, with Lady Kestrienne leaning on her with every step. Jena dimly sensed a groundswell of servants hastening toward the head table to set it to rights.

As soon as they were outside and around a corner of the building, Lady Kestrienne stopped to lean against one of the walls. "You felt it?" she said, her voice hoarse.

"Yes. Not nearly as much as you."

"Thank you for getting me out of there." Lady Kestrienne smiled faintly. "I owe you too much to quarrel with your methods, although I doubt I'll ever wear this gown again."

"I'm sorry—"

"Not important. Not as important as this." She turned her face blindly up to the sky.

"What is it? Do you know?"

"I am not sure," the answer came slowly. "But it's big. Oh, yes, it's very big."

Jena waited. Lady Kestrienne's harsh breathing eventually slowed. "I think . . . it has to do with the Emerald."

"The Emerald?" Jena echoed.

"Yes. Something has happened, something terrible, which has wrenched all the possibilities in Piyanthia on a scale I have never felt before."

"Do you think we will hear what it was?"

"Oh, yes, we will hear." Lady Kestrienne turned and fixed her with bleak eyes. "We will hear what has happened, never fear."

CHAPTER
TEN

"NOTHING?" LADY KESTRI-
enne asked.

Jena sat back with a sigh. "Nothing." Her talisman stone sat, silent as a stone could be, in the center of her worktable in her tower room.

"Are you done, then?"

"I think so. For the moment."

"You've forgotten something. Again." Lady Kestrienne looked very severe.

Jena started guiltily. "Oh—the wards." She shut her eyes, reaching out with silent words to cut the three layers of protective lines around herself and her mentor, around the table, and around the perimeter of the room. After three weeks of practice, she was beginning to catch glimpses of the ward lines at the instant they dissolved. Soon, Lady Kestrienne had assured her, she would be able to see them clearly whenever she shut her eyes during the spell, like narrow bands of colored smoke. Or like the fragments of light, Jena thought, reflected from a prism or scattering from the heart of a brilliant-cut gem. That image pleased her more; it seemed to capture the hard edges of the lines in her mind and the way they disappeared abruptly when she cut them, not like the lazy wafting and eddying of a plume of smoke through an air current.

When Jena had finished, she rested a fingertip on her stone. The sparkles caught the light shining through the narrow window; they had not decreased in size any further after the second day here in Duone Keep. "The bond is still there. Why can't I find him?"

"Your bond is with Morgan, but it is through your talisman stones. If Morgan's ring is a large distance away from him, that could confuse the spell."

Jena slammed a fist down on the table, hard enough to make the stone bounce. She got up and began to pace back and forth angrily. "This is ridiculous. I'm not getting anything accomplished here. I'd be gone in an instant, if I only knew where to look for him!"

Lady Kestrienne raised an eyebrow. "It's good to have strong emotions, Jena. Of course, it sometimes can be a little difficult to see possibilities if you let those emotions clutter up your reason entirely."

Jena stopped abruptly. She folded her arms over her stomach, taking deep breaths to try to compose herself.

"Hand at your sides," Lady Kestrienne said. "Unclench the fingers. There. Breathe more slowly."

Jena shot her a venomous look, but obeyed. After a few moments of inner struggle she felt the knot inside her begin to unclench. "Morgan has a *terrible* temper."

"Hmph. Judging from your behavior, no doubt he is a sweet lamb now, wherever he is, thanks to your influence."

Despite herself, Jena smiled.

"That's better," Lady Kestrienne said. "Sit down again, dear."

Smoothing her skirts out of the way, Jena plopped down on the worktable bench and blew out a long sigh. As she scooped up her stone and tucked it back into her sleeve pouch, she studied her mentor, sitting across from her, drumming her fingers on the table with an absent air. In the last few weeks Jena had seen very little of Lady Kestrienne, who remained busy with the keep's domestic management while Lady Duone was bedridden. Consequently, the moments stolen for Jena's magical study sessions were always short—

frustratingly short, it seemed to Jena, although practically everything frustrated her these days. Although dressed impeccably as ever in an embroidered gown of icy green, Lady Kestrienne was pale, her face pinched with fatigue and worry.

"Forgive me for saying so, my lady, but you look as if you could use about three days and nights of uninterrupted sleep."

Lady Kestrienne smiled wearily, massaging her temples. "That, my child, is a simply splendid idea. Unfortunately, I shan't be able to indulge in such a pleasure anytime soon. It makes me feel old, I must admit, that Lady Duone's duties seem so taxing to me."

"You've had other burdens, too, what with the baby and helping me search for Morgan." Jena hesitated and then added, "I haven't asked . . . I know you have had so many pressing concerns, but have . . . have you heard anything from Arikan about . . . about what happened?"

Lady Kestrienne brooded for a few moments. "Yes," she said finally. "The news became known in Piyar quite quickly, and he passed it on to me immediately. Messengers are traveling to bring word to every corner of the country even now. The news is this: the Emerald is dead."

Jena let out her breath slowly; she hadn't even noticed she had been holding it. "I didn't realize the death of one of the Gems would have such a great magical effect."

"A large part of what we felt—perhaps most of it, I think—was the death of his unborn son. He would have been an adept, you see." Lady Kestrienne shook her head, her face etched with sadness. "A potential adept in direct line to one of the Council seats; there hasn't been one for many a year. An opportunity for change, cut off at the root."

"I don't understand. You said it was the Emerald who died?"

"He perished trying to rescue his pregnant wife in a boating accident," Lady Kestrienne said, "and of course, the baby died with her." She sighed.

Jena's eyes filled with tears. "How terrible." She shuddered at the thought of it: how terrible to struggle, screams and coughs cut short by water pouring down the throat, frantically reaching out for a hand that wasn't there until exhaustion won. The clarity of the vision chilled her, and she reached for her talisman stone for comfort, thinking sadly of the Emerald Consort's baby, drowning, too, before ever drawing breath.

"There are no legitimate heirs left to assume the Emerald's seat," Lady Kestrienne went on. "The Emerald House is no more."

Jena gasped. "The entire House?"

"Yes. I have not plumbed the depths of it," she said thoughtfully. "The House is gone; there will be only six Council seats now. Yet although these possibilities have been closed, others have opened up I cannot yet see. Perhaps my perceptions will be clearer after the baby is born."

"When will that be, do you think?"

Lady Kestrienne smiled. "Soon. I'm quite hopeful that all will go smoothly."

"I wish I could do more. You've been bearing the brunt of it." Jena sighed. "Kestrienne, why can't I support the baby when I'm awake?"

"Be patient with yourself; you're still learning. You've done well at learning to guide your dreams, and dreamwork is better than nothing."

"Maybe, but it still means you have to monitor when I sleep," Jena said glumly. "No wonder you're so tired lately. Morgan might have been more help."

"Perhaps, but then he's linked by blood." Lady Kestrienne looked thoughtful. "Or perhaps . . . sleep is a time heavy with magic. In the dream mind, anything is possible; nothing is automatically rejected as too outrageous to consider."

"So?"

"You may not see those same possibilities when awake, which means your magic is blocked. That may be your trouble: something about the baby is right in one of your blind spots."

"I can't imagine what it could be."

"Well, of course not," Lady Kestrienne replied, amused. "What do you think a blind spot is? Morgan might be able to help you find it, if he were here." She considered Jena through narrowed eyes, like a jeweler choosing the angle to cut. "It may not be entirely coincidence that he was speaking to you about leaving home, just at the point you partnered. Leaving the womb, so to speak. Tell me, Jena: is there a part of you that feels trapped?" Jena opened her mouth to answer, but she held up her hand. "No need to answer right now, my dear. Just think about it."

And Jena did think about it in the days that followed. The green, gold, and blue waning summer slipped away, hurrying toward Equinox. The nights grew colder. Jena's life eased itself into a routine. She arose early and broke her fast and then would spend her mornings with the other fosterling girls. She didn't like all of them, particularly the ones who did nothing but gossip, but Liselle, at least, showed signs of becoming a good friend. Drawing interested Liselle, so Jena spent some time teaching her about perspective and composition. In return, Liselle gave Jena a few lessons on the lute, although Jena's new disequilibrium often made her lose her temper at her own clumsiness, and she quickly concluded she would rather hear Liselle play.

Liselle often was called upon to sit at Lady Duone's bedside, and Jena sometimes joined them. She found the lady of the keep to be soft-spoken but friendly, and interested in Jena's stories of life in Piyar and Chulipse. Lady Duone sometimes spoke of the baby, but without hinting at the anxiety she must have been feeling. Often, around midmorning, Lord Duone would come to see his wife. On one or two occasions, watching Lady Duone's gentle face light up as Lord Duone approached her bed, Jena had a fleeting sense of touching the waiting presence of the baby. Close—but not quite.

Seeing Lord Duone still made Jena uneasy, and she would customarily curtsy and withdraw immediately upon his appearance. She probably needn't have worried, since he usually only had eyes for his lady. But he did speak to her once, inquiring courteously about her planned project.

"I can show you some sketches, if it would please you, my lord," Jena answered. "It is a gift for Lord Morgan to give, a lady's girdle buckle, shaped as a truelove knot." His eyebrows went up at this—the truelove knot was a traditional betrothal and wedding gift design—and she went on with what she thought was the proper touch of arch carelessness: "I will set it with rubies, of course, although the central stone could be replaced with another at a later time, should that prove necessary." The widening of his eyes told her he understood her meaning. For the rest of that visit and the ones that followed, she would sometimes catch him watching her with an intent expression, as if considering her in a new light.

Following dinner at midday, if Lady Kestrienne could not spare time for a surreptitious lesson, Jena sometimes helped the ladies of the keep with the mending and embroidery, but usually she turned to her own work. After drawing and fretfully rubbing out dozens of sketches, she finally had a design for the girdle buckle which she transferred to paper. She planned to use the lost-wax casting method to make it. The first step was to make a wax model of the buckle. The next step, which would have to wait until she could gain access to a goldsmith's shop and tools, involved attaching wax rods, called sprues, to the model, and encasing the model in plaster. The mold would then be baked in a furnace to melt out the wax, leaving a hollowed-out impression of the model, with tunnels left in the plaster by the sprue rods. Liquid gold would be poured into these tunnels to cast the buckle.

For now, Jena spent hours shaping and reshaping her model, improvising with the tools she could borrow from the keep's doctor, which were patently inadequate. With no gems to cut, and nothing to cut them with anyway, she planned the design around stones she had back at Piyar, which could be mounted later.

Only when will that be? she wondered to herself irritably as she worked. *Trapped? No wonder I feel trapped. It's almost Equinox. Lord Duone would have reached Piyar by now if it weren't for the baby. Will he leave with a party I can join after it's born? Or will he remain here? I could be here to stay all winter when the mountain passes snow in. Unless anybody would travel on the river after it freezes? If only I understood how I did that travel spell and could do it again. But there's no chance I'll be able to do it without my partner, and it's the fact that he's missing that's the reason I need to travel in the first place.*

Going to Piyar would be best. Bram is there, and Father and Arikan and even Lady Rhuddlan. But even if I could join a party leaving for Piyar or Chulipse, I still don't have the faintest idea where Morgan could be. The thought tormented her, almost as if embedding itself further into the wax with every stroke of her tool:

Where is Morgan?

One night, two weeks after Equinox, Jena dreamed she was holding Lady Duone's baby and walking by the Spangle River with Bram again. "The child's cold," Bram insisted. "I'll make him some Festival clothes." From out of the air, he drew out lengths of beautiful soft material, Chulipse silks in a dazzling profusion of colors: cerise and amber, cerulean, lavender, melon, and pale rose. He began sewing the silk around the baby, his needle dancing through the fabrics as quick as thought. She tried to pull the child away, exclaiming it would be smothered, but Bram only laughed and said, "Oh, no, he'll like it, let me show you, let me sew something for you, too." And before she could protest, he was pulling the cloth around her tightly and sewing her in, saying "Let me do it, Jena, I love you, I love you," until she fought for breath.

She gasped and started awake and stared for a long time into the velvet silence of the night until her heartbeat slowed. Still uneasy, she lit a candle to drive the darkness back and reached for paper and charcoal. *It seems as though I've done nothing lately but sketch.*

Under her hands, Bram's face came to life on the paper. His expression looked reproachful; perhaps it was the shadows. She took another piece of paper and drew a rapid sketch of Morgan. He was a less familiar subject, but the picture seemed better. The eyes looked more real.

She dropped the sketches on top of the bed, side by side, and buried her face in her hands, her knees drawn up into a hump under the coverlet. *Trapped. Not here, but at home. Why didn't I realize it? No wonder the baby's in my blind spot. When Bram talked to me by the river the walls were closing in around me, and I couldn't even see them!*

Partnering broke me out of that, but out into what? If I

*find Morgan now, what will happen between Bram and me if
I have a wizard partner who just happens to be a Gem Consort? And if I go back to Piyar, who knows what new possibilities I'll find there?*

The truth hit her like a blow to the gut. *When I go back to
Piyar, my life will be completely different than it was.* She
moaned, and the pain twisted in her like a live thing. It took a
moment for realization to penetrate the surprise: Lady Duone
was in labor. Lady Kestrienne had warned her that the baby's
magic would be at its peak at the time of its birth. Jena raised
her head, sweating, and through clenched teeth spoke the
words of the spell Lady Kestrienne had taught her.

The pain drained away quickly like ice melting on a hot
stove, leaving her gasping in relief. But the baby was still
there, and now she could sense it clearly, its thoughts un-
formed, chaotic. Possibilities. She tried to reach out toward
it, the way her mentor had taught her. *Don't be afraid. You
just have to find your way out. Your mother and father are
waiting to welcome you. We'll be here to help you.*

Something eddied around her like a swirl of black gauze,
and when it lifted as suddenly as it came, Jena saw her
mother. *No,* she thought, feeling first surprise and then a sudden lump in her throat. *No, I can't. Forgive me, Mama, but I
mustn't remember the way you died now; it could hurt the
baby.* She wanted to turn away, but her mother moved her
head on the pillow wearily, holding up her ashen face for
Jena to kiss. "I'm sorry to leave you now, darling, but I know
you'll be a good girl, won't you? And you'll help your father
and your brother? Promise me?" Her tears blinding her, Jena
kissed her and promised. What else could she have done?
Was that why the net had started closing in, because of
something as innocent as a promise made in love to a dying
woman?

Jena got up and dressed quickly, her hands shaking, and
hurried from her room, a candle held high. Lady Kestrienne
would be with Lady Duone in the family quarters by now.
She could feel the magic pressing through them and through
herself, thick and heavy, the multitude of outcomes like so
many tendrils being woven skillfully together under Lady

Kestrienne's hands into a single golden cord, guiding Lady Duone through the pain, guiding the baby to safety.

On her way along the corridor, she heard shouts drifting up through the windows facing the inner ward, and then the thin silver voice of a horn, echoing from the parapet. She frowned, her steps slowing. *What in the— At this time of night?* She went over to a window and looked down. Men were running toward the southern gate leading to the outer ward. Through it, she could hear the sound of horses' hooves approaching, and after a moment, a rider entered at a slow canter into the inner ward.

At the sight of him, every pore in Jena's skin came to attention. He was surrounded by four of Lord Duone's men from the outer ward on horseback. An honor guard? The unfamiliar rider slowed his horse to a trot and then stopped in the middle of the ward, clapping his mount on the shoulder as men carrying torches ran up, their boots clattering on the stone. The rider raised a spear, and she saw the silhouette of silken tokens fastened to the top, rippling in the night breeze. The possibility—no, the certainty—burned clearly in her mind with enough magical power to light the entire ward: *It is the messenger come with news from Piyar. Go down, hear what he has to say.* She hesitated, glancing over to the family quarters, but the call tugged at her too strongly to be denied.

Jena's feet flew down the corridor, so quickly that her candle went out. She blundered her way down the staircase in the dark, feeling her way along the wall, skidded around a corner, and then ran again to the ward doorway. She raced to join the small crowd gathering in the center of the yard. Lord Duone was coming, too, striding across the yard, hastily pulling a jerkin over his doublet and shirt. As they approached, Jena saw the rider hand his spear ceremoniously to the castellan and dismount. The spear tip flashed in the torchlight, and the two attached silks fluttered with the movement. As best as Jena could tell in the ruddy glare, one was white, so thin as to be translucent, and edged with a green border. That was the token of the Diamond; the border was green because the Diamond had ascended to the Adamant Throne from the Emerald House.

The other silk was black.

The messenger, young and travel-stained, bowed to the castellan and spoke, raising a firm tenor voice so that all assembled could hear his words. "I bring news from Piyar. I must beg leave to speak with Lord Ranulf Duone immediately, upon order of the Diadem."

The castellan made a reply, too low for Jena to hear, and then turned.

"I'm the man you seek," Lord Duone said, stepping forward into the torchlight. "What is this news?"

"My Lord Duone," the messenger said formally. "I am ordered to bring these tidings, to you and your household: the Emerald is dead." There was a pause and a collective sigh from the crowd. The messenger continued, after the whispers had died away: "With him died his wife and unborn child, the last of that line. The Emerald House is no more."

Lord Duone's face grew pale in the torchlight, stricken by this news, so near to his fears for his own family. *Oh, don't,* Jena found herself thinking to him. *Don't despair for them, my lord. It isn't an omen. Don't allow your fear to hurt them now.*

"I grieve for the passing of the Emerald House," Lord Duone said. His voice sounded stiff and harsh with the effort at self-control. "And for the Diamond upon the death of his noble son."

"You are commanded by the Diadem to come to Piyar," the messenger went on, "to present yourself to the Council at the opening of the Winter Solstice Festival—"

"But that's impossible," Lord Duone interrupted sharply, and then stopped himself. "I would wish to honor the Emerald," he went on in a milder voice. "Were I closer to Piyar, I would come." He glanced involuntarily toward the family quarters. "But I can't leave my—There are many cares in my household that require my presence at this time." A puzzled frown crossed his face. "They are going to wait that long for the funeral?"

"No, my lord. The Diadem, having convened in Council, now summons its candidates for the new Emerald House from among the minor noble households. Your name has been presented to the Council as the formal candidate of Lady Vianne Rhuddlan, the Ruby." He drew a sealed dispatch from a dispatch pouch behind the saddle and handed it to Lord Duone. The seal was of ruby-red wax, like a drop of blood.

In the breathless silence that followed, Jena realized, *This is the new possibility, the one Lady Kestrienne could not yet see. Not six Council seats instead of seven, but Lord Duone as the new Emerald!*

Utterly taken by surprise, Lord Duone looked at the parchment in his hands and asked, in a carefully neutral tone, "I am the Ruby's candidate to be the new Emerald?"

"Yes, m'lord."

"But the Diadem commands, you say, not the Diamond?"

"My lord," the messenger said gently, "I am not yet done with news. I am also ordered to bring these tidings: when the Diamond received the news of the death of his son and his son's family, the bitterness of the blow ravaged what little remains of his health."

Lord Duone frowned. "Is the Diamond—"

"A stroke, my lord. Although alive, he has not moved nor spoken since being stricken. It is not known whether he can hear or understand." In the little swell of excited murmurs that followed this, Jena could hear the horses chewing on their bits and the sound of their hooves as they shifted on the flagstones.

"This is grave news, indeed," Lord Duone said, his face bleak. He slit the wax on the letter and read the enclosed message. Then he slowly turned and walked a step or two back to the family quarters, and then stopped. The castellan exchanged a puzzled glance with the messenger and hurried to his side. "My lord?"

"I cannot go."

The messenger took a step forward. "My lord . . . in order to be considered, you must be in attendance when the candidates are presented at the beginning of the Festival. Otherwise—"

"I cannot leave her," Lord Duone said without turning around. "She needs me. It is impossible for—"

"Lord Duone!" The call across the courtyard made everyone turn. Lady Kestrienne was walking toward them quickly, her face wreathed in smiles. As she approached Lord Duone, she reached out to clasp his hand. "My dearest boy, you have a son."

Lord Duone seized her hands in both of his, the parchment fluttering forgotten to the ground. "A son? And is he safe? Is my lady well?"

"Your lady is safely resting. And your son is strong and healthy, but as for resting—hmph! The lungs on that boy!" Lady Kestrienne laughed. "He will keep us all from getting any sleep for many nights to come, you may be sure of that, my dear."

"A son," Lord Duone repeated, savoring the words.

"A new Emerald Heir, my lord!" Jena cried out, and others around her took up the call. "A new Emerald Heir!"

Lord Duone looked at them, startled, and then he laughed, a rich, rolling laugh proclaiming his joy and relief. "Aye, a new Emerald Heir, and a new Emerald House. One of you, see to it that this man's horse is stabled, and that he is fed and shown a place to sleep." He gestured to the castellan. "Ready stores for a party to ride to Piyar. We are due at the opening of the Winter Solstice Festival, you say? Then we must leave within the week. There will be a new Emerald House rising!"

CHAPTER ELEVEN

INSINUATING HERSELF INTO
Lord Duone's traveling party took Jena almost three days of
steady maneuvering and argument.

Craftily, she first broached the subject with Lady Duone
during a lying-in visit. This was patently unfair of her, considering her target was still weak as a kitten and plainly distracted by the glow of first motherhood. Lady Duone was
sitting up in bed when Jena came to see her, eating broth
served on a fine inlaid birthing tray (a present from Lady Elladine) while keeping a careful eye on the nurse changing her
new son's nappies. "I do think he looks like his father, particularly around the eyes, don't you think?"

"Oh, yes! But I think I can see you around the mouth."

Lady Duone's spoon hung suspended in midair as she
watched her son kick and squeak. "Such tiny hands he has!"
she marveled.

Jena smiled at her tender expression and bent over the
baby in the nurse's lap. "He's truly beautiful, my lady. Lord
Duone must be so proud! Is Garrett a family name?"

"Yes, one of my lord's uncles on his mother's side." She
came out of her reverie with a shake and began sipping her
soup again. "Now, what were you saying about accompanying Lord Duone to Piyar?"

Jena held out a finger for the baby to grasp as she explained again. "I did hope for your ladyship's permission."

"I think my lord could include you in the party, unless you'd prefer traveling with me?"

"You'll be going then, too, my lady?" Jena was surprised. "Are you sure that's wise, so soon after—"

"Oh, I won't be going overland," Lady Duone hastened to assure her. "No, no, the midwife won't allow that. My route will be entirely by boat, east on the Orbo, and then south along the coast, by way of Niolantti. It's a much longer journey; Lord Duone needs to cut overland through the Zorin Pass and then travel south down the Koh by boat to arrive in time for the ceremony to present the nominees. But although my route is slower, it will undoubtedly be more comfortable. I should be glad of your company. I do expect to arrive in time for the installation of the new Emerald, at least."

"Lord Duone, of course." Jena smiled.

Lady Duone's lips twitched. "If fortune favors us. I do think he would make a worthy addition to the Diadem Council."

"I am honored by your invitation, my lady. But if the journey by sea is slower, I'm sure you can understand why I'd prefer to go overland: my father and fiancé must be very worried about me by now."

"Ah, yes, I remember; you weren't able to notify them you were leaving, were you?" Lady Duone answered absently. "Well, of course then you must return as soon as possible." Her gaze strayed over to the baby again. "I know how important family is."

Emboldened, she presented her case to Lord Duone next, coming to see him the following afternoon in the Great Hall, where he was meeting with his seneschal, going over the last details of the management of his estates during his absence. He listened to Jena's request and then leaned back in his chair, frowning. "Travel with me? I don't think the journey would suit."

"I understand it will be arduous. Lady Duone has mentioned the less direct route she will be taking."

"Yet you still wish to go overland?"

"I, too, have time constraints, my lord. Journeyman elevation occurs at the end of the Winter Solstice Festival, and I must have enough time to resubmit my application piece, if I wish to avoid waiting another year. I cannot work on it here, despite your generosity: I've no equipment and few supplies. And of course, the sooner I reach Piyar, the sooner I leave your charge."

"You wouldn't have equipment and supplies until you reach Piyar again, in either case."

"I would reach Piyar faster traveling with you, if you would permit me to accompany you. I understand you will be going through the Zorin Pass?"

"Yes, we will spend at least one or two days in Tenaway."

Jena smiled in relief. "I can get some of what I need there from the goldsmith Master Rolly, and that would give me a head start. One of my father's former apprentices is working with him as a journeyman. Besides, I think my father would consider it my duty to pay his colleague a courtesy visit."

"I have employed Master Rolly's services myself," Lord Duone said slowly. "He has made several pieces for my family. As a matter of fact, I was thinking of calling upon him during this trip." He smiled, despite himself. "I need to buy a birthing gift for my lady."

Finally she gritted her teeth and tackled the hardest case of all: Lady Kestrienne.

"Overland with Ranulf's party! Certainly not!"

"Why not?"

Lady Kestrienne looked up from a pile of folded chemises stacked in front of an open trunk. "Let you loose to go haring off across the country? Courting who knows what sort of mischief?"

Jena smiled her sweetest smile. "Why, I imagine that is exactly what Lord Duone used to say to Morgan, isn't it?"

Lady Kestrienne opened and closed her mouth, looking confused. "Oh, pish!" she managed finally. "You're simply not ready."

"I wasn't ready to become a wizard, either. That didn't stop me."

"This is different," Lady Kestrienne said, so crossly that

Jena knew she'd scored at least one hit. "It would be best for you to go with Lady Duone's party, by boat."

"Kestrienne, you taught me I must learn to distinguish between what I think is best and what other people think is best for me. I know, I know," she said, holding up a hand to forestall a retort, "I'm only a beginner. But the feeling arose in me as strongly as a flame when I first heard the messenger: I must return to Piyar as soon as possible. And I think I must go with Lord Duone."

Silent for a moment, Lady Kestrienne smoothed a pleat of a gown spread out in her lap. "I can't leave Metissa now," she said finally.

"I don't expect you to."

"If you would only stop being so stubborn and go by the Orbo," Lady Kestrienne said stubbornly, "at least I'd be there to help you."

Jena pounced on that opening. "Help me how? By teaching me magic? You said you couldn't teach me too much as long as Morgan remains missing, or our partnership would become imbalanced. Or would you find Morgan for me? Remember, his partner can do that best—and with all due respect, my lady, I am his partner, not you."

Trapped by her own words, Lady Kestrienne glared at Jena.

Jena waved a gently admonishing finger. "Now, now. Remember, it's hard to see possibilities when you let strong emotion clutter up your reason."

Lady Kestrienne, if possible, scowled even more ferociously—and then the corner of her mouth began to twitch. "Oh, bah! You learned too well, I suppose. Hand me those cloaks, if you please. Oh, and you might as well take that one lined with fur off the top of the pile. No sense in dying of chill while you're crossing the mountains."

Three weeks later, on a crisp fall morning, Jena rode with Lord Duone's company into Tenaway. Twenty men-at-arms and retainers made up the party, besides Lord Duone himself, Jena, and three serving women Lady Kestrienne had managed to foist onto the group at the last moment. "They'll be needed to open up the house in Piyar," she had insisted.

"Goodness knows what condition it will be in after being shut up half the year. Of course, it can't be entirely set to rights until Metissa and I arrive, but at least they can make a start. It would be simply dreadful, Ranulf, if you arrived at the presentation ceremony with a nasty head cold from sleeping on damp sheets." Lord Duone, like others of his class, was not averse to measures taken to ensure his comfort and so had agreed—rather to the amusement of Jena, who suspected Lady Kestrienne also intended to provide her with some female chaperonage.

The journey had been hard, and Jena's muscles ached with unaccustomed pains, despite the sheepskin saddle pad one of Lord Duone's retainers had kindly provided for her. Despite her weariness, Jena sat up a little straighter in her saddle as they entered the city gate and looked around curiously at the narrow, tall houses. Tenaway was smaller than Piyar, but much more compact, as if the buildings jostled each other to stand at the bend of the Tulio River. All the buildings were built of cream and sand-colored brick and stone, and they stood flush up against one another, rising three and four stories over the narrow, crooked streets. The sounds of the horses' hooves rose in weird echoes, startling cats sunning themselves on upper-story window ledges. Gap-toothed old men sat on tipped-back stools in the cool doorways, sipping wine from pottery cups as they played games of nine-peg and straw-and-hay on carved boards balanced on their laps. A dank, muddy smell rising up from the river and the rain gutters mingled with the aroma of vegetables cooked in olive oil with the fiery local sausage. Jena looked around for gardens but saw none; perhaps there were private courtyards inside the houses. But window boxes provided color, splashes of golds, oranges, and reds of late-blooming fall flowers, set off by the somber green of dangling ivy. A woman busy pinching off dead leaves at one leaned farther out of her window to watch them pass. At the intersection of every two or three streets, the thoroughfares converged into small plazas, with stone benches and public fountains where women gathered to draw water and gossip. Finally, at a plaza larger than the rest, where a spill-off spout from the fountain filled a stone trough with water, Lord Duone called a halt.

Jena gingerly dismounted with the rest and led her horse to the lineup at the trough. She checked the saddlebag where she kept her wax model, which had been painstakingly wrapped in layers of silk, feathers, and velvet and then carefully packed into a small wooden box. The box looked undamaged. She tucked it back into the saddlebag. Lord Duone stood off to one side, speaking with Taras, his taciturn second-in-command on this journey. "I've always stayed with my cousin, Lord Nevatt Marstimore, whenever I've been in Tenaway," he was saying. "He can undoubtedly put up some of the men, but not all."

"His stables won't accommodate all the mounts, either, I suppose?" Taras asked.

"No. That means an inn for at least some of the group." Lord Duone broke off as he noticed Jena listening. "And you, Jena Gemcutter? Do you wish to stay at the inn, then, or do you hope to stay with the goldsmith?"

Blushing a little at having been caught eavesdropping, Jena replied, "I'm sure Master Rolly will have a place for me, if he's in the city."

Lord Duone nodded. "Once we've settled the men, I can take you there."

"Thank you, my lord," Jena answered, faintly surprised. "That's very kind of you."

"Not at all. We'll be here in Tenaway several days to resupply. If I give Master Rolly my commission this afternoon, hopefully he will have it finished before it's time for us to leave again."

To reach Master Rolly Goldsmith's shop, visitors off the street first entered a cool atrium with a richly tiled floor, lit by sunlight falling in tinted circles through small roundel windows. Lord Duone spoke a quiet word to the two men-at-arms who had escorted them, and they withdrew to wait there. The door leading into the shop itself was of heavy wood, richly carved, and it boasted an ornate bronze knocker shaped like a grotesque mask, holding a ring in its bared teeth. Inside, a quick glance around the shop confirmed Jena's impression that Master Rolly's business was doing very well indeed. He had been able to afford a fine paneling for the walls, trimmed with a delicately gilded frieze. Instead of being made of humble masonry, the ceiling was also paneled, with bold dish-shaped bosses embellished with rosettes. Well-polished brass lanterns hung suspended from the crossing points of the heavy ribs, lending a warm glow to the room. The furniture—two wooden counters, a pair of chairs with richly upholstered seats and comfortably curved backs, and a table—were all of fine quality.

A young man wearing a journeyman badge was seated on a tall stool behind one of the counters, explaining something in a low voice to an apprentice. The journeyman was lanky, with straight, dark hair he kept brushing back absently from his forehead, and frank, muddy hazel eyes. As he spoke, he gestured animatedly with a chasing tool at an elaborate gold salt cellar on the counter before the two of them.

"Baldesar?" Jena said.

The journeyman dropped his tool with a start as he looked up and saw her, and he broke into a delighted grin. He rose respectfully and spoke to Lord Duone first, as was proper. "Good afternoon, my lord. Your visit brings honor to this shop. May I be of service to you?"

"Good afternoon," Lord Duone replied affably, pulling off his gloves and laying them on the counter. "I would be pleased to speak with your master about a commission, if it can be finished within the next two or three days."

"But of course, that will be no difficulty at all," Baldesar said smoothly. Jena smiled, thinking he sounded like a true journeyman now, ready to pronounce any and all demands perfectly achievable. He looked at Jena again.

Lord Duone gestured toward her. "And I have also brought someone I understand to be an old friend of yours."

Having been given implicit permission to recognize her, Baldesar stepped forward and warmly took her hands in both of his. "Mistress Jena," he said, a grin glowing on his earnest face, "I'm delighted to see you so well. But what a surprise! What in the Guild's name are you doing in Tenaway?" Jena had to bite back the urge to laugh. Baldesar had called her "Mistress Jena" since she was eleven years old, as if she were twenty years older instead of a year younger than he. It seemed to be a spillover from the awe he had always held for

Collas. He explained to her seriously once, when she had objected, that he called her that out of respect for her father, an explanation which had seemed rather ridiculous to her at the time, if certainly in keeping with Baldesar's habitual nicety of manners. Perhaps it was part of the reason she had never been in love with him, but rather felt toward him the affection of a sister.

"It's rather a long story," Jena said, giving Lord Duone a sidelong glance. "I've been traveling with his lordship's party. I'm glad to see you, too. How are you, Baldesar?"

"I'm well, and I'm learning so much. Master Rolly is a fine teacher."

"Is Master Rolly here?"

"Yes, in the main workshop." Baldesar addressed himself to Lord Duone again. "I will go and tell him you are here, m'lord . . . ?"

"Duone."

Baldesar bowed and hurried off and in a moment returned with Master Rolly. At the sight of him, Jena again had to suppress a laugh. When the goldsmith had first visited Collas in Chulipse years before, Baldesar had privately pointed out to her that Master Rolly was so bowlegged he could step over his grinding wheel without even separating his heels. He was older than Collas, with handsomely silvering hair, cheekbones that jutted out as sharply as knife edges, and startling blue eyes. "Welcome, my Lord Duone." His warm smile included Jena. "And welcome, too—Jena, isn't it? Kipp, some refreshments for our guests." As the apprentice withdrew, the goldsmith continued, "It's a pleasure to see both of you again. How may I be of service?"

"We are en route to Piyar, but will be here in Tenaway several days," Lord Duone said, "and Jena, who has been traveling with my party, mentioned she would be glad of the opportunity to see you again."

"Indeed, an unexpected but very welcome pleasure. Is your honored father traveling with the party as well, Jena?"

"No," Jena said, "but I'm sure he would wish to be remembered to you."

"If you're going to be several days in the city, Jena," Master Rolly said, "I hope you'll consider staying here, if my lord will allow it."

Jena smiled gratefully. "You're very kind. I must confess I was hoping I could trespass upon your hospitality."

"No trespass indeed! We'll have the chance to talk over trade secrets, no?"

Jena laughed. "I'd love to hear yours, although I doubt I have very many to offer you. In the meantime, Master Rolly, I think Lord Duone also wishes to speak with you about a commission."

The goldsmith bowed deeply. "My lord, I am honored."

"If you can have something done by the time we leave the city," Lord Duone said, "I would like you to make something for my lady."

"But of course. Did you have something specific in mind?"

"I would be open to suggestion. Something that would be appropriate for a birthing gift for my wife."

Jena wondered whether it was her developing magical sense that made the carefully concealed pride so clear to her behind the casually spoken words.

Master Rolly smiled. "My heartiest congratulations, my lord." Lord Duone acknowledged his words with a genial nod and the smallest of smiles. "I would be proud to make something beautiful to please your lady," Master Rolly went on. "Would a pendant suit, perhaps, or a set of bracelets?"

Lord Duone looked mildly perplexed, like any man being quizzed about his wife's tastes. "I'm not certain," he admitted, and unexpectedly turned to Jena. "What do you think?"

She blinked, surprised at being thus applied to for an opinion. "Master Rolly is famous for the quality of his enamel work," she replied. "I remember one day when Lady Duone snapped the teeth on one of her ornamental hair combs. Those were a light orange, but her hair is dark enough that I think a rich blue might suit her coloring better. Or perhaps a mirror?"

Master Rolly's face lit up. "Yes, a mirror! I have some mirror forms already cast. I could enamel the back of one with a motif that would match the combs. Look here . . ." and he seized a slate from a shelf over the counter and began a deft sketch. "This would be a pleasing design for a mirror set in an oval. I have just the blue for the enamel. It could be embellished with lapis, or onyx, perhaps, if your lady's hair is particularly dark."

Or emeralds, Jena forbore from adding. Lord Duone accepted the pottery cup of wine the apprentice offered him and bent over the sketch. His absorption allowed Jena to freely study his face. *He doesn't know how much his eyes give him away whenever he thinks of her,* she thought. *It's strange . . . I've always been a little frightened of him, I think. He could be very dangerous to me. But it's somehow hard to be afraid of a man who loves his wife so tenderly.* She smiled to herself as she watched Master Rolly sketching furiously and listened to Lord Duone's questions. *And I'll wager Master Rolly can smell that on him. The goldsmith will make a tidy sum on this sale.*

At that moment, one of Lord Duone's escorts pushed open the door to the shop. "Forgive the interruption, my lord," he said respectfully, "but a messenger has come looking for you. He says he was redirected here by Lord Marstimore's house steward."

"A messenger?" Lord Duone frowned, puzzled. "Show him in."

Some words were exchanged in the doorway, and the other escorting man-at-arms stepped into the shop, followed by an unfamiliar man dressed in dark britches and a rough linen shirt. His swarthy skin, etched with fine lines, and hair bleached the color of bone suggested many years of exposure to the sun. His gaze quickly scanned the shop and rested on Lord Duone. "Lord Duone?"

"I am he. What news?"

The man bowed respectfully. "It's grave. My lord, your wife, the Lady Duone, lies very ill of a fever in Niolantti. She's feared to be at the point of death."

In the dreadful chill that fell over the room with this pronouncement, Jena gathered her horrified wits and reached out with all her senses. *Can it be true? Gentle, kind Lady Duone—is she really near death, after we thought the danger past?* In the breathless silence, her heart could feel no answer.

Lord Duone's face turned as white as milk, all his quiet joy shattered into shards like glass. He would have dropped his wine cup if Jena had not hastily snatched it from him and placed it on the counter. "Metissa? What . . . how . . . ?" he breathed hoarsely.

"My lord, even now she's calling for you. Your brother begs you to come immediately."

"My brother," Lord Duone repeated in a dazed voice.

"Lord Morgan. Here is his token." The messenger stepped forward, reaching out to put a large gold ring into Lord Duone's trembling hand.

Except that Jena seized it first.

It would have been difficult to say who was most stunned by her audacity, but one touch told her what she needed to know. A surge of power flared, beating back her fear and giving her the cold quickness necessary to see the path to follow. "Forgive me, my lord," she burbled, knowing she sounded like an idiot, "but I do so admire the design." Master Rolly's jaw dropped, and she saw Lord Duone gathering himself for an explosion.

No, don't speak! she willed fiercely and said hastily to the messenger, "But you've said nothing of the other person close to Lord Duone's heart. What of his newborn daughter, the apple of her father's eye? Is she healthy?"

To her profound relief, Lord Duone's mouth shut and his eyes narrowed. He turned abruptly to the messenger. "Well?" he snapped.

Now the messenger's face looked confused. He hesitated and licked his lips. "Your daughter, too, is very ill. That is another reason your brother begs you to hurry."

Lord Duone's face flushed a murderous red. A quick tic of his eyes, a jerk of his chin, and the two escorts, after a heartbeat of surprise, seized the messenger by the arms and held him fast. The stranger's face registered shock and then twisted in rage as he realized he had been tricked.

Lord Duone wheeled to face Jena. "How did you know?" he cried. "How could you possibly know he was lying?"

"It had to be untrue. This isn't Lord Morgan's ring."

Lord Duone looked blankly at the circlet of gold in her outstretched hand. "How can you tell?"

Then Jena saw the trap into which she had almost fallen. Of course she couldn't tell him that when she touched it, the ring had no memory, no trace of Morgan's hand. She looked at the ring for a moment, panicking, and then saw how to bluff her way out. "It's the wrong size."

"What?" Lord Duone reached for the ring and turned it over.

"I saw my father size Lord Morgan's hands. Master Rolly, could we see a mandrel?"

The goldsmith reached under the counter and produced a tapered stick cut with evenly spaced notches. Jena slipped the ring over the top and down the shaft. "There, you see? The largest Lord Morgan could wear would be a ten. This ring is size twelve. It can't possibly be his." *That's even true.*

Lord Duone leaned over the stick to look. Beside him, Master Rolly stiffened. He was opening his mouth, he was shaping the words, but Jena had felt the surge of danger and was already turning, her eyes widening.

"My lord!"

The words of warning floated toward her over an impossible distance and time, like a wave poised, suspended, before crashing upon the shore. There must have been noises, she realized afterward: the grunt of pained surprise from Lord Duone's guard when the false messenger brought his bootheel down hard on the man's foot, the swift intake of breath and thud as a leg lashed out, the crash as the second guard somersaulted into the table. But all she would ever remember hearing through the deadening silence was her own heartbeat. Then there was a knife, the blade dazzling her eyes with shifting patterns of light. Where had that come from? Had he seized it from the first guard's belt? The messenger hurled himself forward at Lord Duone, but he seemed to move so slowly, so slowly. Slowly enough for her to think, *No, not Lord Duone.*

At her mental shout, the messenger's knife swerved in midair as if hitting an invisible wall, just as Jena started forward. At the same moment, the first guard lunged forward and stabbed the messenger. The momentum of the thrust bowled the man into Jena, driving her back into Lord Duone's arms. The messenger's knife plowed a searing furrow over the skin just above her breast, and as it jolted sickeningly against the collarbone, she saw in a flash that she stood on the deck of a ship, looking far off to sea. No—she stood in a lady's luxurious sitting room, hung with rose-colored silk. She blinked and saw the messenger's face before her, flaccid with shock. She had time for one peevish thought: *Well, you didn't need to hurt me, either.* And then the magic rose up to overwhelm her. Frightened, she struggled against it, but it sucked her under into blackness. There wasn't enough pain to bring her back.

CHAPTER TWELVE

SHE WAS LYING ON THE FLOOR, which was wrong. She could feel the coolness of the marble through her dress, and something wet dripping from her collarbone. Someone had an arm under her head and shoulders and was trying, with difficulty, to hoist her up, like a half-empty sack of grain.

"Jena, can you hear me?" Baldesar's anxious voice said. "Can you try to swallow this?"

Her eyes fluttered open as she smelled wine in a cup held to her lips. She took a swallow and half choked as it ran down her throat too fast. The cup withdrew as she coughed and then came to her lips again at a shallower angle. She held it steady with one hand and drank gratefully. Finally she pushed the cup aside and looked up at the faces crowded around. "What happened?" she managed to croak. "Was there—oh." A few feet away from her, the erstwhile messenger lay on the floor, blood running from the side of his shirt down to a pool on the floor. His eyes stared at her unseeingly. Jena had to clamp her teeth down over her lower lip to keep the wine from coming back up. "Help me up."

Baldesar studied her face skeptically as he pressed a folded polishing cloth over her cut. The pain from the pressure brought tears to her eyes. "Are you sure you can manage?"

"It's not my legs that are hurt," she said shortly.

Baldesar looked questioningly over at Lord Duone. "You fainted," Lord Duone told her gruffly, almost accusingly.

"How very silly of me," Jena said. She felt giddy.

"Not as silly as trying to rush a desperate man wielding a knife."

"You should be grateful I did," Jena said even more tartly. "My lord." *I sound just like Lady Kestrienne.*

Lord Duone smiled. "Perhaps. Are you really sure you wish to stand?"

"No, my lord, here's a stool," offered Master Rolly. "Kipp's gone to fetch the mistress, Jena, so she can tend to your cut immediately."

They hauled her up and sat her down upon the stool, careful of her injury. Jena squinted down at the blood on her dress and suddenly wished she hadn't. "Poor Liselle. She won't be lending her gowns out after this," was the first thing she could think of to say. She began to shake and was grateful for Baldesar's supporting arm behind her back.

In a moment, Kipp returned with a short, stout woman wiping her hands on her apron, who stopped and sucked in a breath at the sight of the body on the floor. "My word! I don't suppose there's anything we can do for him."

"No," said Master Rolly. "Jena, this is my wife, Leani. Could you look at her hurt, my dear?"

Leani's sharp, kindly eyes turned to her. "Why, you poor little mite! Here, let me see it, Baldesar." She knelt at Jena's side, parting the slit cloth with gentle fingers to look at the wound; Baldesar shifted aside to make room. "Well, now. You were lucky. Not deep—a slice rather than a stab." Jena hissed softly at the touch of her cool fingers. "Still, you'll need stitches." She quickly untied her apron and began rolling it up into a soft pad.

"Can I fetch anything for you?" Baldesar offered.

"No, stay with her. Here, take this and press it over the cut. Keep the edges closed. Kipp, run and bring the large shallow blue bowl, the one on the shelf by the windows. And some clean soft cloths, and the kettle on the hearth. I just boiled that water this hour; it should still be hot. I'm going to get my needle and thread and some herbs." She gave Jena a sharp look. "You look white as muslin, poor lamb. I have some wine that will help."

As Baldesar pressed the cloth against her shoulder and Leani bustled away, Lord Duone stooped down and took Jena's hand. "Jena Gemcutter, you put your own body between me and steel. I will not forget."

She turned away from his gaze, embarrassed, remembering why that steel had entered her body instead of his. *Stupid, stupid. Oh, well.* "Who is he?" she whispered, looking over at the body.

"I don't know," Lord Duone said grimly. He stood. "I must leave for Niolantti immediately."

"Niolantti!" Jena sat up straight in alarm. "Why must you leave for Niolantti?"

"He knew Metissa was headed there. He was willing to draw a blade against me. What might the others who conspired with him do to my lady? Or my son?" He paled at the very thought. "I've no time to lose."

"My lord, wait! Stop!" She held up her arms to him and, wincing, dropping the left one. "Think, my lord. They don't have Lady Duone."

"How can you know?" He sounded like a man pleading for hope.

"They would have used *her* ring to lure you, if they had it. They didn't." He moved restlessly as if he might speak, but she overrode him: "Think, my lord! Why was this done? What was the purpose?"

He stared at her.

"They hoped to make you lose your chance to become the Emerald. There are other candidates, aren't there, nominated by the other houses? If you can be drawn off the trail, chasing a wild story to Niolantti, you would never arrive at Piyar before the Solstice Festival begins. They don't need to really threaten Lady Duone. In fact, that might taint the candidate they hope to win. I doubt Lady Duone has even reached Niolantti yet—and don't forget, she's traveling with an escort to keep her safe, too." *Not to mention Lady Kestrienne—*

I doubt anyone could sneak up on her. "Now the lie is exposed. Don't fall into the trap anyway!"

Lord Duone hesitated, gnawing his lip. "You really think she will be safe?"

Jena pondered. Could she get a message to her mentor? She didn't know of any way to do it magically. "You should send some of your escort immediately down the Tulio River to intercept Lady Duone at Niolantti," she answered finally. "They can warn her and ensure her security." And it would alert Lady Kestrienne to be on her guard, at least. "But you must go on to Piyar."

Lord Duone considered this for a moment and then glanced at the body. His face hardened. "Search him," he said crisply to his men. "See if we can find out anything about who might have sent him."

The two guards carefully rolled the corpse over onto its back. The movement made one of the arms flop heavily into the spreading pool of blood, spattering it on one of the guard's boots. Baldesar made a strangled sound in his throat and squeezed Jena's hand; she squeezed back, swallowing. She wished she could stop her hands from trembling.

"No pockets in the britches or pouches on the belt," one reported. "Here's a small pocket in the shirt. That's where he carried the ring, maybe, but it's empty now."

"Are there any scars or other marks?"

The guards worked quickly, stripping off the shirt and turning the arms to look. Jena averted her eyes from the sight of the wound in his side. "There are some moles. No scars or tattoos."

"Anything about his clothing?"

The first guard shook his head. "The shirt and britches are plain enough. Sun-rotted, though. He must have spent most of his time outside, what with that tan and all."

The second leaned forward to peer at the corpse's boots.

"These are Nyarian leather. See the hand-tooling, like a stamped row of circles? Good stout waxed stitching, too—he saved awhile to buy these. It won't tell us much about where he's from, though. That sort of leather gets traded all over."

As Lord Duone bent over to scrutinize the boots, Leani and Kipp returned. Grunting, Leani knelt down beside Jena and reached for the kettle, filling the bowl Kipp held out. She glanced over at the body with distaste as she filled a cotton bag with chamomile flowers and dried vervain and tossed it into the water to steep. "Here, now, I'm going to need a little more room."

Shrugging, one of the guards grasped the body under the armpits and pulled it several feet out of the way. "Look," Baldesar said suddenly as the head lolled. "He's wearing an earring."

Jena craned her neck to see over Leani's shoulder as the first guard pushed back a hank of hair where Baldesar pointed. There, a glint of gold flashed.

"Give it here to me," Master Rolly said.

Clumsily, the guard removed the earring, about the size of a squashed pea, and brought it over to the goldsmith. Master Rolly fitted a loupe to his eye and drew a lantern on the countertop closer to examine the small disk. It was difficult for Jena to see his face from her seat on the footstool.

Leani nudged her shoulder with another cup of wine. Jena accepted it and took a swallow as Leani held the cup steady, and at the widening of her eyes, Leani grinned. "I know. I laced it quite heavily. You shouldn't care too much as I'm stitching you up." She helped Jena drink the rest of it and then pushed Baldesar's hand aside, parting the top of Jena's dress and tearing away the top of the chemise. Baldesar politely averted his eyes as she began daubing at the oozing line left by the knife. At first, Jena set her teeth against the sting, wishing with all her might for Bram's hand to hold. She eased her right hand surreptitiously into her left sleeve to finger the pouch holding her stone. That seemed to help stop the shaking. Eventually, as the drugged wine began to work, she relaxed, leaning back into Baldesar's supporting arm and blinking slowly. The water in the bowl turned red.

Above their heads, Jena heard Master Rolly grunt in satisfaction. "See how the lines outlining the design are silvery black, my lord?"

"How is that done?" Lord Duone asked, leaning over the counter to look.

"Whoever made this etched the design and then placed silver sulfide in the lines and heated it until it could be pressed into the crevices. It's called niello work; it's a specialty of the Niolantii goldsmiths. It could be that—yes, here's the master's mark. If you would be so good as to reach for the Guild book there, my lord, from that stack on the other counter, against the wall? The red one, third from the top."

They bent over the book, turning the heavy pages, as Leani threaded her needle. "Feeling a little muzzy, hmm?" she asked Jena.

"Yes," Jena forced herself to answer after a pause. Her tongue felt thick.

"If it's any comfort, I was a seamstress before I married my Rolly." She smiled kindly at Jena, patting her hand, and then raised the needle. "And I was reckoned quite skillful with the needle. Now, then. Hold still, if it please you."

It didn't please Jena, or it wouldn't have if the wine had allowed her to object, but it didn't, so she didn't. She stared at a point on the opposite wall and tried to think of possibilities that would keep the needle from seeming *quite* so sharp. Nothing came immediately to mind.

"Look, here's the mark registration," Master Rolly said, scattering her feeble attempts at concentration. "Master Chevrin of Niolantti." She could hear him tap a finger heavily against the page. "Perhaps . . . We goldsmiths and jewelers trade pattern books back and forth containing the designs we use. I have some from the Niolantti Guild. That fish and crown device might be in one of them." Jena heard his footsteps retreat to another room.

Lord Duone asked his guards, "Have you found anything else?"

"No, my lord."

Leani paused to daub again at a trickle oozing from the tracks of her needle as she glanced again over her shoulder at the body. "Kipp," she said, wrinkling her nose, "put down that bowl and go fetch the old gray blanket at the bottom of the oak chest in the workroom. They can use that to roll him up and carry him outside until someone can go fetch the watch."

While the apprentice went away on that errand, Master Rolly returned, thumping several more books down on the counter. "Here they are. It will take me a while to go through them."

"Two will make the job go more quickly." Lord Duone pulled one of the books toward him and began turning pages, too.

The drugs in the wine were making Jena sleepy. She watched through half-lidded eyes as the apprentice brought the blanket, and the dead man was taken away. She could tell the blood on the floor pained Leani, but although the goldsmith's wife sent the apprentice to fetch more rags, Leani didn't set him to work cleaning.

"Go back to the workroom now, Kipp, and finish up some of your sketches," she said as she snipped off another stitch. "I'll see to this mess; you're too young to have the stomach for it. Oh, but send Celya to me once she is back from market: I could use her advice on a poultice, and I want her help putting Jena into bed, too. Certainly Celya's nightclothes would fit better than mine."

More borrowed clothes, Jena thought.

"Patience, now, Jena, I'm almost done."

Just then, Lord Duone made a soft sound of recognition. "Here it is," he said, and swung the volume around on the counter for Master Rolly to see.

"'Fish and Circlet'," Master Rolly read aloud. "It's the device of a shipping consortium. 'Mark of trade, House of Palani.' Perhaps they employed him as a sailor?"

"Palani?" Lord Duone repeated sharply.

"You recognize the name, my lord?"

"I know I've encountered that name recently." There was a moment of perplexed silence. "Palani . . ." Lord Duone muttered. "Palani! That was the candidate—they would *dare*—!" he stopped and cursed under his breath.

"My lord?"

"Never mind," Lord Duone said impatiently. "Tell me, do you know if one of the seven houses of the Diadem is involved in the ownership of this shipping company?"

"I'm sure I wouldn't know," Master Rolly said, his tone skeptical. "Although . . ."

"Yes?"

"Well, this pattern book lists a number of commissions

Master Chevrin has done for the Topaz, Lord Guilford Ose-lare."

"The Topaz! That would make sense," Lord Duone said softly. "The Topazes are involved in shipping and fishing, aren't they? And they do have investments in Niolantti." He thought it over for a moment and gave a short, hard laugh. "Yes. That certainly makes sense."

Leani cut the thread on the last stitch. "Now, then," she said briskly, as she gave the site a last blot with her cloth, "are you able to stand up?"

Jena tried and gave up abruptly.

"Very well, then, you carry her, Baldesar," Jena heard faintly through the spreading haze.

"I feel like such a fool," Jena mumbled. "It—mm, only some stitches."

"No, it's the drugs in the wine as much as anything, not to mention the shock. You'll sleep awhile now. In Celya's room, Baldesar." Baldesar was carrying her up a narrow staircase. "Set her down on the bed carefully—that's right!" Presumably then Baldesar retreated, because she could feel someone easing her out of her clothes and into a nightgown. She managed to snag the pouch holding her stone, crumpling it in her hand as her arm was pulled out of her sleeve. The neck of the nightgown was left untied so a cool poultice could be applied over the stitches. She would have sneezed at the pungent herb smell if she hadn't been so very tired. Thrusting the pouch with the stone under her pillow, she slid gratefully into a deep sleep.

She awoke the first time because someone was changing her poultice. The light from the single candle beside her bed made her blink as she squinted up at Leani.

"Well, now!" Leani said softly. "Awake? Do you need to use the chamber pot?" Jena nodded, and Leani threw back the covers and helped her onto it. When Jena was done, she noticed her knees still shook a bit as she slid back under the blankets.

"Ah, you must be hungry: that's why you're feeling weak."

Jena consulted her stomach. "I am hungry, I think. A little."

"Eh, well, you've slept away the day and a good part of the night. I have some soup here that should hearten you up a bit." Leani uncovered a bowl on the table by the bed, and a spicy steam rose up, curling in the candlelight. Then she helped shift the pillow so Jena could sit up and handed her the spoon. To Jena's relief, Leani didn't seem inclined to try to feed her. The soup was thick with beans and potatoes and tasted very good going down.

"There, now," Leani said, taking the bowl when Jena was done. "Go back to sleep. That's the quickest way to put you on the mend." The last thing Jena remembered before drifting off to sleep once more was Leani's touch as she checked the position of the poultice again. Her hands were warm and soft.

When Jena next awoke, daylight was streaming in through the oiled window cloth, bringing a glowing luminosity to the narrow, low-ceilinged room. The bed in which she lay was short and simple, just a straw ticking on top of planks supported by trestle stands. A wooden chest and bedside table were the only other furniture. After a short scramble through her memories, she identified where she was: at Master Rolly's in Tenaway, in the room of someone named Celya. The housemaid? She shifted her blanket and winced as something pulled. She turned her head at the sound of a thump on the wooden flooring and saw Baldesar, who was placing a saddlebag just inside the doorway. As she raised herself up on an elbow, he saw she was awake and smiled at her.

"Good morning. I'm sorry I woke you."

"No, that's all right. What time is it?"

"Almost midmorning."

"Well, then I've had more than enough sleep." She yawned, and then, noticing that Baldesar seemed embarrassed at the sight of her nightgown, drew the covers up farther. At her motion, the stitches pulled, and she winced once more. "I suppose this poultice needs changing again."

"The mistress said she'd have Celya do that, once you're awake. I just came in to leave the saddlebag. One of Lord

Duone's men dropped it by this morning, so you'd have some more clothes."

"Mmm. Thank you for bringing it up." Jena drowsily pushed hair out of her eyes. "Did they find out who sent that messenger?"

"No. I know Master Rolly and the Lord Duone's men talked with the watch, but they haven't been able to find out anything yet."

Jena shook her head. "Strange."

Baldesar gave her a sidelong glance. "I heard a little of what they were saying. Do you happen to know what it was all about, then?"

"Maybe I do," replied Jena cautiously. "But maybe I don't. Anyway, I don't know how much Lord Duone would appreciate having his private business discussed."

Baldesar shrugged agreeably. "Suit yourself. It's just that we don't often have people come in and try to carve up our customers. You can't blame a fellow for being curious. Oh, Lord Duone also sent this." He tossed her a large pouch.

Jena caught it before it thumped her on the nose; it was very heavy. She opened it and gasped. "It's gold, and a lot of it." She pulled a small square of parchment out of the pile of coins and squinted at it in the morning light. "To Jena Gemcutter," she read aloud, "as a token of gratitude for your help yesterday on behalf of myself and my House. I hope and trust you will be ready to ride again in two days' time when we continue on to Piyar. Lord Duone." She hefted the pouch and grinned up at Baldesar. "He must be planning to take my advice, then."

"His lordship is generous," said Baldesar, suitably impressed.

"Yes, very. And his timing is wonderful. Do you think Master Rolly would allow me to cast something in his workshop before I leave? I can use this gold for a project I have in mind."

"Depends on how big it is."

"Not big. A belt buckle. The model's in that saddlebag, in a wooden box near the top. Could you get it out?" She pointed, and Baldesar lifted the bag's flap, fished out the box, and handed it to her. She opened it and unwrapped the protective layers to show him the wax design.

Baldesar studied it carefully for a few moments. "This is the final model, then, you think?"

"Yes, it's done. I'll need to add the wax sprue rods for the casting, of course."

"A betrothal or wedding gift, I suppose?"

Jena nodded.

"Good traditional design," Baldesar said. "I'm pleased to see you're finally returning to the old forms." Jena managed not to smile. For Baldesar, "traditional" was the highest possible praise. She hoped he would not be too disappointed when he learned she intended to leave the buckle free of enameling.

Baldesar carefully packed the model back into the box. "After you're dressed, come down to the kitchen. It's at the foot of the stairs, to the right. Celya or the mistress will give you something to eat and check that knife slash, and then you can speak with the master in the workshop."

Master Rolly's shop was smaller than Collas' in Piyar. To Jena, it felt more disorderly, although certainly everything had its place, either stacked on tables and shelves or hanging from hooks on the walls. Perhaps the impression came from the way equipment crowded the working space. The goldsmith apparently didn't worry if the sketches tacked up on the wall hung crookedly, either. Baldesar's grinding and polishing wheels stood tucked into one corner. Light poured in through two glass roundel windows and an open doorway leading to a small internal courtyard where the furnaces stood. The room smelled of wax, hot metal, and glue.

Master Rolly sat on a stool tipped back against a wall. He was studying Jena's letter from the Jewelers' Guild while eating a late breakfast. He took his time reading it, brushing fallen crumbs off the parchment as Jena and Baldesar waited. Eventually he refolded the letter and looked gravely at Jena's model in the center of the table. "And so this is intended as your reapplication piece?" he said through a mouthful of bread and sausage.

"Yes, if you're willing to let me cast it here, Master Rolly."

The goldsmith leaned forward and turned the model, studying it from another angle. "What mixture of metal do you want?"

"Gold, if you please. Eighteen-carat weight, since it's to be set with gemstones. I'd like it alloyed with equal proportions of copper and silver—not too green, not too red." She gestured to the pouch on the table next to the model, full with the money given to her by Lady Kestrienne and Lord Duone. "Will this be enough to cover your fee, as well as the cost of the raw material for the buckle?"

"Well, now, how do you suppose we could find how much metal you'll need to cast it?" He took the last bite of his breakfast and leaned back on his stool again, grinning up at her as he chewed.

"Weigh the model, once the sprues are set," Jena answered promptly. "Then multiply by the specific gravity."

"Ah. And for eighteen carats gold, yellow mix, that would be?"

There was a tiny pause. "Fifteen and a half."

"Very good." Master Rolly hefted one of the pouches and then placed it back on the tabletop. "My guess is you'll have plenty here. Will you be enameling the piece?"

"No, I'll just be doing a bit of flat chasing."

"How do you intend to set it?"

"Faceted gems in claw settings. Rose cut, I *think,* although the central stone will be brilliant cut. I'll be getting the stones from Piyar."

"Not cabochon or table cut?"

Jena shrugged. "I like the challenge. It is meant to be an exhibition of my best work, after all."

"Would you like me to make the foils, too?"

"Thank you for the offer, but I don't plan to use them."

Master Rolly's eyebrows went up. "Oh?"

"I believe," Jena said politely but firmly, "if a stone is properly chosen and properly faceted and polished, the color will be sufficiently rich without tricking out the setting with foil backing."

"The Guild could regard such a position as a bit eccentric," Baldesar ventured.

"Possibly. Or they might consider it a sign of confidence in my own work."

Master Rolly rubbed his chin as he thought that over for a moment. "They might," he admitted finally. "What gems do you plan to use?"

"I must keep that to myself for now, Master Rolly, since the engagement is still secret. But I can tell you the piece is intended as a gift for a prominent member of one of the Diadem Houses."

"Ah, I see," Master Rolly said, a slow smile growing. "Intriguing. How could I turn down a commission like that?"

"It must be pointed out, I suppose," Jena said, after a little hesitation, "that since I've already been rejected by the Guild once, helping me with this piece might be . . . well, politically delicate. You understand, don't you, that I'm asking the Guild to overturn a long-standing tradition?"

Master Rolly's keen blue eyes shot her a look of hawklike amusement. "Well, now, tradition is all very well," he said, throwing Baldesar a significant glance, "but I believe in keeping the Guild from becoming too hidebound. That comes from being a goldsmith, maybe."

"Goldsmiths are more . . . flexible?" *More open to possibilities?* She wondered if Master Rolly was an adept.

"If you like. You see, goldsmithing has always been the training ground for all the other artistic fields: sculpture, painting, architecture. A goldsmith who wants to be successful must always be open to new ideas." He leaned back on his stool. "Besides, I have daughters of my own—although the Founders know they've never wanted to become goldsmiths."

"So you'll help me, then? Even if it might mean trouble?"

"If trouble comes, I think I'm equal to it. The cast can be done here, and I'll give you a letter for the Guild certifying it was done under your supervision."

"Thank you, Master Rolly!" Jena said with a rush of gratitude. "Oh—did Lord Duone ever settle on his commission? Will you have enough time to finish that if you're helping me?"

"He ordered the mirror and the set of combs. I'll be able to finish both projects easily before you go."

"Good. Oh, and Master Rolly, I also have a stone I'd like to cut, if I may have permission to use some of your equipment?"

"Well, I could hardly begrudge you that, could I, now, what with the fine fee you'll be giving me for the casting of that belt buckle, hmm?"

CHAPTER THIRTEEN

MAGIC, JENA DECIDED WHILE preparing her belt buckle model for casting, could be very useful when making jewelry.

It also could be terribly distracting.

Since metal casting wasn't Jena's specialty, she had only practiced the minimal level to satisfy the general journeyman requirements, not nearly as much as a journeyman specializing in silver- or goldwork. On the rare occasions she had cast metal in the past, her work had usually turned out well, but once or twice in the learning process a cast had been ruined by bubbles in the slurry or by an incomplete pour. She had never known what the result would be until she cracked the mold and saw the cooled metal—until this time. Even as her new magical sensing helped her "see" the end result, she could also "see" potential disasters at each step in the process. Sorting out the difference took real concentration.

In the workshop, as Jena began setting the sprue rods on her model, Baldesar polished enseigne tokens and Master Rolly worked on polishing the mirror back for Lord Duone's gift, both ostensibly ignoring her. That left only Kipp to sit by her side, watching, and she understood this was part of her evaluation, since a journeyman's responsibilities included supervising and instructing apprentices. She could tell that Master Rolly, at least, seemed to be listening.

"Why'd you remove that sprue?" Kipp asked her as she worked. "Don't you need it to feed gold to that section?"

"You're right, I do, but I have to reset the angle," Jena told him. "If the rod is set at a straight perpendicular, the gold won't flow easily around the bend, and the metal might cool before filling the cavity completely." She probably would have been satisfied with the first position of the sprue herself, but for the subtle warning the wax rod gave her under her fingers. Belatedly, she thought to put up a weak ward over herself and the model as she worked. This business of mingling magic with the practice of her craft was new territory, and she didn't want to risk affecting Kipp in case the boy had any sensitivity to what she was doing.

When she had finished setting the sprues, Jena began painting the model with a coating of debubblizer. "How do you like working in a goldsmith's shop?" she asked Kipp. "Do you want to switch to another specialty later on?"

"Goldsmithing's fine with me. Better than playing with rocks, *I* think," Kipp said with the cheerful scorn of the young. "And I like the master, too," he added, lowering his voice. "He don't beat me."

Jena gave him a startled look as she dipped her brush into the pot. "*Beat* you?"

"Lots of masters do," Kipp said stoutly. "Nothing strange about it, I s'pose. Even my father did. Didn't yours?"

Jena shook her head.

"Course," Kipp said after a moment's reflection, "the master *did* throw a bucket of cold water over me in bed one morning when I overslept. So I know he wants what's best for me."

"How fortunate you have a master looking after your welfare," said Jena, only a slight tremor of laughter in her voice betraying her.

"Uh-huh. I've only just started with the master this year, of course. He still says my sketches look like cat scratches. Do you want me to mix the slurry?"

Jena carefully set the model on the table to cool. "It's my

piece so I'm supposed to do it, but why don't you show me where it's kept?"

After preparing the slurry, Jena placed the model in a metal cylinder and poured in the paste very slowly, so as to avoid air bubbles. When it was full she took a metal rod and began tapping the side. Kipp watched her do this for several minutes and then said impatiently, "That should be good enough. You've surely shaken out all the air by now."

Jena placed her fingertips against the flask, closing her eyes. After a moment, she opened them. "No, I don't think so," she said with a small smile and began tapping again.

Eventually, though, she stopped and set the flask aside. "The furnace needs firing up," she said. "We can do that as we wait for the plaster to dry."

When the plaster had set, Jena carefully flipped the flask over and removed the tapered bottom, leaving a funnel-shaped depression in the plaster. The hole at the bottom of the funnel led, deep within the mold, to the convergence of the wax sprue rods.

She donned thick leather gloves and took the flask outside to the courtyard, where Kipp worked busily applying the bellows to the fire in the furnace. "Hot enough, I think," he said cheerfully, stopping to rub his sleeve over his flushed forehead. "Ready to put it in?"

"Where are the tongs?"

"Oh, there. Hanging from a hook on the side."

Opening the furnace door, Jena placed her flask into the interior on a trivet, with the hole facing down. A crucible had already been placed inside the furnace to preheat. She closed the door with a clank of the latch and stripped off the gloves as Kipp continued working the bellows. "Don't pump it too hot, Kipp."

"I won't."

Jena stared at the furnace until it seemed she could see through the door, into the very mold itself. Why had she never seen the beauty in metal casting before, in the fascination of empty space, waiting for her to fill as she chose? All that potential . . . She blinked, gave herself a little shake, and the exhilarating rush of magic ebbed. *Better not keep lapsing into dreams like this,* she told herself firmly, *or you'll end up burning yourself, or worse.*

"I'm going in to get my poultice changed again," she said. "Once the wax is all melted out, take the tongs and turn the flask on its side for the burnout—the fire has to be built up for that. I'll be back to spell you on the bellows, as long as it doesn't pull my stitches too much."

After her cut had been tended, Jena returned to the courtyard to fetch the heated crucible. When she reached into the furnace with the tongs to pick it up, however, a sudden surge of warning magic almost made her drop it. Startled, she put it down and stepped back, fumbling with the tongs. "What's the matter?" Kipp asked.

"Just clumsy." Jena picked up the vessel with the tongs again, steeling herself against the wash of impressions flowing into her hands . . . the crucible shattering, pouring molten gold over her fingers, searing . . . She looked more closely. "Kipp, did you check this crucible before putting it in the furnace?"

The apprentice looked startled. "Why?"

"It has a hairline crack, see? Right at the base. It could break apart in the centrifuge and send liquid gold flying everywhere."

Kipp came over to examine it and gave her a guilty look. "I thought I did. I know I'm supposed to."

"Well, it might have cracked here in the furnace, too," Jena said, although she knew quite well it hadn't. "I'll ask Master Rolly for another one."

Inside the workshop, Master Rolly gave her a measured look at her explanation and reached up to a shelf for another crucible, handing it to her. Jena looked it over carefully. It felt cool and safe in her palm. She checked it against the centrifuge counterweights and then slid the meticulously preweighed piles of gold, silver and copper into it.

"Call me when you think the gold is read for the pour," Master Rolly said as she carried the crucible out to the courtyard.

From her pouch Jena surreptitiously took a tiny button of gold knocked from the nugget in Morgan's room. *Who knows? Maybe it will help.* As small as the fragment was, she could still faintly sense in it the longings that had permeated the nugget as a whole. Jena shook her head, dropping the bit of gold into the rest of the small heap of metal. *Where are you, Morgan? We both need you, Lady Rhuddlan and I.* She deposited the crucible inside the furnace and watched the gold in the dull red of the coals until the heat made her close the door. *Who knows what the Guild will think, but I hope . . . I hope Lady Rhuddlan will like it. I really hope she will.*

"So, this is the right temperature, you think?" Master Rolly said. He had the crucible out of the furnace and was expertly swiveling it with the tongs to watch the viscosity of the molten gold against the sides of the vessel.

"Oh, yes," Jena said eagerly. Master Rolly looked at her sharply, but she couldn't help it, aroused as she was by the eager yearning of the gold. *It feels so ready. I sensed it partly when I put the mold in the furnace. That was one possibility, waiting for fulfillment, but this gold holds so many! Why, it could be molded into a thousand different patterns.* Well, she had the form prepared that would shape it now.

"We'll see if you're right," Master Rolly said with a small half smile.

"I need an apron," Jena said, trying to regain her composure.

"We all do. And eyeshields and gloves."

"Kipp, run and get them," Jena commanded, remembering belatedly that she was in charge. "And please ask Baldesar to come outside; I would like his help for the cast."

Baldesar joined them, and Kipp brought out the protective leather gear and the wooden disks cut with narrow slits to shield their eyes. After they had garbed themselves, Jena said, "Baldesar, take those tongs and get the flask from the furnace—Kipp, open the door for him. Master Rolly, if you would be so kind as to bring the crucible?"

She led the small procession back inside to the centrifuge and quickly wound the casting arm into the cocked position. "Slip the mold in first, Baldesar. Quickly, now, but be careful." The journeyman clamped the flask into position and then Master Rolly stepped forward, placing the crucible into the crucible shoe. He pushed the pouring lip up flush to the funnel formed in the plaster and closed the second clamp.

"Are they both secure?"

"They are. Let fly."

"All right, then." Jena had to fight to keep her voice calm. "Everyone step back." She punched the release knob.

With a thunk, the spring released and the arm began spinning in a rush, too rapidly to allow them to see the gold flying from the crucible into the mold. But Jena could feel the jubilant surge of metal into the crevices left in the plaster, rushing from formlessness into embodiment, into this-is-what-is-meant-to-be!

Gradually the arm slowed. The other watchers, rapt as she, sighed and stirred. "You had it well balanced," Master Rolly commented, removing his eye shields. "Not a single wobble."

Jena removed her shields, too, and watched, blinking, as the centrifuge came to a halt. "Kipp, I need some water from the cistern."

By the time Kipp returned, slopping water all over his feet from the bucket he lugged, the flask had had several minutes to cool. With the tongs, Jena unseated it from the clamps on the centrifuge arm and then plunged it into the water, which boiled with the force of the violent disintegration of the plaster. A dull bronze color gleamed up at her through plaster crumbs. She reached in with the small tongs and pulled it out—an intricate knot of unburnished gold, still caked with plaster, set on thin rods like a strange bouquet of flowers. She laughed aloud in triumph and held it up for the others to see.

"Ah," said Master Rolly, his voice sounding pleased. "Scrub it clean, and then we'll see what we have."

A few minutes later, more details emerged from Jena's scouring brush. "It's all here," she announced with satisfaction. "The pour was complete."

"Let me see it," said Master Rolly. He took the buckle to examine, pulling a lantern close for more light. "Only one or two air bubble nodules, and they'll be easy enough to remove." He rotated it, flicking away a fleck or so of plaster with his thumbnail. "No pitting except for this spot on the underside, and that can be rubbed out without any noticeable thinning of the gold. Eh, you've a fine cast here, Jena Gemcutter. Worthy of a journeyman stamp, at the very least!" He smiled and handed the buckle back to her. "And when you pickle it and saw the sprues off and polish it up, I'll write a letter to the Guild for you telling them so. But of course, since your specialty is cutting, it will depend in the end on the stones with which you set it."

"Trust me on that. It's going to be beautiful. You'll see."

Late in the evening, after the household had gathered for supper and then retired for the night, Jena stayed alone in the workshop to cut the stone Morgan had given her.

She suspected that if casting metal felt different now that she was in touch with her magic, cutting would be a revelation. Or was it merely that this was her talisman piece, the link with her partner? She didn't know. She only knew that for the first time, she didn't even need to dip the stone in oil and "cut a window" to see the angle of cleavage and check for imperfections inside. She already knew: there were no flaws—no inclusions, no bubbles, no feathers, no structure lines. She didn't even think of her customary grumble that wasn't it a pity the Glass Guild couldn't grind lenses with greater magnification. She didn't need to look at the stone the way she ordinarily did. She *knew* it.

Lady Kestrienne had said her stone should be shaped the same way Morgan's stone was shaped: the brilliant cut. Jena turned the stone slowly in her fingers. *Perhaps it's not quite as simple as that. The talisman is supposed to form my link with my partner. Then . . . in a way, the way I shape this shapes that link. But it's also the focus for my power. Will the cut also shape that? Perhaps I should think about this a little further rather than simply following what Morgan has already done.* She held the stone up to the candle. *There is more than one possibility here. Which is the best to choose?*

Within the rough angular form of the stone, she shaped lines of light with her mind. It was simply a way of perceiving the gold flecks within as if strung like infinitesimal beads on beams of light, crisscrossing at facet angles. One of the table cuts, like the square? *No, not a square. The angles at*

*the girdle are like . . . someone turning a shoulder, refusing
to listen. It makes you think you can only go at a limited
number of angles, in a limited number of directions. I've had
enough limits.* She reangled the lines within the stone. *A
combination cut, like the heart?* She held the form for a moment, and then the lines rescrambled themselves, as if uneasy
at the very idea. *Now, I know that's wrong. Morgan's heart
belongs to someone else. I have a tie to him, yes, and it's just
as strong, but it's different. Besides, I don't want my magic
limited only to matters of the heart.* One of the round cuts,
like the rose? *Closer. Round would be good for scrying, I
think . . . but the rose cut doesn't let in enough light.*

Well, what about *the brilliant?*

The lines dissolved again, and the flecks glittered like
sand reflecting shifts of light as a clear wave rushed out over
it. Jena took a deep breath and then, trustingly, plunged in.
"The widest part of a facet-cut gem, the edge, is called the
'girdle,' Jena. The part above the girdle is called the 'crown,'
and it includes the large flat facet on top, called the 'table.'
Below the girdle is the 'pavilion.' Sometimes there's a tiny
facet at the tip of the pavilion, cut parallel to the table; that's
the 'cutlet.'"

It was her father's voice. She sat as a very young child in
his lap as he held a knife in her chubby hands, carefully
guiding her in carving a potato into the shape of a roughed-
out gem.

"This is how you'll start learning, Jena, when you're an
apprentice. My father taught me how to cut facets this way,
and now I'm teaching you." Mama objected, Jena remembered: "But she's so young, she'll cut herself!" Collas only
laughed and ruffled Jena's hair (he had laughed so much
more before Mama died) and said they'd be very careful.
Sometimes young children see things beyond their years:
Jena understood that even if her parents took opposite sides
on the question, they both cared for her and wanted what was
best. Knowing that made her feel special, and loved—but she
was still glad when her father won in the end.

"The brilliant cut has fifty-seven facets, Jena. Fifty-eight,
if you include a cutlet. We cut the table first—a long flat
slice. All the angles have to be just so when you're doing the

brilliant cut, to make the light reflect through correctly. You'll learn about that when you're older; right now we're just practicing the shape.

"There are three rows of facets on top—that's the crown, you'll remember—and two rows below the girdle, on the pavilion. Every time you cut a facet, the next cut is on the opposite side. So we'll start with the first facet from the girdle to the crown. Then the opposite side. That's right. Now two more, one opposite the other. See the squared table? These first four facets are called the 'bezel' facets. The next four are the 'corner' facets, and that turns the table into an octagon. That means it has eight sides, now; can you count them? One, two, three, four, five, six, seven, eight. . . . All together, these first eight facets, the bezels and the corners, are called the 'crown' facets."

How patient he had been! The potato juice oozed over her fingers and the knife, making them slippery, but she trusted him utterly; she knew he would never, never let the knife slip.

Could she learn to trust Morgan that way if they ever found one another? Would he trust her?

"The second row above the girdle is made up of the 'star' facets. We cut off the eight corners on the table, leaving triangles with points facing downward. Remember, we need to cut each facet opposite the other as we go around the table.

"The last row of facets on the top of the gem is the hardest. These will be the 'break' facets. See what we're doing as I guide your hand: we're making sixteen kite-shaped cuts in each main facet. It's easy to become confused."

Collas' hands, holding hers so carefully, were gentle. The heavy scent of clove and wintergreen clung to his fingers— he kept dishes of the expensive spice oils in the workshop to check the reflective angle of light in gems. The smell always reminded Jena of him.

"Now we're done with the crown, and we must start on the pavilion, so turn it over. The eight 'pavilion' main facets are cut just like the crown main facets, except they come to a point. We don't cut any star facets at all in the pavilion. The break facets on the bottom part are longer than the ones on top. See, they take up half the distance between the girdle and the point of the pavilion. They are more diamond-shaped than kite-shaped. Now, do you want to put a cutlet in, too? You do? Then it's just a tiny slice . . . and there, it's done. When you cut a real gem correctly, and all the proportions are right, then the light will reflect up again through the crown, rather than being lost in the pavilion. The cutlet will make a tiny point of light, and you want as much light in the stone as possible."

This is the right cut after all, she realized. *Doing the brilliant cut in Father's lap made me realize what I was meant to be: a gemcutter. I'm not simply copying the shape of Morgan's stone—no, the brilliant cut is in me. It has always been so, right from the beginning, and so it makes as much sense to say the way Morgan's stone was already cut was what attracted his magic to mine.*

"Light is what you want," her father's voice said, fading away. "Light is what the gemcutter always wants. . . ." The facets gleamed in hard-edged perfection, and then the light blazing up from the cutlet all but blinded her. When it died down and she could see again, she seemed to be looking through a window in the stone, far out to sea.

A man's face swam into view in the pale, pearly light; she appeared to be looking up at him from a peculiar, cramped angle, at about his waist level. He was a swarthy man in the prime of life, stocky, with a short, dark clipped beard and powerful shoulders. In one ear swung an earring, a gold post set with a fine, black baroque pearl. The man frowned, his attention caught by something, and then his tired, weather-lined eyes turned straight toward her. In the first instant of mutual shock, they simply stared at each other, and then a gleam entered his eye.

"I didn't expect to see you so soon," he said quietly. "You've been learning quickly."

Jena couldn't think of a thing to say.

"What is your name?" he asked.

"J—Jena," she answered, to her own surprise. She hadn't intended to say anything, but it was as if her name had been dragged up out of her throat on a string. She felt a cold sheen of sweat break out on her forehead. Oh, what a fool she'd been: she wasn't examining the stone anymore, she was scrying it. And now she had stumbled upon the enemy. Morgan's ring allowed her to see him; this stranger must have put it on one of the fingers of his own hand, the one resting on the ship's rail.

"Jena," he said thoughtfully. "A pretty enough name, I suppose. Where do you live, young Jena?"

"In—in Piyar and Chulipse, with my father." She barely managed to stop herself before blurting our Collas' name. Even exerting that much control was excruciating. If only she had put up a ward before starting! But how could she have known this would happen after all her failed attempts to scry the stone?

"Ah. And do you love anyone, Jena?"

She didn't even think to wonder at the strangeness of the question. "I love . . . I love . . ." She stopped. The man's gaze bored into her. Struggle as she might, she had no escape, but she wasn't even sure of the answer anymore. "I love . . . Bram. Bram Tailor. I'm . . . betrothed to him."

This seemed to please him. "A tailor. Excellent. So you don't love *him*."

"Love . . . who?" she forced out between frozen lips.

"Lord Morgan," he answered with a sneer, making the title an insult. "You're wiser than I was, not to want someone so far above you. Yes, a tailor is quite perfect. Where does this fine, upstanding tailor live, Jena m'dear?"

Don't tell, don't tell, a frantic portion of her mind chanted, but it came out anyway. "Three Blossom Lane, on the Fifth Rim on the Sweet Bank." She closed her eyes, overcome with shame at her own weakness.

"That would be in Piyar, then, wouldn't it? Good. Look at me, now. Look at me!" Compelled, she opened her eyes again. "Go and find your tailor, Jena. Settle down and breed brats with him. Have a long, long, happy life that adds up to nothing in the end. I suppose I couldn't wish a worse curse on you than that, eh?" Even in the midst of her anger and panic, the thought occurred to Jena that she had never seen anyone with eyes that looked quite so miserable. "Forget about magic and about Lord Morgan," he went on. "He's of no concern to you now."

"He does concern me. He's bound to me." She felt rage

and stung pride rising within her, warming her like heat from a forge. "Since you know my name, tell me who you are."

"Me?" Her question surprised him into a harsh crack of laughter. "Why, I'm nobody, of course, nobody at all." Her fury rose higher, and a current between them hesitated and began flowing the other way. "I'm Kett. A ship's captain." He blinked, as if surprised at himself, and she pressed her advantage.

"Where is Morgan? Why do you have his ring? You don't have any right to it."

"Oh?" he said, amused again. "And who will force me to give it up?"

"I will."

His smile wavered and then strengthened. "Lord Morgan doesn't need it anymore." He waved his hand, and the sea and ship disappeared. She had a glimpse of rose curtains, of a lady's bed and chair. Just as quickly, they were gone, and something sucked Jena down, down, into the maelstrom of the spinning facets of the stone.

And then, abruptly, the walls of Master Rolly's workshop in Tenaway appeared around her, bumping her to a halt. She trembled, her breathing ragged in her ears. Dawn was near; she could hear birds beginning to sing in the small trees in the courtyard beyond the workshop door. The lantern had gone out. She fumbled with the flint and steel and lit the wick again. *Light is what the gemcutter always wants.* Then she looked down at her hand and opened her fingers.

Nestled in her palm, golden flecks sparkling up at her, lay her talisman stone: a perfectly faceted and polished brilliant-cut gem.

CHAPTER FOURTEEN

HUGGING HER CLOAK AROUND herself, Jena stood on the deck of the barge as the deckhands poled it to a halt at a market loading dock, on the Sweet Bank just below the Fifth Bowl Bridge. After quiet weeks of travel down the Koh River, the noise pressed on Jena's ears as a pleasant cacophony. Voices shouted, ropes flew through the air, and boxes were hauled out of the hold for unloading once the gangplank went down. Overhead on the bridge, foremen bellowed orders as workmen scrambled over arches and trusses, hanging heavy white banners for the Winter Solstice Festival, beginning in three days. Over everything else rose the muted roar of the Two Bridge Market crowd.

Being home again made her stay at Duone Keep seem like a distant dream. Yet, in a way, even the previous summer in Piyar had been strange, Jena suddenly realized. After all, until this year she had always spent her summers in Chulipse. To her, Piyar meant hot mulled wine, heavy cloaks, breaking the ice in the bucket in the morning, sometimes even fingerless gloves in the workroom—not the alien city she had come to know in the past summer, prostrate with humidity, redolent with the scent of flower gardens.

But this Piyar, readying itself in its gaudy finest for the

Winter Solstice, looked achingly familiar in the pale morning sunlight. Jena's gaze roved over the crowd, as her breath plumed out in the crisp, cold air. Through the dank scent of river water and wet rope, steam wafted down from the costermonger wagons on the bridge above, bringing the aroma of roasted caselnut meats and tiny holiday mincemeat pies, baked apples, and currant-studded Solstice loaves. Children raced up and down the lanes adjoining the piers, bright in their new festival jackets, dodging the servants and housemaids bargaining loudly at the edge of the docks over fish, oysters, and mussels. A man strode through the throng, heading for the stairs leading up to the bridge. The pole on his shoulder bristled with dozens of the small white paper lanterns people hung outside their houses during the two weeks of Festival.

Jena felt her heart lighten a little. Ever since scrying her stone in Tenaway and encountering Kett, she had been beside herself with anxiety over Bram, although she had done her best to keep anyone from seeing that anything was troubling her. But now she was finally home, and in a very little while she would see her father and fiancé again.

"Jena Gemcutter?"

Jena turned and saw Taras making his way toward her across the deck, sidestepping hurrying crewmen. "Yes?"

"Will you be disembarking here, or at the Golden Docks?"

"This is closer to my home, so I'll be getting off here, as soon as they're done unloading cargo."

"Lord Duone would like to see you before you go."

She followed him to the bow, where Lord Duone stood, also watching the crowd. With a nod, Taras withdrew, and she stepped forward, clearing her throat to alert the nobleman to her presence. She curtsied deeply as he turned. "I'd like to offer you my thanks once again, my lord, for allowing me to accompany your party."

Lord Duone waved this off. "I think we can agree that debt has been repaid. But I do wish to ask a favor of you."

"Of course, my lord," she answered, surprised.

"About what happened in Tenaway—would you be willing to come before the Council to testify to the events there?

I do think," he added grimly, "this incident should be considered in the evaluation of the candidates."

"The Diadem certainly wouldn't want to add anyone to their circle who practices treachery like that," Jena agreed. "Just as I wouldn't want such a person ruling." She hesitated and then decided to speak her mind. "My lord, forgive my frankness, but I'm surprised you thought it even necessary to ask my permission."

Lord Duone chuckled. "I could simply order you to testify, eh?"

Jena found herself smiling. "Well, yes, you could."

"I won't insist, Jena Gemcutter. We don't know who did this; although I have ideas, I might be wrong. You want to practice your trade among patrons at the Court, but if you come forward as a witness, you could create some awkward enemies for yourself."

"I would say instead that someone has made an enemy out of me," said Jena firmly. "That knife left a scar, my lord. Yes, I'll testify."

"Good." Lord Duone heaved a sigh—of relief, she realized with surprise. "Thank you. The Diadem Council will meet the candidates on Solstice Eve, at sunset. I will make arrangements at the palace for you to be admitted to the Diadem Chamber. Where can you be reached until then?"

"I'll be at my father's, Collas Gemcutter. We live on the Sweet Bank in the Third Bowl, on Goldberry Lane."

"Very well, then. Until the night after tomorrow, then, Jena."

"Until then, my lord." Jena curtsied again and left him. She walked back to the stern, where Taras joined her again.

"Lord Duone told me to make arrangements to have your luggage delivered," he said, "if you'll tell me where you'd like it sent."

"His lordship is very kind, but that's hardly necessary. I was, uh, traveling rather lightly when I arrived at Duone Keep, and most of what I have with me now I borrowed from Liselle, one of Lady Duone's fosterlings. Could you see that my bag is returned to her?"

"Don't you have anything to take with you?" he asked, surprised.

"I have everything in that small bundle set against the rail there, and in the pockets of this cloak."

"Very well, then." He gave her a little nod and a smile. "A happy end to your journey, and a good Solstice, Jena."

"Good Solstice to you, too."

The gangplank had cleared, and so after retrieving her bundle, Jena disembarked. She paused on the wooden pier, enjoying for a moment the sensation of a surface that didn't move beneath her feet. *Bram's first. Then home.* Tucking her pack under her arm, she began striding toward the stairs leading up to the bridge.

The people coursing through the market were in a leisurely preholiday mood, and the sheer mass of bodies forced Jena to slow down. Although she meant to pass by the market vendors without stopping, a herbwoman's stall hung with Solstice pomanders and pillows caught her eye, and she halted there.

"Well, now, missy," said the woman, smiling broadly as she sensed a potential customer, "d'ye need something to make the new year smell sweet?"

Jena hesitated. "Maybe I do." It was true she had only a few coppers left, not enough for a proper Festival gift for Bram. But she could get one later in the week, and it would be nice to bring him at least something today, even if it was only a small holiday token.

"How about a Solstice pillow for your true love?" the herbwoman said, whisking one off the counter to show her. "Place it under his pillow this Solstice Eve, and he'll dream of only you for a year and a day. A-course," she added, winking broadly, "you have to get it into his bedroom first. D'ye think you can manage that?"

Jena blushed. "How much?"

"Four coppers, missy."

"And how much for that pomander, the small one?" She could bring it to her father, to hang in his workshop.

"That one is five; 'twill smell sweet and fresh throughout the holidays." The herbwoman unhooked the pomander ribbon from a nail on the wall of her stall. "It has oils in it, too, to make it burn bright colors when you put it in the fire at Festival's end." She gave the herb ball an exaggeratedly appreciative sniff and proffered it to Jena. "Lovely smell, ain't it?"

Jena leaned forward, inhaling the scent, and nodded. "I'll take both, then." She dug the last coins from her money pouch and offered them to the herbwoman, who wrapped the pomander and pillow in a scrap of muslin and handed them to her.

"Thank you, then, missy, and a merry Festival to you."

"Good Solstice." Jena picked up her bundle again and walked on, breathing the pungent fragrance of the small package which she tucked into the sleeve of her cloak.

It took Jena the better part of an hour to thread her way through the throngs of children, servants, nobles, buskers, and merchants on her way to Three Blossom Lane. As she turned down the corner leading to Bram's house, she found her heart was beating quickly. She had shied away from thinking much what she and Bram might say to one another at this reunion—she had deliberately avoided scrying it. But the issue couldn't be avoided now. She would have to tell him why she had left and about the changes she had undergone. But how? Magic was a real presence in her life now; would Bram accept that? Her steps slowed.

What would happen if he couldn't?

She was almost within hailing distance of Bram's house, but her courage ebbed more with every step she took. What *was* going to happen? She tried to see the possibilities in her mind and remembered the little herb pillow she had in her sleeve. Bram would take the bag, and he would smile at her and take her in his arms, and everything would be all right again. Wouldn't it?

She shook her head, not sure the picture was altogether convincing. *It may take more than a little charm bag to get me through this meeting.*

Suddenly Jena gasped and stopped. That figure—frantically she scrambled for her ward-building spell. She slammed the ward up as fast and powerfully as she could, and ducked behind the corner of a leatherworker's shop, two doors down from Bram's house. When she was sure the spell was complete, she cautiously edged her head around the corner to look.

The sea captain, Kett, was going into the tailor shop.

Jena raised the hood of her cloak and withdrew. If Bram was in there . . . and if the wizard hurt him . . .

Stop it, she told herself firmly. *Enough. Panicking won't help. I need to know what he's up to, and to make sure Bram's safe without giving myself away.*

But if I get too close, Kett might sense the possibility that I'm nearby. He might even be able to sense me now, at this distance. What can I do?

Jena hesitated and then drew together her magic. A ward . . . something to prevent Kett from choosing a possibility that might hurt Bram . . . *I have to try, even if it means risking the chance Kett might sense it and trace it back to me.* She spun together a web of protective magic and, with a whispered word, sent it wafting out in search of her lover. *Bram? It's Jena. Let me hold you closely, love. Let me enfold you, protect you, keep you safe from anyone who might wish you harm.* She stood rigidly in the cramped space between the houses, sweat beading on her forehead as she strained, reaching.

But the spell came eddying back to her, untouched and empty. Jena's eyes flew open.

Bram wasn't in the house.

The discovery threw her thoughts into a turmoil. Perhaps Kett made him disappear somehow, like Morgan? After a moment, she resolutely set her fear from that thought aside. *There's one consolation, at least: if Bram isn't here, I won't have to risk giving myself away by protecting him.*

Perhaps she could try to eavesdrop on Kett using her link with Morgan's ring? She pulled her cut talisman stone from its pouch and stared at it. *I didn't have any barriers in place when I scried this in Tenaway. Will my ward be enough to protect me this time?* It would be terribly risky. . . . Her hand tightened over the stone, and then she put it away again. Perhaps there was another way.

She thought the problem through slowly. When she met Kett through the stone, he seemed to be . . . lying in wait for her to use magic. Now he must be hoping Jena had given up.

*But perhaps . . . perhaps if he only expects to encounter me
magically, he may miss me if I choose to do something that
doesn't involve magic?* She craned her neck out around the
corner of the building again. *Something so simple as listening under a window, for example?*

Jena hesitated and then stepped out from around the corner
of the leatherworker's shop. She reminded herself to keep the
ward up as she walked forward. The tailor shop window facing the street was made of oiled linen stretched over a window frame of wood. It could be raised or lowered but was
lowered now to keep out the chill. Jena stopped beside it,
careful not to let her shadow fall across the fabric, and pretended to be checking something inside her pocket as she
leaned against the wall to listen.

"I'm extremely sorry, sir, but I tell you, my brother isn't
here," came a young girl's voice from inside, speaking with
an impatience that was only thinly veiled. *Carina,* Jena
thought.

She heard Kett say something but couldn't make out the
words.

"Oh, yes, for quite some time," Carina replied. "He left
the city at the end of summer."

Jena's jaw dropped. From within the shop came another
masculine rumble.

"No, I'm sorry, I don't know when he'll be returning; he
hasn't contacted us at all. Would you like to leave a message
for him to receive when he returns?" Jena heard an impatient
exclamation and then the scrape of boots coming toward the
door. She straightened up and hurried around the corner of
the shop, drawing back into the shadows behind a water barrel.

After a pause, Kett strode by her without so much as
glancing in her direction. She could see the black pearl
swinging from his ear. He headed down the street in the direction of Lowertown. After waiting a few moments, Jena
eased her way out from between the shops and followed, trying to keep several heads in the crowd between the two of
them in case he turned around. But rather than slowing down
or stopping, Kett only walked faster, impatiently elbowing
people out of his way. He kept to the main lanes, where the

crowd was becoming thicker, and Jena had to hurry to keep him in sight.

But after a series of turns and a descent down a public staircase, she lost him. He had disappeared into the Sailor's Knot, a tangle of narrow, dark streets lined with taverns frequented by seamen, not a section of the city where any young woman could explore for very long without attracting unwanted attention.

"Shatter it," Jena muttered under her breath, her eyes scanning the shadowy doorways along the street. But it was hopeless. Kett was nowhere in sight. She toyed with the idea of dropping her ward and risking a magical search after all, when she remembered Carina.

She turned and hastened through the crowds of people going the other direction, retracing her steps up the stairway and back to the tailor shop. Carina was alone in the front room when she came in, and her face paled a little at the sight of Jena, her mouth opening in an *Oh* of surprise.

"Carina?"

"Jena!" The younger girl came out from behind the rough wooden counter to give her a hug. "My stars, I was so worried! But . . . is Bram with you?" she asked, looking eagerly past Jena's shoulder.

"With me? Why . . . no," Jena stammered. "I thought—that is, I came expecting he would be here."

A sound in the back room of the shop made Carina glance over her shoulder. She seized Jena's elbow and hurried her toward the shop doorway. "Hush," she whispered into Jena's ear, pressing a finger against her lips. "I don't want Father to hear you."

"Carina, what—"

"Here," Carina said, bringing them to a halt in the tiny sheltered entryway to the shop. "They won't hear us here, if we keep our voices down. Oh, Father was so angry when Bram left, Jena. I've never seen him in such a rage. I . . . I don't think you should see him, at least until Bram comes back. He blames you, you see."

"But why?"

"Because Bram left the city to look for you."

"*What?*"

"About two months ago, several weeks after . . . after you left." Carina's gaze dropped to the floor. Jena wondered what Bram had told his family about that.

"Two months ago," she repeated numbly, putting her bundle down.

"He asked directions from that magician, the one who's a friend of your father's?"

"From *Arikan*?" Jena gaped at Carina, her mind in a whirl.

"Bram came home late one night, and when Father asked him why he was packing a kit, Bram said he was leaving to go find you. He'd already arranged for passage to a city called Nio—Nio—"

"Niolantti? He went by sea?"

"Yes, he was going to work his way up the coast as a cutter deckhand. And when Father told him he'd only end up drowning himself by going on such a madcap chase, Bram told him Arikan had given him spells to keep him safe."

"Oh, no," groaned Jena, appalled at the thought of the tailor's reaction to this statement.

"Exactly. For Bram to have anything to do with a magician—well, I've never seen Father so furious in my life. Oh, how he scolded! But Bram couldn't be stopped, and in the morning he was gone. And Father hasn't mentioned his name since."

Gone . . . and it was all her fault. Yet, for pity's sake, what could she have expected him to do, once his fiancée had gone tearing off after some mysterious nobleman and then disappeared into thin air? Did she really think Bram would simply stay put, sewing, until she decided to come back?

That's exactly what I thought, she realized with a sinking sense of shame. *Or rather, I didn't think at all. What a fool I've been! Steady, homebody Bram, who's never been away from Piyar in his life—it never even occurred to me he would do something like this!*

One of the shop cats twined around Carina's ankles, *mrrow*ing an interrogatory note, and Carina stooped to pick it up and bury her face in its fur. "Do you think Bram'll be all right?" Jena heard her say in a muffled voice.

With a pang, Jena put her hand on the younger girl's shoulder. "I know how your parents feel about magic, Carina. But believe me, if Arikan said his spells would keep Bram safe, they will." *And Arikan, don't you make a liar out of me.*

Carina looked up at Jena with sad, puzzled eyes. "Why did you leave, Jena?"

"It didn't have anything to do with Bram and me. And it was totally unexpected and . . . not entirely voluntary on my part."

Carina frowned. "But if Bram—"

"Never mind that now, Carina, please. The important thing is, I'm back and I want to see Bram safely home, too. By the way . . ." she said hesitatingly, "there was a stranger who was just in here, asking for Bram. Did he say what he wanted? Has he been here before?"

Carina let the cat jump down from her arms. "Stranger?"

"Rather stocky, with a close-cropped beard, wearing a dark green cloak and a mariner's cap. You were just speaking with him."

Carina frowned and shook her head. "I don't remember . . . but I don't think there's been anyone in the shop like that today."

"Well, it's not important," Jena said lightly over her stab of uneasiness. *Hiding his possibilities, was he? Well, Bram wasn't here, and maybe that's for the best, after all.* "If you don't think it's a good idea for me to speak with your parents at the moment, perhaps I should go home now. I haven't even been there yet. And I need to find Arikan, so he can tell me more." *I have to have more information before I can scry the possibilities.* "After I've talked with him, perhaps . . ."

"I don't know if there's anything you can do," said Carina gloomily.

"Maybe. Maybe not." She gave Bram's sister another hug. "Don't look so forlorn, Carina. Bram'll be fine, and home before we know it."

Carina managed a small smile. "I hope you're right."

Jena raised her arm to lift the hood of her cloak and stopped, arrested by the feel of the small bundle in her sleeve. "Oh—could you do a favor for me?"

"Of course, Jena. What is it?"

Jena took out and unwrapped the muslin package the herbwoman had made up, and pressed the small herb pillow into Carina's hands. "Could you please put this under the pillow on Bram's bed? She stopped and took a deep breath, but her voice cracked anyway. "It should be there, waiting for him, when he returns."

Carina nodded and pressed her hand. Jena picked up her bundle and turned to go, the sudden tears in her eyes making her stumble a little at the threshold as she left the shop.

The sight of the house on Goldberry Lane brought a lump to her throat. All the blossoms in the acacia grove were gone. She had barely set foot in the garden when the door to the house opened and out came Collas, striding toward her. He swept her into his arms and held her close. "Jena, Jena. Oh, *child*," he said, with a catch in his voice. "I've been beside myself all day, waiting for you to come home."

Jena dropped her bundle and hugged him back with all her strength, squeezing her eyes tightly as she savored the feeling of his arms around her. "I'm here," she choked. "I'm finally here. Oh, Father, I'm so sorry."

She hastily dried her eyes with the back of her hand and pulled away to look up at him. Collas' soft blue eyes were filled with tears, but he was smiling as he softly pushed back a strand of hair from her forehead. Did his hair look slightly grayer, his eyes just a little more worn? Tenderly, Jena kissed his cheek. "How did you know I was—oh." Over Collas' shoulder, she saw Arikan step out into the garden and come toward her with his hands extended, a warm smile in his eyes.

"Welcome home, Jena," he said, enveloping her hands in his. "I knew today would be the day."

"Arikan," she murmured, and gave him a hug, too. She sniffed and laughed. "I need a handkerchief."

Collas picked up her bundle and waved them forward. "Come inside, come inside. There's some hot mulled wine, all ready and waiting. Are you hungry, my dear?"

"Famished," Jena replied.

They trooped into the house. Inside the doorway, Jena unfastened the catch of her cloak as she looked around, drinking in the sight of the familiar, beloved room. Collas put her bundle in a corner and hastened down the hallway, calling for the servants to bring in the wine. Arikan seated himself at the front table and regarded her steadily. At his look, she smiled self-consciously. "Do I look very different?"

"I know you are different," Arikan replied gravely. "Aren't you?"

"More than I even know myself yet, I suppose." She nodded toward the hallway where Collas had gone. "Has it been very hard on Father?"

Arikan raised an eyebrow. "Well, now, I suppose you'd have to ask him."

"What have you told him?"

"That when you discovered magic within yourself, you became caught in a spell which took you far away, but that you were under the protection of people who would teach you and be good to you."

"The simple truth is best, I suppose," sighed Jena.

"No: it's not simple. And it isn't entirely the truth. I said nothing, for example, about wizardry."

"Did he—" she began, and then broke off because Collas was returning, followed by a servant girl Jena didn't recognize, carrying a tray with wine and honey cakes.

"Sit down and eat, Jena," said Collas, drawing two more chairs up to the table. "This is just a morsel; we'll be having a proper meal served within the hour."

"Thank you, Father." Jena hung her cloak on a hook by the door and seated herself along with him as Arikan adroitly appropriated the wine jug from the servant girl's hand and began pouring. Jena picked up a cake and bit into it, scattering sticky crumbs. "Delicious," she said through a mouthful, smiling at Collas as she accepted the cup Arikan handed her. A little silence fell as she drank. She could all but see the questions hovering on Collas' lips, and the difficulty with which he restrained himself from asking them. Arikan simply ran his fingers through his beard with a small, inscrutable smile.

Jena broke off another corner of the cake as the servant girl left. "Has . . . has business been going well, Father?"

Collas seemed to need a moment to shift his thoughts from the channel they had been following. "Ah, yes . . . well, quite well. Oh, of course, commissions have been down in general because everything is in hiatus with the Court until the Diamond's condition is clarified. Still, there have been Solstice orders, including some big pieces."

"Have the servants been keeping the workshop in order? Has the household been running properly?"

"Why, yes," Collas replied, slightly puzzled by the question. "As satisfactorily as always, I think."

It took Jena a moment to recognize the feelings this report caused, and once she did, she allowed herself a little private amusement. *It seems Father can get along without me. Does that disappoint me? Perhaps I expected the shop would fall apart once I'd left?* "I'm glad," she said, her voice carefully neutral, "that everything's been going well since I left."

Arikan said nothing, although his smile became more of a grin.

"Except for missing you, of course," Collas replied.

"Well, I'm very glad to be home."

"I've taken on another apprentice," Collas went on, "a lad named Stephano, from Cheversee."

"Does he look promising?"

"Clever fingers, although he's a lazy little urchin. We'll see. Also, I've been negotiating with the Guild about having another journeyman posted here." He took a sip of wine, avoiding her eyes.

But Jena replied easily enough, "Yes, that would be best, since I still want the Chulipse post. Of course, we'd still be together in the summers."

Collas looked at her then, with surprise and a dawning delight. "So you've decided to appeal after all. You're not . . ." he added hesitantly, glancing at Arikan, "going to be concentrating on magical studies full-time?"

"I'm a gemcutter, Father, whatever else I may be."

"This year's deadline for reapplication is very close, you know."

"I cast my piece at Master Rolly's shop at Tenaway, and it just needs a bit more burnishing and the setting of the stones. I'll use some I've already cut." She got up, went over to her pack, and pulled out the carved wooden box which held the buckle. Collas' eyes lit up as she unwrapped it for him to see.

"Ah." He carefully took it from her, and turned it around in his fingers. "Well done, my dear. I'll be anxious to see the finished piece." He reached for his wine cup again. "So you were in Tenaway, then?" he asked with a cautious casualness.

"No. I only came back via that direction." She glanced at Arikan, who only sipped his wine with a suspicious innocence, uncharacteristically quiet and obviously unwilling to help. Jena sighed. "I was farther north, at the Duone Keep on the Orbo River. Have you heard of Lord Ranulf Duone?"

"Lord Duone?" Collas frowned. "I've heard that name recently."

"Probably because he's one of the Emerald candidates," put in Arikan.

Collas turned to Jena with a look of surprise. "Indeed?"

She nodded. "Yes. That's how I got an escort home: his party was traveling here to meet with the Diadem Council. His brother . . ." she stopped and took a sip of wine to steady her nerves. "His brother, Lord Morgan, was the lord who brought the stone Arikan advised you not to cut."

"Shortly before you . . . you left. Is this Lord Morgan involved, somehow," Collas said slowly, choosing his words with care, "in why and how you ended up at Duone Keep?"

"Yes."

Collas waited, but Jena didn't elaborate. "Well," he said finally, "I'd gathered that the nobility didn't generally consider pursuing magic to be terribly proper, much less teaching it."

"I didn't say he was my teacher, Father," she replied. She remembered what Lady Kestrienne had said, that magic could be muddled by lies. *Well, it's the truth.* "I did receive some lessons in magic at Duone Keep, but from someone else. Frankly, I don't think Lord Duone would have approved, had he known. And as for Lord Morgan, as a matter of fact I haven't seen him since the end of summer myself, and it's rather urgent that I locate him again. I was hoping Arikan could help me."

"Perhaps I can," said the wizard.

"Why do you need to find him, Jena?" asked Collas. "If you don't mind my asking." His expression seemed to say that whatever it was, he hoped it wouldn't mean more trouble.

"For one thing," Jena said lightly, "he commissioned my reapplication piece. I'm going to be giving it to the intended recipient tomorrow, and so I'll be offering a sketch for the reapplication rather than the piece itself. I suppose the Guild will wish to speak with Lord Morgan about it and to inspect the piece, to make everything official."

"We can work on determining his whereabouts tonight, if you like, Jena," offered Arikan.

Jena certainly wanted to spend some time with Arikan alone, to talk with him about Bram at the very least. But she also needed to see Lady Rhuddlan as soon as possible. "We might, but I think I should concentrate on finishing the buckle tonight instead. And Father," Jena added, lightly touching the pouch holding her talisman stone through her sleeve, "I also need a gold setting, if you have one to spare.

"I want to make myself a ring."

CHAPTER
FIFTEEN

ARMED WITH A LETTER OF IN-
troduction from Lady Kestrienne, Jena presented herself late
the following morning at Lady Vianne Rhuddlan's palazzo
on the Golden Rim. Unlike some of the Diadem families, the
Ruby family maintained its central seat, Rhuddlan Palazzo,
in Chulipse. But the family's Piyar residence was impressive
enough, with a gracious, well-proportioned limestone facade
and neatly landscaped grounds. Jena was admitted at the
front entryway by a servant in elegant livery who requested,
politely enough, to know her business.

"My name is Jena Gemcutter," Jena replied as confidently
as she could. "And I'm the daughter of Collas Gemcutter,
who has received commissions from the Ruby in the past.
I've been out of the city until only yesterday, and so I don't
have an appointment, but I wish to request an audience with
her grace." She flourished the carved box she held. "I've
come to convey Solstice greetings and to bring Lady Rhuddlan a gift from my patron, someone whom I trust is a dear
friend of hers."

"And that person is?"

Jena hesitated. "I'd like to tell her privately, if you please,
but I have here a letter of introduction from the Lady Kestri-

enne, lately of Duone Keep. Would you take it to her grace and convey my request for the kindness of a meeting with her?"

The servant accepted the letter and escorted Jena to an anteroom to wait. Jena sat down on the seat provided and tried to distract her nerves by looking around. Remembering some of the rueful comments her father had made in the past about the former Ruby's taste for garish ostentation, she was a bit surprised by the restrained style of the room. The heavily gilded panels and sentimental, gaudy mosaics Collas had described were nowhere to be seen. Instead, a simple white and black marbled floor, polished to a high gloss, and finely carved cypress panels and pilasters gave the room an easy elegance. Apparently, Lady Rhuddlan had taken it upon herself to redecorate since ascending to the family seat. *Even if Lady Rhuddlan's opinions about magic differ from Lord Morgan's, at least her tastes will blend nicely with his.*

One especially luxurious touch was a mirror in a richly carved frame on one wall. Jena, who had never seen one so big, went over to examine her reflection. Critically, she smoothed the narrow pleats at the waist of her dark blue wool skirt and plucked a bit at the edge of her chemise to even out the narrow ruffle. It felt strange to be wearing a dress with pockets again, rather than pouches, but she still wore one of Liselle's hair snoods. It did flatter the shape of her face, she thought, softening the line more than her old hair braid did. Her dark blue eyes looked a little anxious, perhaps, but other than that, she thought she presented a pleasing picture. Jena took a deep breath and stared at the new ring on the fourth finger of her right hand, a simple gold hoop set with her talisman stone. *I hope she will listen to me. Surely she will. Only . . . what am I going to say?*

A sound behind her made her turn. It was the servant again, who bowed as Jena stepped forward. "Her grace will see you now," he said, and turned to lead the way.

Jena followed him to the door of a morning room adjacent to the central courtyard. Here, the servant knocked, opened the door, and announced her. A woman's voice from within answered, courteously bidding Jena to enter, and the servant bowed and withdrew. With the underside of her sleeve, Jena surreptitiously wiped the top of the box she held and then stepped over the threshold.

The brightness of the light pouring through the courtyard roundel windows made Jena blink, and it took her a moment to see the Ruby, seated at a writing desk near the fire. As the sunlight fell across the books and parchments on the desk, it turned the soft blond of her hair to a warm honey gold. The noblewoman swiveled in her seat to face Jena, and the erect posture of her slender figure and the set of her chin gave her an air of quiet dignity. She was older than Jena would have expected: women of the nobility usually married in their teens, but if Jena was any judge, the Ruby had to be in her late twenties at least. A generous forehead balanced the firm set of her jaw and fine curve of her mouth. She had a warm, delicately golden undertone to her skin and hair, which meant that the traditional deep red color of her house would not suit her, and she had sense enough to know it. She wore a dress of muted aquamarine, with only the red ribbons attaching her sleeves and a red band at the neckline acknowledging her hereditary station. Pinned to her bodice was the Sunburst, the famous suite of stones set in a brooch in a graduated rainbow array of colors, traditionally worn by each year's Diamond Heir. She was also wearing the parure set Collas had fashioned for her, including the belt for which Jena had designed her buckle.

The lady's cool jade eyes studied Jena with a grave intelligence. Something about her gaze aroused Jena's hopes as she stepped forward and curtsied. "I am deeply grateful to you for agreeing to meet with me on such short notice, your grace."

At the sound of Jena's voice, a rust-colored terrier that had been sleeping in a pillowed basket at Lady Rhuddlan's feet raised its head and sprang to its feet, giving a short, sharp bark. Lady Rhuddlan reached down to restrain it as it started forward.

"Hush, Marzipan, sit. Quiet, if you please." She patted the dog's head absently as it reluctantly obeyed and then turned her attention back to Jena. "Lady Kestrienne is an old family friend. I'm happy to do her the service of granting your request."

Jena opened her mouth to answer—and stopped. Something about the room nudged at her memory, yet when had she ever been here before? Suddenly she realized: the walls of the room had been hung with rose silk. She had seen a vision of those hangings before, twice, when attempting to scry her talisman stone to find Morgan. Jena felt herself begin to break out in a sweat. *Lady Rhuddlan couldn't possibly be in league with Kett.*

Could she?

She reached for a protective ward, but some instinct stopped her. *No. Don't react with defensiveness. Trust, and be open. Don't shut her out.*

"Jena Gemcutter? Is something amiss?" Lady Rhuddlan's voice held no threat, only a mild curiosity.

Jena pulled herself together. "A bright Solstice season, your grace. I've brought something which my patron hopes will bring you pleasure." She stepped forward and carefully placed the box on a marquet table.

Lady Rhuddlan rose gracefully and came forward to look at the box, but had to stop to grab for the terrier's collar, who had seized the opportunity to start forward eagerly toward Jena again. "Down, Marzipan," the Ruby exclaimed. "You bad dog!" Thwarted, the terrier began barking noisily. "I'm sorry," Lady Rhuddlan said ruefully above the din as the dog danced and twisted, trying to escape her grip. "He doesn't usually act this way."

Another servant, a woman, entered the room, carrying a hot chocolate tray. "Ah, Heredia," Lady Rhuddlan said. "Could you please take this noisy playmate of mine away? He needs to learn to behave himself better when company calls."

But as the servant stepped forward, the terrier immediately stopped barking and sat up on its hindquarters, waving a paw in the air. "You rascal," Lady Rhuddlan said warmly. "So you're promising to behave yourself now, sir? What if I decide it's too late?" Marzipan gave a little yip and then, with an agile spring, did a backflip. Lady Rhuddlan burst out laughing as Jena gasped. The terrier then settled meekly at its mistress' feet with its head on its paws, eying Jena, however, with a keen look that made her uncomfortable.

"Never mind, Heredia," amended Lady Rhuddlan, seating herself. "Please leave our refreshment there on the table and draw up another seat for my guest. If this little fellow continues to behave himself, he may stay."

After pouring out the chocolate and adding more coal to the fire, the servant left. Shyly, Jena sat down and accepted the delicate porcelain cup Lady Rhuddlan offered her, raising it from its saucer in a toast. "To your very good health, your grace." She took a careful sip. The chocolate, spiced with a hint of cinnamon, tasted delicious.

Lady Rhuddlan gravely accepted the salute with a nod and drank, too. "I remember your father," she remarked as she put down her cup. "Such splendid work. He made this carcanet and belt, you know, and they have pleased me much."

"Yes, your grace. In fact, the piece I've brought you today was designed to blend with that set."

Lady Rhuddlan eyed the carved box between them curiously. "And this was commissioned by a friend of mine, you say, as a Solstice gift?"

"Not . . . exactly, your grace. I mean—not as a Solstice gift. Would your grace care to open it?"

Lady Rhuddlan's fingertips brushed the lid of the box and paused. Her voice sounded politely perplexed. "And whom do I have to thank for this gift, Jena Gemcutter?"

Jena stared at the box—and panicked.

Her magic had told her Morgan and Lady Rhuddlan were betrothed. *But what if she were wrong?* What if she were making a terrible mistake? The repercussions, the possible political embarrassment for Morgan, if ever he could be found . . . Jena squeezed her hands tightly together and opened her mouth, wondering how she could possibly back out now. For a long pause, no sound escaped—and then she managed to force out one word from between frozen lips.

"Guess."

Lady Rhuddlan raised an eyebrow and opened the box.

For a long moment, she said nothing. Then, gently, her finger stroked the glistening surface of the belt buckle and ran over the central cut ruby. "It's exquisite," she said in a low voice. "A truelove knot . . . " Suddenly her finger stopped and her face grew rigid with surprise. "Morgan?" she breathed.

Jena let out her breath in a tiny gasp of relief.

One, two, three heartbeats—and then Lady Rhuddlan's face crumpled. Blindly she seized a handkerchief from her sleeve and buried her face in it, her shoulders shaking.

For a moment, Jena was too astonished to speak. "Your grace," she gulped finally, appalled. "*Lady Rhuddlan! I . . . I—*"

Lady Rhuddlan looked up, tears streaming down her face, and seized Jena's hand. "Oh, have you seen him? Have you?" she implored.

"I . . . I—no, my lady—I mean, your grace," Jena stuttered. "Not since—not since before Equinox."

Lady Rhuddlan's terrier hastened to its feet again and stood up on its hind legs to paw at her skirt, whimpering. Lady Rhuddlan picked it up and held it close, and the terrier licked at her chin. "I'd hoped—it's been so long. There hasn't been a word for him, not one. And there was no one in whom I could confide. No one!" She looked down at the dog in her lap and tried to smile. "No one but Marzipan, that is. I trust him to keep his own counsel." She looked up again at Jena, her eyes brimming. "Morgan told you, I see."

"I—you may trust me to keep the secret, Lady Rhuddlan," Jena said.

"I thought he had disappeared without a trace because of our last quarrel. And yet, after all the dreadful things I said to him," Lady Rhuddlan said wonderingly, touching the buckle again, "he still sends me a truelove knot." A desperate sadness crossed her face as she gently stroked her pet's ears. "If only I could see him again, to tell him how sorry I am, and how much . . . how much I love him." Her dog snuggled closer into her waist, crooning at the distress in her voice.

Jena shifted uncomfortably, hoping she wasn't wooing the lady for a match Lord Morgan had decided he didn't want after all. "I . . . I think I know a little about what your quarrel might have been about. You'd discovered something about him that made you uncomfortable, made you doubt your future together?"

Lady Rhuddlan's cheeks turned pink. "Yes," she admitted in a low voice.

"Something not generally accepted by your family and friends," Jena went on. "Something like . . . like magic?"

Lady Rhuddlan was silent, but Jena didn't need to scry to see she had spoken the truth.

"Your grace," Jena said gently, "I'm very sorry. My fiancé is far away at the moment, too, so I know a little bit of how you must be feeling." *It's different for me, though,* Jena thought, looking at Lady Rhuddlan's lowered head. It had been Bram's choice to go north to find her, Arikan had told her the previous night once they were alone. Pushed a little further, the wizard added he had sensed the possibility of danger for the tailor in Piyar, and so he hadn't tried to talk Bram out of the journey. Remembering Kett's appearance at the shop, Jena couldn't be angry. But Lady Rhuddlan didn't even have the comfort of knowing why her fiancé was gone, and what was worse, she had to hide her worry and self-reproach from everyone.

"Don't blame yourself for Lord Morgan's silence, your grace," Jena went on. "I believe he would have returned to work this out with you long ago—except he is being prevented from doing so."

Lady Rhuddlan looked up quickly. "Prevented?"

"I have reason to think so, yes. I need to find him, too, and I have some ideas about where to start searching. Perhaps, if we put our heads together, we might help each other."

Lady Rhuddlan smiled slowly and nodded. She gave her eyes another wipe with her handkerchief and settled her dignity around her again. "Your present has given me hope, Jena Gemcutter. I—" She looked down at her girdle, as if struck by a sudden thought. "I should like to try it on. Will you help me?"

"Gladly, your grace."

Lady Rhuddlan unbuckled the girdle and handed it to Jena, who unhooked the old buckle from the chain and set it carefully on the table. She took the new buckle from its box, hooked it to the fasteners, and handed the reconfigured belt back to Lady Rhuddlan.

"Marzipan, my love, you'll have to jump down." As the

terrier hopped down off her lap, Lady Rhuddlan stood up and refastened the girdle about her waist.

"Is it comfortable, your grace?" Jena asked.

Lady Rhuddlan nodded and started to speak—and then stopped. Her smile disappeared, and she slowly turned pale. Her hands began to shake.

"Your grace?" Jena said. "Are you all right?"

Lady Rhuddlan abruptly turned and walked to the window. She stood with her back turned, rigid for a moment or two.

"Your grace?" Jena tried again.

"Is this magic?" Lady Rhuddlan said, her voice hushed and tense.

"What?"

"This . . . this feeling, this knowledge." Lady Rhuddlan turned to face her again. Now her face was ash-gray. "The buckle is . . . is ensorcelled! It tells me that . . . that . . ." She swayed, and started blindly forward, stumbling over a stool as Jena watched with growing alarm. "Morgan?" Lady Rhuddlan said in a voice tight with fear. "Morgan, Morgan, where are you?"

"My lady, I—"

"He's in the room!" Lady Rhuddlan cried hoarsely. "It tells me he's in the room!" She blundered forward again as Jena stared, bewildered. "Morgan? Morgan, answer me!" Lady Rhuddlan's terrier began barking and running around her in circles, and then leaping into the air in a frenzy.

"Your grace, please sit down." Jena helped Lady Rhuddlan back into her chair as Marzipan continued barking. Lady Rhuddlan started fumbling at the belt buckle, but her hands were shaking too hard to remove it herself. "If you will allow me to help you, your grace?" Jena knelt and reached for the buckle—and then sat back in surprise as Marzipan leaped into her lap. Before she could push the terrier off again, it placed a paw delicately on top of Jena's talisman ring, looked up into her face, and spoke.

"It's about time you got here!"

Lady Rhuddlan clapped a hand over her mouth with a stifled cry.

"*Morgan?*" Jena gasped.

CHAPTER SIXTEEN

"WHO ELSE WOULD IT BE?" growled Morgan.

Jena didn't know whether to laugh, cry, or wring his scruffy neck. Partnering, which had worsened her temper, apparently hadn't soothed his—but then, she supposed being turned into a terrier must be extraordinarily provoking. "I wouldn't know. I've never talked with a terrier before."

Morgan/Marzipan blinked, and the most extraordinary expression crossed his face—if a dog could be said to have an expression. "I *am* talking," he said, astonished. And he was, in a strange, rough voice. Almost a furry voice, Jena thought a little wildly. Some of the words weren't entirely clear; they must have been more difficult for a dog's mouth and throat to shape. But he could be understood.

The ring, Jena thought. *It happened when he touched my ring. After all, the talisman is supposed to be the instrument of communication between partners.* "And if you're going to keep talking, I'd better go lock the door. If . . . if you will get down?" Morgan hopped off Jena's lap, and she went over to turn the key in the lock. Then she came back and simply stared.

"Would you look to my lady?" Morgan said quietly.

Jena glanced up quickly and, seeing that Lady Rhuddlan's color had gone beyond ash-gray to a kind of sickly green, picked up the Ruby's hot chocolate cup to offer it to her. It seemed a laughably inadequate restorative, under the circumstances.

"There's some wine there on the sideboard," Morgan offered.

Jena went to get it and poured out a glass for the Ruby, who took it mechanically and tossed it down in one unladylike gulp, and then choked. Jena swatted her deftly between the shoulder blades as Lady Rhuddlan gasped and wheezed. "I'm sorry, your grace," Jena said. "I suppose this isn't exactly the reunion you had imagined."

"All this time . . . while I was—" Lady Rhuddlan started, and then began coughing in earnest. "You were—oh, my—" After a moment or two, she managed to catch her breath, and a little color crept back into her face. Both women stared at Morgan, sitting on the floor, the tip of his tail moving restlessly. Lady Rhuddlan's knuckles whitened around her wine cup. "I . . . I *undressed* in front of you for almost three months!"

A dreadful silence fell.

Morgan looked down at his paws. "I honestly tried not to look."

Jena felt a gurgle of laughter welling up. She tried to suppress it, but in the end collapsed into her seat, doubled over in convulsions of mirth. Lady Rhuddlan, if anything, looked more distressed as Morgan's hackles bristled. "How can you laugh so?" cried Lady Rhuddlan, her face flaming scarlet. "It isn't funny!"

Jena wiped her streaming eyes. "Oh, forgive me, your grace, but yes, it is. If you two marry, you'll be undressing in front of each other anyway."

"But how can we marry?" Morgan exploded. "I'm a *dog*!"

Jena went off into another peal of laughter. Lady Rhuddlan shook her head and went off to the sideboard to pour herself more wine. She brought back a cup for Jena, too.

"Thank you, your grace. I'm sorry, truly. I didn't mean—" her lips twitched, and she took a swallow of wine and went on hastily. "But how did this happen, Morgan? And how did you end up in her grace's, er, custody?"

Morgan shook his head. "I'm not entirely sure. I remember being at Duone Keep with you, and then, suddenly, I found myself . . . on a boat? In some kind of cabin. I only had a moment to look around and see the room, when something hit me on the head." He winced. "I . . . I woke up quite some time later, I think. A man brought me a tray of food."

"Did you know him?"

"I'd never seen him before in my life, but he certainly knew about me. He said things . . ." Morgan broke off and looked away.

"What?" asked Jena.

"I don't want to talk about it right now," Morgan answered crossly.

"But if—"

"I *said,* I don't choose to talk about it."

The two women looked at each other.

"What did he look like?" Lady Rhuddlan asked.

Morgan wrinkled his nose. "Tall. Dark beard. Don't know if it was brown or black, because I had little light to see by. Thick chest, well-developed arms, but not fat."

"Did he have an earring, a black pearl set on a gold post?" asked Jena.

"I . . . I don't remember, but then, it was so dark."

"Do you remember seeing a woman?"

Morgan thought. "I never saw a woman . . . but maybe . . . I heard a woman's voice, at one point?" His tail beat the floor in concentration. "Things were hazy then, for quite a while. And the next time I came to myself, I was . . . I was changed . . . " His voice trailed off on a pained note.

"It must have been Kett," Jena muttered.

"Kett? The sea captain?" Lady Rhuddlan asked, frowning.

Jena gave her a quick look. "You know him?"

"Why, of course. He's the captain of the *Windspray,* one of ten ships in the Golden Fleet." The Golden Fleet traditionally transported the Diadem families when the Court moved between Piyar and Chulipse. "He gave me—" she stopped and looked at Morgan.

"He gave you *Morgan*?"

"That's *Lord* Morgan to you," said the dog icily.

"I'd sent a gift to the Mariner's Guild," Lady Rhuddlan went on in a puzzled voice. "Since the Golden Fleet wouldn't be getting its usual fee this year because the Court wouldn't be moving. And Captain Kett came to call, to tell me the Guild was grateful I had remembered them, and they wanted to show their appreciation by giving me a gift in return." She stopped, embarrassed.

"A terrier," Jena prompted.

"He said he'd found . . . the dog . . . on his travels, and that it was a breed well-known for its, uh . . . "

"Its what?" Morgan demanded.

Lady Rhuddlan turned red.

"Tell me, Vianne," Morgan said, baring his teeth.

Lady Rhuddlan clearly didn't want to, but Morgan insisted. "Its docility," she said finally. "He said you would make a very good pet."

Jena had to fight to keep her composure as Morgan snarled. "That bastard! That tar-eating scum! If I ever find him, I'll nail his guts to the wall!"

"I wonder why he hates you so," Jena said when she could trust herself to speak. "The wretch! He must have known you two were engaged and found a way to torment you by putting you together and yet keeping you apart."

"But how could he know?" Lady Rhuddlan demanded. "I never told anyone, whereas you—" she looked at Morgan speculatively.

"No," he said. "Well, I hinted to Ranulf, I will admit. I had to. But he would keep it to himself."

"But Jena knew," Lady Rhuddlan protested.

"No, he didn't tell me," Jena said. "I had clues I used to put it together. The same way Kett did, I expect: he's a wizard, and he scried it. But that still doesn't tell us: why should he have done this?"

Morgan looked blank.

"He's a what?" asked Lady Rhuddlan.

Jena would have bitten off her tongue, if she could. "Uh . . . well . . . " she floundered. "It's something I'm not sure I should explain to you, your grace."

"Why not?"

"Please. If I might, uh . . . speak with Lord Morgan alone?"

Lady Rhuddlan set her lips together mulishly. "If you have something to tell him about why this happened, I have a right to hear it, too."

"Well, yes, perhaps," Jena said lamely, "but it would involve also telling you some things I'm not sure you should know. Some things you might not want to know, given your, er, strong feelings about magic."

"I already told you," Lady Rhuddlan said slowly, "how sorry I am for what I said about that. Morgan, you heard me."

"Jena, what—" Morgan began.

"Hush, Morgan. Let me think."

Apparently surprised by her peremptory demand, Morgan fell silent as Jena thought furiously. "By telling you," she said finally, "I'd be putting both my life and Lord Morgan's into your hands. I'd be giving you a kind of power over us I'm not sure is altogether wise. I can only do it if I have your promise you won't harm us. Choose whatever oath you think most binding, your grace, and if Morgan trusts it, I'll tell you."

Morgan swelled with noble fury. "You would *dare* doubt the word of Lady Vianne Rhuddlan? You are my pupil, under my authority, and I order you—"

"I'm not your pupil, Morgan—" Jena began.

"*Lord* Morgan," he practically barked.

"I'm your partner."

"You're his what?" asked Lady Rhuddlan.

Jena narrowed her eyes. "Only if you swear."

Lady Rhuddlan considered, and then lifted her chin proudly. "Very well, then. I won't use whatever you might tell me to hurt either of you. I swear by . . . " she glanced at Morgan, "by my love for Lord Morgan."

Jena hesitated. "Such an oath might prove a double-edged sword if that love doesn't survive the telling of what I reveal."

Morgan looked as if he were considering biting her.

"Then I swear by the Sunburst—and by the Adamant Throne. Will that do?"

Jena looked at Morgan, who nodded, apparently unable to

trust himself to speak. "Very well, then. Listen carefully. I have much to tell you both."

The telling took a long time. At midday, Lady Rhuddlan ordered a meal, and her servants brought in a luncheon of cold pheasant, served with dressing and jellied quince. After the servants left and the door was locked again behind them, Lady Rhuddlan looked at Morgan in some embarrassment. "Would you like to, er, get up on the table and join us, Morgan?"

"No, thank you," he answered with dignity. "It would be fine if you would just put a plate down on the floor for me, please."

Lady Rhuddlan cut some pheasant into small pieces, arranged them on a plate for him, and set it down. He waited politely for a moment or two, and then stepped forward and daintily began his meal.

Lady Rhuddlan forced her eyes away and deliberately picked up her fork. "What you have told us, Jena, is remarkable," she said finally, after seeming to search for a moment or two for something to say. "It will take a while to absorb it all. But the question is, what do we do now?"

Morgan looked up from his plate, licking his chops. "Find a way to change me back."

"Of course," Lady Rhuddlan answered gently. "That goes without saying. Only how?"

A little pause fell as the two women uneasily looked down at Morgan. *This is simply dreadful,* Jena found herself thinking. *He can't possibly stay this way; it's just too ridiculous and humiliating for all of us. But what if he can't be changed back?* She broke the silence first. "First let's add up what we know, and what we still need to learn. We should also think about how to use the advantages we have."

"Advantages?" Morgan said skeptically.

"Part of the spell over you has already been broken," Jena pointed out, trying to sound confident. "You can talk now. That shows us it may be possible to break the rest of it, too."

"How did that happen, anyway?" asked Lady Rhuddlan. "Is it because he touched you?"

"Not exactly. I think it happened because he touched my ring."

"What ring?"

Jena sighed and held up her hand. "My talisman ring. You can't see it, can you?" Lady Rhuddlan shook her head. "It's here, on the fourth finger of my right hand." She gave Morgan a curious look. "You were already a magician before we partnered, but you didn't know about wizards or their talismans, so how did you know to touch it?"

"I'm not sure," Morgan admitted. "But I felt the aura of power around it drawing me as soon as you walked into the room."

"The same way yours drew me, I suppose," Jena said. "If we could get your own ring back from Kett, that might break the rest of the spell."

They considered this. "This is my dispute to settle with him," Morgan said slowly, shifting his weight from paw to paw. "I don't like the thought of either of you getting involved."

The two women exchanged glances, and Jena rolled her eyes.

"We appreciate your concern, Morgan, but we already are involved," Lady Rhuddlan said mildly.

"It's bad enough he did this to me! What if he tries one of his spells on you?"

"I've already had at least one magical encounter with him," Jena pointed out, "and it didn't turn out so dreadfully. At least I learned a little. I think he may be overconfident." She tapped a finger against her plate. "Consider, Morgan: somehow you're a threat to him, or he wouldn't have done this to you, but now he thinks you're neutralized. He told me to go away and forget you. Perhaps he thinks he succeeded with me, too."

"Your partnership must interfere with his plans somehow," Lady Rhuddlan said, nodding. "What he doesn't know, at least not yet, is that the two of you have found each other again."

"Now we can act together as a team, which is the way wizards are meant to work. You're a part of this, too, your grace."

"Me?"

"Kett had Morgan in his power, a prisoner on his ship. But because he couldn't resist a cruel joke, he turned Morgan over to you." Jena raised an eyebrow. "The Ruby, the Diamond Heir, Lady Vianne Rhuddlan, one of the most powerful women in the land. Tell me, how can he get that little dog back from you now, once he's given it away as a gift? Particularly since you've grown so very fond of it?" She watched as her words sank in. "I think it would be safest, your grace, if you take your pet with you everywhere you go from now on until we can decide how to proceed. You may get a reputation of being a little eccentric, I'm afraid, but the two of you can protect each other."

"I'm not sure we could do anything to stop him," Morgan said. "He was able to seize me magically before. He might try to snatch me back again if he figures out we know the truth, and how would we find each other then?"

"My belt," Lady Rhuddlan said suddenly. She picked up the girdle from the table and stroked the buckle. "Morgan, as long as I'm wearing this, I'll always know where you are."

Jena blinked. "Are you sure? I tried the buckle on myself when I was finishing the fastenings, and I never noticed such an effect on me."

"I'm certain."

"Perhaps it depends on how far away the wearer is from Morgan? If you'd permit me . . ." Lady Rhuddlan handed the belt over and Jena experimentally wrapped it around her waist. "No," she said, shaking her head, "I don't feel anything."

"Let me see that belt here," Morgan said.

Jena placed it down on the floor beside him. He sniffed at it a bit, nosing the buckle, and then placed a paw on it, sitting still with half-closed eyes. "So this was your journeyman reapplication piece for the Guild, Jena?" he said finally.

Jena nodded.

Morgan grinned, showing sharp teeth. "It looks as though it was your journeyman piece as an adept at the same time. You've managed to work a very wide-ranging finder's spell right into the substance of the buckle."

"Did I?" Jena said, astonished. "But how?" She thought.

"I suppose—I remember I was wondering where you were when I worked on the model. Could I have worked the magic into it that way without knowing it?"

Morgan considered, tapping his tail absently. "I'm not sure. Why would the spell be specific to Vianne?"

"I did use a little gold from the nugget she gave you as a gift to make it. That might be the reason."

"Not the whole nugget, I hope," said Morgan.

"No, no," Jena hastened to assure him. "Just a tiny piece."

"Well, I'm indebted to you, in more ways than one," Morgan said, his voice a little amused. "You did a splendid job in making it to my, er—specifications. Thank you for executing your commission so faithfully." Jena wasn't sure, but she thought he winked at her. She let out a tiny sigh of relief.

"Now, as for getting rid of this transformation spell," Morgan went on briskly, "you're probably right, Jena. The first step is recovering my ring from Kett."

Lady Rhuddlan frowned. "I could come up with some kind of excuse that would require him to call upon me again," she said. "Then perhaps I could . . ." she trailed off uncertainly.

"We might eventually resort to a plan such as that," Jena said, overriding the beginnings of Morgan's protest, "but to do it safely, we first need to learn about Kett's blind spots."

"If I understand correctly what you've told us," said Morgan, "that means finding his partner, doesn't it? She's the one who guards them."

"How do you know it isn't the partner, not Kett, who's behind all this in the first place?" Lady Rhuddlan demanded.

"We don't, your grace," Jena admitted. "But if we can find out who she is, maybe that will give us enough pieces of the puzzle to figure out what they're up to."

"Or enough to play one partner off against the other?" Lady Rhuddlan asked.

"To interfere with the partnership, in other words?"

"Just as they've interfered with yours."

"That is, after all, why wizards keep their partners secret," said Jena. She thought for a moment. "When I encountered Kett through the ring, he said . . ." she paused to remember the exact words, and saw again the pained, gnawing loneliness in his eyes. "He said I was wiser than he had been, not to love someone too far above me." Morgan gave Lady Rhuddlan a quick look.

"Could it be you he loves, do you think, Vianne?" he said hesitantly. "Is that why he did this to me?"

The Ruby looked immensely startled. "I should think not! That is . . ." she stopped and considered and then shook her head. "No, I don't see how it could conceivably be me. I know who he is, but I've only seen him once or twice, and we've never had a truly private conversation together."

"Hmm." Jena leaned forward and thoughtfully picked up a sugared nut to nibble. "Well, how about this as an idea? If he's been hurt by someone above his station, what if it was his partner? After all, the strongest wizards are those from very different backgrounds, and we know Kett and his partner must be very powerful indeed to have created the spell that spirited Morgan away."

"His partner might be someone below him in social class, not above," said Morgan doubtfully.

"Maybe. But when he spoke of loving someone above him, I had a feeling, a hunch, that . . . a kind of balance needed restoring. And it seemed . . . tied in with his magic somehow." She looked at Lady Rhuddlan and Morgan. "So let's suppose Kett's partner is someone very high above him."

"If he's a member of the Golden Fleet," Morgan suggested, "perhaps he partnered with someone he met during one of those yearly trips."

Jena nodded. "That's another reason to suspect his partner's above him rather than below. What if the imbalance I sensed had something to do with the partnering relationship itself? What if the imbalance happened because Kett fell in love with her, but she rejected him?"

"A sea captain in love with a noblewoman? You can't be serious!" said Lady Rhuddlan.

"If I'm right, I can imagine she might have said the very same thing," Jena observed wryly.

Lady Rhuddlan looked at them both as if they'd lost their minds. "But . . . someone among the *Diadem families?* Using magic?" A look of distaste passed across her face, and she seemed to shudder. "No! There's never been anyone . . ." she stopped and glanced at Morgan, turning red.

"Until now," Morgan said. Lady Rhuddlan looked away, unable to meet his eyes.

"But that isn't even necessarily true," Jena said. "I have reason to know the perished Emerald Heir would have been born a potential adept." Lady Rhuddlan opened her mouth, as if to protest, and then shut it again.

"If there have been others, they've kept it secret," Morgan said, watching Lady Rhuddlan narrowly, "just as I plan to do."

Lady Rhuddlan closed her eyes in genuine pain. "Morgan, we've had all this out before—"

"Your grace," Jena broke in gently, "if we're successful in breaking the spell and you two marry, you can't simply ask Morgan to give up his magic. It's a part of him now. It may even be a part of what he'll bequeath to your children."

They waited as Lady Rhuddlan swirled the wine in her cup in silence. "Magic is one thing," she said finally in a low voice. "Morgan, if . . . if you were only a magician, maybe I could learn to accept that. All the thinking I've done since we last spoke has brought me to that point at least. But wizardry . . ." Lady Rhuddlan looked at them both with a haunted expression. "Wizardry means there's another . . . another factor in your life."

It took Jena a moment to realize that Lady Rhuddlan meant her. She thought of Bram, who would be facing the same problem, if she ever found him again. *I'm not your rival, your grace,* she wanted to say, but she kept silent. Morgan and Lady Rhuddlan had to work this problem out themselves.

Morgan looked up at Lady Rhuddlan. "Wizard or no, I'd hoped my gift would at least reassure you where my heart lies, Vianne. And that you'll never lose me again." He nosed the belt across the floor until it rested beside Lady Rhuddlan's shoe. "That is, if you still want me?"

Slowly Lady Rhuddlan picked the belt from the floor and fingered it in her lap. "A finder's spell . . . Even if I'm not entirely sure about magic, I can see how such a spell might be useful for a wife to have." The wry smile tugging at the corner of her mouth dissipated the tension that had been building in the room.

"Well, let's suppose for the moment you are correct, Jena," Lady Rhuddlan said with the air of someone changing the subject. "Suppose Kett's partner is a noblewoman, maybe even someone among the Diadem families. That still leaves the question: what could possibly make your partnership a threat to them?"

"The partnership may have been the precipitating factor—the reason why they decided to act," Jena said thoughtfully. "But the actual threat to them might lie elsewhere."

Morgan cocked his head. "What are you talking about?"

"Kett knew about your engagement. Perhaps the difficulty lies somehow within the links Morgan's entire family is forging with the Diadem. After Lord Duone's experience—"

"What?" Morgan said sharply, his ears swiveling forward.

"Lord Duone?" Lady Rhuddlan said simultaneously, sitting up straight. "What has happened to him?"

"You don't know? I mean, hasn't he contacted you?"

"Why, yes, he has. He sent a message saying he wished to call upon me this afternoon. In fact," Lady Rhuddlan said, glancing at the small golden clock on her desk, "I was expecting his arrival very shortly."

And so Jena told the tale of what happened in Tenaway. By the time she had finished, Morgan was sputtering in rage. "Of all the despicable, cowardly, loathsome . . ." and the rest of what he meant to say was lost in a series of ferocious snarls. When he had recovered somewhat, he shook himself all over fiercely. "It seems my brother owes you his life, Jena."

"Indeed, I am grateful, too," said Lady Rhuddlan, shock visible on her face. "I had no idea this had happened."

"No doubt he intends to tell you about it when he meets with you. He'll also be asking for the Council's permission to call me as a witness to testify at tonight's meeting."

"He shall have it," Lady Rhuddlan said with swift assurance. "The Diadem must hear this tale." She stared into space for a moment with narrowed eyes, drumming her fingers on the table. "There are some I could have chosen as candidates who would react to such an attack by withdrawing from the Council's consideration, but I don't think Ranulf will." She gave Morgan a sly look. "Morgan likes to harp on their differences, but that's one way the two brothers are alike, at least. Being crossed tends to get their back up."

Jena nodded. "Lord Duone was shaken and angered, naturally. But I think this has only solidified his resolve to win the seat."

"He will win it," Morgan declared loyally. "He's by far the best candidate."

Lady Rhuddlan shook her head. "That's no guarantee, my innocent, especially when you're dealing with the Diadem. Ranulf must also have the best support. I'll do my utmost to give it to him." She cocked her head at Jena. "Do you know if Lord Duone has any theory about why this happened?"

"Well," Jena said, remembering the earring worn by the messenger, "I believe he has ideas—but I don't think I should speak for him, your grace."

"Of course." Lady Rhuddlan nodded. "Well, Morgan, if Jena is correct in thinking Kett or his partner is behind this, too, you must see that the quarrel now includes me, beyond the simple fact that you are my fiancé. Ranulf is my candidate. A blow aimed at him because I have put him forward is a blot against my House's honor, too." She looked determined. "It will be answered, never fear."

Morgan flattened his ears back against his head. Jena thought he wanted to argue further, but he said nothing.

"Well, if Lord Duone is coming to call soon," Jena said, rising, "perhaps I'd better go. After all, I've given you two much to think about." *And you might want to be alone for a while,* she added mentally.

Lady Rhuddlan nodded and rose, too. "Perhaps we might discuss our next steps some more tonight, after the Council meeting."

"It won't cause too much comment if you're seen speaking with me?"

"I'd be expected to want to question you individually about your report of events in Tenaway." Lady Rhuddlan looked down at the belt buckle in her hand and smiled. "And who knows? I might look in my jewelry box this afternoon and decide to commission another piece or two."

CHAPTER
SEVENTEEN

THAT NIGHT, WHEN JENA walked into the reception room adjoining the Diadem Chamber, ablaze with the light of dozens of tapers and crowded with the members and retinues of all the Houses, she was glad she had followed Collas' urging and worn dark gray.

"Formal Court occasions are when they bring out the most glittering colors," her father had told her. "The servants and attendants, on the other hand, usually wear pastels. You don't want to be perceived as trying to ape or outshine anyone. And you might create offense if you chose a color that indicates an alliance with a House that you don't intend or, mercy forbid, clashes with some haughty lady's new gown. If you want everyone in that quarreling bunch to listen to you and not treat you as a servant, sober neutrality will garner you the most respect and credibility."

Certainly the gathering of splendidly coiffed, bejeweled, and adorned lords, ladies, and retainers dazzled her eyes. The air, cloyingly fragrant from the scented tapers and jumbled mix of perfumes, hummed with conversation. Some glanced at her curiously. As Jena looked around a little helplessly, wondering where she was supposed to go, she saw Taras making his way through the crowd toward her. He gave her one of his curt little nods when he reached her side.

"Thank you for your promptness, Jena."

"I don't see his lordship. He's here, isn't he?"

"They're keeping the candidates sequestered in another room until presentation to the Council." He flourished a piece of parchment. "Here's the warrant that allows your entrance into the Council Chamber. As soon as the—oh, there it is." A bell chimed three times, sweetly, over the crowd's hubbub. The murmurs died down for a moment, and then a few people began drifting away from the sweetmeat and confectionery tables and toward the Diadem chamber, where the double doors stood flung open wide.

"Am I to go in now?" Jena asked Taras, who nodded, and gestured to her to join the people headed toward the Council chamber.

"I'll show you where to sit," he said.

At the door, Taras displayed the parchment to the usher stationed at the door. After a low-voiced conversation, the servant allowed them to pass. "Over there," Taras said in her ear, directing her with a touch on her elbow to the right as they entered the high dome-ceilinged room. Jena followed, craning her neck to study the brilliant fresco panels lining the room underneath the sweep of the dome, depicting scenes from the Founders' War. Eventually she realized Taras was indicating a bench along one of the walls, and she seated herself.

"Here's the parchment; give it to the steward when you're called upon to testify. I must leave you now to join Lord Duone's party."

"Thank you, Taras." He strode off, and Jena employed the minutes as other people settled onto the benches to study the crowded room.

Four chairs, now empty, stood in the center of the room facing the Diadem Council table, with several rows of benches ranged behind them. The Council table itself was made up of a short trestle table flanked by two longer ones set at an angle. Chairs for the Diadem members lined the outside table edges, each with a silk banner attached to the back indicating the House color. The seats for the heirs formed another row behind those for the heads of house-holds. The ornamented chair for the Diamond at the central short table was empty.

Lady Rhuddlan stepped up through the crowd and sat down in the smaller chair beside it; as the Diamond Heir, she would be presiding over the proceedings tonight. Besides Collas' parure set and Jena's buckle, she wore a tightly fit-ting gown with a bodice of ivory white brocaded silk, set with rubies at the juncture of the sleeves. The color of the skirt gradually changed from white just underneath the bodice to a deep crimson at the hemline. A servant appeared at her elbow and placed a large embroidered cushion on the table.

Seated on the cushion was Morgan.

Jena could tell that Lady Rhuddlan's companion was at-tracting some stares, but the Ruby simply settled herself back in her chair, magnificently at ease, scratching Morgan's ears with one hand as she reached for a wine goblet with the other. Jena bit down the urge to laugh.

Lady Rhuddlan's appearance at the Council table appar-ently was the cue for the other members of the Diadem and the heirs to find their places, too. Lady Julianna Golpier, the Amethyst, sank into the chair on Lady Rhuddlan's immedi-ate left. Twenty years the Ruby's senior, Lady Golpier had for decades been publicly praised for the beneficence of her works and privately ridiculed for the homeliness of her face. A portly woman with coarse features, she wore her fading chestnut hair in an elaborate arrangement of waves, puffs, and curls, in the vain hope (it was said) of detracting atten-tion from a prominent overbite. She was known to listen to any and all petitions for her attention with a degree of empa-thy that sometimes exasperated the more ruthless members of the Diadem. Those who tried to cross her, however, quickly learned she was nobody's fool.

Next to the Amethyst sat the oldest member of the Coun-cil, Lord Sebastian Alcide, the Sapphire. Despite the meticu-lous cut of the Sapphire's doublet and jerkin, his slight frame and scrawny neck made him look frail, and his blue-veined hands had a fine tremor. But his narrow eyes with beetling eyebrows missed nothing; he was widely known to have one of the most powerful voices on the Council.

In the last seat on Lady Rhuddlan's left was Lord Dolan Fedreggo, the Aquamarine. Mild-spoken and cautious, Lord Fedreggo had succeeded his late father to the Aquamarine's seat on the Diadem Council only two years before, and he still tended to defer to the more senior members. He sat with arms folded, watching the room through half-lidded eyes, his chair pulled back from the table to give his long legs room to stretch out before him. He had an athletic build with narrow, sloping shoulders and a handsome face set off by thick, prematurely graying hair.

To Lady Rhuddlan's immediate right, Lord Guilford Oselare, the Topaz, leaned over to speak with Lord Burne Teutaine, the Citrine. The two were second cousins, and a faint family resemblance could be detected in the breadth of their foreheads and the slight droop at the outer corners of their eyes. But where the Citrine was dark-haired and fleshy, even corpulent, the Topaz was blond and spare, his compact frame animated by an intense energy. Lord Teutaine idly picked at his teeth and stared off into space as he listened to the younger man. He shook his head at a question. Lord Oselare turned abruptly away, lips thinning as he poured himself a glass of wine.

To Lady Rhuddlan's far right, at the end of the table nearest to Jena, the chair for the Emerald remained empty, draped with green and black.

A man in white livery stepped into the space formed by the conjoining tables, bowed to Lady Rhuddlan, and rapped his staff three times on the marble floor. The last dawdlers hurried to the benches lining the walls. Jena had to shift over to make room for a stout gentleman who settled himself beside her.

"Silence!" said the master steward. "Silence for the Diamond Heir!"

The buzz died down, allowing Lady Rhuddlan to speak, and the excellent acoustics created by the architecture of the domed room carried her words to everyone. "The Diamond, my lords and ladies, remains unable to attend our meeting tonight. I shall preside in his place. Master Steward, please name those in attendance."

"Their graces the Diamond Heir and Ruby, Lady Vianne Rhuddlan; the Topaz, Lord Guilford Oselare; the Citrine, Lord Burne Teutaine; the Aquamarine, Lord Dolan Fedreggo; the Sapphire, Lord Sebastian Alcide; and the Amethyst, Lady Julianna Golpier."

"All are not named, Master Steward," Lady Rhuddlan replied ceremoniously. "Where is the representative for the Emerald House?"

The master steward bowed. "His grace the Emerald, Lord Torian Bestett, is deceased."

"Where is the Emerald Heir, so that he may take his place among those of the Diadem Council?"

"There is no heir from the House of Bestett to be presented and seated, your grace."

"Thank you, Master Steward." The steward again bowed and went to stand at one end of the Council table. "A new Emerald House must be selected," said Lady Rhuddlan. "The candidates will please present themselves."

At a gesture from the master steward, a door facing the Council table opened, and four men came in and walked forward. One was Lord Duone. Each carried a parchment, which they presented, one by one, to the master steward, and then went to stand at the four chairs facing the Council. A stream of their attendants came in, too, and went to sit at the benches ranged in rows behind the candidates' chairs.

"Lord Reuven Agnolle," announced the master steward, "is presented as a candidate by the Citrine." Lord Agnolle, a young man dressed in a doublet and slashed jerkin of dull bronze, bowed jauntily to the Council table. Rings decked his hands in a display that would have been more impressive had there been less of them. As he sat in the first chair he flicked the tail of his cloak aside, revealing a lining of vivid green silk sewn to the fabric, as if the wearer had already been installed. Jena noticed Lord Teutaine's slight wince at his candidate's demonstration of poor taste, and a low mutter of disapproval arose, dying down finally as the master steward raised his hand for silence.

"Lord Ferrin Signo is presented as a candidate by the

Amethyst." Straightening up from his bow caused a slight crease of pain to furrow Lord Signo's forehead, but he seated himself with an old soldier's military crispness. He wore a doublet of muted blue-black, with no jewelry other than the knotted clasp pin proclaiming his service with the Order of the Protectorate.

"Lord Ranulf Duone is presented as a candidate by the Ruby." Someone must have given Lord Duone the same advice Collas had given Jena, for he wore a velvet doublet and jerkin of charcoal gray, set off with gold and onyx jewelry. It suited his auburn hair and gray eyes well, Jena noted approvingly, and the cut flattered his form splendidly. Next to him Lord Signo looked rather frail, and Lord Agnolle looked like a fop. Lord Duone bowed to the Diadem with respectful poise, but his eyes studied Lord Oselare a little narrowly as he seated himself.

"Lord Maxil Palani is presented as a candidate by the Topaz." The fourth candidate, short and rather pudgy, looked the most ill at ease. He bowed with a nervous jerk, wiping his palms surreptitiously on the hem of his burnt-orange doublet. After he was seated, his fingers crept up to fidget with the knife handle on his belt.

"My lords," Lady Rhuddlan said, "we bid you welcome and offer our thanks to you for coming to meet with us tonight." She swept the four with a deliberate look and raised an eyebrow. "But we seem to be missing two candidates."

Lord Alcide, the oldest member of the council, cleared his throat. "The Sapphire nominee is Lord Aric Wode. A rider was sent to his estate with the Council's summons, but Lord Wode was apparently unable to journey here in time for Solstice. My apologies to the Council; I'd thought the travel time would be sufficient."

"The Aquamarine candidate, Lord Niall Scroop, is also missing," offered Lord Fedreggo, frowning. "I've been told he received an urgent message several weeks ago requiring his presence at one of his western holdings, and the Council's emissary was unable to locate him in time."

"Perhaps," suggested Lady Golpier in her reedy voice, "in all fairness, the Council should wait until these two other candidates can be located?"

The Ruby looked inquiringly down at the other Council members. "Well, your graces?"

"I would prefer that the Diadem wait, but will not insist," Lord Alcide said stiffly, drumming his frail, blue-veined fingers on the tabletop. "The Council's intention when it set the schedule for this meeting was quite clear: candidates who arrived late would lose their chances for consideration."

Lord Fedreggo looked disappointed but didn't argue. The Topaz, Lord Oselare, said nothing, but Jena thought his shoulders relaxed a little.

"I'm against allowing more time," Lord Teutaine said.

"But after all, Teutaine," the Amethyst tried again, "the Diamond is, er, not in a position to elevate a candidate at this time anyway. What harm can there be in waiting?"

This reminder of the Diamond's condition prompted an uncomfortable silence. "The presentation of the candidates is the issue now," Lord Teutaine said finally. "Not the elevation. The nominations should be considered closed so Council members can complete their evaluations and make their recommendations to the Diamond."

"If you're so concerned about keeping to the schedule set by this Council," asked Lady Golpier bluntly, "what if the Diamond is still unable to act upon those recommendations by Solstice's end? Who will elevate the new Emerald in that case? The Diamond Heir?"

"It could hardly be considered proper," Lord Oselare put in smoothly, "for the Ruby to elevate her own candidate."

Many pairs of eyes turned to Lord Duone to see how he reacted to this remark, but he appeared to be listening with only polite interest. "We're getting ahead of ourselves here," Lady Rhuddlan interposed. "As Lord Teutaine remarked, the question at hand is simply which candidates are being presented, not elevated. I agree the Council's intent was clear when this meeting was scheduled: only candidates who stood before us this evening could be considered."

Looking doubtful, Lady Golpier sat back. Lord Alcide sighed, his face disappointed but resigned. "If the Council would only consider . . ." Lord Fedreggo started, and then stopped, scowling, as his nephew Lord Rodric leaned forward to whisper in his ear. On the other side of Lady Rhudd-lan, Lord Oselare permitted himself a small smile.

"If you please, Lord Fedreggo, I wasn't quite finished," Lady Rhuddlan said. "As I was saying, the Council's intent was very clear. But it has been brought to my attention that there is another factor to consider: it may be that some candidates are not here because they have been deliberately delayed. We must take this into account when we consider what to do about the missing nominees—and perhaps even some of those present as well."

Lord Oselare's smile abruptly disappeared.

"Deliberately delayed?" said Lord Teutaine blankly above the rising swell of murmurs. "Whatever are you talking about?"

Lady Rhuddlan didn't even look at Lord Oselare. "Lord Duone," she said. "If you please, tell the Council what happened to you on your journey to this city after receiving the Diadem's summons."

Lord Duone rose and stepped forward, bowing again. "Your graces," he said, his firm tenor voice filling the hall, "my journey to Piyar was uneventful until I reached the city of Tenaway. There, while I was visiting a goldsmith's shop, a messenger arrived looking for me, purporting to carry a message from my brother, Lord Morgan. The message said that my wife was near death in the city of Niolantti. Detouring there would have delayed my arrival here past the beginning of the Winter's Solstice feast."

"And so you chose to ignore your brother's message?" said Lady Rhuddlan.

"That so-called message was a lie, your grace. It was sent to me, I'm convinced, in order to delay my arrival here and prevent me from presenting my candidacy to the Council."

"What evidence do you have for this assertion?" asked Lord Oselare roughly.

Lord Duone looked him squarely in the eye. "One of my traveling companions proved that Lord Morgan couldn't have sent the message."

"Oh?" Lord Oselare said haughtily. "How?"

Lord Duone shrugged. "If the Council permits, I will call her as a witness."

"You may do so," Lady Rhuddlan replied.

Lord Duone turned toward the master steward and said something to him in an undertone. "The Diadem calls upon Jena Gemcutter to present herself to the Diadem," the master steward said.

Taking a deep breath, Jena rose, pulling out the parchment Taras had given her as heads turned in her direction. She offered it to the steward and went to stand beside Lord Duone. The sight of Morgan sitting quietly on the cushion on the table stopped her inner quaking, and she lifted her chin and spoke. "My name is Jena Gemcutter, your graces," she declared firmly.

"Let your words before the Council be truth and any oaths you make be binding," said the master steward.

"I swear it shall be so," Jena replied.

"Jena Gemcutter," Lady Rhuddlan said, "how did you know the message brought to Lord Duone was not from his brother?"

"The courier offered as a token a ring which he said belonged to Lord Morgan. I am a jeweler by trade, and I know the size of Lord Morgan's hands. The ring was obviously too big to fit Lord Morgan. And so I concluded the messenger must be lying. To uncover the hoax, I asked if he had news about the health of Lord Duone's newborn daughter. The messenger said she was also ill, and that made the lie apparent to everyone: Lord Duone's child was a boy, not a girl. Once the courier realized he had exposed himself, he drew a knife and attempted to kill Lord Duone."

This last statement wrung an exclamation from the Amethyst and the Citrine and provoked a buzz among the spectators. "Order!" cried the master steward, pounding his staff on the floor. Lord Oselare sat absolutely still, his face draining of blood.

"Do the members of the Council have any questions for this witness?" asked Lady Rhuddlan when the noise had died down somewhat. There were none, and so Jena curtsied and returned to her seat. "Please continue with your story, Lord Duone."

"The false messenger didn't hurt me," Lord Duone went on, his eyes never leaving Lord Oselare's face, "but he did manage to wound Jena Gemcutter before my guards killed him. We searched the body afterward and found this." He drew something from a pouch at his belt and stepped forward to present it to Lady Rhuddlan.

She accepted it and held it up for examination. "An earring, marked with the device of a fish and a crown," she said, passing it on to Lady Golpier. Behind Lord Duone, Lord Palani started violently. "Do you know the significance of this pattern?"

Lord Duone drew another piece of parchment from his doublet. "I have here an affidavit from the Tenaway goldsmith Master Rolly describing the mark and its origin." He paused. "The fish and crown is a commercial sign for the shipping house of Palani."

A roar rose up. "Order!" cried the master steward again, "Order!" Lord Oselare flushed a murderous red.

Lord Palani sprang to his feet. "Your graces!" he cried. "I swear to you on my life's blood I had nothing to do with this!"

Lord Duone turned to face him. "That messenger was an employee of yours, *my lord.*"

"I had nothing to do with it!" Lord Palani insisted, all but on the verge of tears. "Your graces, please!" The master steward continued pounding until the room fell silent. "Lord Oselare's nomination came as a complete surprise to me," Lord Palani went on. "I didn't seek this nomination. I never expected to win it. Such a stain upon my House's honor . . . " he drew in a shaky breath and then drew himself up as tall as his stature would permit. "Your graces, I am innocent," he said with simple dignity. "And to prove it, I wish to withdraw my candidacy from consideration immediately! I offer my profoundest apologies both to the Diadem and to you, Lord Duone, and I swear that I will offer all the resources available to me to help you find who did this terrible thing. I will never rest until my House's good name has been restored."

Lord Duone hesitated and then inclined his head to him, stiffly. Lord Palani bowed to the Council and then turned and walked over to the spectators' sitting section. There, he sank down onto a bench, his face like pasty ash, to the accompaniment of excited whispers.

The Topaz sprang to his feet. "My candidate has been falsely maligned!" he cried, his voice shaking with fury.

"As I understand it, Oselare," said Lord Alcide caustically, "he isn't your candidate anymore."

"Do you dispute the evidence Lord Duone and his witness have presented?" demanded Lord Fedreggo.

After a short struggle, Lord Oselare appeared to get a grip on his temper. "Your graces," he said after a moment in a quieter voice, "treachery thrives in changing times such as these, creating great dangers. Obviously the seriousness of the . . . the incident Lord Duone experienced speaks for itself. The crime is compounded if your candidate, Lord Fedreggo, or yours, Lord Alcide, have been harmed in any way. I, too, will volunteer the means to help find the guilty culprits. And I will gladly send additional riders to make sure the Lords Wode and Scroop are safe."

"Your own men, I suppose?" Lord Fedreggo said in a careful neutral voice.

"If the Council doesn't trust me," the Topaz retorted, "I shall provide the necessary monies to equip messengers picked by the Council. But I firmly believe that my candidate, an honorable and honest man, has been maliciously slandered. Who knows but that earring may very well be a counterfeit, planted to embarrass me and to force Lord Palani to withdraw!"

Lady Golpier snorted. "I very much doubt the messenger was so obliging as to allow himself to be killed so Lord Duone could find it."

"I tell you, Lord Palani is also a victim of treachery here!" Lord Oselare snapped.

"We do not question, Lord Oselare," Lady Golpier said coldly, "that we speak of treachery. We are simply trying to find out who is responsible, and your indignation on Lord Palani's behalf—"

"Who is responsible?" Lord Oselare interrupted, his voice rising. "That is my intent, to find out who is responsible for these threats to the Emerald candidates—*including* to Lord

Palani's reputation. Uncovering that treachery may even lead us to the reason the Emerald House failed in the first place."

"Whatever are you talking about?" Lord Fedreggo said, puzzled. "The Emerald House failed because Lord Bestett and his lady drowned."

"I speak of magic, your grace," Lord Oselare replied icily. "I speak of black acts of the filthiest sorcery. Lord Torian Bestett was renowned for his skill as a swimmer. It is obvious to me at least that dismissing his death as mere accident is willful blindness."

"Come, come, Lord Oselare," Lord Teutaine said. "What happened to Lord Bestett was an accident. Terrible, yes, and tragic, but an *accident*. And Lord Duone was threatened by a knife, not a spell. Your opinions regarding magic are well known, but I think you are allowing your fears to, er, get the better of your reasoning."

"Oh, am I, your grace? If my concerns are so absurd, then tell me this: why have I been receiving anonymous reports warning me of a sorcerous threat to the life of the Diamond?"

As if in response to the Topaz's words, magic stirred somewhere in the room, and Jena lost what was said next. *Another possibility vision?* was all she had time to think, and then she heard a surprised yelp from Morgan. Something like a wave of sheer terror swiftly crashed over her, beating back all her senses, and she gasped and almost cried out, too.

For an unknown period of time the searing wash of panic and dread dimmed everything else and then slowly, slowly, sight and hearing returned. Someone was saying something in her right ear, the words like a buzz; she turned her head jerkily in that direction.

"Madam? Are you ill?" It was the stout gentleman beside her, studying her face with concern. She forced herself to smile as her face flushed with embarrassment.

"I . . . I'm quite well, thank you. Something poked me, a splinter on the bench, doubtless." Deliberately, she turned her attention back to the Council table until the man next to her did, too.

Morgan was on his feet, whining softly, with Lady Rhudd-lan's hand on his shoulders. When he caught Jena's eye, he slowly lay down again and put his head on his paws, and Lady Rhuddlan's hand withdrew.

Well, whatever it was, both of us felt it. What was *that?* Jena looked around the room, but didn't see anyone getting up to leave or having a fit or doing anything else to call attention to themselves. Lady Rhuddlan was speaking, and finally, with an effort, Jena forced her attention back to what was being said.

"... nor rumors being fed with wild accusations. The Diamond's guard can be increased, given your tender concern for his safety."

"What good are swords and spears against sorcery?" the Topaz all but spat.

"What else would you have us do?" the Ruby retorted crisply. "When you have solid evidence of a magical threat to the Diamond, Lord Oselare, and not just vague anonymous warnings, then by all means, this Council will wish to see it. In that event, perhaps your helpful informant might have some suggestions."

Lord Oselare bowed, his face stony, and slowly sat down again.

"But until then, let me assure everyone here," Lady Rhuddlan continued, "that the Diamond's condition is unchanged, and has been since the news came to him of his son's death. He is frail, yes, and he cannot speak. But he is able to take nourishment, and he is under the best care of our most highly skilled physicians. We all hold out hope that he will eventually recover."

A silence fell while Lady Rhuddlan waited for the Topaz to respond, but he avoided her eye.

"Well, then," the Ruby said finally. "Given Lord Duone's news regarding interference with Emerald candidates, I suggest that in all fairness we extend the time nominations remain open until the night before Solstice Festival ends. Hopefully, two weeks will give us more than enough time to send out messengers to find Lord Wode and Lord Scroop and fetch them back. Will this be acceptable to all?"

After some cursory further discussion, the recommendation was ratified by the other Diadem members.

"Now, then," Lady Rhuddlan said. "The current candidates for the new Emerald House have presented their credentials to the Diadem Council. I trust, your graces, you will all take the time to meet and speak with these gentlemen, starting with the opportunity presented by tonight's banquet, and with the Lords Wode and Scroop when and if they arrive. I am sure you will make your evaluations carefully. Council will reconvene to present its recommendations two weeks hence."

"To the Diamond?" asked the Topaz pointedly.

"If the Diamond is not able to make his choice at that time, we will deal with the question then. Unless you have an alternative suggestion?"

The Topaz glared, but Lady Rhuddlan stared him down, and he turned away. "No. Not at this time."

"Then all that remains tonight is to conclude our meeting here and begin the night's revels. Again, I thank all the candidates for their appearance before us and wish you good fortune in the decision which we will be making. Master Steward?"

The master steward advanced and bowed to the Council and then rapped his staff on the floor. "This session of the Diadem Council is now concluded." He nodded to the ushers at the doors, and the doors were opened as people began rising and making their way out of the rows of benches.

Catching Lady Rhuddlan's eye and small hand motion, Jena remained seated until the room was almost empty. Then she rose and made her way slowly past the Council table as Lady Rhuddlan turned away from a bevy of hovering noblemen. "Jena Gemcutter?" the Ruby said in her coolest public tones.

Jena faced her, schooling her face to show only the most formal respect, and curtsied. "Your grace?"

"A word, if you please. No, no," she said, turning back to the viers for her attention. "I am sure you have a point, but we will discuss it at a later time. Speak with me at the banquet, Lord Riaro, and Lord Ercole, perhaps you might call upon me tomorrow?" After the gentlemen took their leave, with many obsequious murmurings (Morgan's lip curled at some of the more fulsome compliments, Jena noted), Lady Rhuddlan waved at the master steward to withdraw and shut the doors. As soon as the three of them were alone, Lady Rhuddlan turned to Jena and Morgan and said in a very different tone, "What made both of you jump while Oselare was raving on?"

Jena and Morgan exchanged uneasy glances. "I sensed something terribly strong. . . ." Morgan said, and trailed off.

"A magical fluctuation," said Jena. "It was in the room, don't you think, Morgan?"

"Was it something having to do with Lord Oselare?" Lady Rhuddlan pressed. "He was talking about possibilities, after all. Could you tell whether he was lying?"

Morgan screwed his eyes shut and his tail thumped as he considered. "He knew something, before Ranulf and Jena told their stories."

Lady Rhuddlan's jaw tightened. "So he was angry that someone he'd sent botched an assassination attempt?"

Jena shook her head. "I . . . I don't know."

"He wasn't surprised Ranulf encountered a messenger," Morgan said slowly, his nose twitching. His eyes flew open. "But Lord Oselare was as shocked as everyone else in the room when Jena said the messenger tried to kill Ranulf."

Lady Rhuddlan frowned, puzzled.

"But that wasn't even what we were reacting to," Jena went on. "It was afterward, when Lord Oselare was talking about . . . about the threat to the Diamond. I felt . . . terror. *Magically.* It wasn't Lord Oselare; it was someone else responding to what he said."

"Who?" Lady Rhuddlan demanded.

Jena and Morgan looked at each other. "It was someone who was between us, don't you think?" said Jena.

Morgan nodded.

"A woman or a man?" Lady Rhuddlan asked. "Could you tell?"

"A . . . a woman," Morgan said after a moment. "Here, stand aside for a moment." He hopped down off the table and trotted off, sniffing at the floor and the legs of chairs. Lady Rhuddlan and Jena exchanged uneasy sidelong glances. Morgan slowed as he approached one chair, his nostrils flaring. "Here."

"Where?" asked Lady Rhuddlan, walking toward him. Jena hastened after her.

"Who sat here?" Morgan asked as they came up beside him.

Lady Rhuddlan glanced at the silk banner on the back of the chair. "It was Lady Rinnelle. The Topaz Heir."

"Lady Rinnelle, eh?" Morgan sat down and raised his nostrils, sniffing in deeply; he sneezed. "The fear-stink is . . . well, it's overpowering." He looked up at the two women solemnly. "She was petrified."

They stared at the empty chair and then at each other. Lady Rhuddlan drew herself up. "Come on." She wheeled sharply and headed for the Council chamber entrance leading to the banquet room.

"Uh, where are you going, Vianne?" asked Morgan, trotting at her heel.

"To have a little chat with Lady Rinnelle about jewelry," Lady Rhuddlan said grimly. "I want you two to sense whatever possibilities about her you can."

"Wait, your grace," Jena said, touching her elbow as the noblewoman was about to push open the door. "I'm not sure confronting her is the best idea."

"If she presents a danger to the Diamond, I must."

"But—"

"It would be safest now, in a crowd. She cannot dare to practice magic too openly."

"Then let me put up a ward over you, at least. Over all of us. Just in case?"

"A ward? What's that?"

"A protection spell, against any magic that might cause harm."

Lady Rhuddlan winced. "Must you?"

"Please, Vianne," Morgan said. "Let her do it."

The Ruby sighed. "Very well."

The spell was the work of a quick moment or two. Once the lines were safely drawn and tested, Jena stepped back and nodded toward the door. "After you, your grace."

The crowd, with Lord Duone and the two remaining candidates in the center of the throng, still lingered over the sec-

ond hors d'oeuvre course being offered in the space before
the set trestle tables. Over in the corner, Lord Oselare was
speaking urgently to Lord Palani. Apparently the conversation was not a happy one; Lord Palani seemed to be disagree-
ing vehemently with something Lord Oselare was urging.
Roving servitors wove their way through the people, carrying trays offering minced chicken and goat livers, candied
crabapples, and sweetbreads garnished with gilded pome-
granate seeds.

"Do you see the Topaz Heir?" Jena asked Lady Rhuddlan
in an undertone. Lady Rhuddlan shook her head.

Morgan scratched a paw along Lady Rhuddlan's shoe and
pointed with his nose. The two women looked in the direction he was indicating, far over to one side. "There," murmured the Ruby. Beside one of the pillars, a dark-haired
woman perhaps two or three years older than Lady Rhuddlan
listened reluctantly to a gentleman speaking earnestly to her.
She was shaking her head and trying to extricate her hand
from his.

"That direction," Lady Rhuddlan said, "along the wall.
They won't see us coming up with the pillar in the way, and
I don't want to give her the chance to escape."

They edged their way closer, Morgan keeping close to
Lady Rhuddlan's heels. "Who's the man talking with her?"
Jena whispered.

"That's her intended, Lord Woric," Lady Rhuddlan whispered back.

Soon they could hear snatches of the low-voiced conversation: ". . . understand why you haven't answered my letters.
Rinnelle, please: you have to tell me what is happening."

"I can't." The woman's low voice was full of misery.
"Woric, forgive me, but I can't. Please, just be patient with
me a little while longer."

Somebody else with love problems, Jena thought. She
could see a little of the back of the man's head around the
pillar's curve. Dropping Lady Rinnelle's hand, he drew back,
and although Jena couldn't see his face, she heard the hurt
dignity in his next question.

"Are you . . . weary of me? Do you want me to withdraw
my suit?"

"No! Woric, how can you say that?" Lady Rinnelle stammered with tears in her voice. "I . . . I want to marry you." She continued speaking, but her voice dropped to inaudibility.

Jena reached out and squeezed Lady Rhuddlan's elbow. "Perhaps it wouldn't be wise to interrupt them now," she breathed in the noblewoman's ear.

Lady Rhuddlan frowned, and opened her mouth to whisper something back, when a short, low growl from Morgan made them both look down. When Jena looked up again, she gave a hasty tug to Lady Rhuddlan's sleeve, and the two women ducked farther around the pillar. Lord Oselare was walking toward his sister and her betrothed. "Lord Woric, if I might have a word with you, please?" he called.

"Go, go," Lady Rinnelle whispered in a strangled voice. Peeking out cautiously around the pillar again, Jena saw Lord Woric bow deeply and then stalk stiffly away to join the Topaz.

Jena glanced uncertainly at Lady Rhuddlan, but the Ruby was already moving out around the other side of the pillar. "Lady Rinnelle?" Lady Rhuddlan said.

The Topaz Heir, who stood with her back toward them wiping her eyes with a handkerchief, turned at the sound of her name, startled. She had vivid coloring: midnight-black hair and fair skin softened by a slight plumpness, and wide eyes of an unusual blue-violet color, now puffy from crying. She gave them a last hasty dab, tucked the handkerchief into her sleeve, and mustered a tremulous smile. "Yes, Lady Rhuddlan?"

Lady Rhuddlan held out her hand toward Jena peremptorily, and reluctantly, Jena came forward, too. "I have someone I'd like you to meet: Jena Gemcutter. You heard her testimony earlier, of course. I have been telling her about your exquisite collection of gemstones. Jena, Lady Rinnelle."

And if Lady Rinnelle believes that, then I have some fool's gold she might like to buy, Jena thought as she curtsied. She raised her eyes to meet Lady Rinnelle's.

But in fact, Lady Rinnelle appeared to be too distracted or perhaps too rattled by her conversation with Lord Woric to find anything strange in the introduction. "I—er—I'm pleased to meet you, of course . . . although I've never thought myself much of a connoisseur. . . ." her voice trailed off uncertainly. She obviously wished herself well away from them.

"You're far too modest," Lady Rhuddlan said with a brilliant smile. "Lady Rinnelle is renowned for her taste."

"Perhaps my father, Master Collas, has cut some pieces for you?" Jena said.

"I'm not sure . . . that is, my pieces are mostly heirlooms, actually. They've been in the family for years." Her hands fluttered vaguely, indicating her rings and bracelets and a pendant shaped like a ship, pinned to her bodice. And then Jena saw.

That pendant. Jena had seen many like it; it was a motif that had been fashionable for years. The delicate goldwork and colorful enameling captured all the features of a ship's fittings and riggings with exquisite detail.

"That lovely ship pendant, now," Jena said. "How appropriate, given your family's fortunes. What a marvelous piece of work."

Lady Rinnelle fingered it, and a little smile crept to her face. "Yes, I'm very fond of it. It was given to me by my grandmother, and I think her mother gave it to her."

"The pearl, though, I imagine, is something you've added."

Lady Rinnelle's hand, fingering the pendant, froze.

"Pearl?" Lady Rhuddlan said. "What pearl?"

Jena smiled. "Why, the absolutely exquisite baroque pearl hanging from the bottom of the ship. I suppose you can't see it, Lady Rhuddlan, but I can. Lady Rinnelle isn't accustomed to having anyone notice it. Are you, Lady Rinnelle?" Lady Rinnelle looked quickly at Jena, her eyes widening in surprise.

"Such a fine white pearl is very rare indeed," Jena went on, more and more sure. Prickles of magic told her she was right: Lady Rinnelle's terror was rising again. "I know one man who deals in such exceptional items; perhaps you know him? Captain Kett of the *Windspray*."

"I've met him myself," Lady Rhuddlan said, her voice like

ice. "He's the one who so kindly gave me my beloved little dog Marzipan as a gift." She picked up Morgan and held him close, her eyes boring into Lady Rinnelle's.

The Topaz Heir gave Morgan a startled glance, and, if possible, her eyes opened even wider. She reached out an uncertain hand, and then blanched as Morgan growled. "But he's a . . . he's a . . ."

"He's a what, Rinnelle?" Lady Rhuddlan said with poisonous sweetness.

Lady Rinnelle picked up her skirts and fled.

CHAPTER
EIGHTEEN

IMMEDIATELY MORGAN LEAPED
out of Lady Rhuddlan's arms and tore off after Lady Rinnelle. The Topaz Heir shoved people aside in her frantic haste, bowling over a servitor, which sent a shower of hors d'oeuvres over the startled bystanders, as Morgan dove through men's ankles and ladies' skirts in hot pursuit. "Mor—uh, Marzipan, come back!" Lady Rhuddlan cried out in a strangled whisper.

It was useless; the two quickly disappeared through one of the banquet room doors. Jena clutched Lady Rhuddlan's sleeve and tugged it. "The belt. We can follow them. Hurry!" They followed the route Lady Rinnelle had taken, threading their way through the jostling, indignant crowd, trying not to walk too quickly until they were through the door and out of sight of the banquet room. Then they ran.

"Which way?" Jena cried as they came to an intersection of corridors at the top of a staircase.

Lady Rhuddlan hesitated for a moment, her hand on her belt buckle, and pointed to the right. "Not the stairs. Down there." The hall was dark, and they half ran, half trotted, their hands out before their faces to keep themselves from running into anything. Jena strayed near one of the walls and caught her foot on a small table set up against it. She went crashing down.

Lady Rhuddlan's voice called out in the darkness, "Are you hurt?"

"No." Jena's hands, scrabbling to extricate herself from the table legs and pull herself up, encountered a familiar shape. "Here's a candle. Now we just need to find a light."

She pulled herself up and the two went on, more cautiously. After turns down two more corridors and a short trip up a flight of stairs, they saw an open doorway. Inside the empty room, they could see the remains of a fire. "Wait," Jena whispered. She darted into the room and lit her candle with a coal taken from the fireplace with tongs. Coming back out, she could see Lady Rhuddlan staring farther down the corridor, her face transfixed.

"I think I hear Morgan."

Jena paused and listened, and then she could hear it, too: a thunderous growling and a scrabbling sound. When they went around a corner, they saw Morgan partway down the hall, ruining the finish on a shut door with his frantic paw scratches and throwing himself against it. Picking himself up off the floor after one particularly enthusiastic charge, he saw them. "She's in there," he snarled. "She got in there a second before I did and smashed my nose when she slammed the door. I'll bite her knees off, I'll rip her throat out, I'll—RRRRaarrrgh!"

"Morgan, stop it," Lady Rhuddlan said, going swiftly to join him. "That won't work. Jena?"

"Wait, Morgan. Let me check the wards again." After another quick test, she nodded and sighed. "They're up, and still strong," she said in a low voice.

"I know this room," Lady Rhuddlan whispered. "Morgan must have been getting too close, and she panicked and shut herself in. She can't get out any other way."

"Maybe she can," Jena said grimly, remembering her own inadvertent trip to Duone Keep. She placed a hand on the door, but failed to scry any hint of spell preparation on the other side. *If we're lucky, she's too frightened to think of it, or doesn't have enough magic to do that. Lady Kestrienne*

*said it took a tremendous amount of power, after all. Or
maybe she doesn't know how.*

Still, the fact that she was cornered probably made Lady
Rinnelle even more dangerous. "Are you sure we want to go
in there, your grace?" Jena whispered. "She's a wizard, and
even with the wards—"

"If she knows something about a threat to the Diamond,
I'll walk through fire to face her. And anyway," Lady Rhuddlan said firmly, stooping and catching Morgan as he tried to
butt his way through their skirts to throw himself at the door
again, "I know Rinnelle; she's a rabbit at heart."

"There's no crowd to protect you here," Jena warned.
"Don't underestimate her, your grace."

"I won't. Morgan, stop it. You're certainly not going in
there if the only thing you can think to do is to bite her."

Morgan abruptly stopped straining against Lady Rhuddlan's grip and sat down, panting. He was shaking all over.
"I'm fine," he said grouchily after a moment. "I'll control
myself."

The two women eyed each other dubiously. Lady Rhuddlan's hand crept up and tried the door latch. "It's locked,"
she said, shaking her head.

Jena smiled. "It's possible for locks to break, you know."
She put her hand on the lock and pushed firmly, allowing her
magic to flow out to nudge the latch. With a snick, it gave
way, and Jena allowed herself a small surge of triumph. She
lifted her candle high and led the way in.

The room, a small music salon, was all but empty of furniture, except for several gilt chairs and a music rack holding
lutes and sheet music. Lady Rinnelle was scrabbling at the
bars covering the small latched window, but it was too small
for her to climb out.

"Rinnelle," Lady Rhuddlan said in a deceptively gentle
voice.

The Topaz Heir wheeled to face them and cowered back
into a corner. "Oh, please . . . please . . ." she whispered brokenly.

"Please what, Rinnelle?" Lady Rhuddlan said, walking
slowly into the room, her eyes burning. Jena hastily lit candles on the table beside her and shut the door after Morgan.

"Please, forgive me. Don't expose me to the Court, I beg you. Guilford will—" she stopped and gulped. "I never meant any harm."

Morgan laughed bitterly, the sound ridiculously incongruous, coming from a dog. "Never meant any harm! You can look at me after what you've done and say that!"

Lady Rinnelle started violently at the sound of his voice. "Kett did that! I didn't! I didn't know! You must believe me." She turned appealingly to Lady Rhuddlan. "Please believe me."

"Why should I?" Lady Rhuddlan said coldly. "You know something about the Diamond, don't you?"

"I . . . I . . ." Lady Rinnelle faltered.

"Answer me! Did you or did you not swear an oath to the Council when you were installed as the Topaz Heir? 'By the Sun and Star that protect and defend—' "

" '—the Heir and the Diamond—' " Lady Rinnelle choked and stopped. She shrank against the wall, turning her face away.

Lady Rhuddlan waited, but the silence stretched on. "Are you an oathbreaker then, Lady Rinnelle?" she demanded finally, her voice a whiplash of scorn.

Lady Rinnelle looked at the three of them, and in the dim light, Jena saw that all her terror had burned itself away into something that left her with nothing but the truth. "No," she said quietly in a different voice. "I'm no oathbreaker. My loyalty has always been to the Diamond. And in return for my loyalty, I can only implore your brilliance's protection."

Lady Rhuddlan stared at her, breathing hard. "What did you say?" she said finally in a curiously flat voice.

"You heard me," Lady Rinnelle said, nodding and pushing herself up stiffly. "Your brilliance." She gave a half laugh that sounded hysterical. "You hold the Sunburst, but it's the Starburst you should wear now. The Diamond—the old Diamond from the Emerald House—has in truth been dead since Equinox." She closed her eyes, her face still and set, a muscle in her cheek twitching. "Or he would be except for the spell Kett and I put over him that . . . that *forces* him to continue."

Jena heard Morgan swear softly. Lady Rhuddlan pulled up a chair and sank into it, her eyes haunted. "You lie."

Lady Rinnelle laughed again. "Oh, yes, I do, your brilliance. I have. But not about this, believe me." She shuddered and all but fell.

"Sit down," Lady Rhuddlan snapped. "And explain to us what this is all about."

Lady Rinnelle groped her way to another chair. Jena sat, too, and Morgan hopped up onto Lady Rhuddlan's lap. Jena wondered at this at first, and then realized that somehow he knew it was the right thing to do, that letting her stroke his fur would bring Lady Rhuddlan back out of her shock.

"I'm . . . I'm what Guilford would call a sorceress," Lady Rinnelle began.

"A wizard," Jena corrected.

Lady Rinnelle gave her a surprised look. "I've never heard that word before."

"Haven't you?" Jena's eyes narrowed. "How did you meet Kett? Was it when you sailed with the Golden Fleet?"

That brought her another surprised look from Lady Rinnelle. "Yes. I knew who he was for about five years or so before we ever exchanged a word, when I was still married. The year after my husband died, he . . . he approached me for the first time, and said he had something he wanted to give me, because I looked so sad." She blushed, and ducked her head down, looking at her hands twisting in her lap. "Something white, he said, because it hurt him to see me dressed all in black. And then he showed me the pearl. I knew better than to take it, but he pressed it into my hand. And when I touched it, I saw the black pearl hanging from his earring for the first time. Something made me reach out for it." Her voice trailed away, as she looked off into the distance, remembering. It was very much like the look of someone scrying, Jena thought.

"And then what happened?" Lady Rhuddlan prompted.

Lady Rinnelle looked at her, her eyes full of shame and sadness. "As soon as I touched it, I knew that somehow, we had the same soul. He felt it. He knew it, too. I saw it in his eyes."

The three listeners exchanged looks.

"Soon after that, I discovered the sorcery," Lady Rinnelle said in a low voice. "I tried to ignore it, to fight it, but I couldn't. I felt it all the time. And I could . . . could *feel* Kett. I found out the next time the Court moved, when the Golden Fleet sailed again, that he'd discovered it, too." She flushed, and Jena had to strain to catch her next words. "We started exchanging messages after that, sometimes even meeting secretly. He learned things on his travels, and then he'd teach me."

"Before you met Kett, did you know anyone else who used magic?" Morgan asked. "Or did you talk with any adept about it afterward?"

"No." Lady Rinnelle shook her head, her face rigid with self-loathing. "No, I never talked with anyone cursed like me."

"It's not—" Lady Rhuddlan stopped and cleared her throat, her fingers tightening in Morgan's fur. "It's not a curse, Rinnelle," she said in a louder voice.

"You never were catalyzed by a tutor," Jena said in wonder. "And you never had a mentor."

"Is that possible?" Morgan asked doubtfully.

"Lady Ke—I mean, it's rare, but I've heard it can occur."

"What are you talking about?" Lady Rinnelle asked, her eyes widening.

"Lady Rinnelle, you've never heard about wizard partners, or blind spots, or scrying, or anything like that?"

Wordlessly, Lady Rinnelle shook her head.

She's even more a babe in the woods about magic than I was, Jena realized wonderingly. *Would it be foolish to explain to her?* She studied Lady Rinnelle with narrowed eyes, searching for guidance from the inner voice of instinct Lady Kestrienne had taught her to heed. Somehow, Lady Rinnelle wasn't the enemy she expected, but someone in desperate need of information and guidance. Perhaps giving it to her now would encourage her to help them in return?

Then again, maybe not. And yet, I think . . . I think I have to try. "Magic is all about possibilities," Jena said. "People who are adepts—magic users, that is—can work alone exploring possibilities, as magicians. But it's much more powerful when a man and a woman meet and partner, like you and Kett have. . . ." Lady Rinnelle heard her out without interruption.

When Jena had finished, Lady Rinnelle nodded slowly, fingering her pendant. "Well," she said mildly. "That explains a good deal, doesn't it?"

"And you think Kett didn't understand this, either?"

Lady Rinnelle considered in silence for a few moments. "Maybe he did," she admitted finally. "Maybe he learned about it on his journeying, when he was trying to find out all he could about magic, but he didn't completely explain it to me for some reason. He told me about Lord Morgan—" She stopped herself.

"What about Morgan?" Lady Rhuddlan said, her voice cold again.

Lady Rinnelle stared at the terrier on the Ruby's lap. "I'm so sorry," she whispered. "I've been such a fool." She took a deep breath. "Kett came to me and told me that the Ruby had become betrothed to a sorcerer."

"How did he learn that?"

"I don't know. I didn't ask. He just . . . knew things. I trusted him when he told me things like that. And he told me . . ." her gaze dropped to her lap and she turned red.

"What, for pity's sake?" Lady Rhuddlan exclaimed impatiently.

"I—you have to understand: I told you, my loyalty is to the Diamond. You're the Diamond Heir, and Kett told me Lord Morgan would use his sorcery to . . . to kill the Diamond. So you would become the Diamond instead, and he would be your Consort."

"And you believed him?" Lady Rhuddlan said, her voice rising. "You would believe such an accusation of me, when you've known me all my life?"

"No! Not of you! I didn't believe it of you. But I don't know Lord Morgan, and what would prevent him from doing it, even without your knowledge? I believed Kett, and if Morgan is a sorcerer—"

"You couldn't trust a sorcerer, obviously," Jena murmured, shaking her head. *She was raised to hate and fear magic so blindly—how she must hate and fear the magic in herself!*

"And so you put this spell on me?" Morgan said, showing his teeth.

"No! I wouldn't have done any such thing, Lord Morgan. It wasn't my intention to hurt you, but to protect the Diamond. Kett had a way, he said." She fell silent for a moment, apparently gathering her courage to say what came next. "Together, the two of us put a spell on the Diamond. We bound him to live safely through the end of the year, until the danger that he might be murdered so that the Ruby House could inherit was past." She looked up, her eyes pleading. "You see now, don't you, that I did it because I wanted to help? Because of my oath to the Council, not in spite of it?"

"She's telling the truth, Vianne," Morgan said in a low voice.

"Yes. Yes, I do see, Rinnelle." Lady Rhuddlan looked down at Morgan, who was lying quietly in her lap, and then her face hardened. "Then what happened?"

Lady Rinnelle couldn't meet her eyes. "My next message from Kett was urgent. He told me Lord Morgan might be close to gaining a new kind of power soon. And if he did, he would be able to detect the spell we put over the Diamond. He might be able to break it or expose me as a sorceress. We had to be ready to act in case that happened. We set up the spells and then, two days later, Kett and I felt the surge of power that tripped them." She looked at Morgan again. "My spell snatched you away to Kett's ship. And then Kett was responsible for . . . for taking care of things from there."

Jena gave Morgan a glance. *And take care of it he did.*

"He must have known about partnering, then," Morgan said thoughtfully.

"I . . . I think you're right."

"But how could he have known I was so close to doing it?"

"Perhaps he perceived the potential when, uh, your partner looked into your ring the first time," Jena ventured. "That must have convinced him you were about to forge the bond."

"Yes, but why? If he's so skillful at scrying, how could he believe I might murder the Diamond? Why was he watching me so closely, anyway?"

"Wizards can be misled by false possibilities," Jena said, remembering her run through the streets of Piyar. *I was.*

"No, that's not it," Lady Rinnelle said bitterly. "I found out the real reason at Equinox, when the Emerald died. They brought the news to the Diamond, and his heart failed, too. I . . . I felt it." Her eyes welled up with tears again. "It was horrible! He longed to die, but he couldn't. Our spell now bound him past the point he was meant to live.

"It almost drove me mad. I contacted Kett and told him we had to break the spell now to let him go. But he refused." She gave an ironic laugh. "I hadn't thought it all the way through, you see. The Ruby is the Diamond Heir this year . . ."

"But the Topaz is the Diamond Heir next year," Lady Rhuddlan exclaimed softly. "And so Kett wanted you to wait until next year to let the Diamond die, so your brother would become the Diamond, and you the Diamond Heir?"

"Worse than that." Lady Rinnelle's lips trembled. "Kett came to my rooms late at night when he received my message. He told me he loved me. All we had to do was wait until next year. Except for one little thing." She closed her eyes, and the tears began slipping down her cheeks. "We would have to kill my brother, Guilford, so I would become the Topaz. Kett wanted *me* to murder him. And then after the new year, once the Diamond was released from the spell, he would die, too, and I would ascend the Adamant Throne.

"And Kett would become my Diamond Consort."

"By all the Founders . . ." Lady Rhuddlan whispered. The three of them stared as Lady Rinnelle groped in her sleeve for her handkerchief and mopped her eyes with shaking hands. *No wonder she doesn't trust wizards,* Jena thought.

After a moment, Lady Rhuddlan roused herself from her thoughts with an effort. "So what did you tell him?"

"I told him I would never agree to such a thing, of course!" Lady Rinnelle gasped. She looked down at the handkerchief twisted in her hand. "It . . . it had never crossed my mind we should marry." She sounded as if she were trying to convince herself, but the catch in her voice gave her words the lie. "Then—well, he was talking so wildly. And the Diamond's pain pressed me so hard, it made it difficult to think and . . . I made a mistake. I . . . I laughed at Kett. Oh, what could you expect? The idea was so insane, so bizarre! I tried to turn him aside as if it were all some kind of gruesome joke. Woric and I were betrothed, I told him; we loved each other. He had to be mad if he thought I would marry him instead. Kett wouldn't believe me. Not at first. And then . . . he became so angry . . . so angry." Her voice trailed off into a whisper, and pressing the handkerchief to her lips, she got up and paced to the window. "He told me I had no choice but to carry out the plan." She laughed, a grating sound that made Jena wince. "Our plan, he called it. If I didn't arrange to have Guilford murdered somehow, Kett swore he would expose me to my brother as a sorceress."

"Is that such a terrible fate?" Jena asked dryly.

Lady Rinnelle shook her head. "You don't know Guilford, or the Oselare family. If I was lucky, I would simply be disinherited. But Guilford is the head of the family, and he loathes magic so much . . . I'm afraid he would try to kill me."

"Surely not!" Lady Rhuddlan exclaimed.

Lady Rinnelle looked at her solemnly. "There were stories whispered when I was little, about an aunt who died before I was born. It was the coughing sickness, everyone said. But once, my nurse secretly swore to me the real reason she died was because my father caught her with a spell book. He had her smothered." She leaned against the window bars wearily, like a prisoner. "Anyway . . . I haven't seen Kett since that night. But that's why he's been sending those anonymous reports to my brother about magical threats to the Diamond."

"*Kett's* been sending them?" said Morgan.

"Yes, don't you see? That's why the hints to Guilford are getting stronger and stronger all the time: Kett's drawing in the net, trying to force me to kill Guilford and marry him before Guilford's suspicions turn toward me." She shuddered violently. "And Kett says he's doing it because he loves me!"

"No," Lady Rhuddlan said. "Don't torment yourself like that. These aren't the acts of a lover, but a monster."

"A monster . . . then what does that make me? His studies of magic have shown him we *must* marry. The bond we share means we have no choice at all, because our souls are one." She began to cry again. "Because I'm just like him. I *am* him. What does that make me but a monster, just like him?"

Lady Rhuddlan looked down at the dog in her lap, and then at Jena, her apprehension plain in her eyes. *Could it be true?* Jena wondered, feeling a cold finger of fear. *Could it be that partners really have no choice but to marry each other?* Lady Rinnelle continued weeping, and Jena found herself thinking, with some irritation, that as dangerous wizards went, the Topaz Heir was certainly a sodden sponge.

"You've been letting yourself get tied up into knots over nonsense," she said crisply. "You don't have to marry him."

Lady Rinnelle peered at Jena above the edge of her handkerchief, and Jena noted that Lady Rhuddlan, too, looked almost as hopeful. "Truly?" said Lady Rinnelle. "You don't think so?"

"Of course not," Jena said, thinking of Arikan and Lady Kestrienne. "A poor kind of magic this is, telling you that you have no choice! Why, the most powerful wizardry is meant to multiply choices, not eliminate them. And as for being somehow obligated to marry him because you 'share the same soul,' well, that's nonsense. Wizard partners are attracted and bound to one another precisely because of their differences, not their similarities.

"And anyway, Lady Rinnelle," she went on impatiently, "if partners can only marry each other, why was Kett treating Lady Rhuddlan's engagement as such a threat? After all, Lord Morgan is going to marry the Ruby, but he's my partner, not hers!"

"I told you," Lady Rinnelle faltered, "I didn't know about wizard pairs." She looked bewildered. "So you and Lord Morgan . . . uh . . ."

"Now you've done it, Jena," Morgan said in disgust.

"What? Oh." Jena stared at the Topaz Heir, her mind in a cold whirl as she realized her mistake. *She didn't know about wizard pairs. She didn't know Morgan and I are partners—until I told her just now.*

Lady Rinnelle looked at them in confusion and then lifted her chin. "You said wizards keep their partners secret to protect themselves, didn't you? I've told you, I never meant to hurt anyone, if that's what you fear."

"Will you swear to that before me?" Lady Rhuddlan asked, adding pointedly, "By your loyalty to the Diamond?"

Lady Rinnelle winced. "I will. And I do."

Jena tried to swallow her chagrin. *After all, that's the one oath that will probably hold her. I hope.*

Lady Rhuddlan looked at Jena, the question *Can we trust her?* in her eyes.

Do we have a choice? Jena's own look answered in kind. "So you understand now that Kett has been lying to you," she said, "don't you, my lady?"

"I suppose." Lady Rinnelle sighed, her expression a complex mixture of fear, yearning, and even a little dawning hope. "I just haven't known what I should do. You don't know what it's like to feel so trapped, so helpless!"

"Oh, yes, I do," said Morgan bitterly. "Lady Rinnelle, can you break this transformation spell over me?"

The Topaz Heir shook her head. "I don't think I can. It's Kett's spell."

"Try," Morgan urged. He hopped down from Lady Rhuddlan's lap and sat on the floor, looking up at the Topaz Heir hopefully.

Lady Rinnelle shut her eyes and whispered some words under her breath. The air felt thick and heavy for a moment, and then a sweet breeze, smelling like cinnamon, stirred the room's air. It lifted the tendrils of hair over Jena's forehead and ruffled Morgan's fur. His outline shimmered for a moment—and then solidified again. Lady Rinnelle gave a little gasp and then opened her eyes and shook her head. "I'm sorry," she said, looking at Morgan with regret. "But I can't."

Morgan's ears drooped with disappointment. Lady Rhuddlan's hand crept down, as if to tousle the fur on the top of his head consolingly, but she pulled back without touching him.

"We were wondering whether retrieving Morgan's talisman ring might help us break the spell," Jena suggested. "Do you think that could work?"

"I wouldn't know, but . . . maybe."

"Can you help us get the ring back?"

Lady Rinnelle bit her lip. "I don't know. Kett won't answer any of my messages now. But perhaps I can help you think of something. . . ."

"What about the spell over the Diamond?" Lady Rhuddlan demanded.

Lady Rinnelle sighed. "Don't you think I've tried? That took magic from both of us, and Kett won't lift a finger to help me break it. It's not something I can do by myself."

A discouraged silence fell. "I have to be getting back to the banquet," Lady Rhuddlan said, stirring restlessly. "It wouldn't be wise for me to stay away much longer."

"Oh, yes!" Lady Rinnelle said, starting and turning pale. "Guilford and Woric will wonder where I've been, too."

"We have to meet again and talk some more tomorrow," Morgan said.

"Not tomorrow, I'm afraid," Lady Rhuddlan said, shaking her head. "I will have Council business all day, and I'm afraid I couldn't extricate myself without prompting a lot of questions."

"The day after tomorrow, then," Morgan said. "But where?"

"Not at my house," Lady Rinnelle said quickly.

"I know," Jena said. "You two ladies both need to order some jewelry."

"We do?" Lady Rinnelle said.

"Yes." Jena smiled. "At . . . let's say two days' time, at midafternoon, at my father Collas Gemcutter's shop. I think I can have someone there who might be able to offer us some advice."

CHAPTER
Nineteen

"I'M NOT ACCUSING YOU OF luring me here under false pretenses, mind," Arikan said, reaching for a platter of delicate Festival cakes. "But you'll have to admit the distinguished company you promised me is rather tardy in arriving. Luckily, I have the generous contents of your father's larder with which to console myself."

"They were supposed to arrive by now," Jena said. "They will—they *must* come." The two sat in the front room of Jena's house with the brazier pulled up close to drive away the winter chill. When Jena had reported the Diamond Heir and Topaz Heir were expected to call, Collas, although surprised by the singular honor, had ordered refreshment worthy of the expected company, and her father's cook had risen to the occasion admirably. Besides the platter of cakes (Arikan was making rapid inroads through these), the table boasted an assortment of candied oranges and ginger, meringue piped into the shape of swans, dainty quince tarts, and hot mulled wine.

"Must come, you say? Is it your magic telling you that, or simply your wishes speaking? If the Ruby is like most nobles, she may have fears—"

"You're the one who told me not to generalize about people, Arikan," Jena said a trifle sharply. "I trust Lady Rhuddlan. She'll be here." She hesitated. "But I'm not at all sure about Lady Rinnelle."

"Excuse me, miss." The new servant girl, Terza, stood at the doorway. "The guests you've been expecting have arrived, and the master's greeting them now."

"Oh. Er, thank you." As Terza left, Jena turned to Arikan with some alarm. "I didn't think—oh, but of course Father would assume they came to see him."

"Don't worry, Jena," Arikan said. "I've already spoken to Collas. He knows your visitors have a purpose other than spending appalling amounts of money on the fruits of his labors. He'll extend the courtesies of the house and then bring them here. Be easy," he added, raising a hand to forestall her shocked objection. "I haven't told him anything about Court politics, or magic, for that matter, which isn't his business to know."

Jena tried to draw comfort from that assurance. "Thank you, Arikan. I think."

Within a few moments Jena heard footsteps in the hallway and Collas' voice coming toward them. She and Arikan stood. ". . . here to receive you. Jena," Collas said, coming through the doorway first and then stepping aside so Lady Rhuddlan and Lady Rinnelle could enter, "if you will attend? It's my understanding, your grace, my lady, that you've both already met my daughter Jena?"

"We have indeed." Lady Rhuddlan, who was carrying Morgan, smiled at Jena with perfect self-possession. She stooped to place him carefully on the floor. Morgan sat down at her feet and looked up at Jena and Arikan with an innocently doggy expression. Lady Rinnelle appeared subdued; she raised her eyes fleetingly to meet Jena's and then her gaze dropped to the floor again as she nodded slightly.

Jena curtsied. "Your grace, Lady Rinnelle," Jena said, "allow me to present to you Arikan, my former teacher and very good friend. Arikan, her grace Lady Vianne Rhuddlan, and Lady Rinnelle."

"A very great honor and pleasure," Arikan replied, bowing.

As the ladies settled into their seats and busied themselves removing gloves and veils, Collas took his leave. "Your grace, my lady, thank you again for honoring my house." He inclined his head as they murmured the proper things and then left the room, quietly closing the door behind him.

"Did you have difficulty finding my home, your grace?" Jena asked.

"No," Lady Rhuddlan replied. "Morgan knew the way. That is," she added, looking at Arikan, "my friend, Lord Morgan, er—provided directions."

"It's all right," Jena said quickly. "He knows about Morgan."

"Oh. I see," said Lady Rhuddlan. She looked a little distressed.

"Lord Morgan," Jena said, "may I present Arikan? Arikan, Lord Morgan." *And that's undoubtedly the first time I've ever introduced anyone to a terrier.*

"Delighted, my lord," Arikan said, inclining his head gravely.

With dignity, Morgan stood up and "bowed," bending one foreleg as he extended the other out before him. Jena caught Lady Rhuddlan's eye, and at the exchange of glances, both hastily turned their faces away to hide their smiles. Then Morgan approached the table and lay down at Lady Rhuddlan's feet. "There was another problem that made us late," he said, glaring up at Lady Rinnelle.

The Topaz Heir flushed. "I . . . I didn't want to come. I sent a note to Lady Rhuddlan—"

"With an excuse which I judged to be insufficient," Lady Rhuddlan cut in briskly with a smile, but with a dangerous edge to her voice. "And so there was a delay while I went to the Oselare Palazzo and, ah, *persuaded* Lady Rinnelle to join us as planned."

"Well, I'm here," Lady Rinnelle said, and for the first time a note of defiance crept into her voice. "What now?"

"Perhaps that depends on this gentleman here," Lady Rhuddlan replied, eying Arikan.

"Arikan is an adept," Jena said carefully, "who practices as a magician here in Piyar."

"You've acquainted him with the entire situation?" said Lady Rhuddlan, raising an eyebrow. Beside her, Lady Rinnelle turned pale.

Jena refused to be cowed by the Ruby's frosty tone. "Yes. I trust his judgment and discretion, your grace. Surely you see we need the guidance."

"I'm touched by Jena's faith in me," Arikan said as the two noblewomen looked at him expectantly. "Unfortunately, I must blushingly disclaim at least part of her praise. I have not been discreet. I, too, in fact, have consulted another person." He smiled and extended a plate. "Have one of these delicious tarts."

Jena felt the blood drain from her face, and Lady Rhuddlan gasped. Morgan sprang to his paws. "How dare you betray the secrets of her grace the Lady Rhuddlan! Villain! You wretch—you—" Abruptly he broke into a paroxysm of barking.

"Calm yourself, my lord," Arikan overrode him, unruffled. "You offend the ladies' ears." Taking a tart from the plate, he popped it into his mouth. "Once you know all, I doubt you will complain. You, at least, already know the person I've taken into our confidence."

Morgan's barking subsided into a murderous growl. Lady Rhuddlan leaned forward. "Why—" she began, and then jumped at a knock from the hallway door.

The three women exchanged nervous glances, and then Jena got up to answer it. It was Terza.

"If you please, miss," she said, "there's a lady here asking for Arikan."

"Ah," said the magician, getting to his feet. "Show her in, won't you?"

And in swept Lady Kestrienne.

"My *dear* friend Arikan," she said, her eyes twinkling as if she had noticed the stupefied silence and rather enjoyed it. "You've gained weight. Your rapacious taste for sweets, no doubt." She extended her hand to him, and he bowed and kissed it.

"You, on the other hand, are looking as blooming as ever, my lady."

"Hmph. As quick to flatter as ever, too. How commonplace. Ah, well, there is something to be admired in consistency."

"Aunt Kestrienne!" Morgan exclaimed.

"Ah, Morgan. I can't say your appearance is much improved since I last saw you. Still, we must make allowances for the fact it's not strictly voluntary, mustn't we?" She turned to the Ruby. "My dear child. I have come to help you, if I may."

Lady Rhuddlan looked puzzled. "I thank you, but I don't quite see the justification"—she glanced at Arikan—"for consulting you in such . . . er, a delicate affair."

"Why," said Lady Kestrienne, as if it were the most natural thing in the world, "Arikan needed to call upon my expertise as a wizard, naturally."

Lady Rhuddlan sat back in her chair. "A wizard!" she said, astonished. "You?"

"Why, yes, of course."

Lady Rinnelle's eyes widened, and Jena realized that this was the first time it had occurred to the Topaz Heir that other noblewomen besides herself might be adepts.

"But Lady Kestrienne," Jena put in, "how is it you're here? I thought you weren't expected to arrive in the city for several more days at least. This is Lady Kestrienne," she added as an explanation to Lady Rinnelle, "who has been en route by sea from Duone Keep, up north in the Uriat Mountains. Lady Kestrienne, I believe you know her grace, Lady Rhuddlan, and this is Lady Rinnelle of the House of Oselare."

"Splendid to see you." Lady Kestrienne beamed. She removed her muff and sat down in a chair Arikan had pulled out from the wall for her. Arikan poured her some mulled wine and then refilled the other goblets, too.

"Did you use magic to raise a wind to get here more quickly?" asked Morgan, lying down again at Lady Rhuddlan's feet.

"Magic? Oh, no, no, no. Well, I could have," she added as an afterthought. "But prodding the possibilities associated with weather patterns takes immense power, and it would have sent me to bed for a week at least. Fortunately, it didn't prove to be necessary; we were blessed with very favorable winds. It's possible to be favored with simple luck, you know, even if one knows magic."

"Is Lady Duone well?" Jena asked.

"Yes, quite well, and the baby is growing at a prodigious

rate. We were met by Ranulf's escort at Niolantti, and so we learned of your situation in Tenaway. How fortunate you kept your head there, Jena, and kept Ranulf from haring off after phantom dangers! But now," she went on briskly, "I understand we meet today to discuss other matters. Arikan has acquainted me with the situation. My partner—never mind who—and I are at your disposal."

Jena could see Lady Rinnelle was eying Lady Kestrienne's ring. "So you're really a wizard?" she asked timidly.

"Yes. A less troublesome one than you, I think."

A sudden flurry of coughs came from Arikan, who seemed to have choked for a moment on a Festival cake.

Lady Rinnelle blushed deeply. "I've done nothing!"

Lady Kestrienne raised an eyebrow. "Nothing? The binding spell on the Diamond was nothing?"

The Topaz Heir looked away in genuine pain. "But I've explained: I did that out of honorable loyalties. And it wasn't just me! Kett—that is . . ." she floundered to a stop and shook her head.

"Hmm." Lady Kestrienne studied her through narrowed eyes.

"Morgan and I have been wondering," Lady Rhuddlan ventured, "whether someone else could be behind all this. Besides Lady Rinnelle and her partner, I mean."

"An interesting theory," Arikan commented. "Would you care to elaborate?"

"Well," Morgan said, "no one ever taught Lady Rinnelle magic, except for Kett, or so she says."

"It's true," Lady Rinnelle insisted faintly.

"So where did Kett learn it?" Morgan continued. "Someone must have taught him. Could that someone be using him now?"

"Perhaps," said Lady Kestrienne. "Perhaps not. It's entirely possible, as Lady Rinnelle says, that he never had a teacher or tutor. He could have picked up what he learned from experimentation. It's rare, but a wizard can be self-trained."

"Maybe he also discovered some old books on the subject," Arikan added.

"Why are you so sure someone else must be involved?" Lady Kestrienne asked.

Lady Rhuddlan glanced at Lady Rinnelle. "I've known Rinnelle for many years. I don't believe she is, well, capable of being the moving force behind such a conspiracy."

"You mean because she's too spineless," Lady Kestrienne said, smiling. Lady Rinnelle colored angrily.

Arikan gave the Topaz Heir a sympathetic look. "Now, now, my Lady Kestrienne. Be nice."

"And Kett is . . . well, he's only a sea captain," Morgan said.

Both Lady Kestrienne and Arikan began to laugh. "Don't allow yourself to be deceived by aristocratic snobbery," Arikan said. "If you'd stop to think like a wizard, you'd realize lowly sea captains can have high ambitions, too."

"Wild talents are the most powerful," Lady Kestrienne said. "And don't forget: wizard pairs are bound by the attraction of their opposite natures. Lady Rinnelle is cowardly, you think? Too hopelessly scared and suggestible to ever dream up such a plot, eh? Then you must assume her partner is all the more ruthless."

Lady Rinnelle looked down at her hands, breathing rather quickly.

"Which means, my dear," Lady Kestrienne said kindly, "that if you could manage to put some starch into your spine, that would make it all the more easy for us to successfully confront your partner."

Finally Lady Rinnelle looked up and met Lady Kestrienne's eyes. "You want me to betray Kett."

"You may think of it that way, if you so choose." Lady Kestrienne smiled slightly.

"And how do you think of it?" Lady Rinnelle challenged.

Lady Kestrienne's smile disappeared. "I think of it as righting wrongs." She extended a slender, manicured finger and pointed deliberately at Lady Rhuddlan. "Yes, and assisting this woman in claiming the Adamant Throne which is rightfully hers." Her finger swung down toward Morgan. "And helping this man regain his rightful shape. These are two young people who love each other, who are being kept apart by the malice of your partner's spell." She shrugged with elaborate casualness. "Despite what my flattering friend Arikan might say, I am an old woman, and old women must be amused. And it amuses me to help young people who have been wronged, particularly when they are in love."

"Doing what is right is the proper business of adepts," Arikan put in. "Don't forget, we're also trying to release the Diamond from a living death, and to save your brother's life."

"Oh, yes," Lady Kestrienne said. "That, too."

Lady Rinnelle's face crumpled, and she covered it with shaking hands. "But . . . but I'm . . . in love with Kett!" they heard her say in a muffled voice. "That is—I'm marrying Woric, and . . . and I love him, too . . . but Kett and I—" she choked on a sob.

"Ah." Lady Kestrienne nodded slowly. "Then I truly pity you, my dear."

Tears began to leak out between Lady Rinnelle's fingers.

"Listen to me," Lady Kestrienne continued. "I've not come here today because I'm burning to persuade you to betray anyone, least of all your partner. If I'm trying to do anything, it is to make you do your job! Your ability to do magic, to see and act upon possibilities, gives you the potential for great power, and having a partner to cover your blind spots increases that power even further.

"And yet with great power comes great responsibility. Your blind spots are covered by your partner, but you must, in turn, cover his. And what does that mean? It means you're the one who must keep him honest. Your partnership should be a mirror which forces each of you to see the consequences of lies and hurtful actions. By maintaining balance between the two of you, and by being honest, you prevent each other from falling prey to one of the most insidious temptations of the powerful: the temptation to steal magic—that is, to coerce the actions and choices of others.

"From what I'm told, you and Kett have failed to do that. But I believe you can rebuild the equilibrium you were meant to have between you, and the power in your partnership can be guided with training and used for good." She smiled. "And don't forget one of the most important possibilities of all: that Kett might change his mind."

After a moment Lady Rinnelle began fumbling at the cuffs of her moss-colored brocade sleeves. Lady Rhuddlan raised her eyes toward the ceiling in mute appeal and took a handkerchief from her sleeve. She poked Lady Rinnelle on the shoulder with it.

Lady Rinnelle took the proffered piece of linen and used it to wipe her eyes. "So . . . you think . . ."

"Listen to yourself," Jena interrupted gently. "You're always worried about what we think, or the Court, or your brother, or Kett. What about what *you* think?"

Lady Rinnelle sat silently, pulling the damp square through her fingers.

"You're a wizard," Arikan said. "Not a puppet on a string."

Lady Rinnelle took a deep breath and looked up at them all. "So what do we do first?"

"What do *you* want to do?" Lady Rhuddlan asked.

Lady Rinnelle looked down at the dog on the floor. "I think we should start by changing Lord Morgan back into his proper form."

Morgan raised himself up on his forepaws. "As soon as possible!" He cocked his head, tail thumping on the floor. "Only how?"

"Have you thought of a way we could get Morgan's ring back?" Jena asked Lady Rinnelle.

She shook her head. "I don't even know where he's keeping it."

"He's wearing it," Jena said.

"Is he?" said Lady Kestrienne, her face brightening. She exchanged glances with Arikan. "Well, that might make things easier. My, he's rash. Or, I suppose, he doesn't know any better."

"What do you mean?" Lady Rhuddlan asked. "It's a wizard's talisman, after all. Doesn't that give him additional power?"

"He probably thinks so, too," Arikan said, "but after all, it's not *his* wizard's talisman. And it's keyed to someone who isn't his partner. True, as long as Kett holds on to that ring, Morgan's magic is weakened. Morgan's partnership with Jena is unbalanced, too, since she has a ring and he doesn't. But the ring probably unbalances Kett as well, possibly enough to interfere with his command of his own magic."

Morgan's ears went up with surprise. "You say my magic is only weakened?" he said. "When I was first transformed, I tried to do spells, but I couldn't. I thought Kett's spell was blocking me. And then when Jena explained wizardry to me, we assumed that the problem was that I no longer had my ring."

"Oh, for goodness' sake, Morgan!" Lady Kestrienne exclaimed. "The ring doesn't contain your power. You were a magician before you met your partner, before I'd even given you that ring. Have you forgotten all the lessons I taught you?"

"I'm telling you, I did try, but I couldn't use my magic at all! What does the ring do, exactly, if it doesn't hold my magic?"

"It serves as a focus, intensifying your ability to see and manipulate possibilities." Lady Kestrienne selected a candied orange and nibbled on it. "And it binds your connection with your partner, meaning the two of you can use it to communicate."

"So that's why I encountered Kett when I tried scrying my own ring," said Jena. She shuddered. "I'm not anxious to try that again."

"But if my ring doesn't hold my magic," Morgan said, "does that mean even if we get it back, it won't break the spell?"

Arikan stroked his beard. "There is that possibility. You won't know until you try."

"Forgive me, but that brings us back to the same point," said Lady Rhuddlan. "How are we going to retrieve it?"

"First we need to find Kett," said Arikan.

"Preferably in a public setting," Lady Rhuddlan said, glancing at Morgan, who nodded. "That will limit his ability to use magic against us, won't it?"

"He'll be participating in the flotilla of ships during the Union of City and Sea Ceremony the day after tomorrow," Lady Rinnelle said, "with the rest of the Golden Fleet."

"Of course!" Lady Rhuddlan exclaimed. "He'll be coming on shore for the parade and the civic ceremony."

"How very fortunate," said Lady Kestrienne.

"The next question is, how do we get him to take the ring off so we can get it away from him?" said Arikan.

They pondered for a moment. "I could bite his hand off," Morgan said, not entirely in jest.

Lady Rhuddlan smiled a little ruefully and shook her head. "I think not."

"Well, what reasons do people have to remove their rings?" Morgan said.

"Sometimes people take them off when they sleep," Jena suggested.

"Perhaps, although I doubt Kett will be napping at the ceremony," Arikan observed.

"Maybe . . . if he got something on his hands. Might he take it off to clean it?" suggested Lady Rhuddlan.

"Nooo," said Morgan dubiously.

They thought some more. "People remove their rings to give them to someone," Lady Kestrienne said. She looked at Lady Rinnelle. "Could you convince him to give it to you?"

"But . . . but I can't approach him in the middle of a public ceremony!" Lady Rinnelle stammered. "Think how suspicious it would look if I were seen talking to him!"

"Why would it?" Jena said. "After all, he's the captain who ferries the Oselare family. It would simply be regarded as a gesture of courtesy to someone who has performed a service to your household."

"But what could I possibly say that would make him relinquish it?"

"Perhaps if you said you've changed your mind, that you want to marry him," Jena said slowly. "Could you ask him to give it to you as a troth ring?"

"But I tell you, I'm going to marry Woric!" Lady Rinnelle exclaimed, looking even more terrified.

"No," Lady Kestrienne said quickly. "That's a poor way to rebalance Kett's partnership with Lady Rinnelle. And it would destroy any chance of persuading him to undo the spell on the Diamond."

"Aunt, you can't believe he'll ever agree to release that spell on his own," Morgan said.

"It's a slim possibility, I agree, but it's there. We have to give him that chance, but you'll spoil it forever once you encourage his partner to begin lying to him. Lies twist magic and unbalance things even further. No, don't even think of it."

"Just tell him the truth," said Arikan. "Say you know what he did to Lord Morgan and try to persuade him to give you the ring back so you can break the spell."

Morgan snorted. "Oh, that will certainly work."

"Really, it might," Lady Kestrienne insisted. "He should have the opportunity."

"I really don't think he'd take it, my lady," Lady Rhuddlan said, and grimaced. "From what he said when he gave Morgan to me, I think he's deriving too much pleasure from what he's done to us."

"But really, if you would just try . . ." Lady Kestrienne's words trailed off as heads were shaking around the room.

"He'd get angry, I know he would," said Lady Rinnelle. "And then he might start arguing with me, loudly, about spells and magic. . . . It would expose me in public!" She shuddered. "Oh, no, no, I can't risk it!"

Lady Kestrienne sighed.

Arikan picked up the last Festival cake from the platter and then stopped with it halfway to his mouth. "A person might take off a ring to put on another one."

Jena sat up straight. "That's right!" She thought hard for a moment. "Listen: there's one person who has a reason to approach Kett during the ceremony without making him suspicious."

"Who?" asked Lady Rhuddlan.

Jena smiled. "You."

"Me?" Lady Rhuddlan looked stunned.

"No," said Morgan. "Absolutely not."

"Wait, Morgan, and listen." Jena turned back to Lady Rhuddlan. "You're not a wizard. Kett doesn't think you have any reason to know about wizardry. As far as he knows, you still don't have any idea about the true identity of your little dog. Goodness, if you're right and he's gloating about the spell he put over Morgan, he might even relish the prospect of getting close and exchanging a word or two with you about how you're enjoying your pet."

Lady Rhuddlan nodded doubtfully. "Go on."

"You're also the Diamond Heir, and since the Diamond is ill, you're going to be presiding over the ceremony. We can put wards over you for protection." She thought for another moment. "Now suppose, just suppose, that at the ceremony itself a special tribute is given to all the captains of the Golden Fleet." She smiled. "In honor of their faithful service to the Diadem, and in recognition of the special, honored part they have in the ceremony, each is going to receive a golden ring from the hand of the Diamond Heir herself."

"Ah!" Lady Kestrienne exclaimed.

"You wouldn't want to let it be known beforehand," Jena continued, warming more and more toward the idea, "because you want him to arrive at the ceremony still wearing Morgan's ring."

Lady Rhuddlan frowned. "Yes, but if I understand you correctly about wizard talismans, I won't even be able to see it."

"That's even better. Since he knows that, he's not likely to be wary of you." Jena grinned. "But you'll be carrying your little dog. You take him with you everywhere, don't you? Morgan can see the ring, and he can place his paw over the finger on your hand that's the correct one, and no one will be the wiser."

"That might work," said Morgan, sounding a bit surprised.

"Have the captains all lined up in front of you," Jena continued, "make the announcement, and then go down the line, placing a ring on each finger. When you get to Kett . . ." she hesitated.

"Well?"

"Hmm. Well, either he'll take off the ring—"

"In which case I'll jump up and grab it!" exclaimed Morgan.

Jena gave him a look. "Do you really think you can do that?"

Morgan began panting with excitement. "I can do it. I know I can! And then, well, I suppose I'll change back as soon as I touch it, won't I?"

"But what if Kett doesn't take it off?" Lady Rhuddlan said. "He might think that since I can't see it, it would be safe to leave it on and let me place the new ring on his finger right on top of Morgan's."

"In that case, when he extends his finger toward you so you can put a ring on it, you reach out and grab Morgan's ring off his hand. You may not be able to see it, but I'll wager you can feel it."

"Try touching Jena's," Lady Kestrienne suggested.

"It's here, your grace, on the fourth finger," Jena said, extending her right hand toward Lady Rhuddlan. "Can you feel it?"

The Ruby hesitantly reached out a finger. "I can," she said, surprised.

"But his magic!" cried Lady Rinnelle. "What if he sees the possibility of what Lady Rhuddlan intends?"

Jena tapped a finger to her lips. "I might make a point of being there at the ceremony, but over to one side. He would focus his attention on me instead."

"Possibilities are much more difficult to scry in a crowd," Arikan said, "simply because there are so many of them. And I think Jena is right: Lady Rhuddlan would be the least likely to arouse his suspicions."

Lady Rinnelle shook her head. "But once Lady Rhuddlan tries to seize the ring . . ."

"What can he do?" Jena said. "Try to wrestle it away from her? He'll have half a dozen Palace guards on him in seconds."

"But he might attack her magically!"

"That's why we'll place the wards over her. Lady Kestrienne and Arikan can help me, to make them especially strong."

"It still sounds quite risky," Arikan said, and then slowly began to smile. "But it might just do the job."

"Are you willing to try it, my child?" Lady Kestrienne asked Lady Rhuddlan. "We'll do our best to protect you, of course, but you'll still be assuming most of the danger."

Lady Rhuddlan looked at Morgan. "Yes, I'll do it. Anything to change him back."

For a moment, Morgan looked as though he were going to begin barking again out of sheer exultation. Instead, he took a deep breath and put his paw on Lady Rhuddlan's shoe. "Thank you, Vianne," he said. "I hope it works."

"We all do," Lady Rhuddlan said, and then frowned. "What can be done about the Diamond?"

"I'll try again to break the spell on my own," Lady Rinnelle offered. She sighed. "I *have* been trying."

Arikan eyed the empty Festival cake platter with regret and pushed it away. "Why don't you come to my home now with me, my lady? I've some books that might contain an answer to the problem, and we could go through them together."

"A magician's house?" Lady Rinnelle fluttered nervously. "Oh, er, that is—I need to be getting home again—"

"Nonsense," said Lady Kestrienne, waving a hand. "Do go along with him. I assure you, Arikan won't bite!" She glanced at the dog on the floor. "You can't say that of everyone, you know."

Morgan bared his teeth at her. "Aunt—"

"But if my family were to find out!" Lady Rinnelle exclaimed.

"Oh, pish posh," Lady Kestrienne said. "If they do, simply tell them you went there to get your fortune told. They can hardly hold that against you: all brides-to-be are considered superstitious!"

"What if the two of you can't break the spell?" Lady Rhuddlan asked.

"Then we try to find some way to force Kett to do so," Jena said, "although I think we should wait until we see whether we can change Morgan back once we have his ring. If I have to tangle directly with another wizard, I'd rather do so with my partner at my side."

"You might want to come along with us as well, your grace, my lord," Arikan offered. "We can do some research on the spell over Lord Morgan, too."

"Splendid!" said Lady Kestrienne. "Lady Rhuddlan can have her fortune told at the same time."

After a bit more discussion working out the details of the plan, Arikan took his leave, accompanied by Lady Rinnelle, Lady Rhuddlan, and Morgan.

Left alone with Jena, Lady Kestrienne turned her attention

to the remaining refreshments. "How fortunate Arikan departed before ravaging all of the tarts," she remarked, selecting one dusted with almond slivers and taking a bite. "Mmm. Delicious. I'm so pleased to have the opportunity to see you in your father's home." She went to the window to unlatch a shutter and push it open. A burst of cold air made Jena shiver, but Lady Kestrienne breathed it in deeply. "That garden must be charming in the spring."

"Yes, it is." Jena came to the window to look, too. The winter silence in the garden was thoughtful and still. A fine rime of frost encrusted the bare twigs of the bushes and trees, lacy patterns of silvery white against the crisp blue of the sky. Jena thought of all the hours she had spent there, walking along the path or sitting on the bench at sunset, looking down toward Lowertown. She and Bram had shared the bench sometimes, talking quietly or just being silent together. She sighed.

"You're going to miss it, aren't you?"

"I'm sorry?"

"When you leave, to set up your own household. After all, you're a bride-to-be, too, aren't you?" She looked over her shoulder with an expression Jena couldn't quite decipher. "Perhaps you'd like your fortune told as well?"

"I don't know if I am a bride-to-be anymore," Jena said slowly. She shivered again, and with one last look at the garden reached out and closed the shutter. "Bram is traveling. He left to look for me. We last spoke months ago, and since then, everything has changed."

Lady Kestrienne said nothing.

"I think Lady Rhuddlan may be a little worried, too," Jena said, giving Lady Kestrienne a sidelong glance. "Lady Rinnelle said Kett told her partners could only marry one another."

Lady Kestrienne looked genuinely startled. "Did he indeed? Gracious! I certainly hope you told her it's not true."

"Well, I did. Still, I wondered. Arikan's never married, as far as I know, and you—"

"I'm a widow, my dear."

"Oh. I'm sorry."

"Don't be. I'm not."

"Er—"

"So, you see, your partnership with Morgan isn't an obstacle. There's no reason why you and your young man shouldn't marry." She cocked her head. "Unless there's something else?"

For an instant, Jena hated Lady Kestrienne for the questions she was asking, questions Jena had avoided asking herself because she hadn't been sure whether she could bear the answers. "It took becoming a wizard to make me see I really want to be a gemcutter. It's strange: when I found out the Guild was making obstacles for me, I was ready to give up. If I hadn't been cornered into making up that fib that Lord Morgan had commissioned a piece from me, I don't think I would have challenged their ruling at all.

"Now I'm not just following my father's path anymore; I'm ready to fight for the right to cut gems. But I'm beginning to think marrying Bram would create even more obstacles." She shook her head. "It sounds like an awful thing to say. But it's true."

Lady Kestrienne pursed her lips. "Why should marrying your young man keep you from doing what you want to do?"

Jena sighed, thinking of her conversation with Bram by the river, the day she partnered with Morgan. "If I'm going to take on the Guild, it would help if my husband was supporting me." *Maybe it's for the best,* he had said. "I'm not sure Bram would.

"And if I marry, there would be children." She felt a lump begin to rise in her throat. "I want to have them, but how could I raise them and still run a shop? Even if I do manage to wrangle from the Guild the right to cut gems, my license would be hereditary, in trust for a son. If I have a boy, the Guild would use that as an excuse to deny me my trade again."

"I believe I've already expressed my opinion about having to get the Guild's permission. About anything."

"It's not that simple!"

"Besides, Jena, you have the power to decide whether or not to have sons, or whether to have children at all. If it would be easier, you can simply remain childless."

"What?" Jena stared at Lady Kestrienne. "Of course I'm going to have children if I marry."

"You are a wizard," said Lady Kestrienne, enunciating the words slowly, presumably in deference to Jena's stupidity. "You can see possibilities and learn to manipulate them. That means you can control your own fertility." She smiled. "I'll teach you. It takes concentration and care, but the precepts are very simple."

"I can decide?" The idea stunned Jena.

"Yes, you can. A very useful skill—valuable if you choose to take a lover on the side, for example; you never have to worry about an inconvenient pregnancy."

"I would never do that!" Jena exclaimed. "I don't believe in that."

"Ah, well. That was always one of the chief attractions of wizardry for me, but to each her own. And that's the point, Jena," she went on serenely, oblivious to Jena's shock. "You can choose. You don't have to let yourself be buffeted around by circumstances beyond your control, like 'the Guild won't let me,' or 'once I have children I can't.' Being able to see and manipulate possibilities clarifies the choices available to you, but you still have to make the decision: do you *want* to marry your fiancé?" She went back to the table to refill her wine goblet.

Jena hesitated. "I think—"

"No, no; don't speak. You haven't had enough time to think about what I've told you yet. If you said one way or another, you might change your mind, and that would be embarrassing, wouldn't it? I do so dislike buying wedding presents and then discovering that they aren't to be used. And you'd want to speak to your young man again before deciding, hmm? What was his name again?"

"Bram." Jena wondered whether he would agree to marry knowing he would never have sons, or perhaps children at all. Or would she even tell him? Yes, of course she would.

But what did *she* want?

She looked at Lady Kestrienne speculatively. "Did you and Arikan ever—" She stopped, and reddened.

Lady Kestrienne twirled her wine in her goblet. "Did Arikan and I ever what, dear?"

"Never mind. I mean, I was just wondering about something, but it's really too personal to ask."

"Did we—oh." Enlightenment appeared in Lady Kestrienne's eyes. Her lips twitched, and then she began to laugh. "Did we ever? Oh, yes, we did." She continued laughing, not at all discomfited, unlike Jena, who blushed furiously. "Arikan is one of my dearest friends in the world. But just because you're friends and partners doesn't mean everything should go that way. Yes, we tried it, but it didn't work out. Oh, no, it really didn't work out at all." She stopped laughing to take another sip of wine and considered.

"And besides: he snores."

CHAPTER TWENTY

TWO DAYS LATER, THE MORN-
ing of the Union of City and Sea Ceremony dawned with
reckless splendor, bright and crystalline. The sun touched
with fire the roof of the Winter Palace and edged with gold
the sails and rigging of the tall ships tacking proudly across
the harbor. It reflected off the choppy water of the bay, dazzling the eyes of the throng jamming the wharves and ferry-
boat rails to watch the flotilla and the swimming races. At
the Golden Market Piazza, it caught silken shimmers in the
crowd's Festival finery. And, at the dais set up at the piazza's edge, overlooking the water, angled rays glinted off a
narrow tray of golden rings, casting glimmering lights over
Lady Vianne Rhuddlan's honey-blond hair.

By special arrangement, Jena stood to one side, at the
steps leading up to the dais where the Diadem and other no-
tables sat. Kett would be sure to see her there. She couldn't
spot Arikan but knew he stood in the crowd, protective
wards ready. The task of safeguarding Lady Rhuddlan had
fallen to Lady Kestrienne, who stood with the gathering of
nobles ranged on the other side of the dais.

The morning had seen an assortment of swimming and
boat races, and Festival speeches and presentations from sev-

eral city leaders and Council members. The crowd, in a fine holiday mood, jostled around Jena constantly, not always paying very close attention to the orations coming from the dais. With such a shifting mass of people, Jena was hard-put to keep her chosen place, not to mention her temper. Small boys dodged between legs to catch glimpses of the jugglers; young men with their giggling sweethearts vied for the attention of the strolling vendors selling Festival tokens and sweets. A pair of sailors elbowing their way through the press stopped directly behind her, and she winced as they cheered, whistling piercingly in her ear for one of the winning swimmers receiving a medallion up at the dais.

And then, a flourish of trumpets announced the arrival of the small fleet of boats carrying the captains' cortege. Jena craned her neck to see as eagerly as anyone around her. A ragged cheer rose up, and another mass of people who had been milling about at the boat landing surged back to let the procession pass. As the crowd parted, Jena saw Kett in the midst of the other captains, coming toward the dais.

He wore a pourpoint of cream-colored linen trimmed at the shoulder with a rosette of the Diadem colors. The matching ribbons trimming it trailed down his arm, fluttering in the breeze. All the captains had a rosette like it, she saw, and the rippling streams of color made a brave, festive show. But Kett's expression was somber; unlike the other men with whom he walked, who smiled and waved to the crowd, the wizard stared straight ahead, seemingly unconscious of the people immediately around him. As the procession came closer, Jena saw that he was scanning the dais with quick, darting glances—looking, no doubt, for Lady Rinnelle.

His searching made the chance that he would see Jena an easy possibility to manage. As the procession reached the head of the piazza and turned so the captains could walk toward the stairs leading up to the dais, she stepped forward and stared at Kett boldly, directing her magic toward him in a mental command: *Look at me, Kett.* He raised his head and saw her. At first she wasn't sure whether he knew her, but then his eyes widened in recognition and perhaps even alarm, as Arikan's power reached out to join her in agreement and warding: *Behold your challenger, Kett.* She was sure Kett was aware of the warding lines, but she didn't bother making any explicit threat. Let him expend all his magic trying to scry what she was planning to do.

Now the line of captains was mounting the steps and marching forward. She kept her chin high and smiled a very small smile at Kett, who shot her an inscrutable look as he passed her.

Wondering, eh? She concentrated her stare on the middle of his back, noting with satisfaction the tense set of his shoulders. *Go ahead and sweat, Captain.*

Lady Rhuddlan rose to her feet and came forward, carrying Morgan. She regarded the line of men ranged before her, and Morgan shifted in her hands. Jena couldn't see what he was doing with his paws, but whatever it was, it seemed to give the Ruby the required signal. Lady Rhuddlan smiled and placed Morgan on the ground at her side. "Good captains of the Golden Fleet," she said in a strong, carrying voice. The sounds of the crowd gradually died down as the people fell silent to hear her words. "At the behest of the Diadem Council and the citizens of Piyar, I wish you a joyous Festival and extend to you and your crews our warmest hospitality.

"The celebration of the bonds between Piyar and the sea has a long and rich tradition. We have always been a seafaring people. Piyar itself was founded here because of the conjunction of navigable rivers with a deep sea bay. Through us, the Founders splendidly fulfilled their hopes to establish our country as a great sea power. And as the fortunes of those who love and serve the sea have prospered, so have those of our city.

"Today we choose you as our representatives of all those who have helped fulfill the Founders' dream for us by bringing us the sea's blessings. Accept, then, these rings as tokens of our most heartfelt thanks."

Kett had been looking sidelong at Jena during this speech, but now, as Lady Rhuddlan signaled to her side, he turned his attention forward. A young girl came to stand a little behind the Ruby with the tray of rings. Lady Rhuddlan picked one up and stepped over to the first captain, Morgan following closely at her heels. She reached out to clasp the captain's hands warmly, and then raised one and slipped the ring she had selected on his right forefinger. They exchanged a few words in an undertone, and then the captain bowed deeply, his hand pressed to his chest. The crowd sighed in approval, and a ragged spatter of applause rose up.

The next captain, one of the youngest in the line, knelt swiftly as the Ruby turned to him, and seized her hand and kissed it. As the crowd roared, Lady Rhuddlan, laughing, drew him to his feet again and slipped a ring on his hand. Then she continued down the line, giving the rings to each captain, until she reached Kett, the third man from the end.

Standing straight at attention, Kett smiled at the Ruby, and then inclined his head in a courteous half bow. Jena thought he said something to her. With commendable self-possession the Ruby returned the smile and took his hand. Jena held her breath and sent her magic to join Lady Kestrienne's ward. Lady Rhuddlan reached toward the tray of rings, and as Kett glanced in that direction, she wrapped her fingers with a quick movement around the base of his right forefinger and pulled hard.

What followed next happened very quickly. Kett's face registered surprise for only a moment, and then he twisted his hand underneath Lady Rhuddlan's grip and hissed something. Jena braced herself for a counterblow to the wards, even as she began pushing forward, trying to see. *Did she get it?*

Lady Rhuddlan staggered back, and then the wards collapsed. Jena's heart lurched. *Oh, no!*

A quick flash erupted at Lady Rhuddlan's throat. As Jena blinked, unsure whether she had really seen it, she felt something wrench and gasped. Whatever it was that had crashed through their safeguards, threatening to swallow the Ruby, abruptly vanished.

Kett gave a hoarse cry and began scrabbling at his right hand. At the same moment, Jena looked down at her talisman ring in surprise; it was suddenly unaccountably hot. Hastily, she eased it off partway to keep it from burning her finger. When she looked up again, she could see Lady Rhuddlan still standing on the dais, apparently unhurt, but not Kett. The palace guards were fanning out over the platform. Jena began fighting her way frantically through the press of people.

"Ho, Jena!" she heard over to her right. It was Arikan. He was at her side in a moment and seized her wrist. She had to grab at her ring hastily to keep it from bouncing off the tip of her finger. It was already cool again, and she pushed it back on.

"Where's Kett?" she demanded. "Did you see?"

"He shoved his way through the people on the dais and jumped off the back."

Jena groaned. She turned and craned her neck. "Is Lady Rhuddlan all right? What happened?"

"I think he tried a spell," Arikan said in her ear, "but it backlashed on him."

"What?"

"Come on." Arikan turned and began cutting a swath through the crowd, Jena following in his wake. Arikan used his height and weight to good advantage, and perhaps a spell to find the fastest possible way through the throng, so that they reached the edge of the dais within a very few moments. "Your grace," he called as Jena stumbled up beside him.

The dignitaries and captains were milling around in confusion, getting in the way of the guards hurrying forward to hear their commander's orders. Lady Rhuddlan, who was speaking urgently to Lady Kestrienne, turned and saw Jena and Arikan. She said something in an undertone to Lady Kestrienne, who came forward to stoop at the edge of the platform. "Morgan has the ring," she told them in a low voice, "and Kett's trying to catch him."

"He's been transformed back?" Jena cried.

"Hush! No," Lady Kestrienne said with a glance over her shoulder. "Kett took it off as if . . . as if it *burned* him—and Morgan jumped up and grabbed it," she continued hurriedly, "but he didn't change back. When Kett tried to seize him, he bolted off the back of the stage. I think he might have jumped in the river." She lowered her voice again. "Morgan always did say he wanted to try the Festival swimming races sometime."

Lady Rhuddlan pulled away from the knot of nervous guards and came up to join them. "My dear Lady Kestrienne, we must find my little dog right away," she said anxiously. *Before Kett finds him,* her eyes pleaded.

"Are you hurt, your grace?" Jena said quietly. "I thought I saw a flash at your throat." That was where the Sunburst was pinned, below the ruff of the Ruby's gown, she realized; it appeared undamaged.

"Never mind me, I'm fine!" Lady Rhuddlan cried in an agonized whisper. *"Find Morgan."*

Jena eyed the Ruby's belt. "Do you know which direction he's heading, your grace?"

Lady Rhuddlan closed her eyes briefly and then opened them. "Upriver, following the waterline." She glanced at Lady Kestrienne. "Did you say you saw him swimming?"

"Dog-paddling," Lady Kestrienne corrected. She stood, glancing over toward the courtiers, some of whom were eyeing their conference curiously. "Your grace, you must finish the ceremony." She nodded briskly at Arikan and Jena. "Good luck," she said, turning away and drawing Lady Rhuddlan back to the center of the dais.

Arikan tugged at Jena's elbow, and they headed back through the crowd in the direction of the waterfront. They began to run once they were well away from the piazza.

"Now what?" Jena cried when they had passed several warehouses and were approaching the quays where the *Foamdancer* and the *Silverwake,* two of the ships in the Golden Fleet, rode at anchor.

"Wait . . . wait a moment," Arikan wheezed, flapping a hand urgently. He slowed to a lumbering walk and then stopped to lean against a corner of a stack of crates piled at the shore end of one of the nearby jetties. "By my beard," he panted after a few moments, "I wasn't planning on joining any races myself today."

Jena bit her lip and hurried a short distance farther down the street to peer around the corner of a lane leading back to the upper bowls. She saw a few people; there was a tinker trundling his cart of swaying pots and pans down the hill, and a pair of gap-toothed laundresses gossiping by the small public fountain. In a narrow patch of sunlight, a trio of girls bundled in quilted jackets argued shrilly over a game of ball-and-catch-stone, their voices reverberating against the house

walls. But there was no sign of either Morgan or Kett, and
Jena shook her head in vexation. *This is stupid. I could take
weeks looking through every street in the city this way. If
only Lady Rhuddlan were here, so we could use the belt!* She
ran back to Arikan. "I don't see either of them in that direction," she said.

Arikan nodded and pulled out a handkerchief to wipe the
sweat off his face. "A moment, please, to catch my breath.
Then we can continue the hunt." He eyed her as she danced
from one foot to another in impatience. "Feel free to use the
time to recheck the wards over us."

Jena made a face at him but forced herself to stand still.
He was right, she knew, damn him: time and time again
Lady Kestrienne had warned her that the easiest way for a
wizard to forget the wards was to become too impatient—
and that, of course, was usually the time when safeguards
were needed the most. Which reminded her . . .

"Arikan, what did you mean when you said that Kett's
spell backlashed? I mean, I thought I felt our wards over
Lady Rhuddlan fail."

"They did," Arikan said grimly. "The backlash was caused
by something else, not our work at all."

"Something else?" Jena repeated blankly. "Do you mean it
was a spell Lady Rinnelle did?"

"I don't think so."

"But something—or someone else?" Jena's eyebrows
rose. "Another wizard, helping us?"

"I don't know, I tell you," Arikan said, sounding irritable,
perhaps because he was worried or hadn't entirely recovered
his wind.

Jena looked down at her ring, remembering how it had
heated up against her hand. She opened her mouth to ask if
the backlash might have caused that, but then stopped, struck
with the realization: "Arikan, I can scry my ring again, can't
I? Since Morgan has his back now?"

Arikan straightened up. "Confound it, you're right." He
seized her elbow again and hustled her to a shadowed doorway where they could see up and down the street without
being seen themselves. There, a scruffy ginger cat that had

been gnawing at a fish head flinched and ran off. "Do it now—you're already warded."

Jena raised the ring and looked into the stone. The flecks in the facets winked up at her in a shaft of the cold winter sunlight. The shimmers grew more rapid, and she remembered the vision of the dark well she had experienced when Morgan's ring had drawn her in, the first night they met. *But my ring is clear. Think instead of a spring, deep in a forest.* She took a deep breath so her mind would be as calm as the pool she was trying to imagine. Use the details when you're trying to build a scrying vision in your mind's eye, Lady Kestrienne had told her. *The spring is surrounded by sprays of wildflowers . . . pink hearts-of-lace and lavender glimmerbells . . . and lined with stones overgrown with a deep emerald-green moss. White water-smoothed pebbles line the bottom. The waters are so fresh and crystalline that they bring visions when you peer into them.* The part of herself that was the observing student adept wondered briefly why water images were so common in magic. Perhaps the fluidity of water suggested the fluidity of possibility? *I want to see one whose fate is tied to mine,* she told the pool, *who carries another ring, with a black stone. My partner. Where is he?*

The pool showed her quick glimpses: the shadowy underside of a wooden wharf, its pilings rimed with barnacles; a bobbing cork boat mooring; the side of a ship swaying at anchor, the sunlight flashing on seaweed undulating from its side below the water level . . . she strained to see the name painted on the stern.

"Where's the *Waterlily* moored?" she asked Arikan, lowering the ring.

"The *Waterlily*? I haven't the least idea. Why?"

"Morgan's near it. We've come too far, I think—oh!"

"What is it?"

"He sees Kett's getting quite close," Jena said. She clenched the hand wearing the ring. "Arikan—"

"Go, go." Arikan waved her on. "You'll have to run, and I can't keep up. You're warded, so go!"

For the barest of moments, she hesitated, and then she nodded tensely and picked up her skirts and ran, leaving him behind. Beyond the warehouses she turned down the path along the quays used by the fishermen and shippers. Only a few quay folk passed her, mostly fishwives in leather aprons, toting baskets piled high with herring and scrod. She had to slow down to avoid slipping on the odds and ends littering the path from the continual parade of crates unloaded here: cabbage leaves, the offal gutted from the night's catch of fish, packing straw and rotten potatoes. *Stay safe, Morgan,* she willed in a silent plea as she swerved around a sodden pile of rope. *I'm coming.*

Finally, as Jena rounded a mound of nets, she slid to a stop, arms flailing, and ducked behind a stack of boxes loaded with glass fishing floats. Kett stood at the end of a wooden pier with his back toward her, scanning the water. Several fishing ketches were moored along the pier. She squinted, trying to make out the letters painted along their sterns. Yes, one was the *Waterlily.*

She looked at her ring again. *Morgan is near. In the water, shrouded by the darkness underneath the pier, hiding.* He was very tired, she realized. Surely Kett would go away soon, so he could come out?

Kett paced restlessly from one end of the pier to the other. As she watched, he tapped a gloved fist against one of the supporting piles, apparently thinking. After a moment, he seemed to come to some decision; he wheeled and headed toward the shore, the heels of his boots sounding in thumping echoes on the timbers. Jena drew back farther beyond the lee of the stack of boxes, scarcely daring to breathe. *That's right—you need to search elsewhere.* She glanced back toward the Golden Market. *Back by the piazza where you lost him.*

But Kett stopped at the head of the pier, hesitating, and then turned toward the water again. He stood there for a moment, and then waded a few feet in, stooping to look under the pier. Jena cursed inwardly.

And then, floating over the water from her right, she heard Arikan's voice. "Look, there goes Lady Rhuddlan's dog," he bawled. "It's heading for the ferries. Ten gold pieces to the man who catches it for her! Don't let it get away!"

Kett's head came up. After a moment, he waded back to shore and headed back downriver at an increasing run. Cautiously, Jena eased around the boxes and then hurried down to the water's edge when Kett had disappeared from view. She looked around, but no one stood nearby. "Morgan," she called in a low voice, "it's Jena. Arikan's drawn Kett off. Come out of the water."

After a few moments, she saw a small dark shape glide out from underneath the pier and swim toward her slowly. It was Morgan. He staggered out of the water, clearly exhausted, and shook himself, drenching Jena's skirt and cloak with a malodorous spray. Then he collapsed at her feet, sodden and shivering. Filthy water dripped from his muzzle and oozed out through the pads of his paws. With his fur plastered to his ribs, and his saturated tail, skinny as a rat's, he was about as sorry a sight as she had ever seen.

Jena unbuttoned the hood from her cloak and knelt to wrap him in it. He shuddered under her hands as she rubbed him briskly, and then his nose poked out of the fabric, looking under her knee. "Behind you," he said in a low voice.

Jena stood, fast, and turned to see a hooded figure approaching them. She tensed, ready to grab Morgan and run—and then the person threw the hood back. It was Lady Rhuddlan.

"Is he safe?" the Ruby said eagerly, hurrying forward. "He's here, isn't he? Does he have the ring?"

"Yes, he's here," Jena said. She sighed and stepped back so the Ruby could see. Lady Rhuddlan looked down at Morgan, a stricken look on her face.

He stood, shakily, and opened his mouth. Jena clearly heard the metallic ping as the ring bounced off a stone.

"I've got it," Morgan said, his voice tired. He placed a muddy paw over the gold band and nudged at it with his nose.

"But dammit, I'm still a dog."

CHAPTER
TWENTY-ONE

"JENA? WHAT IS IT, CHILD?"

"Hmm?" Jena came back to awareness of the workroom around her with a start. "I'm sorry, Father, what were you saying?"

"I just asked you for the third time whether the cement was set on those peridot stones."

"Oh." Jena looked down at the roughed-out gems on the table in front of her and guiltily reached for the rack of dopping sticks and a pot of cement. "I'm so sorry. I haven't—that is—I haven't even dopped them yet."

Collas sighed. "My dear, you've been staring into space for a good part of the evening. What's troubling you?"

What was troubling her? The answers to that were so manifold that Jena almost laughed. Bram was still missing; Morgan was being tormented by the most ridiculous spell imaginable; Lady Rhuddlan had only a few days left as the Diamond Heir, and they still had no idea how to break Kett's spell over the Diamond; and her ring—Jena lifted her hand and looked at it. Her ring. It was her ring; that was what had been gnawing at her attention.

"I have to go to the palace," she said slowly.

"What?"

"Now." Jena looked up at her father. "Tonight."

Collas looked stunned. "But why? What makes you think you must go there?"

"I'm needed. It's my magic—it's difficult to explain." In truth, she had no explanation. In the three days since the Union of City and Sea Ceremony, all of the attempts made by Jena and her friends to restore Morgan to his true form had failed. Even though they had recovered his ring, Morgan still couldn't seem to use his own magic. Yet their rings remained linked talismans, and he was her partner. And despite the spell over him, there was no mistaking the urgency of the message Morgan wanted to convey.

Since doorkeepers do not generally heed the commands of terriers, it was doubtful that Jena could have gained admittance to the palace at all had it not been for Lady Kestrienne. Jena had just reached the palace entrance and dismissed the servant escorting her when a covered carriage rattled to a halt in the torchlit courtyard. A groom ran up to open the carriage door and pull down the wooden steps. Lady Kestrienne alighted first and then turned to assist her fellow passenger. It took Jena a moment to recognize Lady Rinnelle beneath the heavy cloak and veil.

Lady Kestrienne quickly spotted Jena and motioned her over without the slightest hint of surprise. "The young lady is with us," she said with a grand wave to the door warden, who, knowing his match when he met it, bowed and withdrew. "Let Lady Rinnelle lean on your arm, if you can manage it without being too obvious," she muttered as she led the way to a corridor off to the right. "Did Vianne send for you?"

"No." Jena lowered her voice. "I think Morgan did." She waggled a gloved hand to indicate her talisman.

Lady Kestrienne gave her a sharp look. "Oh? Any contact that he achieves with you at all may be a hopeful sign. Hmph. Well, for whatever reason, you're here, and I intend to put you to good use. Perhaps you can talk some sense into this wilted gillyflower here."

Jena gave Lady Rinnelle a sidelong glance. The Topaz Heir walked with her eyes closed, allowing herself to be passively drawn along by Lady Kestrienne's firm grip on her elbow. She didn't say a word. "But whatever has happened?" Jena asked.

"Morgan didn't tell you? The ninny tried to kill herself."

"I thought it was the only way."

They were in the reception room set aside for Lady Rhuddlan's use. Lady Rinnelle sat by the fire, still deathly pale, with shadows like purpling bruises under her eyes. She massaged a spot between her eyebrows, avoiding Lady Kestrienne's irate eye. Jena sat beside Lady Rinnelle, bathing her temples with lavender water. Lady Rhuddlan sat opposite them, a little pale herself, but composed, with Morgan lying, watchful, at her feet.

"I don't know how you became a wizard," Lady Kestrienne fumed as she paced, "if the only solution you can think of for a vexing problem is swallowing poison. Such an appalling lack of vision."

"I never asked to be a wizard. And it would have worked! The Diamond would have been free by now! That is, if what Kett told me is true," Lady Rinnelle added with a note of uncertainty, "that a spell can't survive its maker's death."

"Oh, so only now do you pause to consider that little detail," Lady Kestrienne said. "Wouldn't you have felt foolish if you were dead right now, and Kett had been lying?"

Jena smothered a nervous laugh. Lady Kestrienne threw a glare in her direction and addressed herself again to Lady Rinnelle. "Well? Wouldn't you?"

"Was he lying, then?"

That brought Lady Kestrienne up short. "As a matter of fact, he wasn't." She stalked over to the sideboard and poured herself a goblet of wine.

Lady Rinnelle nodded. "And if I'm dead, Kett's entire plan to infiltrate the Diadem disintegrates. There would be no point in his attacking Guilford, and no reason for him to keep the Diamond alive anyway." She leaned wearily against the back of her chair. "It was tonight's Council meeting that decided me. I couldn't face hearing Guilford circle closer and closer to the truth that I'm . . . I'm a sorcerer."

Lady Kestrienne gave an impatient exclamation. "That you are a *wizard*. Forget all the claptrap about 'sorcerers' you heard while you were growing up. You're an adept. That doesn't mean that you're cursed, or that you've suddenly grown fangs, or that your touch kills."

Lady Rinnelle shook her head, apparently not wanting to argue the point. "You are the rightful ruler, your brilliance," she said to Lady Rhuddlan. "And I felt that if I must do this to make it clear for all to see, then so be it."

"No!" Lady Rhuddlan leaned forward. "Do you think I want to be established as the Diamond with your bloodguilt on my hands?" She shuddered. "If Kestrienne hadn't been monitoring you and gotten suspicious, if she hadn't gone to fetch you—"

"All your problems would now be over," Lady Rinnelle said stubbornly.

"There would still be the spell over me," Morgan said quietly.

Lady Rinnelle fidgeted in her chair. "I'm sorry, but I haven't been any help in breaking it anyway."

"And what about Lord Woric?" Jena added. "How would he feel?"

Lady Rinnelle sat silently for a moment, and then a slow trail of tears began dripping down her nose.

Lady Kestrienne *tsk*ed in exasperation. "That's quite enough. We're in no danger of drought this year, so you may turn off the fountains, if you please! We are sorry if it doesn't suit you to be alive. We intend to keep you that way, however, and so you had better make the best of it."

"I want you to swear to me," said Lady Rhuddlan, "that you won't try to do anything like this again."

There was a long pause, with no sound but the crackle of the fire. "I'm sorry," Lady Rinnelle said. "It's precisely because of my loyalty to you that I can make no such promise."

Jena raised a hand to forestall another outburst by Lady Kestrienne. "I don't agree with you, my lady, that your, er, solution is a necessity. But there isn't any reason to take such a desperate action until the end of the year. After all, we might succeed in breaking the spell over the Diamond before then, and then such a recourse would be totally unnecessary. Isn't that true?"

Lady Rinnelle reluctantly nodded.

"Jena, what are you saying?" Lady Rhuddlan exclaimed. "You're all but telling her to go ahead and kill herself at year's end!"

"No, Vianne, Jena's right," Morgan said unexpectedly. "I'm not sure anyone can be prevented from ending their own life if they're really determined to die. Jena is simply trying to win us a reprieve, a period of time where we won't have to worry about that possibility. Until year's end."

Jena nodded. "Hopefully, the problem will be solved by then."

Lady Kestrienne snorted. "Well, then, Lady Rinnelle, perhaps you might redirect your attention from dramatics to spell-breaking. I would rather not have to spend another afternoon resorting to purgatives and restoratives again. Such a messy business."

A timepiece on a side table chimed, and Lady Rhuddlan threw it a worried glance. "We need to talk further, but meanwhile the Emerald is being chosen at the Council meeting tonight. Both Rinnelle and I have to be there."

Lady Rinnelle sighed. "Must I really?"

"All the heirs have to appear."

"Quite true," Lady Kestrienne said. "But I want Lady Rinnelle to change her clothes first."

"I beg your pardon?" Lady Rinnelle looked at her blankly.

"That green color you're wearing, dear. It makes you look positively bilious. One look at you in that dress and everyone will know you've been up to something dreadful. Hardly the picture of the radiant bride-to-be. Why, it would be a terrible affront to Lord Woric. And besides," she added briskly, with a rapid gesture behind Lady Rinnelle's chair that Jena caught out of the corner of her eye, "I'm afraid you couldn't possibly appear in public with that stain on the back of your skirt."

"A stain?" Lady Rinnelle turned in her chair, looking over her shoulder.

"Yes," Lady Kestrienne said, going over to the corner and pulling a bellrope, "My wine goblet slipped. Quite careless of me. Yet I'm sure her grace could lend you something that would be most suitable. Perhaps that rosy sarcenet I saw you wearing to the revels a few evenings ago, Vianne, dear?"

"But—but—you—" Lady Rinnelle sputtered.

"Oh, yes, I know. I'm so very sorry. Please do send the bill to me."

"She couldn't possibly have time to change," Lady Rhuddlan exclaimed.

"Oh, my, the time is very short. You'd best hurry, then, hadn't you, my lady?" Lady Rhuddlan's servant entered the room at that moment, and Jena watched with a kind of bemused admiration as Lady Kestrienne dismissed the Topaz Heir over to the servant's care with a rapid list of instructions and admonitions. *I know just what that befuddled expression on Lady Rinnelle's face means. Lady Kestrienne seems to be an expert at volunteering the use of other people's clothing.*

"Why did you do that?" Lady Rhuddlan asked when the door closed.

"Because I thought it best that Lady Rinnelle not be in the room while we discuss one important point about the Council meeting. I hope Jena has convinced her not to do anything stupid, at least for the next several days. But if not, and she is still as desperate as she seemed this afternoon, it might occur to her to stand up in Council and say, 'I'm the one you're looking for.' "

"Because she thinks Lord Oselare will kill her!" Morgan exclaimed.

"Yes. That would achieve the same goal, you see, breaking the spell over the Diamond in a way that would be much more difficult for us to stop."

"Yes, I do see," Lady Rhuddlan said thoughtfully.

"What do you suggest?" Jena asked.

"I think I had best monitor her during the Council meeting. There are ways I could stop her, if necessary, if I am nearby. Is there a place close to the Council chamber which would be sufficiently private?"

Lady Rhuddlan looked as if she could not believe her ears. "Are you suggesting that you—what is the word—*scry* the Council meeting?"

Lady Kestrienne raised an eyebrow. "You have an objection, then?"

"An objection!" Lady Rhuddlan for a moment appeared to be torn between unbelieving laughter and outrage. "That any member of the Diadem would allow magical—" She glanced at Morgan and fell silent for a moment. "Ranulf is my candidate," she began again finally. "And of course I want him to become the Emerald. Yet I must know: will you agree not to interfere with the Council's decision? Either one of you," she added, looking at Jena.

"Interfere?" Lady Kestrienne blinked at the question. "It would never have occurred to me to do so. I do believe the country would be well served if he were one of its guardians—although of course the dear boy can be quite tiresome at times. But I assure you, I won't interfere."

Lady Rhuddlan looked at Jena.

"I suppose I want Lord Duone to win the Council's vote, your grace," Jena said. "And yet, I don't know anything about any of the other candidates, or for that matter what the criteria for evaluation should be. Being an adept means not only knowing what choices to make, but recognizing who should make them." Lady Kestrienne gave her a sidelong glance, and Jena remembered their conversation about that very point, the night they had talked in Morgan's room. Lady Rhuddlan still seemed to be waiting for something more, her mouth taut, and Jena felt a wave of impatience. "Shards, your grace," Jena went on, "it's not our choice at all! It's yours—yours and the Council's. And the Diamond's." She remembered, and winced again. "You can handle the politics, if you don't mind," she mumbled. "Personally, I'd rather cut gems."

After what seemed an endless moment, Lady Rhuddlan relaxed and finally smiled again. "I'm sure you understand my bluntness. I had to be certain. Very well, I'll make arrangements for you to wait in the garden."

Lady Rhuddlan gave the servants instructions, and in a short while she led Jena and Lady Kestrienne, with Morgan trotting at their heels, outside through the garden entrance and past the covered flower beds to one of the topiary walkways skirting the palace's formal garden. In the summer, Jena knew, thick walls of lovingly tended and shaped boxwood covered the walkways, but now, during the winter, only a framework of densely interwoven twigs remained.

They followed the pathway until they came to a topiary pavilion, at the point where the avenue intersected with another. There, Morgan hopped up onto a stone bench, which had been covered with a carpet. A lit torch had been set into a bracket attached to the pavilion's framework, and a charcoal brazier burned, too, warming the chill air.

"I think you can wait here safely," Lady Rhuddlan said. "It's quite private in the winter, much more so than any of the public reception rooms. I hope you will be warm enough." She gestured toward a tray on the small ornamental table that had been pulled up close to the bench. "I told them to bring you some mulled punch, which should help; it's quite good."

"Your grace is very kind," Jena said as she seated herself.

"You'd best go in, my dear," Lady Kestrienne said. "You still need to retrieve Lady Rinnelle."

Lady Rhuddlan nodded and turned to go. "Morgan?" she said questioningly, when Morgan didn't move.

"I'll follow you in a moment, Vianne." After a brief hesitation, the Ruby nodded and walked out under the topiary archway toward the garden's entrance. "Wish us luck," Morgan said when the sound of her footsteps had died away. "And Jena, would you loosen my collar a bit?"

Surprised and a little embarrassed, Jena gently parted the fur at his neck with her fingers. As she searched along the strap for the buckle, she touched something and suddenly understood. It was his talisman ring, of course, strung on the collar and dangling over his throat. Morgan nudged Jena's talisman ring on her hand with his nose. "I didn't want Vianne to be worried further," he said softly. "But I'm sure I can depend on you to help Aunt Kestrienne if necessary. Can't I?"

Jena nodded. Morgan hopped down from the bench. She watched him go, a small rust-colored shape trotting away briskly until the darkness beyond the torchlight swallowed him.

"Pour us both some punch, won't you, dear?" Lady Kestrienne said. "I would appreciate having something warm in my belly, since we're going to be here awhile."

Jena did so, and then watched as her mentor detached a

small mirror from a chain hanging from her girdle and placed it on the table. Lady Kestrienne then extricated one of the vials from her pomander and poured a thin film of liquid onto the mirror's surface. "Not as large a mirror as I would have wished," she muttered. "And rosewater instead of almond oil . . . I hope it won't freeze. Still, we must make shift to use what is at hand."

"Will that allow you to see into the Council chamber?"

"No, it won't work the way your ring will, but then, I'm merely monitoring. There are patterns in the fluid which tell me what I need to know, rather than pictures. I'll have to depend upon you to tell me what's said."

Once they had set and carefully checked the wards, Jena bent over her ring under the guttering light of the torch and reached through it for the connection with her partner. The stone was a tiny window that she drew close to her eye, until it filled her vision. All she could see in the scry-sighting, however, stare as she might, were two reddish, oblong shapes. They puzzled her, until one of them shifted, and then she almost laughed. Of course: Morgan's talisman stone dangled over his forepaws. *Wonderful. This will certainly be a tremendous help.* Gradually, however, she realized that although she couldn't see anyone else in the Diadem Chamber from her peculiar angle of vision, she could hear voices.

"Gentles, if we may start?" It was Lady Rhuddlan. There was a change in the angle of mumbled conversations and the scrape of wood against stone as benches were rutched back, and then a gradual silence. "You know our business tonight. We must reach consensus, in Council, as to our preference for the new Emerald." Jena repeated this, but as Lady Rhuddlan continued talking, the scrying link between the rings enveloped Jena even more firmly, until she gradually lost her awareness of the dark garden, Lady Kestrienne, or even that she was repeating what she heard. She was only a listener.

Lady Rhuddlan continued: "The candidates available for consideration are: Lord Reuven Agnolle, nominated by the Citrine; Lord Ferrin Signo, nominated by the Amethyst; Lord Ranulf Duone, nominated by the Ruby; and Lord Niall Scroop, nominated by the Aquamarine. By the agreement reached at our last meeting, Lord Scroop's candidacy is acceptable, even though he did not arrive into the city until two days after the beginning of Festival. Lord Maxil Palani, the Topaz nominee, has withdrawn. I understand that Lord Aric Wode, the Sapphire's nominee, has still not been located.

"Each of us has spent these two weeks interviewing the candidates and their supporters. Now, if the ballots can be passed, we will see if the field has been narrowed by our investigations."

"One moment," said a man's voice gruffly. It was the Topaz, Lord Guilford Oselare. "I must renew my previous objection. If the Diamond remains unable to state his preference, then I presume Lady Rhuddlan, as the Diamond Heir, will be determining the new Emerald. I maintain that it would be grossly irregular, not to mention unfair, for her to elevate her own House's candidate."

"If the fact that Lord Duone is Lady Rhuddlan's candidate troubles you," said another voice (Lord Sebastian Alcide, the Sapphire, Jena identified after a moment), "then I propose a solution: let me adopt Lord Duone as my candidate."

"What?" said Lord Oselare, obviously startled.

"You heard me," the Sapphire said crisply. "My intended nominee, Lord Wode, cannot be found. My House has the right to present a candidate to the Council. If I sponsor Lord Duone any perception of conflict for Lady Rhuddlan is eliminated."

"You can't do that!"

"Why not? Lord Duone was present at the required deadline."

"But—you—" Lord Oselare was reduced to sputters.

"I will second Lord Alcide's suggestion," said someone, either the Aquamarine or the Citrine, "that Lord Duone's candidacy be transferred to the Sapphire House."

The proposal was put to a voice vote and ratified. Jena fancied she could hear Lord Oselare's teeth grinding as he abstained. *Why is he so intent on thwarting Lord Duone's candidacy?*

"Now," said Lady Rhuddlan, "we will proceed to the vote for the Emerald. Master Steward, if you will distribute the ballots?"

A silence ensued, broken only by the harsh scribble of

pens and the sound of Morgan's tense panting. *I do hope Lord Duone wins,* Jena thought, and then remembered her promise to Lady Rhuddlan and grimaced. *Oh, well. I only mean to wish him well, not to influence votes.*

After the ballots had been checked, the master steward announced the results. "Lord Reuven Agnolle, with no votes, has been eliminated. Otherwise, the tally stands as follows: Lord Signo—two votes. Lord Scroop—one vote. Lord Duone—three votes." Scrying the vote was easy: the Citrine had given up on his own candidate and thrown his lot in with the Sapphire and the Ruby. Lord Oselare had joined with the Amethyst in supporting Lord Signo.

"And now?" asked Lord Fedreggo. "We present the two top candidates to the Diamond and have him decide?"

"That is the procedure." Lady Rhuddlan sighed. "I must admit, I had hoped we could reach a consensus on one candidate."

"Perhaps we still can after some more discussion?" Lord Fedreggo said.

"The fact is, we're all feeling our way along here, lad," Lord Alcide said. "The Diadem hasn't had to elevate a new House for a long, long time—certainly not in my lifetime."

"This is ridiculous," Lord Oselare said roughly. "You speak of presenting the decision to the Diamond as if he is capable of making it. Well, he isn't. So I suppose that means the Diamond Heir will be stepping in to make it instead, eh?"

"No one but you is even suggesting that the Diamond Heir will elevate the Emerald, Guilford," Lady Golpier said irritably.

"I assure you, Lord Oselare," Lady Rhuddlan said, "that I do not intend, as the Diamond Heir, to attempt to elevate any candidate to become the Emerald. Only were I to become the Diamond would I presume that authority. If there is no Diamond able to make the choice, then I think the chair really should remain empty."

"It cuts the same way for you, too, Lord Oselare," the Amethyst remarked. "In only a few days you'll become the Diamond Heir. Lady Rhuddlan has made clear she will not elevate an Emerald unless she's the Diamond, so you should be bound by the same condition, too."

"In that case," the Citrine was heard to mutter tactlessly, "it's just as well that he doesn't have a candidate anymore."

"Besides, we all still hope for the Diamond's recovery," said the Amethyst.

"You fools," Lord Oselare growled. "You might as well hope for the skies to rain potatoes. The Diamond will never reawaken. The spell that holds him—"

"I have said we will hear your evidence of sorcery in good time, when you have evidence to present," said Lady Rhuddlan.

"I insist—"

"But meanwhile, we are still discussing whether the Council's choice has been determined."

"Everything in its proper order, eh?" Lord Oselare's voice dripped derision.

"Would you have it any other way?" Lady Rhuddlan replied coolly. Jena would have given much to see Lord Oselare's face at that particular moment.

"Oh, yes, very convenient for your candidate, *your grace*, that my accusations should be silenced now."

"What are you insinuating, my lord?" Lady Rhuddlan said in her frostiest tone.

"I merely point out how monstrously convenient it is for Lord Duone that you stand ready to usurp the Diamond's powers—"

"I have told you, I have no intention whatsoever—" Lady Rhuddlan began, but Lord Oselare overbore her:

"—ready to raise him up to sit among us! I shouldn't wonder if that wasn't his sorcerous plan from the beginning!"

By the Founders, Lord Oselare has read Kett's clues wrong! He thinks Lord Duone is the wizard, not Lady Rinnelle. Could it be that before he transformed Morgan, Kett tried to center Lord Oselare's suspicions on the Duone family, in order to prevent Morgan's marriage? Or else Lord Oselare's still trying to deflect attention from himself? The idea of Lord Duone, as wary of magic as he was, being an adept would have been laughable if it wasn't such an alarmingly incendiary accusation within this group.

The outcries greeting the Topaz's statement were drowned out for Jena by the rumbling reverberating through her head from Morgan's growls. *Shut up, Morgan, please*. He must have heard her, because gradually she could hear the angry babble of voices again.

"Lord Oselare, how can you suggest—"

"Are you saying Lord Duone set an assassin on *himself*?"

Above all the other exclamations, Lady Rhuddlan's laughter rang out. "La, your grace! Lord Duone a sorcerer! How very droll; I do believe it's the best joke I've heard since Equinox. Or it would be," she said, her voice suddenly taking on a deathly chill, "if your accusation didn't also impugn my candidate's honor. I think you should consider yourself fortunate that you aired this theory here first with us, rather than in front of Lord Duone. He's quite a competent swordsman, and although he is very even-tempered, he might be tempted to adjust the fit of your doublet at such an insult. Frankly, I wouldn't blame him in the least."

"If you need proof," Lord Oselare all but spat, "I'll give it to you."

"Oh? How?"

Jena held her breath. *Here it comes*. She hoped Lady Kestrienne would be ready in case Lady Rinnelle's nerve broke.

"With this." There was the sound of a scrape of wood, a key turning in a lock, and the creak of a hinge. Morgan began rumbling low in his throat again.

"What," said Lord Alcide, his distaste evident in every word, "is that thing?"

"This orb detects sorcery—spells. Pass it over a person's heart, and the fluid inside will glow if a spell has been laid upon him."

Oh, no. Morgan had better keep away from it, then. Lady Rhuddlan, too, if she's wearing the belt.

"Where did you get it?" Lady Golpier asked.

"My informant provided it—so we can prove that a spell has been placed on the Diamond."

He must still be trying to force Lady Rinnelle to follow his plan.

"Are you mad, man?" exclaimed the Citrine. "Placing that upon the Diamond, sick as he is? Who knows what it might do to him?"

"How dare you bring it in here!" shouted someone else.

"It's not ensorcelled," Lord Oselare insisted. "It detects sorcery."

"But how do you know that? What do you know about this informant anyway? Can you be sure he isn't a sorcerer himself?"

A very good question, Lord Fedreggo.

"He could be using you to try to put a spell on the Diamond," said Lady Golpier.

I wouldn't put it past him.

"Test it." Lady Rhuddlan's voice cut through all the tumult. "On something else. Take it down to a sorcerer's shop—you should be able to find one still open tonight, somewhere in the city. Make him cast a spell and see if it works the way Lord Oselare says it will."

"You can't be serious, your grace. Are you telling us to *hire* a sorcerer?"

"If you don't, you can believe I will never allow you to bring Lord Oselare's little toy into the Diamond's bedchamber. Of course if we do try the test, I trust Lord Oselare's suspicions will finally be put to rest. On the other hand, if this orb shows that a spell does exist, something further would certainly be needed to prove that Lord Duone is the one involved."

"If we're going to do this at all," Lord Alcide said roughly, "let's do it quickly. I want it out of the palace."

"How much time will you need to find a sorcerer to test it, Lord Oselare? Never mind," she said quickly, before he could answer. "We will give you until tomorrow morning. The Council will reconvene at the Diamond's chamber at first light tomorrow morning."

At this, talk in the chamber splintered into several conversations. Morgan scrambled to his feet, making Jena's view of the tabletop careen crazily, as the Ruby said casually, "Oh, Lady Rinnelle, a word in private with you, please?"

Jena and Lady Kestrienne had only a few moments to wait. Morgan arrived first, trotting out of the darkness, shivering. "Did you see everything?" he said, jumping up on the bench.

"Well, no, but we certainly heard everything. Whatever possessed Lady Rhuddlan to agree?" She lowered her voice. "We already know there's a spell on the Diamond. Now we only have until tomorrow morning to remove it!"

"Pressure can work in more than one direction." Lady Rhuddlan appeared suddenly in the torchlight, dragging a rebellious Lady Rinnelle by one wrist.

"Let go of me!"

"Very well," Lady Rhuddlan said crisply, suiting the action to the word so abruptly that Lady Rinnelle stumbled back. "There. Now. You can run and try to hide, if you think you can escape your brother. Or . . ."

Lady Rinnelle rubbed her wrist, refusing to meet any of their eyes. "Or?"

"You can break that spell."

"You're mad! I tell you, I can't!"

"Perhaps she is mad," Lady Kestrienne said calmly. "Or perhaps you haven't been desperate enough until now."

"Did that orb come from Kett?" Jena asked. "Will it work as Lord Oselare says?"

"Yes, it will." Lady Rinnelle covered her face with her hands. "I've never seen it before, but he told me about it. He learned how to do that spell on his last voyage. He was always looking for ways to increase his power."

Lady Kestrienne sniffed. "He would have been better served if he had concentrated on learning appropriate ways to use the power he had."

Lady Rinnelle shuddered. "Kett doesn't know what he's done, giving that orb to my brother."

"Why?" Morgan demanded.

"Because Guilford wants to start a hunt for sorcerers. If the orb reveals a spell on the Diamond, he'll have all the excuse he needs to begin, and then none of us will be safe." Already crying, she began to sob in earnest. "I tell you, he'll hunt every wizard down—hunt them down and kill them all!"

"Stop it!" Jena snapped in exasperation. "This isn't helping."

"He'll kill us all! He'll drown us and burn us, he'll—"

Jena took Lady Rinnelle by the shoulders and shook her

until her teeth rattled. "Stop it, I tell you!" Lady Rinnelle gulped and hiccuped, trembling. "Her grace is right. You must break the spell, right now."

"But I can't!" Lady Rinnelle said mournfully. "Not without Kett."

"You haven't actually been close to the Diamond when you've tried before—right within his bedchamber—have you?" asked Morgan.

"No." Lady Rinnelle looked frightened. "I didn't dare."

"We must try that, then," Jena decided. "If you can get us in, your grace?"

"If we wait several hours, so there are as few servants around as possible—yes, I think so."

"Good. Maybe it will give Lady Rinnelle enough of an edge to accomplish the task. Well?"

"All right," Lady Rinnelle whispered. "I'll do it. I'll do it." She drew a wavering breath. "But if that doesn't work . . ."

"What?"

"Well, if I attack the spell, Kett just might come running. And then you can tell him to remove it yourselves."

CHAPTER
TWENTY-TWO ☉

THE DIAMOND WAS DEAD, AND
yet he breathed. Worse, each breath came with a little sigh
ending in a whistle, as if the spell mocked his age and frailty.
He lay perfectly still upon his richly carved bed, so thin that
his body barely made a bump under the samite bedcoverings,
dwarfed by the room's grandeur. Only a few scraggly tufts of
hair remained on his mottled scalp. His wrinkled skin was
waxy and pale as parchment, and the blue veins in his
gnarled hands pulsed with infinite weariness, as if to say: *if
only the burden could be put down.*

Jena stared down at the motionless figure and felt her eyes
grow hot. *So still—and yet I can feel a tiny part of him struggling to free himself. Ugh, how horrible! No wonder Kett
was afraid to let Morgan near the Diamond. No adept could
have missed this spell.* "How long—" Jena stopped and
cleared her throat, "how long did you tell the attendant to
stay away?" Her own voice unnerved her, making her heart
beat faster. The sound jarred so, mangling the perfect stillness of the room, and she wondered if it would startle the Diamond, too, making him forget to take the next labored
breath.

But nothing changed; the spell still forced air in and out,

in and out. Lady Rhuddlan sat on the edge of the bed. "I told her we'd send for her when she was needed again," she said. "No one will think it strange; I usually send her away when I sit with him." She took the Diamond's hand and squeezed the fingers slowly and deliberately. "Your brilliance?" The shadows up at the ceiling and around the bedcurtains seemed to breathe, too, edging away from the candlelight spilling from the tapers Lady Kestrienne had lit, but still there, still waiting.

"He can't answer you," Lady Rinnelle whispered.

"I know." The Ruby tightened her fingers around the Diamond's again. "Your brilliance? It's Vianne. I've some other people with me who wish to help you." She looked up at Lady Rinnelle. "Try it now," she urged softly.

Lady Rinnelle came forward and pressed her hands on the Diamond's temples. She closed her eyes, and a small crease of concentration appeared between her brows.

Morgan hopped up onto the top of one of the chests pushed up against the bed and settled himself there. "Some wards should be set up for her," he said.

Jena nodded. She and Lady Kestrienne sketched the lines, with Lady Rinnelle and the Diamond together in the center and Morgan, Lady Rhuddlan, Lady Kestrienne, and Jena in a protective square around them. When the lines were strong and steady, Jena opened her eyes again.

Lady Rinnelle was already shaking her head and withdrawing her hands. "No, it's impossible. I can't do it. The spell's like a big, hopelessly tangled knot."

"Unless you have something else to occupy your time," Lady Kestrienne said, "I suggest you keep trying." She raised an eyebrow. "At least until the Diadem gathers here."

Lady Rinnelle flinched.

"Like a knot," Jena said slowly. "Was that the metaphor you used for the spell, then? That you were tying the Diamond's life to yours?"

Lady Rinnelle wrinkled her nose. "I remember that Kett spoke of it as something like a net."

"And now the Diamond is entangled in it, is that it?" Jena came and sat down, gingerly, on the other side of the bed. The heavy silk felt cool and rich under her hand. She fingered a fold of it, thinking of Bram's mother working at her loom. "What if you changed your approach? Instead of a net, think of it as a woven fabric. Kett's part of the spell is the warp, and yours is the woof. It would be faster and simpler if you cooperated in breaking the spell, but if that's impossible, well—if you break the threads running one direction in a piece of cloth, it can eventually be unraveled, even if the threads in the other direction remain intact. So you should just concentrate on breaking your part of the spell."

Lady Rinnelle looked puzzled for a moment, and then reached out to touch the Diamond again. "Very well."

Her rhythm of breathing matched the Diamond's. She remained in that position for a long time as Morgan and Lady Rhuddlan and Jena watched. Slowly, a faint silver glow appeared, like cold starlight, so gradually that Jena wasn't sure at first it was really there. But it strengthened, beginning at the pearl Lady Rinnelle wore and spreading out from there over her hands and the Diamond's face and head. Lady Rinnelle's breathing quickened, and the glow flickered—and then her eyes snapped open and her hands jerked back. The glow vanished. The Diamond continued the same slow, steady rate of breathing.

"He's coming," Lady Rinnelle said. She looked up at them with panic in her eyes.

Morgan raised his head from his forepaws. "What?"

"Kett. He's coming here. He's already quite near."

"Are you sure?" asked Lady Rhuddlan.

"Let him come," Morgan snarled. He stood up and shook himself fiercely. "I'm ready to face him."

Wonderful. That certainly puts my mind at ease. Jena took a taper and went over to the door of the chamber. "If the ward lines are—" she stopped. After a moment, she bent and examined carefully the line of dripped candle wax she had placed in front of the threshold.

"Jena?" said Lady Rhuddlan. "What is it?"

Jena didn't answer. She could see two shadowed shapes at the crack at the bottom of the door. She knelt down to look more closely, and then pulled back hastily.

Something was coming under the door. It was bright orange-red and flowing, like molten metal. At the first contact with the drops of candle wax on the floor, the wax hissed, smoking and bubbling. Jena felt the outer ward lines surrounding the room weaken and fade away, and as she stumbled to her feet, the light from under the door vanished. She blinked to help her eyes adjust to the candlelight again and the door opened.

Jena took a deep breath and straightened up. "Good evening, Captain Kett. Won't you come in?"

His eyes, cold and set, glittered in the light of her candle, as did the pearl swinging from his ear. His gaze went past her to Lady Rinnelle, who still sat on the bed beside the Diamond, her eyes wide and wary.

"Rinnelle," he breathed. He made a sound in his throat, half a gasp, and half a sob, and then a fierce joy sprang to life in his eyes. With smooth efficiency he drew his sword, and the ringing rasp made Jena start. He pointed the tip at Jena's throat, and she felt her hands turn to ice. "Stand aside," he said with deadly softness.

Jena stepped back slowly as he advanced into the room. Lady Rhuddlan followed her. Lady Kestrienne, a little over to one side, remained perfectly motionless. Morgan, still on the chest at the foot of the bed, obeyed Jena's hand motion and stayed where he was, tense and trembling.

When Kett reached the bed, he took Rinnelle's hand, swiftly drawing her up as he kept his eyes on the others. "I'm getting you out of here. Rinnelle . . ." He pressed her fingers to his lips as she shrank away from him, but he didn't seem to notice. "I thought you were dying. I was at sea, and I turned the ship around as soon as I felt—Rinnelle, I thought I'd lost you."

Lady Rinnelle tried to extricate her hand. "Kett. They know. They know about the spell."

Lady Kestrienne took a step forward. "Captain Kett—"

Kett immediately dropped Lady Rinnelle's hand and shoved her behind him; she almost fell. "Keep away from her," he growled, his blade raised and ready.

"Young man, I'm sure Lady Rinnelle appreciates your heroics, but they're hardly necessary—"

"Keep back, all of you!" he shouted, feinting with his

weapon. "Damn you, if you try to hurt her again, if you touch one more hair on her head—"

"Is that what you think?" Lady Kestrienne said. "That we would try to kill her to break the spell? How interesting."

"Kett, don't." Lady Rinnelle seized his arm. "Please! It wasn't them!"

"What?" He half turned his head to her, still keeping his eyes on Jena and Lady Kestrienne.

"They didn't do anything to me. It was me, Kett. I . . . I tried to kill myself. Lady Kestrienne there stopped me."

"What?" He half lowered the sword and looked at her, disbelief in his eyes. "You tried—Rinnelle, *why*?"

"Because she didn't think you had left her any other options," Lady Kestrienne said. "She's wrong, of course, but—"

"You," Kett interrupted. "Lady Kestrienne, is it? What business do you have interfering?"

Lady Kestrienne snorted. "Would you have preferred me to have let Lady Rinnelle's family discover her dead in her bed the next morning?"

"No, of course not," Kett said, scowling.

"And you're a fine one to complain about interference, considering that spell you put over the Diamond."

Kett gave his partner a piercing look. "Rinnelle has been spilling secrets, I see." He sheathed his sword with a look of disgust.

"I hardly think you can hold that against her," Lady Kestrienne retorted, "since you've been talking to her brother."

"Nobles. They always side with their own," Kett went on bitterly, as if he hadn't heard. "That's it, isn't it, Rinnelle? Highborn friends, a blue-blooded husband . . . Nobles will turn their backs on anyone to protect one another."

"Rinnelle didn't turn to me because I'm a noble," Lady Kestrienne said, "but because she needed help, which she certainly wasn't getting from you." She studied him for a moment, her head cocked to one side. "Tell me, Captain: do you think of yourself so meanly because you're not a noble? Is that what this is all about?"

"A nobody," Jena said suddenly. "That's what you said

you were, when I . . . first encountered you, through my ring."

He nodded, almost absently. "Yes. It can be useful, sometimes, to be nobody. It's almost like being invisible."

"That's how you got past the guards, I suppose?" Lady Kestrienne said.

Kett smiled, a cold smile which didn't reach his eyes. "I know myself to be beneath notice, which means I can go anywhere, practically unseen." The smile vanished. "And yet I find I grow weary of invisibility."

At his words Jena felt a stab of empathy, which surprised her. She looked around at the others; their blank, wary expressions told her they didn't understand. *They can't even see it. They have no idea what it's like, to endure a lifetime of little disdainful shrugs, condescending dismissals. But I understand.* She thought of all the subtle snubs she had seen her father receive over the years from his highborn customers, because he was only an artisan. She thought of the Jewelers' Guild, with their incomprehension that a mere girl might want to cut gems. *Oh, yes, I understand.*

But still—"You're a wizard," Jena said evenly, "and a ship's captain—a leader of men. That isn't enough?"

He waved that aside. "Ah, but you see, I'll never be . . ." he paused to consider, "someone of real political significance"—he gestured toward the Ruby—"like Lady Rhuddlan here, for example." He looked at Lady Rinnelle, who glanced away quickly to avoid his eye. "Never be worthy," he added, his voice colorless, "of a fine lady's passing glance."

"You can see so many possibilities," Lady Kestrienne said incredulously, "and yet you really believe that somehow you don't matter unless you're pulling the strings running the country?"

Kett raised his arm, and Jena tensed, ready to guard against an attack on the wards around them. Yet it wasn't a spell he was casting, but a possibility vision. *Behold: the new Diamond, with Consort at her side.* . . . Rinnelle stood before them, no longer a timid, pale woman, eyes puffy from weeping, but a slender, raven-haired queen clad all in shining white. A nimbus of light surrounded the famous diadem of the Seven Houses that she wore, and beneath the diadem her violet eyes regarded them with calm wisdom. Jena felt her heart pound in response, and she gladly knelt, lost in awe. *Can you doubt she is the one meant to lead us? Listen to her words; they are music in the hearts of her subjects. Her judgment is peerless, her heart utterly pure. . . .*Rinnelle smiled, a majestic figure extending a hand graciously toward her people. But in that same motion Jena also seemed to see a young widow in black, shivering from the touch of cold sea spray as she reached out tentatively to take a pearl from a sea captain's hand. His answering love for her, Jena knew, was what shone through the vision, giving it shape and power.

Kett, also clad in white, turned to face Rinnelle's subjects. *Since the Founders, all the Diamonds have chosen their consorts only from among the nobility—until now. I was born as humbly as any of you. I have grown up among you, worked among you, felt hunger and frustrated desire, like you. And yet . . . she has chosen me.* How clearly the wonder, the joy, came through behind those proudly spoken words. *Trust me. Trust us. I will be your voice, your advocate before her. Our decisions will bring peace to this land, prosperity to its people.*

Something inside Jena stirred in uneasiness. There was something wrong here, hidden below the surface, like fault lines in a beautifully shaped stone. It would shatter if tapped with just the right force in the right place. *Choices. Kett wants to appropriate all choices to himself.*

Yes, she heard Lady Kestrienne say. *Even who must live—and who must die.*

The vision changed, and the Diamond, the old Diamond from the Emerald House, appeared at Rinnelle's feet. His bones showed through rotting flesh, and he stank horrifyingly of the grave, and yet he still breathed that terrible moaning breath, each ending with the little whistle. Rinnelle shrank back with a little cry, only to all but stumble over Lord Guilford Oselare. The Topaz had been almost cut in two by the dripping sword now held in Kett's hand. Lord Oselare collapsed forward, groaning, his face twisted in an agonized grimace, and the blood spurting from his wound sprayed his sister's white skirts and soaked her shoes.

"Guilford!" Lady Rinnelle screamed. Her cry rent a veil of mist around them, and Jena jerked back, looking around herself in surprise. They were in the Diamond's bedchamber, and Kett lowered his arms, looking shaken and spent. Lady Rinnelle stared at him with bleak horror in her eyes.

Lady Kestrienne turned her back on Kett and walked back toward the bed. "Lady Rinnelle, I believe you were in the process of removing a spell."

After a last fearful glance at her partner, the Topaz Heir sat back down on the bed and reached out again toward the Diamond's temples, until Kett's voice stopped her. "No."

"Why not?" Lady Kestrienne demanded. "We know what you were trying to do, so what's the point of continuing? Your plan can never succeed now."

"Nonetheless," Kett said through his teeth, "it doesn't suit me to oblige you."

"*Oblige* me? Is that what you think I—" she stopped and pointed at the Diamond. "Look. Look at him. What do you see?"

For the first time, Kett turned his gaze to the figure on the bed. "I see an old man who has lived too long." He shrugged and looked at Lady Kestrienne again. "So he will live a little longer. What of it?"

The Diamond's silent torment, the misery of a life forced beyond its natural conclusion—he didn't even see it. He couldn't. *This isn't working,* Jena realized. *There is nothing we can offer that he wants, nothing we can say that will make him change the course he has charted for himself.*

Lady Kestrienne laughed, a sharp painful sound. "It's ironic, isn't it, Captain Kett? You waited so long and planned this so carefully. And yet your entire design became unraveled because of a simple act which must have seemed unfathomable to you."

He frowned. "What are you talking about?"

"If the Emerald hadn't died, perhaps the Diamond wouldn't have suffered his stroke and been in danger of dying too soon." One look at his eyes told them she was right. "And why did the Emerald die? Because he put another person, someone he loved, ahead of himself. That's your blind spot—the part of you Lady Rinnelle should have challenged and didn't. You don't understand how anyone can think beyond themselves."

"Enough of this," Lady Rhuddlan said sharply. "Captain Kett, you shall remove the spell upon the Diamond."

A sardonic smile curled the corner of Kett's mouth. "Shall I?"

"Yes," said Morgan. "You shall. Immediately."

Kett looked startled for a moment, but recovered quickly. "Ah, so you've found your tongue again, have you, my lord? And you really think anything you could say will make me change my mind?" He shook his head in mock consternation. "My, my. You know, Jena, actually there's one thing worse than being a nobody—and that's being a nobody without even realizing it. Nothing is quite as ridiculous as little dogs who labor under the illusion that their yapping will make some kind of difference."

Morgan got to his feet, growling, hackles bristling, but Kett just threw back his head and laughed.

"You see? Absurd! Really, your grace," he said, smiling at Lady Rhuddlan, who stood stiffly by the bed, trembling with rage, "you should have followed my advice when I first gave him to you, and had him neutered."

Morgan sprang for Kett with a roar. Jena barely had time to say the word to strengthen the ward around him, and then Kett's fist caught him under the ribs. The protective magic absorbed most of the blow, but Morgan still went flying, smashing with a surprised yelp into a tapestry and then to the floor.

"No!" Lady Rhuddlan hurled herself at Kett, clawing at his face. He caught her wrists barely in time to protect his eyes and shouted a harsh, guttural word. Light flared—

And Kett was thrown into a wall himself by an enormous, silent thunderclap of power. With an appalling crash, he fell to the floor in a tangle of limbs.

He lay perfectly still.

"Your grace!" Jena and Lady Kestrienne hurried toward the Ruby as she picked herself up off the floor. She looked dazed but was apparently unhurt.

"Did the ward do that?" she gasped. "I felt something *push* him. Oh—Morgan!" She staggered over to where Morgan was woozily getting to his feet and picked him up. "Are you badly hurt?"

"Nothing's broken, I think," he replied, groggily shaking his head. "What happened?"

"Kett," Lady Rinnelle said in a harsh whisper.

Lady Kestrienne went over to the corner and bent over him. "He's still breathing. Simply stunned, I think."

Jena was still staring at the Ruby. "Look!" she said, pointing. "Look at the Sunburst!" A flutter of sparks still spat and flashed on the brooch at Lady Rhuddlan's throat, and the lace was singed around it.

"What?" Lady Rhuddlan tried to peer down at it.

Gingerly, Jena reached out a finger and brushed the uppermost tip of the brooch. She almost yelped in surprise at the feeling of power that raced through her fingers. "The Sun . . . and the Star," she murmured in wonder. "The *Sunburst* and the *Starburst* that protect . . . the Heir and the Diamond!" Abruptly, she turned away and seized a candleholder. "Your grace, where's the Starburst?"

"The Starburst? Why, I don't know. His brilliance hardly ever wears it. Why?"

"Is it in one of these storage chests?" Putting the candleholder down, Jena thumped the lid back and began pawing frantically through the layers of herb-strewn clothes inside. "Help me look, everyone."

In the second chest, they found the carved casket of polished cherrywood. Nestled in the black velvet inside lay a brooch of white gold, encircled with diamonds in collet settings. *Double-pyramid cut,* the professional gemcutter in Jena noted with a tinge of disappointment. *Fine-quality stones, but barely any refraction at all.* But when she reached out and touched the brooch, she smiled in relief. "I was right."

Lady Rhuddlan frowned. "*What,* Jena?"

"Don't you see? The Sunburst and the Starburst are spellwarders."

"Of course," Lady Kestrienne murmured.

"What?" Lady Rhuddlan looked down blankly at the brooch.

"The 'Sun and the Star which protect' in the Coronation Oath refer not to the Heir and the Diamond, your grace, but to these pieces of jewelry. They were made to shield their wearers from harmful magic." Jena carefully lifted the brooch from the casket and stepped over to the bed.

"Wait! Let me." Lady Rinnelle held out her hand for the brooch. "It's only right."

Jena gave her the brooch. Lady Rinnelle released the catch on the back and pushed the point carefully through the folds of linen above the Diamond's sunken chest. She sank to her knees at his side. "Your brilliance? Can you hear me?"

If the spell had been a mirror they had been unable to break, the touch of the brooch shattered its surface like a pebble dropped into a still pool. The Diamond opened his eyes and looked up at Lady Rinnelle. She gently took his hands.

"Forgive me," she whispered. "Please forgive me!" She touched the brooch. "You're free now, your brilliance."

The Diamond's eyes turned to Lady Rhuddlan. He smiled faintly, and then his gaze fixed on the empty air above her shoulder. A sigh—and then his breathing stopped. Lady Rinnelle tenderly closed his eyes with a brush of her fingers over his face and folded his hands on his chest. "He's with his family again at last."

"No," said Kett's voice behind them. He was struggling painfully to his feet, his face stricken with a strange, bewildered grief, the anguish of a man who has watched all his plans become ashes before his eyes. "Rinnelle, how could you? Don't you know what you've done?"

"I know exactly what I've done," she said, pulling the sheet over the dead Diamond's face.

"You've betrayed me!"

"Yes." Rinnelle stood and walked toward him, her head high, color mounting in her cheeks. "Yes, I've betrayed you, Kett. I betrayed you every time I let you have your own way, when I knew you were wrong but was too much of a coward to tell you. I let you bully me, I let you torment everyone around you, and I never challenged you!" She seized his hands. "Everything I know about magic I learned from you. Why didn't you tell me you had as much to learn from me, too?"

"Rinnelle, take your hands off me."

"Not until you do as a partner should," she replied, pulling him toward her and holding him tightly like a lover. "Look into my eyes and see your own soul there."

"Let go of me, curse you. Let go!" His face rigid with fury and revulsion, Kett tried to turn away from her, but she tore the ship's pendant from her dress and forced it into his hand.

"No! You'll know the truth now, Kett, I swear you will, whether you wish it or not."

Perhaps it was magic, or perhaps it was the force of her will alone that turned his eyes toward hers, but he paled at the expression in them. For one, two, three heartbeats there was a breathless silence, and then Kett gave a hoarse cry, like a drowning man who realizes he is lost. His face twisted in rage, he raised his fist, still clutching her talisman, and smashed her head with a vicious blow, driving her to the floor.

"No!"

"Don't!"

They started forward, Lady Kestrienne and Jena reaching for spells to stop him, but Kett had already fallen to his knees beside his partner and was bringing up his fists again for another blow that would crush her skull. But before they could descend, a gout of flame erupted from his hands. Kett's scream was lost in the thunder's roar. The whole room blazed with fiery light, sparks rushing away from the hot core of power that slammed down, piercing Kett through the heart.

And then the room fell dark and silent—save for a low moan from Lady Rinnelle and the sound of harsh breathing. Jena, Lady Rhuddlan, and Lady Kestrienne slowly straightened up from where they had crouched and Morgan poked his head cautiously around the corner of a chest. Jena stumbled over to the hearth and lit a taper from the coals still burning there.

"*That* wasn't the Starburst," said Lady Rhuddlan, wide-eyed.

"His partner," exclaimed Lady Kestrienne. "I never dreamed he would actually attack his own partner!"

Slowly they drew to the center of the room. There, Lady Rinnelle had painfully turned over and crawled to where the sea captain lay. "Kett," she choked. "Oh, no, no. Kett."

As her hair fell over his cheek, Kett slowly turned his head and reached up to touch her face. His mouth worked soundlessly for a moment, and then the hand fell. The eyes widened slightly and then closed, as if in pain. They didn't open again.

As Rinnelle bowed her head over his body, Kett's black pearl earring crumbled away into dust.

CHAPTER
TWENTY-THREE

"DAMMIT! I'M *STILL* A DOG!"

"But that's impossible!"

"I never thought I'd ever hear you say that word, Aunt," Morgan grumbled.

"But it is! No spell can possibly survive its maker's death."

"Oh, fine!" Morgan snarled. "So I suppose that means I'm really a man again, doesn't it? We all just *think* you see the paws and the tail. In that case, why don't you call my servants to dress me and saddle my horse? I'll bag a deer for dinner and dance a gavotte with Vianne tonight. But no—I think she'd have a little trouble dancing with someone so much shorter than her! Not to mention I'd probably shed all over her velvet gown!"

"But I tell you it's impossible!" sputtered Lady Kestrienne.

"Stop saying that!" Morgan barked.

"Morgan," Jena cut in. "Calm yourself. There has to be some other explanation."

He wheeled on her in a rage. "Oh, by all means, enlighten us, Jena! I'm more than eager to hear it!"

"The spell must have been done by someone else. Not Kett."

That took the wind out of Morgan's sails. He glanced over, panting, to where Kett's body lay on the floor, covered by a cloak from one of the chests. "Not Kett?" he growled doubtfully.

"Or perhaps he did it, but someone else has maintained it?"

They all turned to stare at the huddled figure sitting on the floor beside Kett's body. Lady Rhuddlan, sitting on one of the chests beside the bed, cleared her throat. "Lady Rinnelle—"

"No." Lady Rinnelle shook her head, dry-eyed, her voice lifeless. "No, your brilliance, I swear to you by whatever tattered rag of honor I have remaining, I had nothing to do with the spell over Lord Morgan. I never have."

"Then who did it?" Lady Rhuddlan said helplessly.

Jena studied Morgan, who had slumped down, his head on his forepaws, the picture of ultimate dejection. "Morgan, you must tell us what Kett said to you when this spell took effect."

"I told you I don't want to talk about it."

"Would you rather stay a dog for the rest of your life?"

He sat up, and as best as Jena could tell, scowled at his forepaws. "It had to do with Vianne," he said finally.

"With me?" said Lady Rhuddlan.

Morgan looked up at Jena pleadingly. "Jena, I don't want her to have to hear this."

"Is it that you don't want her to hear it, or you don't want to say it in front of her?"

"Don't stop now," Lady Kestrienne murmured beside her. "I think you've run smack into one of his blind spots."

"Well, Morgan?"

"Kett spoke of my betrothal," Morgan said reluctantly, the tip of his tail twitching restlessly. "I became angry, asking how he knew, and what business it was of his. He laughed. 'Be warned,' he told me. 'Lady Rhuddlan has power, but don't be fool enough to think that wooing her will allow you to share it. You'll only end up—' " Morgan broke off, shifting uneasily from paw to paw.

"As her lapdog. That's what he said, wasn't it?" Jena saw the indignant flush on Lady Rhuddlan's cheek and felt a slow burn rise in her own face. "And you believed him, didn't you? That loving a powerful woman somehow diminished you?"

Yet even through her anger, Jena felt a twinge of sympathetic understanding. Here was a proud and intelligent man with the privileges of noble rank, yet one who had grown up a second son, always in Lord Duone's shadow. Small wonder that he should question whether he wanted to stand in his wife's shadow as well. And Kett had sensed that and exploited it. "So—Lady Rhuddlan wasn't the only one who had doubts about the match. Was she, Morgan?"

Morgan gave Lady Rhuddlan a stricken look. "Vianne, I'm sorry."

"Ironic," Lady Kestrienne observed, throwing a sympathetic glance toward Lady Rinnelle, "that he sneered at you, Morgan, for planning to do the very thing he wanted to do— marry the woman who could become the next Diamond."

Jena stared at Morgan, the seed of an idea taking root. "He told Lady Rhuddlan you would make a docile pet, but he also said that you should be neutered. Now, if you were supposed to be so tractable, why would you need to be gelded?"

"It's a mercy Kett didn't arrange the operation himself," Lady Kestrienne said brightly. "At least, I assume he didn't, did he?"

"Aunt!"

"You're right, my lady," Jena said. "He wanted Lady Rhuddlan to do it."

Morgan actually lay down and put his forepaws over his ears. "I am not listening to this!"

"It's so strange," said Jena slowly. "Kett was a wizard. He could've used his skill to make new opportunities, for himself and others. And yet he exerted power by paralyzing people. He'd find out what they feared the most and then convince them they couldn't escape it—that there were no other possibilities." She felt laughter bubbling up. "Shatter it, it's so perfect. Morgan, don't you see? You're the one keeping that spell over yourself!"

Morgan uncovered his ears and Lady Rhuddlan's jaw dropped. Even Lady Rinnelle looked up, curious. *"What?"* Morgan said.

"Think about it. Metaphor can be magic, can't it? That's what Kett used to transform you. But I think the spell will only last as long as you continue to believe Kett was right."

Morgan sat silently for a long moment. "I want to believe he was wrong," he said, his voice full of shame. "I want to believe I can be a true partner to my lady, offering her as much as she gives me. How can I prove it to myself, so I know it?" He glanced at Lady Rhuddlan. "So we both know it?"

"Morgan," Lady Rhuddlan said brokenly. "I swear to you, I—"

"Wait," said Jena gently but firmly, holding up a restraining hand. "He'll never accept it just because you tell him. He has to work it out for himself."

Morgan sighed in frustration. "Work out *what,* Jena?"

"As long as you're scrying truth," Lady Kestrienne suggested mildly, "you might as well use the tools you have available." She unbuckled the collar around Morgan's neck, slipped Morgan's talisman ring off the leather strap, and handed the ring to Jena.

She accepted it with a little nod and, feeling her magical "hunch" growing, she thought for a moment, striving to put her understanding into words. "Lady Kestrienne explained to me that when wizards first partner, they take on each other's characteristics, acting in opposition to their own natures. It certainly worked that way for me: I'd always been shy, hating to make trouble or take risks. That all changed when I came to Duone Keep. *I* changed. I decided I really did want to be a gemcutter. I stood up to your brother and traveled for leagues to find you. Part of that was because I had partnered with you, but don't you see? Part of it was also because of what Kett did to us. He *exaggerated* the partnering process. There were times I was so frightened and angry that you had left me alone. But if Kett hadn't kidnapped you, I wouldn't have been forced to do things I had never dreamed of doing before. I wouldn't have become as strong as I did."

She proffered the ring. "So look into the stone, and tell me, Morgan: what have you learned from being a dog?"

Morgan lifted his ears in surprise. "You're jesting."

Jena shook her head. "No, I'm not."

He pondered, staring at the ring. "To tell the truth, I've been so angry about the spell that such a thing never occurred to me."

"What did I tell you?" Lady Kestrienne said. "A blind spot."

He rolled his eyes. "Aunt—"

Jena waved a hand. "Shh, if you please, my lady. Morgan?"

"Well," Morgan said uncertainly, "I suppose I've never been forced to just sit and listen before. When Vianne received visitors, I learned to watch the expressions on faces when no one else was looking. It was a surprise, realizing what you can glean from doing that. And I never realized before how much servants notice, and how they gossip."

"That's good. What else?"

Morgan thought some more. "I learned what it's like to be helpless." He shook his head and shuddered. "Vianne, I was so afraid for you. This adept, whom I knew nothing about, had done this to me. What might he do to you? How could I possibly stop him?" He gave a little half laugh. "Didn't you ever wonder why I was always begging food from you?"

Lady Rhuddlan looked away quickly in embarrassment. "Once I realized who you were, I did think it strange for you to do such a . . . a *doglike* thing," she admitted in a low voice.

"I was afraid of poison," he said simply. "I thought, well, if someone tried something, at least you would have some warning that might save you."

"I never realized." A little frown creased Lady Rhuddlan's brow. "You thought you were so helpless—and yet you protected me?"

"Yes," said Morgan with some surprise. "I suppose I did."

Jena nodded. "Keep going, Morgan."

"That's all there is, I suppose. Except . . . except for what I've learned about my lady." He cocked his head, a wondering expression in his eyes. "I thought I knew everything about you, Vianne. We'd all but grown up together, after all. And yet, I never entirely understood what life for a member of the Diadem was like, until Kett's spell gave me the chance to see it for myself."

He shook his head admiringly. "If I've discovered anything in the past few months, it's that Piyanthia is lucky to have someone like you to lead it. You've a quick mind and an open heart, and you know when to yield and when to stand firm. I've listened to you stand up to bullies and fence with liars. I've watched your patience with fools.

"I've seen you merry, and angry, and sad. I've spent hours guarding your sleep, and despite everything, I wouldn't give up the memory of those hours for the world. I embarrass you, I know," he added quickly. "I'm sorry for that. But you know, maybe Jena's right. It's almost a reason to be grateful to Kett."

He lifted a paw, placing it lightly over Lady Rhuddlan's hand. "I love you, Vianne. Whether I remain this way or not, I'd be proud if you'd let me make my place at your side."

And then, something like a breath of warm air swirled around his fur, making the candles flicker, and Lady Rhuddlan was staring down at his hand, holding hers. With a glad cry, she lifted it to her lips and kissed it.

"Morgan!" Jena exclaimed. "Uh, you need some clothes."

Morgan, assessing the situation with a quick downward glance, lunged to wrap a corner of the bedcurtain around himself, his face scarlet.

"I'm sure there's something here that will serve," said Lady Kestrienne, going over to one of the clothing chests. "While we were looking for the Starburst, I saw—hmm, yes. Here's a shirt. Quite a fine-quality linen, if I do say so myself. So wrinkled, though! Would you prefer a pleated or unpleated pourpoint? Perhaps this one? But no, that bright lemon yellow color wouldn't suit you at all . . ."

"Aunt," Morgan said, his voice sounding anguished, "that one will do splendidly, I assure you. Please bring it here."

"No, no. Here we have it!" Lady Kestrienne seized a pourpoint and jerkin of deep olive and waved them triumphantly. "Just wait until you see him in these, Vianne, my dear."

And in a very short time, Morgan was suitably garbed, with hose points tied and a jerkin properly buttoned over his pourpoint. He looked down at his hands with a grin of incredulous delight, and then took Lady Rhuddlan's hand and turned to Jena.

"Well, now," Jena said, smiling, handing him his talisman ring. "That was easy, now, wasn't it?"

Morgan laughed as he put it on. "Well, no, it wasn't. Thank you, Jena." He lifted her hand and kissed it and smiled warmly into her eyes. "Thank you."

"Lord Morgan." Lady Rinnelle had risen, and now came forward. "I'm glad to see you restored to yourself. And ..." she ducked her head. "I'm so sorry. For everything."

"I bear you no ill will," Morgan said gravely.

"Thank you, my lord."

Morgan followed her glance to the still figure lying on the floor. He walked to it and then, after a moment, he stooped and removed something from the hand. It was Lady Rinnelle's ship's pendant, with the pearl still attached. "My lady, I believe this belongs to you."

"No." Lady Rinnelle stepped back quickly. "I mustn't take it back. I can't. It ... it killed him."

Morgan turned the brooch in his hand thoughtfully for a moment, and then came back over to Lady Rinnelle. "No, my lady. His attack upon you was his own choice, and this was the consequence." He handed the brooch out to her. "He was your partner, for good or for ill. Keep it to remember him by."

It looked at first as if she would refuse, but finally, reluctantly, Lady Rinnelle accepted the brooch.

"And now"—Morgan sighed, gesturing toward the two bodies, one on the bed and one on the floor—"the Diadem is going to be looking for explanations for this. I hope they'll accept that the Diamond died in his sleep, but we'd best get the captain out of here." He removed the covering cloak and reached for Kett's arm, pulling it toward himself so as to hoist the body over his shoulder—but then stopped.

"What?" asked Lady Rhuddlan. "What is it?"

"Listen," Morgan said, releasing Kett's arm and lifting his head.

They all heard it then: the sound of footsteps and voices, still distant but coming in their direction. "But it's nowhere near dawn," Lady Rhuddlan exclaimed.

The voices were not coming from the hallway, but from across the outdoor courtyard adjoining the Diamond's bedchamber. Jena flew to the window, opened the shutter a crack, and peered out. "It's Lord Oselare with a few of the other lords, walking along the ambulatory. They're heading around the courtyard toward the far end of the hall." She looked around despairingly. "There's no way out, either through the courtyard or the hall, without them seeing. How can we possibly explain?"

"Quickly!" Lady Kestrienne pounced on a linen cap and apron left on a stool by the bed. "Put these on, Jena."

"What?"

"The attendant left them behind—hurry!"

"But I testified before the Diadem. They'll recognize me!"

"They won't. I'll change your appearance with a glamour," Lady Kestrienne said. "Morgan, where's your sword? Oh, of course, you don't have one. Well, does Kett have a knife?"

As Jena drew on the cap, tucking her hair underneath, and tied the apron behind her waist with shaking fingers, Lady Kestrienne got down on her knees beside Kett's body, scrabbling at his waist.

"Aunt, what—"

"Oh, mercy, Morgan, you weren't always this slow! We have to make it look as though you were trying to foil an assassin. Here's the knife; now do what you have to do."

Morgan took the weapon with dawning comprehension and then glanced at Lady Rinnelle. "My lady—forgive me."

"No!" Lady Rinnelle cried. Lady Rhuddlan tried to draw her away, but the Topaz Heir shook her off. "I won't let you touch him!"

"Wait, Morgan," Jena said hastily. "That isn't necessary." She threw back the folds of the cloak covering Kett's chest to reveal the blackened wound underneath. "All we have to do is to make it look like it was *possible* that he was stabbed."

Morgan's eyes widened, and he nodded. Swiftly he drew up a sleeve and drew a narrow slash across his forearm. He let the trickle of blood drip down from his fingers to the front of Kett's shirt. "Can you do the rest with a spell?"

"I think so," Jena said.

"If she can't, I will," said Lady Kestrienne.

And so it was that as Lord Oselare, Lord Alcide, and Lord Teutaine left the ambulatory for the interior hallway, the sound of shouts made them look at each other in surprise and quicken their steps. As they rounded the corner, they saw a noblewoman and a servant rushing toward them. "Hurry!" the older woman cried, wringing her hands. "We heard the call for help, and Lord Morgan forced his way in, but we can't follow."

"What—"

"The Diamond's bedchamber! The door slammed shut behind him, and now something's blocking it. Her grace Lady Rhuddlan is in there, too! Oh, please hurry!"

The door was indeed blocked. Now thoroughly alarmed, Lord Oselare and Lord Teutaine threw their shoulders against it, and then staggered back as the door gave a couple of inches. Through the crack an outstretched hand could be seen on the floor. "Someone's lying just in front of the door," Lord Alcide exclaimed.

"Help me . . . all together, now—heave!"

Within a few moments, they managed to push their way into the room. There they found her grace Lady Vianne Rhuddlan kneeling on the floor unrolling a bandage, her face set and white. The strange gentleman beside her was tearing away a portion of his sleeve, baring a forearm wound. The man in front of the door was dead, obviously from a stab wound to the chest. Lady Rinnelle stood at the bedside, drawing a sheet over the Diamond's face as she covered her own face with her other hand.

"Vianne!" the noblewoman said, coming in behind the rest. "Are you all right? Morgan—you're hurt!"

"Not badly, Aunt Kestrienne."

"What's all this?" Lord Alcide exclaimed.

Lady Rhuddlan looked up. "Your graces, the Diamond is dead." She stood and gestured to the attendant. "Fill the basin with water, please, and bring it over here with a sponge. His lordship's wound must be dressed." The attendant bowed her head and went over quietly to the sideboard.

"Let me help with that," Lady Kestrienne said quickly.

The lords looked at each other, shocked, and came toward the bed. Lord Alcide reached out to touch the Diamond's still hand with trembling fingers, and Lord Teutaine looked grave.

"How did he die?" Lord Oselare demanded suspiciously. "What happened here?"

"I came to sit vigil by his brilliance's bedside until the Diadem should meet here," Lady Rhuddlan answered readily enough. She raised her chin. "And given the nature of Lord Oselare's suspicions, I thought it best to have Lady Rinnelle join me."

Morgan pulled the shreds of his sleeve out of the way as Lady Kestrienne dipped the sponge into the water basin the attendant held. "I gather that her grace found the Council meeting rather upsetting, and so her previous engagement with me slipped her mind," he said, and winced as the sponge was drawn across the slash on his arm.

"You are . . . Lord Morgan?"

"Yes." He smiled slightly. "Brother to Lord Ranulf Duone."

"My fiancé," Lady Rhuddlan added.

"Indeed," Lord Alcide said in a surprised voice.

"And this is my aunt, Lady Kestrienne."

"I'm here as a chaperone," said Lady Kestrienne, smiling with utmost sweetness as she wrung the sponge out into the water.

Jena could only hope the assembled lords missed the look Lord Morgan gave Lady Kestrienne at that remark.

"We waited for Lady Rhuddlan quite a while," Lady Kestrienne continued, "and eventually made inquiries and were told she was here. I told Morgan we would have to leave in that case, of course, but"—and here Lady Kestrienne managed to look mildly embarrassed—"he begged me to come with him to the Diamond's chamber, to see if we couldn't find someone to take a message in to her grace to let her know we were waiting." Lady Kestrienne sighed. "It wasn't at all the thing, of course, but, well, young lovers can be so impetuous. . . ." She smiled brilliantly at Lord Alcide. "I'm sure you were young once, weren't you, my lord?"

"It's a good thing I did insist," Lord Morgan said hastily. "When we arrived here, I heard a scream, and then of course I rushed in. I found him"—he pointed with his chin toward Kett—"attacking the Diamond, strangling him."

"The attendant had been dismissed," Lady Rinnelle spoke up, to Jena's surprise. "And Lady Rhuddlan and I—well, I suppose we'd dozed off. I woke up suddenly and saw a dark shape bent over the bed, with hands around the Diamond's throat. I screamed and Lord Morgan burst into the room; there was a great deal of noise and confusion, and then just as Lord Morgan stabbed him, I saw who it was. You recognize him, don't you, Guilford?"

Lord Oselare took a step closer and exclaimed softly under his breath. "The captain of the *Windspray*?"

"Why, that's the very same villain who attacked her grace only a few days ago at the City and Sea Ceremony," Lady Kestrienne said as she wound the bandage around Morgan's arm. "The man must have been quite mad!"

"But this is monstrous!" Lord Teutaine exclaimed.

"Yes, indeed," said Lord Oselare, pulling a wooden casket out from underneath the edge of his cloak and opening the lid. "Sorcery frequently is monstrous."

"Lord Oselare—" Lady Rhuddlan began.

"The orb has been tested, as you requested, your grace, and I thought it best to proceed immediately. It may be too late to save him, but at least I can prove it was sorcery that killed him, eh?"

"I believe I told you what happened, my lord," said Morgan stiffly. "I saw no signs of any sorcery."

"Forgive me," Lord Oselare said icily with a very low bow, "if I use my own methods to investigate, rather than take the word of a man who arrived just a moment too late to prevent his betrothed from becoming the Diamond."

"How dare you, Guilford!" said Lady Rinnelle, drawing herself up to her fullest height. "I tell you, it happened the way I say it did. Or do you doubt my word, *brother*?"

Lord Oselare stared at her with an expression of mild surprise, as if he were seeing a totally unfamiliar side of her. Which, Jena reflected, very well might be the case. Then he lifted from the casket a glass orb which appeared to be full of black smoke and held it over the Diamond.

Oh, no. It'll detect the Starburst. Jena held her breath.

But the orb failed to glow, and when Jena saw the surreptitious glance Lady Rinnelle gave Kett's body, she understood. *Of course: Kett's dead, and it was his spell—and so the orb doesn't even work anymore!*

After a perplexed pause, Lord Oselare gave the glass globe a little shake and held it out again. "I was sure . . ." he muttered.

"If you're quite through embarrassing our House, Guilford," Lady Rinnelle said sharply, "please put that away." She held out her hand peremptorily for the orb, and after a moment, Lord Oselare reluctantly gave it to her. Placing it back into the casket, she closed the lid.

Then she knelt before Lady Rhuddlan, her skirts flowing out around her like water. "If I might beg a boon from you," she said, "it would be only this: that you allow me to be the first to swear to you my loyalty and acknowledge you as my true and noble ruler. May your reign be peaceful and prosperous, your brilliance. May you enjoy good health, and long life, and the faithful love of your people."

She clutched the new Diamond's hands. "And please, always remember . . . I was the first."

CHAPTER
TWENTY-FOUR

THE JEWELERS' GUILD NEW
Year's reception honoring newly elevated journeymen and
masters spilled from the two public meeting rooms to the
gallery overlooking the Guildhall's inner court. Jena, with
Collas, threaded her way through the crowd, blushing at the
good-hearted roars of approval that each knot of apprentices
gave her at the sight of the new journeyman's badge on her
dress.

"Eh, good fortune, Jena!" said Skelly, giving her a familiar clout on the shoulder.

"Nothing to do with luck," said Tobio stoutly, smiling.
"She earned it."

"Well, I know that, but—"

"You shouldn't sneer at luck, though, Tobio." Rance whis-
tled. "To have it be the Diamond who ends up wearing your
piece!"

"She's not really the Diamond yet. Not till her coronation."

"Did you see the buckle? I like those flat claw settings."

"No foils, though. Why'd you do it that way?"

"Jena! Congratulations! You'll be opening a shop before
we know it!"

"Well, I hope to someday, but I'm not sure where," Jena said with a little smile. "I thought to have one in Chulipse when I'm a master, but my plans are still changeable."

"Do you think Master Collas will need any more apprentices now?" Skelly asked with an impudent wink.

"I wouldn't dream of depriving Master Brody of your talents," Collas replied with a smile.

A servitor passed with a tray, and Jena asked, "Shall I fetch you some fritters, Father?"

"No, indeed. Today's your day, Jena, so I'll do the serving this time. Excuse me." Collas walked away, amid the mocking ooo's of the apprentices, which dissolved into general laughter.

"Journeyman Jena! How fine it sounds!"

Jena turned to exchange a smile with the rangy woman with the blond braid coronet. "Thank you, Master Elisabetta. I'm proud to be able to follow in your footsteps."

"No, indeed!" Master Elisabetta laughed. "You're making your own footsteps, my dear! Don't be afraid to forge your own way." She squeezed Jena's hand. "Well done. I look forward to seeing much more of your work—and with a master's stamp someday."

Collas appeared shortly with a selection of fritters, seedcakes, and other delicacies. Following closely at his elbow was Arikan. "Your father managed to snag the last of the pickled oysters," he greeted Jena, frowning. "Right from under my nose."

"I saw my chance and took it," returned Collas. "But then, you made it easy by stopping at the wine table first."

"Thank you for coming, Arikan," Jena said.

"Jena, I wouldn't miss the occasion for the world." Arikan leaned forward unexpectedly and kissed her lightly on the cheek. "Especially since the Jewelers' Guild always serves the best pear tarts in the city." A figure in the crowd caught his eye, and he smiled. "There's Lady Kestrienne. Shall we go speak to her?"

"Oh, yes! Father, Master Elisabetta, if you will excuse us?"

Jena took the elbow Arikan offered and went with him through the crowd, exchanging greetings with people as they went. Finally they reached Lady Kestrienne's side, and she greeted Jena warmly. "My dear child, I'm truly happy for you. You'll make us all proud, I know."

Jena curtsied. "Thank you for your good wishes. And my lady, I owe you such a debt of thanks—"

"Oh, pish posh! Whatever for?"

"For helping me see that I really did want to reapply. And for your mentoring—you know."

"Ah, yes. Well, one of the chief pleasures of having a protégée is the opportunity it gives you occasionally to bask in reflected glory. Today I consider myself amply repaid for any trifling trouble I might have taken on your behalf."

Her bright eyes fastened on the necklace around Jena's neck. "What an exquisite piece of jewelry that is, Jena. Is it your work?"

"No, my father made it. He gave it to me just this morning." Jena smiled as she fingered the length of silver links, set with round-cut tourmalines, blue-green in color.

"Those stones are perfectly matched."

"Yes, Father's work has always been splendid. He wanted me to have it as a gift, he told me, because he'd made it for my mother."

"That's not the only reason, Jena," Arikan said, and smiled when she looked at him inquiringly. "That necklace was Collas' reapplication piece to the Guild. The second time, he was accepted as a journeyman."

Jena stared at Arikan, her mind awhirl in a wash of surprise.

Lady Kestrienne patted her hand kindly. "I hope you will have perfectly smooth sailing from here on out, my dear. But remember: we all have to learn, even the ones who always make it look easy. We all have setbacks, and we all make mistakes."

A stirring in the crowd caught Lady Kestrienne's attention. "Ah, here come two others who wish to congratulate you." She stepped back and curtsied, and Jena turned and hastily curtsied, too.

The Diamond-to-be and her declared Consort were walking toward them through the crowd. They both wore white velvet trimmed with ermine and cloth of silver, and the Starburst was pinned just below the small ruff at her brilliance's throat. Jena studied their faces as they approached. No one, she thought, not even the nonadept, could miss the aura surrounding them. It was there in the placement of Vianne's hand on Morgan's arm, and in the smile that hovered around the corners of his mouth as he bent to speak in her ear. It was in the calm joy shining in their eyes. *Possibility.*

"Lady Kestrienne," the Diamond said, smiling, as Lady Kestrienne arose from her curtsy.

"An honor, your brilliance."

Arikan bowed. "Madame, if I may presume?" After a small pause, the Diamond extended her hand to him, and Arikan bowed over it and kissed it with careful courtesy.

"We are pleased to see you among our friends here." The Diamond turned to Jena. "Journeyman Jena, will you speak privately with us?"

Acutely aware of curious eyes, and the delighted nudges her friends among the apprentices were giving each other, Jena joined the Diamond and her betrothed as they continued down the gallery. To her surprise, however, after they passed the second meeting room, people suddenly seemed to cease noticing them. Instead, they simply moved out of their way without a second glance. By the time the three had reached the gallery's end, no one else stood within earshot.

The Diamond smiled at Morgan. "Did you do that, my dear?"

"What? Oh, the crowd? Yes. You did say you wanted to speak privately, didn't you?"

The Diamond shook her head, amused. "I see I'll have to guard my tongue around you." She turned to clasp Jena's hand. "Jena, a joyous new year to you."

"Your brilliance, your kindness to me has made it so. Thank you for your letter to the Guild. It made my elevation certain."

The Diamond tapped her belt buckle lightly, with a mischievous sidelong glance at Morgan. "This piece has proven useful to both of us. But the truth of the matter is that Morgan and I both know ourselves to be in your debt." Her voice grew serious. "You have given my love back to me. And were it not for you"—her fingers touched the Starburst—"I wouldn't be wearing this." Seeing Jena's eyes linger over the brooch, the Diamond reached up and unclasped it. "Perhaps you would like to examine it more closely?"

Jena accepted the brooch and turned it over with great care, feeling the thrum of its protective power between her fingers. "I'd guess, judging from the setting," she said absently after a moment, "that this brooch must date all the way back to the Founders' War, at least." Something about that niggled at the back of her mind.

The Diamond leaned in to look. "How can you tell?"

"One clue is the filigree wire work, combined with the use of those high-relief collet settings."

"Collet?" Morgan asked.

"Boxlike, instead of claw. And there's no sign of the basic S-curve, which became the main feature of design about a hundred years ago. White gold was much more fashionable back then, too." She cocked her head and looked at Morgan. "Doesn't anything strike you as strange about that?"

Morgan looked at the brooch with a puzzled frown. "What?"

"Well, I presume whoever made the Starburst and Sunburst died long ago. *So who's maintaining the spell on them now?*"

The Diamond and Morgan looked at each other, and back at the brooch.

Slowly Jena began to smile. "Somewhere out there, even now . . . it's strange, isn't it? The Founders despised magic, and so when their war was over, they tried to set up the Diadem in a way that would keep magic out. And yet, in all the centuries since then, while the Diadem went on hating magic, somewhere adepts have made sure magic was protecting them."

"But why?" said the Diamond softly, eying the brooch as if she wondered whether she should put it on again.

Jena shrugged. "Who knows? Maybe the adepts were tired of the wars, too, and even though they were shut out in the end, they wanted to make sure that the new government would be safe. Even from themselves."

She looked down again at the brooch in her hand. The

metalwork was exquisite but . . . "It's rather a pity about the stones."

The Diamond blinked. "I beg your pardon?"

Jena blushed. "I'm sorry, your brilliance. I spoke without thinking."

"No, please. What about them?"

"Well . . ." Jena turned the brooch over again. "It's just that they were cut in the old style, the double pyramid. It's easy to do, and common, because it follows the stones' natural crystalline structure. But the double-pyramid cut doesn't do much to reveal a diamond's inner fire, the way a round cut or a brilliant would. Perhaps that's why the previous Diamond didn't wear it very often."

"I see." The Diamond looked thoughtfully at the brooch in Jena's hand, and then gently closed Jena's fingers over it. "Will you recut the stones in the Starburst for me?"

"Your brilliance!" Jena stammered, stunned. "I . . . I didn't mean to imply—"

"I know you didn't. But you're right. The brooch should be recut, and I think the honor rightfully belongs to you."

"Your brilliance honors me immensely, but . . . the Starburst! I'm only a journeyman."

"And yesterday you were only an apprentice, were you not? Yet think about it, Jena. Who else could I trust, who could do the work while still keeping the Starburst's other special properties in mind?"

There was certainly truth in that, Jena had to admit. She looked down at the Starburst in her hand and thought about stones, and magic. She thought about the changes she had undergone in the past several months, and the inner self those changes revealed. "I will honor your brilliance's trust," Jena said finally. "Yet, please, keep the brooch awhile longer. I'll study and learn, and cut it when I'm ready. When I'm a master."

The Diamond accepted the brooch back with a smile and repinned it below her ruff. "I look forward to that day, Jena Gemcutter." She turned to take Morgan's arm as Jena swept her another deep curtsy. "Shall we go, Morgan?"

But Morgan withdrew her fingers and raised them to his

lips and kissed them. "Would you please allow us a few moments?"

The Diamond glanced at Jena. "Of course. I'll meet you at the other end of the gallery when you're ready."

They both watched her walk away, and when they faced each other again, there was an awkward pause.

"I want—"

"Do you know—"

They looked at each other and laughed.

"You first," Morgan said.

"I only wanted to say how pleased I was to hear that the Diadem voted Lord Duone in as the new Emerald."

"Yes, I was, too! Poor Lord Oselare, though." Morgan chuckled. "Vianne said he looked as though he'd bitten into a lemon when the vote was tallied. I suspect Ranulf is going to be crossing swords with him quite frequently in Council."

"Maybe what Lord Oselare needs is a worthy opponent."

"He'd certainly have one in Ranulf." Morgan looked thoughtful. "There's a real antagonism there; I'd give much to know why."

"I'd wondered whether Kett wasn't trying to make him suspicious that at least someone in the Duone family was an adept, in hopes of scuttling your marriage when your betrothal became known."

"And Oselare settled on Ranulf instead of me? I wonder how long it will take him to discover he's yapping up the wrong tree." He blinked, surprised at his own choice of words, and Jena laughed.

"Have you seen your nephew yet?" she asked.

"Yes, I have. He took one look at me and tried to pull off my mustache."

Jena smiled. "I suppose that you . . ." she stopped. "You know, I don't know what to call you."

Morgan shot her an amused look. "I seem to remember your arguing for the right to call me just 'Morgan.' "

"But you're going to be the Diamond Consort now. The last Diamond was a widower for so long that I don't even know: what's the proper title for the Diamond Consort, anyway?"

"Mostly I'm just 'your lordship,' although I gather that if

you want to be particularly formal, it's 'your radiant lord-ship.' " Morgan rolled his eyes. "I'll never get used to it."

Jena grinned. "Are you sure?"

"You might as well just call me Morgan, since we're part-ners. As long as . . ." he gave Jena a speculative glance.

"As long as no one else is around who would think it odd, I know," Jena said quickly. "I have the same arrangement with Kestrienne."

"Do you? Well, actually, that wasn't what I was about to say. What I meant was, as long as you actually want to be my partner."

Jena's eyebrows rose. "Do we have a choice?"

"I've been thinking about that. Doing magic means choos-ing possibilities, and yet we never really chose each other. The bond just *happened* to us. It's a paradox, isn't it?"

"You did ask if I wanted to come with you."

"Yes, to be my pupil, I thought. I didn't understand wiz-ardry then; neither of us did. But now, suppose you were given the choice: what would you say? Would you like to be partners? Or maybe," he added, a touch awkwardly, "even friends?"

Jena gave him a considering look. "I've heard Father say that the noble who tells you he wants to be friends is usually the one who won't pay your bill."

A smile tugged at the corner of Morgan's lip. "Is that so? What do you think a friend is, then, Jena?"

"Someone you can trust. Someone who'll keep promises and keep your confidences. Someone who'll tell you the truth and doesn't expect you'll give them everything for free."

"Fair enough, as long as it works both ways. If those are the terms, I accept. Partners?"

He offered his hand to shake, as if she were an equal—not as if to take hers to kiss, or in a condescending wave, as if he expected her to curtsy. She looked at it for a moment and then accepted it. "Partners."

He looked down at her hand and smiled at her talisman ring. "Aunt Kestrienne gave me the stone you're wearing in your ring at the same time she gave me my own ring. I didn't know why at the time. She only told me that it had come from the same stone as the one used to set my ring. I didn't even know what I was going to do with it when I brought it to your father to cut." He covered her hand with his, and his clasp was warm and strong. "But you knew what to do. It looks lovely, Jena."

"Thank you." After a moment, Jena laughed and withdrew her hand. "Well, what now?"

Morgan shrugged. "I can lend you the books Aunt Kestrienne used to teach me. Arikan's going to be my mentor, so I'll be learning a bit with him. Other than that, I suppose we'll simply live our lives and see how a partnership fits in. My life, at least, is going to be quite different from now on."

Jena looked over back down the length of the gallery and spotted the Diamond in the crowd. "Did what I said help?"

"Yes, it did."

"I'm glad. I like her. I wouldn't have wanted you to lose her."

"I'll tell you a state secret." He tugged at the corner of his mustache. "She still calls me Marzipan once in a while."

Jena's lips twitched. "Never in public, I hope."

"Certainly not." His eye came to rest on the new journeyman badge sewn to the shoulder of her dress, and he tapped it with a fingertip. "Your life is going to be changing, too, eh? Will you be going to work with a master in a different city, or staying here in Piyar?"

Jena's smile faded. "I don't know." She turned away to look over the balustrade.

"Jena?" He came to lean on the railing beside her and looked at her with friendly concern. "What is it?"

"I don't know what I'm going to do." She sighed. "My— the man I was betrothed to, Bram, has been away, looking for me. . . ."

"I know. Arikan told me about him."

"Oh."

"Do you mean you're not sure whether you're still betrothed?"

Jena looked down at her fingers, fidgeting with her talisman ring. "Bram and I haven't even talked since you and I partnered. I don't know what he'll think."

"Is that what it depends on? What he thinks? What about what you think?"

She glanced up at him, her eyes prickling with tears, and angrily she brushed them away.

"What's he like?"

Jena considered for a moment. "He's mostly a quiet person. If he thinks something is his duty, he takes it very seriously. He's one of the kindest persons I've ever known, and he'll always tell you what he thinks is the truth, but . . . he's not . . . not very imaginative. Or ambitious."

"But you are."

"I don't know if I'm imaginative—"

"You have to have some imagination to be an adept. Not to mention a designer of jewelry."

Jena shrugged. "But yes, I am ambitious. I don't know if Bram can be comfortable with that. He doesn't like magic, either."

"Like Vianne. How interesting." His voice sounded amused. "So, what you have to decide is, would building a life together with him be right for you both—even if you're more the type to be the leader? Or perhaps you don't feel comfortable with the wife being the leader, eh?"

"That sounds like what I told you," Jena mumbled.

"Maybe you'd better listen to your own words."

Jena didn't say anything. She was staring at a man who had just walked into the Guildhall inner court below, a seabag slung over his shoulder. Something about him, the set of his shoulders, felt familiar—his gaze swept the hall, and the sound of the crowd on the floor above him made him glance upward. Jena straightened up in shock.

"Wait." Morgan put a hand on her shoulder. "Before you go down to him, remember: I stayed with Vianne, true, but what's right for your partner may not be what's right for you. Whatever you decide, I hope . . . ." He hesitated, and his fingers squeezed her shoulder. "I hope you'll be happy. Good luck."

Jena walked away from him without looking back, heading for the staircase.

Her hand felt cold on the marble railing. He saw her coming when she reached the first landing, and he dropped his seabag at his feet and pulled off his wool cap as she approached. Their eyes met, and her steps slowed and then stopped.

"I like the beard," Jena said shyly.

His hand ran through its short, curling length. "It was terribly scratchy when it came in. But I like it, too. I'll be keeping it, I think."

Slowly she stepped closer and brushed her hand across his cheek, feeling the springy, soft whisker curls. He smelled of salt, and wet rope, and the open wintry air. The texture under her hand, the warmth of his breath across her wrist, made her heart constrict painfully, and she swallowed hard, almost dizzied by the heightening of her senses. Apparently he felt it, too, for he closed his eyes at her touch and, capturing her hand in his, pressed it to his lips. The calluses on his palms rasped against her skin, but his lips were warm and gentle.

After a moment, she pulled her hand away, and he opened his eyes and looked at her. Despite the new tracery of sun lines surrounding them, they were the same warm brown she remembered. He wore a small gold ring in his right ear.

"There's a bench in the corner, underneath the gallery," Jena said a little shakily. "Let's sit down before I fall down."

He smiled, and reached down to hoist his seabag over his shoulder. "Good idea." He held out his hand to her, and they went to sit.

"How far north did you go?" she asked as he set the seabag at their feet.

"All the way to Niolantti. The first week I was on board ship, though, I didn't think I'd make it even as far as Black Needle Point." He laughed. "Hoisting sails and swabbing decks is a lot harder work than sewing shirts. Especially when you're seasick.

"But I got my sea legs eventually. And I learned to love it. Love the sea, I mean." He smiled reminiscently. "There were some nights, you know . . . the crew would be up on deck and the stars would come out . . . I never saw skies like that at night, living in the city. And the sea would be calm and smooth, like dark silk. . . ." He sighed. "A man can do a lot of thinking on a night like that."

"What sorts of things did you think about?"

"About you and me, and how . . ." He rubbed his fingers through his short beard again. "Well, it's hard to explain. I came to see how much I'd let events simply carry me along, instead of deciding things for myself."

Jena nodded slowly. "We'd both been doing it, I think."

"When I found out you were gone, I could have just waited to see what would happen, the way I'd been doing. Or I could make a choice. And I did. I decided I couldn't just let you disappear. I had to find you. Going north after you felt like . . ." he hesitated for a minute, groping for words, "like the first time I'd actually taken my life into my own hands."

Jena's gaze dropped to her lap. "What happened when you came to Niolantti?"

"I disembarked and went into the city to try to arrange passage up the Orbo. But when I asked around about getting to Duone Keep, I found out the Duone household had left for Piyar. Lady Duone's party had passed through the city less than a week before and taken a ship heading back along the coast the way I'd come. The news had come down the Tulio River that Lord Duone was heading overland; all the taverns were gossiping about the attack in Tenaway. So I turned around and found another ship to take me home again."

"How did you know where I was today?"

"I went to your house first. Your father's servants sent me here."

"I think . . . I think a part of me knew you would be returning today."

His eyes became shuttered, careful. "You can tell things like that now, can't you?"

"Sometimes." She swallowed again. "Bram, do you mind so much?"

He looked down at her hand in his. "I don't know."

"Did . . . did Arikan—"

"Yes, Arikan explained. A little."

Her throat hurt. "Bram, I'm so sorry."

He looked up at her again, as if surprised. "Sorry for what, Jena? That you know magic?" He shrugged. "It's not something you did to hurt me. It just happened."

She nodded, a little reassured. "Well, yes. But I'm sorry you felt you had to go chasing north after me."

He snorted. "It didn't make a bit of difference, though, really, did it? You managed to find your way back to your home and family anyway, without my rescuing you. Without my even finding you."

"At least I know you cared enough to try."

"I would have gone to the ends of the earth for you," he said with a sudden fierceness. "I know that now. I love you, Jena."

She flinched and took a deep breath. "You love someone who doesn't exist anymore."

He looked at her with his heart in his eyes, and suddenly she couldn't bear it anymore. "I decided to fight the Guild, Bram, and I won. I'm a journeyman now. The last day we were together, when we walked by the river . . ." she paused, and the tears spilled over and began trickling down her face, "you said you didn't think it . . . it would work out if I had my own gemcutting shop. Between us, I mean." She gulped and paused, but he only held her hand in the same listening attitude, waiting for her to continue. "And I'm . . . I'm an adept—"

"A wizard," he corrected swiftly, and she drew in a sharp breath.

"So Arikan explained that, too."

He nodded. "Well, he told me some. He wouldn't say who was your wizard partner. He said you should be the one to tell me that. If you wanted to."

After a moment, she nodded. "I know how you feel about magic. But I can't give it up." Her fingers tightened in his. "I can't. I won't."

"Jena—"

"I'm not the same person I was when we last saw each other," she said desperately.

"Well, of course not," he said with something like astonishment. "Jena, haven't you been listening to what I've been saying? Did it never occur to you that I could change, too? That I'm not the same person anymore, either?"

Shocked, she stared at him, and then dropped her gaze, ashamed. "No, Bram. It didn't."

"Is that what this is all about? Do you think I won't *want* you anymore, because you're a journeyman and a wizard?"

"You have to understand what it means," Jena persisted. "Even if we marry, I'll always have another bond."

Bram's jaw tightened. "Are you his lover, then?"

"No!" she said impatiently. "He's marrying someone else."

"That doesn't stop some men," he observed wryly.

"It's not like that."

"But it could be like that, I think."

"If we chose to, but we don't. We—"

He placed a hand over hers to still her protests. "I'm not saying this to make you angry, Jena. I'm just trying to make you see that I understand. From what Arikan said, I know there's someone else you're going to feel close to. You'll have things in common with him you won't have with me. Even if you don't intend to be his lover, the possibility will always be there. If I marry you, I'll have to, well, learn to live around that." He gave an impatient exclamation at the look of astonishment on her face. "Jena, don't you see? Arikan explained this all to me months ago. But I still left the city to go after you."

She felt hope stir. A sudden burst of laughter from the crowd in the gallery above them made her remember suddenly where she was, and her shoulders slumped again. "There's also the gemcutting," she said doggedly.

"Yes, I see." Bram hesitated, and then touched the new journeyman badge at her shoulder, just as Morgan had.

"I want to be a master, Bram. I told you about the Guild's rules, that I'd have to give up my membership if we have a son. I've been told that I can use my magic to . . . to *arrange* things so that we have only daughters." She braced herself at the look of shock on his face. "Or even no children at all."

"Jena! Is that what you really want?"

She hesitated. "I want to be a gemcutter."

"Then be a gemcutter," he said firmly. "But children—didn't you want them, too?"

Miserably, she nodded.

"Well, then you'll have to make the Guild bend the rules, the way you did to become a journeyman."

"But Bram—about having children and being a gemcutter—you said—"

"I said a lot of things. But who am I to predict what might happen if we have children, or even if we don't? After all, I've never been as sure as you are about what I want to do. I may just have a shop like my father, or do the silks. On my way to Niolantti, I had some ideas about sailmaking." He shrugged. "Last summer, I was trying to make plans based on one possibility. But there are others, too. Who knows? After two years of journeyman traveling, you may decide in the end you don't want to build a future with me."

"Bram—"

"It could happen, Jena. We might decide to *make* it happen that way."

The words stung, but her magic told her he was right. "We *have* changed," she said.

"Yes, we have. If we stay together, we have a lot to learn about each other. I don't think that even the adept can say for certain what our life might be like. I'm not saying it will be easy. I just know that . . ." He touched her cheek gently. "I think I'd like to get to know this new person you're becoming."

"So you are telling me to fight the Guild?"

"I'm telling you to fight for what you want. Isn't that what I'm doing, Jena? Fighting for you?"

"Because it's worth it to you."

"Jena . . ." his hand brushed a tendril of hair back from her forehead. "You're worth it to me."

She kissed him then, feeling her heart twist with the bittersweetness of a new kind of magic. All her possibilities were still there, as shrouded with potential danger and doubt as ever. But through all of them ran a single certainty, reflected back to her from every angle like the light of a perfectly cut jewel.

What was it—happiness? She laughed as she felt Bram's lips brush against her eyelids, her cheek, and then he took her into his arms for another kiss that left her breathless.

Did it matter?

She pulled back and ran a finger over the edge of the gold ring in his ear. "Now, about your New Year's gift . . . how would you feel about something in garnet?"

About the Author

Peg Kerr lives in Minneapolis, Minnesota, with her husband and two daughters. Her fiction has appeared in *The Magazine of Fantasy and Science Fiction*, *Amazing Stories*, *Weird Tales*, and various other magazines and anthologies.